THE
MULGA MAN

STEVE LANGLEY

Paperback ISBN: 978-1-7641639-6-5
Author: Steve Lanley
Editor: Justine Martin
Cover Graphics: Mylan Carascal

A catalogue record for this book is available from the National Library of Australia.

DISCLAIMER

The information contained in this book is for general informational purposes only. The author and publisher are not offering any medical, legal or professional advice. While every effort has been made to ensure the accuracy and completeness of the information provided, the author and publisher assume no responsibility for errors or omissions or any outcomes or consequences resulting from using this book's content.

COPYRIGHT

All original material in this book is the sole property of the author and Morpheus Publishing.

DISTRIBUTION

This book is distributed by Morpheus Publishing and is available through authorised distributors, booksellers, Morpheus Publishing website.

COPYRIGHT PERMISSIONS

For copyright permissions or any other inquiries, please contact:

PUBLISHER: Morpheus Publishing
www.morpheuspublishing.com.au |
hello@justinemartin.com.au | +61403 564 942 |

AUTHOR: Steve Langley
https://www.morpheuspublishing.com.au/authors/steve-langley

Preface

Born into a fractured, violent family life in the semi-arid Australian bush along the banks of the Darling River, Sean Molloy is a part indigenous boy who, from early childhood, has been appalled by the senseless brutality of his drunken and sadistic father toward him, his sister, and mother, and daily has had to face bullying and torment at school because of his Indigenous heritage. As he grows through childhood, he is mentored by his full-blood aboriginal uncle, who often takes him "bush," where he is taught traditional hunting and tracking skills and becomes trained in the techniques of bush survival in the harsh outback country.

A dangerous incident at school as a young boy, where he saved a schoolmate from a deadly Mulga snake, also known as the King Brown snake, earns him the nickname "Mulga".

As he grows, he forges a strong friendship with an aboriginal stockman, a tribal relative of his uncle, who is a skilled boxer and horseman, who teaches him how to defend himself and to fight against the bullies at school, skills that help shape him for his future adult life.

At the age of twenty, Sean Molloy sees a dramatic change in his life, when he is conscripted into the National Service in the Australian Army in the early 1950s. This transition from his harsh life in the bush into an infantry division and its initial military training suits him. He likes it, learns well and quickly earns a promotion to sergeant within his platoon, and when his National Service training is completed, he is offered the opportunity to join the regular army.

Not wanting to go back to his life in the bush and recognising the army as a great opportunity to better his life, he jumps at the chance and is soon absorbed in the military life of a soldier, learning many fighting skills. It quickly becomes the life he loves and quickly adapts to.

Molloy's platoon officer, when on a jungle training bivouac, recognises his unique indigenous tracking skills when a soldier is lost in the thick jungle and recommends he look at making an application into the harsh training program of the Special Armed Services, known as the SAS. On application, Molloy is accepted for initial assessment. He excels in all aspects of the intense and rigorous training that is needed to become one of these Special Forces, those who are finally selected for the SAS, the military fighting unit, who live and fight by the motto, "He Who Dares Wins".

His skills at hunting, tracking, and bush survival acquired as a child in the harsh outback country and the fighting techniques he learnt from boxing all help him adapt to his military career and lead to officer training. He is selected for specialised training in guerilla warfare and is promoted to the Australian Army Special Operations Force.

Communist forces are threatening global security, and as a military adviser, he is sent to Malaya, where his work is to train the Orang Asli hill tribe's people to help resist Chinese communist military infiltration. From that successful assignment comes a promotion to warrant officer, and he is sent to Vietnam. There, he is engaged in highly secretive and dangerous work when he is assigned to train another group of primitive hill tribes people into becoming anti-communist guerilla fighters in an endeavour to suppress the growing threat of communism and communist incursions in their country.

His training with the SAS allows his natural strength, bush-tracking skills, and fighting prowess to be honed to razor sharpness. Molloy now receives further intensive training in all forms of weapons, martial arts, and hit-and-run ambush killing. His successes in Malaya are recognised; he is seconded to a highly secretive command of the American CIA, engaged in covert operations in the Central Highlands of Vietnam in the earliest days of North Vietnam's invasion of South Vietnam and its victories over the French and their military command in South East Asia.

A high level of secrecy is necessary in this war that is taking place in Vietnam, a war not yet with official Australian government sanction. This highly dangerous mission, which a few members of the Special Operations Force were now put to, took place long before its government officially approved Australian troops to assist American forces and enter Vietnam.

Molloy fits neatly into his new assignment and its unique and highly dangerous mission. Unfortunately, he is wounded in action twice in this hit-and-run war and is repatriated back to Australia for debriefing through ASIO and for convalescence. This gives Molloy time to analyse his future, and recognising the futility of this political war in Vietnam, he considers the possibility of resigning from the military.

While on convalescent leave in Sydney, he witnesses a brutal event, which leads to a meeting with a high-powered criminal barrister. A friendship develops, and in time, Molloy learns his new friend is a man who is very disenchanted by some of the ineffectiveness of the Australian legal system and, in particular, "soft sentencing", as he calls it. This meeting leads to a job offer where Molloy's special skills can be put to use. It is an offer of a type of work that convinces him to resign from the military, and another major change comes into his life. It is a change that leads him into a highly paid position as a "justifier", his own term for a covert moral crusader who brings strong justice, vigilante-style, to those who escape legal retribution.

Because of his belief in the motto of the Special Armed Services, "He who dares wins", and his inherent hate from childhood for mindless brutality and aggression, he now uses his military-trained skills, knowledge of martial arts, and weapons training to administer justice to criminal scum.

Using a nickname acquired in his childhood school days, he now administers justice as lethal as the deadly Mulga snake.

Contents

C H A P T E R   1

The "Mulga" Man

I had carried the nickname "Mulga" since I was eleven years old. It was because of an event that happened on a stinking hot summer day in February 1946, almost a year after World War Two had ended. It was through a potentially dangerous incident about five months before my twelfth birthday that I achieved some small measure of fame from a national news story telling of a boy in a remote country school in a region of the Australian bush along the Darling River that is a rough semi-arid land, colloquially known in the vernacular of the locals as "the Mulga scrub". The newspaper story told of me saving a classmate from a dangerous King Brown snake, which is also known as a "Mulga snake", a nasty inhabitant of that region. The kids at school, as a result of this publicity, gave me the nickname "Mulga Man".

My name is Sean Francis Molloy, and here are some facts about my past eventful life and its change to the highly secretive missions I go on today. I'm sitting in business class on a plane about to take off en route from Sydney to Perth. It is a long flight, and in my mind, I'm mulling over my life, its numerous changes, events, and adventures, since my childhood, growing up in that Darling River country. There is a lifetime of happenings to think about as I settle back into my comfortable seat. The Boeing 707 I am on is just leaving Mascot Air Terminal, and soon it will be doing its long sloping flight up and around Botany Bay to head west on the long flight to Perth, Western Australia.

Seatbelts can now be unfastened, and an attractive flight attendant is taking drink orders. It is time now to relax from the mild uptight feeling I always experience in planes on takeoff and landing, time to relax with a scotch and soda, and now, sitting in the comfort of business class on this Qantas flight, I will have much time to muse over my past life, and I find my mind slipping back in time over a kaleidoscope of memories, reflecting on the past thirty and more years of my life, its changes, numerous adventures, its dangers, near deaths, and all other memorable experiences. It's all running through my mind like a silent movie screen, travelling through the vast number of happenings that have led me to this line of dangerous, high-paid work, which now seems to be my destiny.

I know I must work outside the accepted laws of this country to achieve results, and I often find myself walking a fine line between my conscience and the rights and wrongs of it. But those thoughts are then alleviated by my strong belief in justice, my intense hatred for filth crimes, and ruthless, unjustified brutality. I am good at my work, and I admit to some pleasure in administering retribution and tough justice to the brutal criminals and low-life scum I encounter, and with the bonus of excellent pay. Some could say I was a vigilante hitman. What's in a name? I prefer to wryly think of myself as a moral crusader, a "Justifier", helping to correct some of the inequalities of common law.

The low-lives who are known to be guilty that I track down have often escaped proper punishment through legal loopholes, sometimes because witnesses are too afraid to testify, and are fearful of retribution. There are also weak, ineffectual sentences passed by judges, sentences that are not relative to the mindless brutality of the crime, and, of course, instances of corruption by police, lawyers, or judges. However, there are those who do escape what should have been the "legal justice" of Australian law, and that is where my employers and I come in. First, to microscopically examine the details of the crime, ascertain an appropriate sentence, and then my job is to administer an "appropriate justice".

Once I have been given my brief and studied in depth the details of the crime or crimes, along with all known facts and courtroom evidence, be it whether the accused escaped through lack of reliable witnesses, or witnesses too terrified to speak, or evidence that could not be admitted to court, or whatever legal loopholes, my job is to track down and find whoever, and wherever that person may be, using the information and resources provided to me from a number of sources, and occasionally my own methods of gaining confessions, and then my job is to administer justice deemed relevant to the crime.

In the long hours ahead on this flight, as I muse over my life, I realise I'm looking forward to this next contract and the opportunity to deal with an extremely nasty, perverted and degraded person.

JJ Strong Criminal Barrister

Each assignment starts in a plush mansion cum office stronghold in Double Bay, a harbour-side suburb of Eastern Sydney. It is a unique complex building owned by the man in control, Jonathan J. Strong, who is known to many associates as the "Big Bloke" or mostly called "JJ". That is where I pick up all relevant profile information on the perpetrator, crime evidence, travel instructions, and, of course, payment, which is always cash and untraceable. I am considered a "pro," and any questions on my "modus operandi" are rarely asked, and only the final result is ever discussed. Just do the jobs, leave no trace, and with no come-back to the "Big Bloke".

JJ, Jonathan James Strong, is a high-profile criminal barrister, a "big" man in size, and on the Sydney social scene, with many and varied business interests. He is known as having a "sharp mind", an intuitive mind in high demand by solicitors to legally represent people on various criminal matters, and even when his intuition and intelligence and covert information from his many underworld contacts tell him they are guilty, he does represent them within the laws of the land, and despite having a "strong moral" outlook, he believes in the law, and legal justice when administered correctly. On the other side of the coin, he despises brutal criminality. Whatever, he impartially gets on with the job and does his best to secure legal justice, if deserved, in the normal and accepted way of Australian law. He strongly abhors any that he knows to be guilty and who escape justice with insubstantial sentences. In time to come, these were the cases whose details were handed over to me.

An example of this was a case in Melbourne, the first of many to come, that I attended to. This person was a multiple rapist, murderer, and stand-over thug represented by another criminal lawyer in the late 1970s. His criminal dossier included a number of violent assaults; because of a lack of witnesses, he had been tried and convicted on only one crime, rape and murder. He had been linked to a number of other rapes, but there was insufficient evidence and fear from victims too terrified or emotionally unstable to testify in court. The rapist-murderer's courtroom confession to the one crime of rape and murder was handled by a smart lawyer, and his indictment ended with a lenient sentence of only ten years, with a non-parole period of five years. Needless to say, the extended family of the murdered girl were horrified to learn in time that because of his model prisoner behaviour, and with time already served, plus a parole board of bleeding hearts, these do-gooders saw him released from custody in four years.

Within a month of his release, he was caught in the act of a brutal rape by a girl's brother, who could identify him as the man who was beating and attempting to rape his sister. Sentenced to only four years in jail, he was out in two years. Again, paroled on good behaviour.

One of Jonathon Strong's informants was a leading member of a "Victims of Crime Organisation", and with some assistance from the girl's family, he managed to organise financial remuneration to have this person dealt with. "JJ" passed all the relevant information to me. That particular rapist-murderer will not surface again, and Melbourne women no longer have to worry about this psychopath walking its streets.

"JJ" is an enigmatic man, and yet he has numerous contacts and informants throughout the country who give him a lot of "insider" information, mainly on criminal activities, and he seems to have his finger on the pulse of everything that is happening in the shady underworld dens of the cities and towns of Australia, and even overseas. On some occasions, I would be sent to a "job" outside of Australia; therefore, I have a vast range of aliases, passports, credit cards, and professions, from being a company director to a truck driver. These are all provided on call to "JJ" by his underworld contacts.

He is a big man, possessing great physical strength, and rumour has it that on one occasion, he hung an informer, a man who had turned would-be blackmailer, by his ankles over the cliff face known as the "Gap" at Watsons Bay as a warning. The budding blackmailer disappeared soon after, was not seen again, and was rumoured to have left the country. Jonathan James Strong stands over two metres tall, actually six feet seven on the old scale precisely, and weighs close to 120 kilos. In his penthouse, he has a gym, and is often working out and lifting enormous weights when I call in for my next assignment.

Edith, his personal secretary and confidante, told me that "JJ", in his youth, was an aggressive and tough rugby union forward, playing first grade, and represented our country overseas with the "Wallabies" and still plays a game with the "Golden Oldies". He has numerous awards hanging around the gymnasium, including a number of "best and fairest" players. There were even trophies for amateur boxing as a light "heavyweight". "JJ" always impressed me as a most formidable and yet soft-spoken man, a man to be listened to with respect, and I could well imagine him in a court of law.

Edith is an attractive and well-spoken woman, with a quick wit and beautiful yet shrewd eyes that seem to look clean through you, and is a most likeable person; she is quick-talking and a very elegant well-dressed lady, somewhere in her early fifties, whom I just love listening to. As I got to know her, she would say things like, "Hi Mulga, how is my favourite snake handler?" She is always quick with a joke and a laugh, yet deadly serious when it comes to the business at hand, and as "JJ's" most trusted private and personal secretary, she handles all the assignments and fine details in my line of work from case histories on clients, the targets, and all of his interstate and overseas in and outside the law contacts that includes high-ranking businessmen, politicians, police, ex-police, and private investigators. Edith works from the inner sanctum of "JJ's" private office area and is not involved with the everyday workings of his downstairs legal office staff.

"JJ's" briefs for his general cases and courtroom appearances are relayed to Edith from the downstairs legal staff and then to "JJ". Any high-level, high-profile cases are jointly discussed with his expert legal staff in the upstairs private office.

Over time, I gathered "JJ" was, or had been, legal representative to many of the rich and famous of Australian society—and also its underworld—and in Edith's private work area, she is surrounded by an incredible array of top of the range computer equipment and wide screens and is linked up to every known news monitor there is. This huge array of electronic IT paraphernalia is monitored and maintained by a quiet, shy type of fellow, known only as "Wilson", a self-effacing sort of bloke who seems to be there on a regular permanent basis. He always seems busy analysing information or working on some part of the high-tech equipment that he monitors. He wears thick bifocal glasses that look like the bottom of Coca-Cola bottles. I reckon you could say "Wilson" resembles what is known as the typical, highly intelligent computer "nerd". Always there, glued to the various screens and working on a keyboard, whenever I call in to see Edith or "JJ".

"Wilson" is another person who also seems to be totally devoted to "JJ". I guessed there would be a story there. "JJ" seemed to collect people, most of whom he had helped in some way in the past.

"JJ's" personal living area is a penthouse on the top floor of his office block, and it is cleaned twice weekly by an Asian lady of Malay origin. She speaks little English, and the day that I met her, she almost fell over backwards with shock and then smiled broadly when I greeted her in her native tongue, a language I had learnt when I was with the SAS on special OPs in Malaya. She would often cook and leave prepared meals for "JJ". Sometimes, he eats out in the evenings at a favourite restaurant in Double Bay and occasionally attends some of Sydney's "social set" functions. Then he is accompanied by Eleanor, a very stylish and attractive lady from Sydney's social scene. He is often visited by this lady friend, and I know little about her other than her name. I guessed she was in her mid-forties, having met her here at the Double Bay premises early in the morning on occasions, sometimes coming out of the lift as I was arriving. I guessed she was more than just a friend.

Now and then, and usually at the end of a job, "JJ" would invite me up to the penthouse for a drink and debrief me on the job I had just finished. Even Edith did not sit in on those meetings. JJ prefers the end results and how I achieved them to be for his ears only, so that meeting always takes place when he is alone. Then we would discuss in depth all details of each completed "job", searching for any possible errors or mistakes that could be rectified for future assignments, and based on the important factor that he and I must always remain unknown and anonymous.

The ground floor of this building complex is the mainstream office and reception, where the bulk of the legal and clerical business is handled. This area is staffed by his associate lawyers, researchers, and clerical staff; I rarely need to go in there and take the lift directly to JJ's office. In the building's basement is the underground parking, which is spacious enough for all staff and visitor's vehicles. Access is through massive steel gates; the electrical opening and shutting of them are monitored by a security guard known as George, a solid, burly, and likeable type of bloke, who "JJ" said was once a senior drug squad detective, who had resigned from the force, and accepted to this job. From time to time, George is relieved at his post by another similar type, an ex-policeman named Hector. In time, I was to find that George and Hector also did a bit of covert sleuthing for "JJ", and both kept in touch with a number of informants from their police force days, who continued to feed valuable information obtained on underworld activities back to "JJ", who in turn sees them financially rewarded for this service.

In the office that Hector and George worked in on their alternate shifts, they electronically control the steel gates and have verbal communication with outside visitors by an intercom system. Their office and its electronic systems also have a back room equipped with a bunk, en suite shower and toilet, and cooking facilities. The whole thing reminded me of a luxury concrete bunker, with its thick reinforced concrete walls and bulletproof glass windows, and when a client-visitor or visitors have been visually and verbally assessed, only then were they allowed access into the secure parking area. From there were two small lifts and two separate staircases that gave access to other areas.

One lift and its associated staircase were general access for the public and the legal staff to the ground floor only.

Any special high-priority, legal client visitors would go from the basement in the second lift to the "inner sanctum" office. This second lift has a sign stating: "NO ENTRY. THIS IS A CODE ONLY OPERATED LIFT." That lift went directly to this office, or could be allowed to go one floor more to the penthouse, but operable only by code from JJ.

The adjoining staircase to this lift, also only for emergencies such as fire, went to the "inner sanctum office" and is blocked by two electronically operated, heavy steel fire doors at the top and the basement entrance. These doors can only be opened from the "inner sanctum office" or "JJ's" penthouse. Once the private lift door is opened, there is a code pad that operates a video phone. This phone is constantly monitored from both Edith's desk and the "Big Bloke's" penthouse. No one can get in, move the lift, use the stairs, or use the telephone without knowing the codes, and the code is changed frequently.

A touch of a button on Edith's desk or from "JJ's" penthouse can lock the lift doors and stairway access doors, so if by chance someone had entered either access by devious means, it would trap whoever had gained entrance within the stainless-steel walls of the lift, or the concrete walls of the stairway, and from either they can be observed, and spoken with on video camera. A phone video call from George or Hector to Edith or "JJ" or vice versa could arrange for either to open the door or motivate the lift.

George told me that no occasion of forbidden entry, such as described, had ever arisen, and I felt it was an excellent piece of security, although at first, I found it a little frightening if anything ever went wrong and one was trapped inside it. As an added security, Edith and "JJ" also had an override button that could open or close the main entrance steel entrance gates if anything were to happen to either or both security guards.

Overall, I imagined it like "Fort Knox", the national mint in the USA where only the highly approved could get in or out.

Edith was a brilliant person to work with, full of knowledge and advice on the where, who, and how pertaining to the "job" in my particular line of work.

She had kept information on her personal life to herself for a long time, but as I got to know and like her, I found myself reading between the lines of conversations we had and soon found there were sad times in her life.

"JJ" had helped her to settle a grievous and very painful score with a sadistic ex-partner. A man who had physically, mentally, and sexually abused her and then financially hurt her by taking all her belongings, emptying their joint bank account, and then heading to the Gold Coast with his new lover.

Through a lawyer known to JJ, she was introduced to JJ, who, using his contacts, had traced her ex-husband, living a high life in Surfers Paradise with his new love. There, he was taught the error of his ways. I believe it was a lesson that required him to sign over his bank account and spend some time in a hospital thinking about his misdeeds. Nowadays, he has difficulty walking without crutches.

When "JJ" found out about Edith's previous law school training for a career in law, which was interrupted by her marrying the wrong sort of bloke, he offered her a job, and she soon worked her way into his confidence and into the job of private secretary. In doing this for her, I gathered from the way she spoke that "JJ" had gained her lifelong devotion, loyalty, and gratitude. She also indicated that she had a friend who occasionally partnered her on a date, but no real romantic interest, just seeming to live for her job and the numerous business interests of "JJ." I guessed some hurt was still there and alleviated a little by her work.

Walking away from Edith after our last enlightening conversation, touching on her personal life, I could not help wryly thinking about what sort of social and financial shape the ex-husband was in today.

In the early days after my initial introduction to Jonathan Steel, I mused much over this enigmatic man. A man who could run his whole legal business set up from an extremely secure area and who had a direct line and electronic access to the ground floor secretary and staff for the efficient general day-to-day running of his organisation, and yet they rarely saw him. He was a leader in complete control and would only go down to the main office for important meetings, accompanied by Edith, and only for a special reason. On occasion, a senior lawyer would come to the inner sanctum for a private briefing on a very important case. The complete set-up was most effective and highly efficient, and I admit to being impressed from the first day I started working for this man.

As the plane flew on its long journey to Perth, I let my mind wander back through the years and the numerous sequences of events in my life, a kaleidoscope of events that led me to where I am today.

CHAPTER 3

Bushland Hideaway

On my completing the job in Melbourne and reporting the success of the mission back to JJ, I retreated to my own personal hideaway in the bush for a couple of weeks of rest and recuperation. It's a peaceful retreat that had been purchased from my combined military savings and the excellent money paid to me by JJ and is my special R&R place.

I like Sydney, but to me, it is like all other cities. I am still a country boy at heart and prefer to get away from the hustle and bustle from time to time, and my greatest pleasure comes when the opportunity arrives between jobs to head to the beautiful four-hundred-and-forty-hectare piece of land I now own, situated at the base of a mountain in a secluded valley. It is a scenic piece of undulating land, bordered by a flowing creek and a river on two boundaries, with almost a third supporting a large section of natural hardwood forest. It's very private and only accessible from the nearest small town about twenty kilometres away, partly on a bitumen road, with the last ten kilometres being on my own private, all-weather gravel road, with a locked gate at the entrance. It has no nearby neighbours and is in the northern rivers region of NSW. There is some flat land near the house, and I have toyed with the idea of building a landing strip, taking flying lessons at Bankstown Airport, and buying a small plane for quick access. I think it's a better idea, instead of doing the nine-to-ten-hour drive from Sydney as I do for sometimes short breaks and then have to drive back.

The property previously was a dairy farm, and has two dwellings on it, along with a couple of steel sheds for machinery and tools, horse and cattle yards and dairy sheds. One of the two houses had been the farm owner's house to live in, and the other had been built for a son and his wife, who decided to move to Western Australia for work in the mining boom period.

Both houses were built in the typical Australian homestead style, with wide verandas surrounding them. On buying the property, I had both homes extensively renovated, modernised, and added to: one for me and the other with extensions for their visiting family, which is lived in by the retired farming couple, Melissa and Byron, whom I purchased the property from, and who now act as caretakers looking after the property, my three horses, and a small herd of Angus cattle I purchased. The dairy herd was sold when Melissa and Byron decided to sell and retire; the small herd of cattle enables them to keep an interest, and enjoy the bulk of the income.

With this property being next to an extensive 20,000-hectare state forest, it is my ideal rest and recuperation Nirvana, where I can spend hours between jobs, unwinding, riding and exploring the numerous tracks through the scenic forest, and fishing the river that flows around it. Byron is also a horseman, and although in his mid-seventies, he is an entertaining riding companion with the tales of his youth in the bush, breaking in horses, cattle droving, and riding the rodeo circuit, so I look forward to a visit, and an occasional ride or fish with him.

Suddenly, I was alert, my thought processes suddenly interrupted by some jolting of the plane, and then the pilot's voice coming over the intercom, saying, "The plane was starting to experience some turbulence, and to please fasten your safety belts." As the plane bumped up and down on the thermal updrafts, it set me on a new line of thought, thinking about how my life had seen so many ups and downs, my military training, the dangers and its changes, and currently, the series of events which had led me to this work, and the current mission in hand, and my thoughts skipped forward.

I was now heading to a wealthy suburban waterfront area at Mandurah, not far from Perth, to help "pass away" of natural causes, a rich deviate who had lured a seventeen-year-old girl into his office with the promise of work. It was not long after she started that he showed intentions other than work, and his amorous innuendos, shyly rebuffed by the young girl, turned violent one day when he sexually abused and raped her. The poor girl bravely told her family and then the police. Still, because of corrupt legal representation, his strong political and upper-class social connections, his wealth, and a friendly and also corrupt judge, the bastard eventually walked out of court a free man. In contrast, the poor kid had been made to look like some cheap tart who had offered herself to him. She was now in a mental health clinic facing years of therapy and would possibly never emotionally recover from his filthy attack.

JJ and his informants had spent a lot of time assessing all the media, police, and court records, plus a report uncovered from another young girl who had worked for the same scumbag and who was too terrified to appear in court and tell what she knew about him.

Unfortunately for this evil being, the father of the young girl who had been raped had some connection from past business and legal dealings with a friendly police associate, and that led him to "JJ" and then on to the "Mulga Man", which is the "nom de guerre" that I now work under.

The most important factor, with "JJ's" assistance, is to first establish, without a doubt, the guilt of the perpetrator. This is primarily done through "JJ" and his vast number of investigators and contacts from within and outside of the law. Then my job is to bring satisfaction and, hopefully, closure to devastated defendants and families. Sometimes, the punishment can be as simple as a severe beating, maybe a broken bone or two, or perhaps the destruction or disappearance of valuable property or possessions. On some occasions, and depending on the severity of the crime, the punishment can result in the disappearance of the perpetrator by whatever means available to me at the time. It all depends on the degree of seriousness of the crime or crimes committed.

The pilot is again on the intercom and announcing the plane's turbulence has now ceased. The pilot sounds jovial as he announces we can leave our seats if necessary, and I settle back into my comfortable chair with another scotch and soda and start on another chain of thought, thinking back to my upbringing as a third-generation Australian from an indigenous mother and a white father. My father was descended from Irish farming parents, who were hardworking free settlers. They were a wonderful couple from the south of Ireland who, as small children, had seen their respective parents buried in the 1850s during "An Gorta Mór", the Irish name for the potato famine that blighted Ireland from 1845 into the early

1850s. They had survived solely through the generosity of a tenant farming couple and a sympathetic English landlord, who gave them work and supported them. When the second potato famine blight struck in 1879, the pair, now married, travelled on foot across the country to Belfast, where they took on any form of employment available and scraped together enough money to buy passage by ship from Belfast to Sydney, Australia, arriving in early 1890, and where their son was born.

They were a hardworking couple who took on whatever work they could find while still caring for a growing son, scrimping and saving along the way, and on hearing of the Australian free land selection scheme, they found their way into the vast Australian "outback" where in 1900, they selected five hundred acres of rough scrubby mulga and mallee land along the Darling River, built a wattle and daub, bark-roofed hut, and started their farming life. Their only child, Seamus, now a rebellious ten-year-old, grew to be the man who would become my father.

My dear Irish grandparents were old school, devout, hardworking Catholic Christians and good people whom I loved dearly until the day they tragically died when a huge bushfire swept through the country that they could not escape from when they were caught out in the open country. It burned out their farmhouse and land, leaving only a shed still standing. This happened when I was a small boy during the horrendous bushfires of 1939. Their son was drunk in a pub in the nearby town at the time, but still, the neighbouring landowners rallied to help rebuild the small farmhouse.

Unfortunately, they had lived long enough to see their only son, my father, grow into a drunken, shiftless no-hoper, resentful of his parents and the hard life they had lived, and who shied away from his responsibilities, a dissolute though handsome fellow who wooed and won the girl who become my mother, but after their marriage, was inclined in his drunken rages to beat my dear mother almost senseless. My sister and I were born into this, and often, in these drunken rages, he would then turn on me and my younger sister, and if we were not quick enough to get out of his way, he would severely beat us, and so when we heard him coming, and even at night when we were in bed, we had learnt to run and hide. We would run for cover and lie in hiding, sometimes out in the surrounding scrub or in the old shed that was standing out back, listening to his abuse and blows and our mother sobbing until he had drunk more cheap wine and passed out in a drunken stupor.

We would then sneak back into the house and try to console her, with me swearing through tears that one day, when I was big and strong enough, I would settle the score. I hated him with a rage that carried over into my older years and directed towards any man I saw mistreating or hitting a woman, or for that matter any one person or persons who attempted to brutalise anyone who could not defend themselves; it was and is, an inner rage that I now know from my time in Malaya and Vietnam, helped start me off on the path I follow today.

My mother was a good woman who deserved better. She was one half aboriginal and who, like her full-blood "Uncle Charlie", was of the Barkindji tribe, which was a part of the Paakantji aboriginal nation that inhabited much of the land east and west of the Darling River, that went from Wentworth to the Menindee Lakes country. This aboriginal tribal group had lived along the "Darling" and surrounding area for over 30,000 years, but was eventually fragmented by the advent of the white European settlers.

She only knew of her father as being a white drover who came through their area regularly with mobs of cattle and who seduced her mother. Because my mother, when born, was classified as a half-caste, she was taken from her mother.

She had been raised as a small child in the nearby Pooncarie aboriginal settlement for a time before being removed from her mother.

That is how it was with white man's law then; it was the white man's custom to remove young half-caste aboriginal children and resettle them with missionary families and in Christian institutions, and when my mother was about four or five, a young new missionary couple came into the area to address the Christian and medical needs of the local aboriginal community. As they had no children of their own, they took my mother into their home to live. They gave her the English name of Genevieve. According to my mother, they were good people who treated her well, gave her food, love, and clothing and, most importantly, gave her an education. They did their best to teach her how to live the white man's way, while accepting her aboriginal background, and as a result, my mother grew up believing that was how all white people were. Unfortunately, she had not been exposed to the realities of life for a black person in a white man's world. I reason now that had been a mistake, because when she met the man who was to become my father, she was totally unprepared for what was to come.

As a young woman, she was very pretty, and she had been treated well and fairly by the family she had come to love. She happily lived with them up until her late teens, and when the missionary couple said they were going back to Melbourne to live, their reason for this major move was that they were ageing and feeling the harshness of outback life and that my mother could come with them to live in this big city. That frightened her somewhat because of all the things she had read in newspapers and daily radio news about cities and crime. She felt she would not be safe or happy there, and where she now lived was her tribal land. More so, she was loved, respected, and accepted by the aboriginal community, some of whom were related to her and whom she often worked with assisting the benevolent missionary couple, so she felt comfortable in this small and know-everybody environment she had been raised in. She became terrified at the thought of leaving it to live in a city where she knew no one.

There was nothing the concerned, well-meaning couple could do to convince her otherwise. She told them she could never leave her lovable Uncle Charlie, who was a brother of her deceased mother, and her many other tribal friends and extended family, and she sobbingly voiced her concern, saying she was so frightened of going to a big city to live, and there she felt she would die. There was no way of convincing her, so the well-meaning missionary couple spoke to some Christian friends who owned a boarding house in the small town of Pooncarie and arranged for my mother to work for them.

On the day they left for their new assignment within their Christian missionary and a home in outer Melbourne, after sadly saying goodbye to my mother, she went to their friends' boarding house to live and got her first income-earning job, working as a housemaid at the only boarding house in the town, and that is where "pretty Genevieve" as the mistress of the boarding house called her, met my then handsome father to be.

He was an itinerant farm worker and part-time stockman, and who, when he had money, would come to town to spend it. He was in the habit of staying in the boarding house, and against the advice of the boarding house owners, who warned her against getting involved with him, he wooed her and swept her off her feet with his sweet talk, and then in a short time after he married her, spent the rest of their life together treating her as an object of ridicule and abuse as a useless black bitch, and particularly after me and my sister were born.

I was born in 1941, and my sister in 1944. In this terrible situation, our mother was a hardworking and honest woman who never deserved the abuse and physical violence that the bastard dished out to her. Yet, no matter what happened, she was always there for my sister and me.

The day that I was born was early on a frosty morning, and according to Mum, it was the start of a very cold July day. In later years, I was to find out my father had been too drunk to wake up and drive her to the hospital in his old utility. She was already having regular labour pains, and so she trudged over the frosted ground to the police residence, nearly two miles away, to seek help. She almost did not make it, and I was born in the warmth of the policeman's house, with his wife acting as a temporary midwife. Soon after, at the point of my birth, the local doctor turned up. The local policeman, who was senior Constable Kennedy, I was told many years later, went over to our house after I was born and soundly abused my drunken father for not being with her when she needed him.

We, children, had no idea why our father was such a nasty, selfish man who spent most of the money he earned on booze, and we were dirt-poor, so mum took part-time jobs at the boarding house and cleaning houses for people in the nearby town to keep food on the table, and some clothes on our backs. She would get on her battered old Speedwell push bike that she and Uncle Charlie had repaired after finding it at the local rubbish dump, then pedal half a mile from where we lived into town to do various domestic work. We were living in a rundown old house close to the edge of town, which had been a farmhouse in the early days before the town spread out. It was surrounded by some small properties which had once been large farms, and further out were huge pastoral holdings running mainly sheep and cattle.

Although our father made a reasonable wage working around the woolsheds of the surrounding district as a rouseabout, stockman, and shed hand when he was sober, he would change once he was paid. He would head to the only pub in town, getting drunker and more aggressive, getting into arguments with someone until he was refused service and tossed out by the publican, or was knocked down by someone who had a gutful of his aggressive and "big-noting manner". He would then head to the wine bar in town, where most of the town's no-hopers hung out, and buy wine. He would always have a stash of cheap Muscat or Port planted somewhere and drink from the bottle often as he drove. He would then wend his way home and take his foul temper out on all of us. I supposed as I grew and learnt more about him, he was a non-achiever, his chip-on-the-shoulder attitude had people turning away from him, he was always bragging about everything he fancied himself as, and yet he had never achieved anything of consequence, nor been anywhere. So people saw him as a no-account "skite" who somehow managed to escape the military draft when many other men his age had been sent overseas to fight in the war. He couldn't handle being pushed around or being jeered at by anyone scoffing at his bullshit, so he would come home and take it out on an easier target, meaning us. Christ, how I loathed the bastard! And so, in my early childhood, I often wished he was dead.

CHAPTER 4

Perth, Western Australia

My seat was on the right side of the plane, flying to Perth, and I was looking out the window at the hazy coastline of South Australia off in the distance, and about 35,000 feet below was the ocean. I estimated we were about halfway across the gulf of the Great Australian Bight, and I started on another train of thought of my past life and childhood memories.

Lost in my daydreams of past happenings, the hours on that long Qantas flight had slipped past, and I was again snapped out of my reverie by the plane intercom crackling. The captain was announcing we would be landing at Perth International Airport in five minutes and to fasten our safety belts. There was enough time to collect my thoughts and think about my next movements and the start of the next assignment, my second job as the "Mulga Man". This time, I was travelling as a financial consultant associated with land and housing developments.

I was carrying an impressive portfolio. The initial subterfuge planned was to gain an appointment with the target, who was an extremely wealthy and reputedly ruthless land developer, a man whose greed for money was only surpassed by his perverse sexual needs for very young girls and boys. His perverted needs had led to his arrest on a charge of rape and heinous, allied sexual assault charges, and his subsequent non-conviction due to a huge amount of money paid to, and the sudden disappearance of the main witness, namely his personal secretary, who had overheard the assault. According to information passed on to me, and of course, many things not widely known to the public, it also involved the judge who presided over the case. Allegations had come to "JJ" that some knew of him to be corrupt and who happened to be a friend and member of a group of influential people suspected of paedophilia involvement, a group that included the defendant's lawyer and all with political connections.

The violated young woman's father had hired a top-rate private investigator, a university friend from his past, who previously had been a law school graduate. And who joined the police force and went on to become a senior police detective, noted for his in-depth knowledge of the law and his fringe dweller contacts. After resigning from the police force, he put together his own private investigation business. Over more than a year, he had amassed considerable knowledge of this secretive paedophile ring operating in Perth and its many members, some prominent in Perth society. His portfolio contained names and photographs of some socialising on a large luxury cruiser that the businessman Sinclair owned and kept moored in a nearby boat harbour.

His investigations showed that this property developer, along with his wealthy lawyer friend and the judge, were members. They were the same lawyer and judge whose devious manipulations of the law allowed him to go free. All of this, along with a wealth of information on his business, home addresses, investments, properties, asset ownership, and other activities, had been passed on to the girl's father.

The father was a businessman of considerable wealth and with many connections of his own. On advice from his private investigator, he passed the information on to "JJ", and so it came to me. After intensive study, a plan that had been suggested by the victim's father based on his knowledge of the developer's activities was formed, which would involve me putting to Sinclair, a large but fictitious land and hotel development in the vicinity of the gold mining city of Kalgoorlie with a number of interested investors from the east coast and overseas.

This initial plan was meant to be the means of accessing Sinclair's confidence to assess his movements. However, experience had taught me not to make any moves until I had carefully analysed the situation for myself. At this point, I had not made any contact or appointment. Coming events were to prove that was a wise decision. As the plane was landing, I was looking at a map of Perth and regions and thought my next move would be to rent a motor vehicle and book into a motel in the City of Mandurah, about three-quarters of an hour's drive from Perth. After the plane had landed, I made my way to the airport's Avis Rent-A-Car office, armed with my false credentials. From there, a phone call to a motel, and a short time later, I was behind the wheel of a cream-coloured late-model Valiant, heading away from the airport on the drive to Mandurah City, to the motel.

The motel was situated on the Mandurah Terrace, and looked over the Peel Inlet boat harbour, a short distance away. Checking in, I asked for a top-floor room with a balcony view over the harbour.

Showered, relaxed, and settling in with a beer from the bar fridge, I sat out on the balcony with a pair of high-powered binoculars, one of the keepsakes from my time with Special Operations in Vietnam. It was an excellent vantage point to survey the waterways. The motel was not an opulent one, but quite substantial, and the top floor room I had asked for with its view was excellent for my purpose and fitted in with an idea starting to take shape in my mind

I had an excellent far-ranging view of the boat harbour and what looked to be a marina with a variety of yachts and cruisers moored there; no doubt many of them playthings of the idle rich, and information provided to me indicated one of those playthings belonged to the developer Howard Sinclair. This gave me an idea, and I sat there for a couple of hours, thinking and planning my next moves. Tomorrow was Sunday, and I decided I would head into the city early to find the "target's" office, then spend some time driving around to get the feel of the layout of the city. The surveillance information sent to me said that Sinclair had his main office situated a short distance away in the city CBD and another office in the centre of Perth. He owned a luxury waterfront home near the boat harbour.

The report gave details of the cruiser that he kept at the marina. It was a large, luxurious, though old-style timber cruiser, seen moored in the boat harbour, and I found that piece of information interesting, particularly when I read that the Halverson Company had made it.

The idea I had earlier was now formulating in my mind, a plan aided by the knowledge gained in my Special Operations Force training for Malaya and Vietnam at the Army Water Transport base at Chowder Bay, near Clifton Gardens, in Sydney Harbour. Much of the training was learning boat handling, seamanship, and boat engineering knowledge.

Chowder Bay, and the area of Sydney Harbour I found very interesting. In 1889, it was selected as the site for a Submarine Mining Depot because of the early fortifications built there, and accommodation, storage, training, and operational facilities were since erected. The "Submarine Mining Corp" was responsible for maintaining electrically triggered minefields strung around the harbour as a defence against enemy ships. This "Submarine Mining" was an advanced form of military technology representing the earliest use of electricity for defence purposes. Mines were strung across the harbour and were operational by 1894, but were never fired in anger. The development of submarines made such minefields redundant, and in 1922, the Submarine Mining Corps was disbanded.

Chowder Bay then became a depot and barracks for The Royal Australian Engineers (RAE) until it was occupied by the School of Military Engineering Anti-Aircraft Wing and then from 1943, the school's Marine Transport Wing, colloquially known as the "Army Water Transport Base". There, I did my boat, sea, and engine training on their beautifully made timber Fairmile class boats. These high-powered "Fairmile" Army Patrol boats, built at the Lars Halverson boat building yards on the Hawkesbury River, were well maintained. They were streamlined, fast-moving vessels, capable of twenty knots at full speed, powered by twin Hall Scott Defender petrol engines, each 650 HP with twin screws, and were specially built for the military and used for patrolling our coastal waters and islands during the war, mainly against Japanese submarine incursions, and now were used for training exercises. Their armament consisted of one Rolls Royce two-pounder Mark X1V gun mounted forward and two Vickers 303 Machine guns. Other weaponry carried was one 20mm Oerlikon gun mounted aft, one "Y" gun depth charge thrower, holding two depth charges, fourteen depth charges in chutes with release gears and small arms including Thompson machine guns, .303 rifles, hand grenades, and explosive charges, and manned by a crew of twenty under the command of a lieutenant. They carried no name, and the boat I did training on was ML814.

Chowder Bay and its neighbouring Clifton Gardens is a lovely spot on the western shore of Sydney Harbour, below the plush homes of Mosman, and part of my training involved a number of nighttime pick-ups and drop-offs of military personnel at remote beaches along the eastern coastline with lights out, the craft would be manoeuvred to a safe distance from shore, then a prearranged signal light would flash from the shore, and a man in a frogman's suit would go over the side, or a swimmer would come out to the boat for pickup. Sometimes, in more distant waters, a rubber boat would be launched and paddled from the boat to the shoreline. It was real spy thriller stuff with a certain amount of danger from the elements, and with army military patrols acting as enemy firing with blank ammunition, and occasionally live ammunition would be fired, though safely overhead.

"JJ" had given me a contact phone number in Perth, where I could pick up a weapon if necessary. I knew that person would be one of his "fringe dweller" contacts, so I decided to make that decision after first assessing the situation, finding most times, with the use of my past Special Op skills, a gun was not necessary.

I was hungry, so changing into a pair of jeans, joggers, and a sweatshirt, I went into the lift and down to the foyer. The receptionist was busy checking arrivals, and not wanting to bring attention to myself, I quietly walked out into the street. A short walk brought me to a riverside café/restaurant specialising in Asian food. I sat there, slowly enjoying a seafood combination with rice and surveying the people around me.

The restaurant was almost full, and I saw that a number of families had the appearance of tourists about them. Although one family in particular stood out to me. They were of South East Asian appearance. They were two tables across from me. There were six in the group: an elderly couple I assumed to be grandparents, a younger couple in their early thirties, and two young children, a boy and a girl. The boy looked to be about eight or nine, the girl about seven. They were all noisily chattering away in the singsong way of their language. Straining my ears to hear, I picked up remnants of a language I had some knowledge of, a language I had heard often in sometimes horrifying circumstances. It was the language of a country that had been torn apart by a most terrible political war. A language of Vietnam. A language I had not heard close up since flying out of Saigon, and listening to their accent, I could tell they were from the southern lowlands of Vietnam.

Sitting there in that restaurant, hearing those voices, my mind was transported back to another time and country. I found myself remembering again my military guerilla training, the martial arts, weapons, and killing techniques after being accepted into the SAS and then Special Operations, the covert section for training in top-secret military operations. There was much cloak-and-dagger spying associated with the use of those skills in the Vietnamese Central Highlands, where I worked with and trained the Montagnard hill tribes, and soon, those same skills would again be put to use in my new life as a paid "assassin", the "Mulga Man".

My mind drifted back again, way back again, to the start of it all, before I went into the army.

In one year, I had resigned from my position as head stockman, my miserable father had died, I had fallen in love, and joined the army. A flood of memories came over me, thinking how love had captured my heart and the Australian Military had taken my body and mind. For a time, I dwelled on the kaleidoscopic chapters of my life, its changes and the sequence of events that have led me to this second mission starting tomorrow as the Mulga Man.

CHAPTER 5

Peel Inlet, Mandurah

It's time for the Mulga Man to administer "justice" again. The long plane journey from Sydney to Perth and a restful night in this motel had given me plenty of time to contemplate past history and the decisions made over the years, and now it was time to get down to serious planning and work.

It had dawned a beautiful, clear, sunny Saturday morning; it's 7 a.m., and a glimmer of sunshine is coming overhead as I sit on the balcony of my room watching activities on the Peel inlet below me, a short distance away and the estuary of water that is the boat harbour is sparkling to where it opens out to the Indian Ocean. Some kids are fishing from the jetty, with seagulls wheeling and swooping as they search for any food scraps they can find, each diving in to jostle and screech at the lucky bird that found something. One kid was having the time of his life throwing bread scraps, creating a whirling, fighting, noisy turmoil of these grey and white sea birds.

I had spent most of the previous day perusing all the information given to me that had been gained over the past year's investigation of my next mark. This is to be my second job as Mulga Man, after the successful "doing away" with the Melbourne rapist, who is now resting a few feet under a landfill area west of Melbourne. I trust this next assignment will be just as successful, albeit more complex in detail.

I need to find a way to eliminate a pedophilic scum bag named Howard Sinclair, a filthy rich, nasty person with many assets and one hell of a sick bastard. Divorced a couple of times, with both the ex-wives quoting mental, physical, and sexual abuse, that is just the start of it. There are allegations of shady land and property developments, drug dealing, and numerous whispers around town about his connection with a secretive paedophile ring involving young girls and boys, along with members of the legal profession and high-profile social and business members of the Perth community. Sinclair was definitely someone worthy of my attention.

The portfolio of information I was reading had been gained by an excellent private investigator, who had been hired by the aggrieved father of the young girl who Sinclair had foully assaulted.

The report is very comprehensive. It would have come at a considerable financial cost to the father of the girl, and this knowledge further fuelled my desire to see that justice would be done.

For some reason, obscure to me originally, I had held back on following up on the previously suggested method of gaining inside trust with Mr Sinclair, using a fake property development scheme that had been put to me by her father. This ruse did not sit right with me; I felt I did not want to become known to Sinclair.

This inner gut feeling that had seen me safely through the "behind the lines horrors" of Malaya, and Vietnam, was niggling at me, and I knew there had to be a better way to deal with him.

The more I studied the report and analysed Sinclair's assets, the more I kept thinking back to his luxury cruiser sitting at its mooring, not far from where I sat on the balcony of the motel. The boat was moored in a prime position at the very end of the marina jetty. It was an easy spot to navigate a big boat out from and back to its mooring. I guessed he paid big money for such a mooring, and as I formulated my plan, I felt that the position could be a big plus.

Part of the information I was reading said that each Saturday morning, weather permitting, Sinclair would drive his Porsche to the dock parking area, parking as close as possible to the jetty where his cruiser was moored, and dressed in casual clothes and sneakers, he would unload out of the boot of the car, cartons of various alcohols and food supplies. He would then load everything onto a trolley kept at the marina for the purpose of people taking supplies to their boats. Sinclair would trundle the trolley load along the narrow jetty to his cruiser and load it aboard. He was usually alone or occasionally accompanied by his mate, the judge. This was the same judge who had dismissed the sexual assault charges against him in court. I read he was rather anal in habit and worked very much to a routine pattern.

After loading the supplies aboard, he would turn the radio on fairly high. Obviously, he liked loud music. He would then spend a short time packing the supplies away, usually about a half hour of work. Next, he would start the twin engines, and once the powerful petrol engines were ticking over, he would cast off the forward bow mooring line, then the stern mooring, and slowly move the boat away from the jetty and cruise down the Peel inlet for about another half hour, where he would come alongside a public wharf. There, on most occasions, would be waiting a small group of three or four young girls, sometimes young boys, who were accompanied by two muscular men—pimps, bodyguards? Waiting with them would be a group of three to four middle-aged men. I guessed them as being "partners in perversion". As I read on, it became obvious to me why he acted the way he did. Sinclair did not want to divulge too much of the whereabouts of his private life and private boat mooring to just anyone. His boat, after picking up its motley assortment of passengers, would cruise from its guest pickup onto destinations unknown on the water overnight and, like clockwork, would arrive back to the same public wharf and discharge its passengers around 4 p.m. each Sunday afternoon. On a long weekend, it would stay out two nights to arrive back on a Monday afternoon.

On arrival back at the cruiser's mooring, Sinclair would step ashore after a man or two had caught the lines and moored the boat. He would then report to the marina office, and two members of the marina staff would come aboard and spend the next couple of hours disposing of garbage, cleaning, and hosing the boat down. Obviously, they were trusted employees, and after the cleaning, they would refuel the cruiser's huge petrol tanks, lock up the cruiser, and leave. I guessed an account would be passed on to Sinclair.

The more I studied this detailed information, it got me thinking: could this be the answer, the solution for the job to be done? Reaching for my high-powered binoculars, I decided to pay much closer attention to this part of Sinclair's time on his boat. Scanning the marina entrance, it was 7:10 a.m. on the dot when I saw the Porsche drive up to near the entrance. The man who got out of the car resembled the description given in the report. He was showing some grey hair under a baseball cap atop a ruddy complexion, a build that might have once been athletic but now carried a substantial gut. Broad shoulders and nearly six feet tall. I adjusted the glasses to get a closer look at him. Yes, it was him; he resembled the enlarged photograph I had in front of me. True to the details, he vanished inside the marina's reception entrance for a short time and emerged, wheeling a trolley. Heading back to his car, he went through the motions of unloading various goods, cartons, and bags from the Porsche onto the trolley and disappeared once more in the office for a short period. My next visual of Sinclair was him striding along the jetty, pushing the trolley, and stopping at the large cruiser moored at the jetty end. It took him exactly twenty-five minutes to load the vessel with the supplies and then re-park the Porsche in the main car yard before he reappeared on the jetty and stepped aboard his boat. I did puzzle as to why the marina workers did not assist him with this, but reasoned this was part of Sinclair keeping private his doings, and I thought that with what I had in mind, their non-presence would be a good thing.

A couple more minutes went by, and I watched him take in the mooring lines and disappear inside the cabin. Soon, I heard the roar of the twin engines being started, with the sound travelling up to me from the water, loud at first, then settling down to a low, steady throb. For a couple of minutes, the throbbing of powerful engines softly echoed across the bay, and then I could hear a louder sound as the throttle increased the engine revolutions and the bow of the boat slowly eased away from the jetty and out into the open channel, where it slowly increased speed out to the open water. I followed its passage with the binoculars, watching the diminishing speck of the boat until it had vanished from view.

"Hmmm!" My mind was racing, and my gut was starting to point me in a direction. An idea was forming on what my next move would be. But, first, I needed to do some investigation into more exact details of the type, age, and make of the engines on that beautiful older style cruiser.

I was back at my watching post on the motel verandah when the cruiser arrived back at its mooring Sunday afternoon. At 4:15 p.m., it was moored to the jetty. Sinclair stepped off, and the young marina lads took over.

Monday morning, putting on a baseball cap, dark sunglasses, T-shirt, jeans, and sneakers, I took an idle walk along the marina jetty, endeavouring to look like any other tourist, pointing a camera here and there, taking photographs of the scenery, the pelicans on the water, other boats, and of course the cruiser. Close up, I saw it was bigger than I thought. A few more snaps of kids fishing off the jetty to add further to the subterfuge, and I was away in my hired vehicle to the City of Perth Library. Sitting in the calm of this quiet and large library, I tucked myself away in a corner out of the mainstream of library visitors, armed with the pictures of the cruiser I had on a small table, a number of books on boats and cruisers, and in particular, I had found an excellent book showing the histories on Halverson built boats. After a couple of hours of reading text and studying pictures, I had what I was looking for.

Sinclair's cruiser was a forty-eight-foot "Classic" model, which was built by Halvorson boat builders in 1942 to a Thorneycroft design. Most interesting to me were the twin Rolls Royce V12 Merlin Engines. They were capable of opening up to a top speed of fifty-five knots at full throttle. That type of engine was first fitted to Royal Navy prototype Motor Torpedo Boats. This type of boat had been used by the Australian Navy. I mused considerably over this; the private investigator reports sent to me on Sinclair did mention his occasional overnight trips out to sea, ostensibly to go fishing.

More importantly, the report also said that this same boat, at some time in its past, had been owned and used by an Adelaide businessman with criminal links suspected of drug smuggling. This man had been investigated and now languished in prison, with his assets being sold. The boat had been put to auction, where it was purchased by Sinclair.

The boat had been fully renovated by Sinclair about four years back at a reputable West Australian boatyard on the Swan River, near Perth, at considerable expense. It was then navigated by a hired crew down the coastline to Mandurah and through the entrance into the Peel inlet and its mooring at a marina. I mused, was this a remarkable coincidence, this same boat some years back, known to be used for collecting offshore drugs? Could our bad boy Sinclair and his "fast" boat have another insidious use?

My thinking this way was the original 1942 Merlin V12 Rolls Royce petrol engines had been extensively overhauled and retained in the boat when the renovations were done—but why? Instead of switching the more expensive petrol-guzzling engines over to a lower speed, safer, fuel-economical diesel engine, engines that could easily give a top cruising speed of fifteen knots and be far better suited for pleasure cruising, Sinclair had opted to keep the more expensive and faster-running petrol engines. Why had he decided to have the petrol engines thoroughly overhauled at considerable cost, instead of installing slower but more economical diesel engines? This had me suspiciously wondering why.

I had learnt in my training on the Fairmile boats that petrol engines with age and deterioration have been known to sometimes explode and catch fire due to petrol leaks and fumes, and that knowledge got me thinking.

My previous "just a gut feeling" was now starting to formulate a plan. I knew it was time to head into Perth and do some shopping for what I would need. This was done on Tuesday and Wednesday,

On Thursday, I drove and parked a short distance from the marina and then walked around the waterfront foreshore, looking for a suitable place to enter the water. At a chosen spot, I estimated it was less than a mile, maybe seven or eight hundred yards, swim from the secluded spot I had selected to where the cruiser was moored at the jetty's end.

I knew the marina was closed each afternoon at 6 p.m., and the high-security gate was locked and had motion lights, with a surveillance camera at the entrance, and only boat owners and marina staff had the access code to open the gate. I calculated there was little chance of a boat owner being there or spotting me late at night during the week clambering aboard the cruiser. My calculation was enhanced by the news report that overcast conditions with rain squalls were anticipated late on Thursday.

Earlier that same day, I had made a phone call to Sinclair's office using an assumed name and asked if it were possible to make an appointment for either Friday afternoon or Saturday morning, as I wished to put forward a business proposal and had to fly back to Melbourne on Saturday afternoon. I was brusquely told that Mr Sinclair was away Friday on business, and he made no appointments Friday and would be away Saturday morning for the weekend. I would have to get back to him the following week if I wished to contact him.

That was what I wanted to hear, smiling to myself; I thought soon, our Mr. Sinclair would not be in a position to see anyone at all.

For part of my military training with the SAS, I had been sent to Chowder Bay Army Water Transport, there to do specialised training in the handling of large boats and general seamanship. It also involved studying and working on the high-powered petrol engines of the excellent Fairmile patrol boats. These boats carried no name, only an identification number, and were painted all over with khaki camouflage and built by the Halvorson Company.

The training program covered engine maintenance and safety precautions, and it pointed out the dangers of accumulated petrol fumes, often caused by leaking petrol, lying heavy in the bilges, so it is always necessary to switch on bilge blowers to drive away excess fumes. We were shown the main causes of petrol explosions in boats can be traced to a number of things. For example, old fuel residue can deteriorate over prolonged periods in tanks and fuel lines and can jam the carburettors, and then excess fuel could pour down its throat, fill the manifold, and run onto a hot engine. Another problem can be loose fuel lines, caused by excessive vibration, causing the wearing of a hole or crack leaking fuel, and also, a loose coupling on a fuel line can leak fuel. Combine this with a battery or electrical lead spark when starting, and kaboom! This could be the solution I was looking for.

Fiery accidents like this on old boats are well known, and a number of explosions, fires, and deaths have been recorded over the years.

The weather forecast was correct; Thursday night had turned out perfect for my purpose. It was an overcast, moonless, rainy night with occasional squalls of rain gusting across the bay, and I doubted anyone would not be out on the water when I drove close to a deserted section of beach to don my recently purchased wetsuit, swim flippers, goggles, and waterproof head torch. It was nearly 1 a.m. when I entered the water with the necessary tools and skeleton keys in a tightly sealed plastic bag packed inside the black foam-filled hold-all bag. This was attached by a cord to my waist, and using the bag as a float in front of me, I waded in. There was some windblown wave action, but not enough to worry me as I steadily flipper-swam the distance to the cruiser. I was hoping, though, that the weather would clear up before Saturday for my plan to be effective.

As I swam, I was reminded of a time in the Central Highlands of Vietnam when, with my team of Montagnard hill tribe fighters, we had to swim a river late at night with our equipment to stage an ambush on a squad of Viet Cong and regular NVA, and Chinese Communist Army infiltrators camp. Our ambush was quiet, quick, deadly, and so unexpected there were no survivors. We did not lose a man.

I remember that just before I left Vietnam in 1966 to come home, a captured senior Viet Cong officer told me we were known as the "Ma Rung" or "phantoms of the jungle". Tonight, I hoped that I would be the "phantom of the water", unseen and unheard.

As I approached the boat, there was no sign of life on the jetty, and the faint light coming from a lamp further down was not enough for anyone to get a good view of me as I heaved my bag and myself up onto the transom duckboard, and into the stern section of the boat. Removing the flippers, I made my way to the locked saloon door. It seemed no time before one of my many keys clicked the lock over. Sliding the door silently open, I slipped inside, making sure all curtains were drawn tight.

Fastening a forehead torch to my head, I removed the deck hatch cover and slid down into the bilge and engine area. I noted the two starter buttons for the port and starboard engine. It would be easy enough to trace the wiring through. The big V12 engines did show some sign of their age, but looked to be in relatively sound order. There was some build-up of accumulated grime and grease, only natural, and obvious that Sinclair was not into getting his hands dirty, work-wise.

I found the bilge blowers and, working a wire by hand, managed to create a loose connection, hopefully enough to create a spark. Turning to the fuel connections and lines, I contemplated whether to loosen a connection to create a small and slow drip or to physically manipulate a line to chafe a slight leak. Deciding on the former, I found the connections were relatively tight except for the connection going into the carburettor, a couple of turns with a spanner saw a very slow drip of fuel seeping down the line, and the familiar smell of petrol reached my nostrils. Once the bilge blower was switched on to clear the petrol fumes, there would be a microscopic second before Sinclair passed into oblivion.

I had already reasoned that Sinclair's habit of turning on the radio to his favourite Saturday program would cover the absence of sound, if any, from the bilge blowers, and with the small towel carried in the bag, I removed all traces of excess water from the deck. The damp areas would be dry by Saturday morning. The curtains had already been closed, probably by his cleanup crew, so after a couple of minutes spent looking around for any traces showing off where I had been, I put the deck cover back in place and locked the door. Wiping the outside deck of water, I attached the bag to my waist and slipped over the side with barely a splash. I was feeling good about the night's work and looking forward to the easy swim back to my car.

It was still overcast and very dark, but I had a fix on the faint gleam from street lamps to where I was headed. At the car, I packed away the tools and changed into dry clothing. It was about 5 a.m. when, after a hot shower, I crawled into bed to sleep soundly until midday. The weather had turned fine again when I woke up. Pulling on a T-shirt, shorts, and joggers, I wandered down to the waterfront to enjoy a leisurely brunch.

Sitting outside the small café, enjoying the sunshine and a coffee, I reflected back on the night's work, analysing and dissecting every move, and I felt no uncomfortable niggles. I was confident that my every action was covered.

Assuming everything went according to plan, it would be around 7 to 7:45 a.m. tomorrow morning, and the world would be rid of a very nasty man. Sinclair would disappear into oblivion.

It was just before dawn and a warm, clear Saturday morning when I awoke, deciding to go for a jog down by the boat docks and around the waterfront. I would follow this with a dive into the harbour waters and a brisk swim. I wanted to be back in my room having a light coffee and toast breakfast, ready to take my position with the binoculars for the anticipated fireworks.

Sitting comfortably with my feet up on the middle rail of the balcony, I waited with the binoculars ready, checking my watch. It was 6:35 a.m. People were starting to appear along the waterfront. Mandurah was waking up to a glorious, sparkling, sunny Saturday morning.

It was a few minutes after 7 a.m. when I spotted the shiny black Porsche nose on the pavement's edge. The driver got out, and focusing closer, I saw it was Sinclair, dressed in a boat cruising outfit of white pants, a colourful shirt hanging loose outside his pants, a baseball cap, and sandshoes. Walking around to the pavement, he started through the dock's entrance, no doubt heading in to pick up a trolley, when I spotted a movement on the passenger side of the Porsche. Someone had opened the door from the inside and was stepping out onto the pavement. Holy Christ, who was this? I had not allowed for collateral damage, although I knew it was probable he might bring one of his "partners in crime". I had considered it more improbable based on the surveillance reports I had read. Now, feeling a little uneasy, I focused the binoculars intently on the back of this unknown person. I could see it was a male, average height, heavy build, about to put a cap on a grey-haired head. He was similarly dressed in casual clothes and was slightly stooped as he stood. Just at that moment, Sinclair appeared, wheeling the trolley around to the rear of the Porsche. The figure turned to face him, and that was when his features came into full focus.

Yes! I had certainly seen that face before. His enlarged photograph sat on the glass-topped table beside me. It was none other than his dishonourable justice, Judge Phillip Whitmore.

My mind started racing in light of this. It was too late for a change of plan; I never relished "collateral" damage, and while I was thinking this, it suddenly hit me. It was as if this turn of events were meant to be. That slimy bastard with Sinclair was just as responsible for the poor girl's predicament, just a young kid, barely a woman, who is now facing months, maybe years, of therapy. Maybe she would never recover. Yes, Sinclair committed the crime alright, but that bastard of a judge was just as guilty in helping him to go free, and god knows how many others have gone free of justice over the years due to his foul corruption. I turned again to the information and photographs I had received. The private investigator who had compiled it certainly knew his work. It named this judge and others of the group of high-powered, influential people from various levels of society involved in the paedophile ring.

I was feeling again the cold, calculating fury that always filled my emotions when I was faced with the injustices of life. The answer to my initial dilemma was now clear and simple: an opportunity that might not come my way in the future, and it put a grim smile on my face. What was about to happen may never reverse the damage done to that poor child, but those two evil bastards will pay the ultimate penalty, and what is more, that girl's parents and family will get two for the price of one. Another thought then came to me: it's a bloody shame that the crooked lawyer was not with them. Three birds with one stone. *Ah, well, another time, his karma will come around.*

I figured that it would be another half hour before anything exciting happened. Plenty of time to get a couple of beers out of the bar fridge and settle back for a ringside seat. I watched the unloading of the car boot and the progression of Sinclair and the judge along the jetty with the trolley of supplies. Then came the repositioning of the Porsche to the car park, the loading of the supplies from one to the other person already on the cruiser and then I heard the faint sound of a radio come on. The judge now climbed aboard, disappearing inside the cabin of this luxurious vessel and then nothing. For more than a minute, I waited. Had anything gone wrong?

Puzzled, I watched closely through the binoculars and then smiled as the judge walked onto the deck, putting onto a small table what looked like a beer bottle, and walked to the focs'le to let go of the forward line. Obviously, he was acting as a deckhand while "Captain Sinclair" saw to the engines and would manoeuvre the cruiser away from the dock. The judge was walking back to release the stern rope and was level with the open sliding door of the cabin when he disappeared into eternity, along with a huge sheet of flame.

It was exactly 7:27 a.m. when the very faint sound of a motor came to me across the distance, followed in less than a split second by a massive heat mirage and a mass of flame erupting from the boat at the dockside, and then came the sound wave and pressure of the explosion that hit around me, rattling the windows and the sliding glass balcony door. It was a massive reverberating **wwhooomph!** Not since Vietnam and the American napalm bombs had I witnessed such a fiery explosion.

There were pieces of boat still coming down in every direction, with widespread splashes in the water around the jetty and other boats. Fortunately, there was no one else on the closed-off end of the jetty at the time, and for that, I was glad. What was left of the boat was starting its burn down to the waterline; people were running to the scene along the jetty and from other directions on shore, all headed toward the billowing oily black smoke, their curiosity soon to be followed by the sound of police and fire engine sirens. A little after 8:30 a.m., the remains of that magnificent vessel sank amid the surface flotsam and jetsam to the bottom.

I felt sad about that. What a waste for such a well-made, beautiful timber boat. I could see no sign of Sinclair and the judge.

Watching television that night, the evening news was all about the rich developer and the honourable judge being killed in a tragic boating accident. Police frogmen were still searching for the remains of the corpses. I am not a religious man, but the thought went through me: *Do unto others as they would do unto you.* I was not sure if that was how it was worded. No matter, good riddance to the pair of evil bastards.

Sunday morning, about 9 a.m., I wandered out onto the street and purchased the local Sunday newspaper, headlining the catastrophic event at the dock. It said there was some minor fire and explosion damage to the jetty and the nearby building, with some windows broken and a couple of other boats hit by flying debris, but there were no other casualties. That was gratifying to read. The dock was closed off by yellow police tape, and there were police in overalls combing the dock, with police frogmen in the water examining the remains of the hull below the water and still searching for human remains.

Sinclair was single, divorced from his second wife, with two grown children living overseas. Time would heal their pain, if any, and I found myself hoping that their new inheritance would be put to better use than their father did with his wealth. The judge was a widower whose wife had died a few years earlier; he also had two grown children living elsewhere. I wondered if their remaining family members had any inkling of the shady and depraved lives their esteemed parents had lived.

Folding the newspaper, I went to enjoy a lone celebratory "yum cha" brunch at the same Asian restaurant where I had first heard the familiar language of Vietnam some days earlier. Again, this memory had me reflecting once more on Vietnam, the war and its terrible consequences. I was happy that it was now over and the part that I had played in it finished. I reflected on my initial jungle training and guerilla warfare in Malaya and my attachment to the American Military under CIA command. My thoughts went sadly back to the wonderful Hmong and the raw deal they got from the USA after the war and to my time as a warrant officer, training these warrior hill tribesmen against the Viet Cong. I was filled with a conglomerate of thoughts, and it all had me thinking maybe one day I would go back to look up old friends and places.

Now, with my assignment over, it was time to dispose of all the equipment I had purchased in Perth and head for home. I kept the Sunday newspaper, which had printed the details about the boat explosion and the deaths of a prominent businessman and high court judge.

It seems that the body parts recovered were burnt and beyond recognition. There was no mention of suspicious circumstances, although there would be a coroner's inquest. The newspaper also quoted a similar accident, mentioning a boat accident that took place the previous year in Melbourne. The article said it was suspected the explosion had been caused by sparks igniting fuel leaking into the boat.

I bought two newspapers, cut the relevant sections out of one, and mailed it on to JJ. Checking out of the motel the next morning, I drove until I found a track branching off into sandy scrubland, and digging a hole with a small folding shovel, I buried the now redundant equipment. I then delivered the car back to the airport and flew back to Sydney. On the way, I was thinking I would have a few days, maybe a week, on Bondi Beach after I checked in with the "JJ" and then head to my retreat and the horses in northern NSW.

"JJ" rarely showed emotions, but he clapped me on the back when I entered his office. Edith had even blown me a kiss when I walked in. I handed him the newspaper with the complete story, but it was not necessary. He put it in the shredder. He said it had become a national news item, and the client was extremely happy about the result—so happy, in fact, the "big bloke" handed me a rather fat envelope saying, "He insisted on you having this extra bonus for a job well done". But my planned week on the beach, followed by time out on my property, was not to be the case. It was to be only a three days' rest. As JJ indicated, I would soon be on a plane to Cairns, studying the information he gave me and picking up a weapon in Cairns if necessary. This time, my job was to track down a high-level supplier of illegal drugs, marijuana, speed, ecstasy, and other forms of poison that were finding their way to the children and teenagers in Cairns. Still, a three-day break sounded good. Time for some rest and planning for what lay ahead. Then JJ handed me a phone message from an old childhood friend named Angus, a nephew of my beloved Uncle Charlie, and later, my thoughts drifted back to life on the Darling River.

CHAPTER 6

Growing up
on the Darling River

As I was growing up, I got to know and respect the senior constable, who was now Sergeant Kennedy and still the copper in charge of the town of Pooncarie. He was more like a father who was there from the time he helped my mother with my birth at the police station. He now had a young constable assisting him. Sergeant Kennedy was a big, jovial, strong man who was respected and well-liked by most of the town because of his fair-minded manner of handling situations. Occasionally, he would be called to the pub by the publican, who was tired of the old man's drunken ranting and ravings; he would take away the keys to his old T Ford truck and lock him away for the night. When our father was sober enough, he would let him out with a fine. The whole town knew about the way the mongrel treated Mum and us kids, and I think the landowners only gave him work when he was sober, hoping some of the money would come home to us, but what the town did not know was that Kennedy, the tough, big-hearted, and likeable copper, would put that money from the fine into an envelope and by some means, that he had worked out with our mother, would hand it over to her, and with her small earnings for work done we managed to survive reasonably well.

The country where we lived and where I grew up was outside the town of Pooncarie and close to the Darling River on the edge of the Mulga scrub, hot, dry, semi-arid country with many stands of eucalyptus and red gums, predominantly along the river banks. There was some agriculture, but the main source of income was from the huge sheep and cattle stations. In its heyday, the village of "Pooncarie" had been a major paddle steamer port carrying along the river, the produce of the region. Today, it is a sleepy, though pretty village with a population of around 120 people. Although on the edge of the "Outback", it abounded with rich soils that grew prolifically and many beautiful and varied wild bush flowers when it rained. As a kid, my biggest joys were the river, my Uncle Charlie, and my best mate, Jimmy Collett. I also had a few Koori mates from the Aboriginal settlement outside of town, and very dear to me was my sister Irene, who looked to me as her big-brother protector. My best mate, Jimmy Collett, came from another dirt-poor family who scraped a meagre living from a small mixed farm a short distance out of town.

The small one-roomed school my sister and I attended had about twenty pupils divided into two grades, primary and secondary. At the time I acquired the nickname "Mulga", my sister was eight and was with me in the primary section of the room. We were barefoot bush kids, wearing threadbare hand-me-downs, which our mother somehow managed to keep clean. Our laundry was a dirt-floored tin shed boasting an old "copper" set into crumbling bricks with a wood-burning fire underneath it, and it was my job to keep the split firewood up to it. Alongside the copper was an old twin concrete laundry tub with an old-fashioned "wringer" attached to one end. And there was a single brass cold water tap with a length of rubber hose attached to it so mum could fill the "copper". On one side, away from the dilapidated wooden door, was a galvanised iron tub, which an adult or two small kids could squeeze into on bath night. This was usually Friday night; the rest of the week was what mum called an APC wash, armpits and crutch. Winter or summer, Mum would wield a cake of "Velvet" laundry soap, lathering the respective parts, along with a dousing of cold water from the hose on the brass tap. We would duck and weave, trying to get away from Mum and that ice water in the wintertime, but in the summer, it was a real pleasure. It did toughen us up for the winter cold, though, and we never seemed to get sick apart from measles once.

The summer was great as we could go swimming in the big waterhole in the river near Uncle Charlie's camp. There was a rope that the Koori kids had hung from a big old overhanging river gum, and all of us kids, white and black, would shinny up that tree like a mob of black and white goannas to dive and jump from its limbs and fight each other for a place in the queue to swing out in an arc from the rope. It had its dangers, though; you had to let go of the rope at the right time to drop into the water, or you could slam back hard into the tree.

Another real danger was the deadly Mulga snake, which was prevalent along the river banks. Also known as the King Brown snake, it is one of the deadliest snakes in Australia. If you are bitten by this snake, you have to get medical attention real quick. Many people each year die from the bite of the Mulga snake. The Mulga snake is particularly around in the hot month of February when they are breeding and are very aggressive. As children, we always had to be keeping an eye out for them. One of the kids from an outlying farm got bitten once, and they could not get him to the tiny hospital quick enough, and he died.

Uncle Charlie, as we knew him, was an old full-blood aboriginal of the Barkandji tribe and was related to Mum through her deceased mother. He had his bark and tin "Gunyah" a short distance down the river from the swimming hole and some distance from the main tribal camp. At the main camp, he was well known and welcome as a tribal elder, but he said there was too much trouble and grog there for him to live. He was of the old tribal ways and respected by white and black alike as a tribal elder who lived mainly in the old ways and on a diet of fish, rabbits, and bush animals he could catch in his snares and traps, and some vegetables he grew. He was an expert in the use of the hunting "boomerang", the "woomerah", and spears, and had great skill at bringing down a kangaroo or emu, which he would share with the rest of the tribe after cutting some off for himself. He still lived much like the tribe did in the old days before the white man's coming. His tribal initiation scars used to intrigue me and some other kids as we sat around his camp listening to his stories of the dreamtime. He never touched alcohol; his only concession to white man ways was to drink black tea with some sugar in it, to make bush bread the white folk call damper from flour, and to put on a pair of trousers and a shirt, which he wore when he came to town to see our mother. He kept those clothes scrupulously clean, although unironed by regular washing in the river, and sometimes Mum would put them into our old copper boiler. At his camp, he would be bare-chested and only wear a pair of old long trousers cut off at the knees. For any of the local kids who were interested, he would teach us how to catch fish with woven traps and lines and to track and snare birds and animals. I was one of those kids; I would sit for hours listening to his stories told in his mix of Pidgin English and Aboriginal dialect. It was a unique way of speaking, which I soon learnt and understood. I would watch him set his lines, snares, and traps. At every opportunity, he would take me hunting with him, teaching me the old ways of his tribal life and how to see and recognise different bird and animal tracks, and I became very competent at seeing and recognising the most minuscule of signs. As I grew, he taught me his native language, and we would communicate with signs and talk in a more traditional manner. Many of these skills I would put to good use in the years to come working with native tribes people in Malaya and Vietnam when training them to resist the spreading communist incursions into their country. Uncle Charlie's uncanny skill as a black tracker was well known, and on a few occasions, Uncle Charlie had been called in by the police to help track and find people who had gone missing in the bush in various parts of the country. He once was taken all the way into the high mountains near the Victoria and New South Wales border known as the "Snowy Mountains" to track and help find a stockman lost while out searching for cattle. The man's still-saddled horse had turned up at the mustering camp. It was two days before Uncle Charlie finally arrived at this remote camp, and he immediately started searching for signs by first finding and retracing the remnant sign of horse tracks and then for a long distance over the hard, stony ground for a whole day, seeing signs that others could not see and then finding the man's body on the other side of a narrow, deep gully, its edge hidden behind low thick scrub. Uncle Charlie told the searchers the "signs" told him that the horseman was galloping after cattle and had attempted to jump his horse over the unseen gully at a run. When the startled horse suddenly shied away at the last second, the stockman flew over the head of his horse and landed head-first on the hard ground of the gully on the opposite side, breaking his neck and dying instantly. He received a cash payment and a letter from the government commending him for the part he played in the search and many thanks from the stockman's bereaved family.

I would be excited, thrilled and continually amazed every time Uncle Charlie took me into the bush to teach me how to track, as he could see and identify things that others could not. It was down at the river one hot day that the incident happened, which was to play a major part in my future life and eventually led to my nickname "Mulga". Uncle Charlie, my sister Irene, and I were at the river bank. Uncle Charlie and I were getting ready to fish at a hole full of snags and logs, which was renowned for the big yellowbelly and cod that had been caught there. My sister, who was about seven then, was sitting further up the bank and playing with a doll she had got for Xmas. I was standing at the water's edge looking for a suitable place to cast a line when I heard Uncle Charlie's voice, soft but urgent, say, "Shoon', don' move, boy, don' move!" And startled, I looked around in time to see Uncle Charlie go down on his haunches moving his hand in a circular motion in an endeavour to attract the attention of a big King Brown snake which had its head up, tongue flicking in and out, and its steely eyes focused on me. Uncle Charlie was about two feet from the snake's tail, and his movement caused the snake to swing its head around and focus on his left hand, which was slowly moving in a rhythmic back-and-forth motion, a bit like the windscreen wiper on our father's old car. At that moment, while he had the snake's attention, he moved as quick as a lightning flash, his other hand fastened on the snake's tail, and swinging it up and over his head, he cracked it like a stockman cracks a stock whip, breaking its vertebrae behind the head. He then beat it a few times against the base of a red river gum tree to make sure it was dead. I stood transfixed, not moving a muscle, fearful yet fascinated by Uncle Charlie's feat of skill at disposing of that deadly snake. Uncle Charlie turned to me and, staring at the open-mouthed look on my face. His very black, white-bearded face broke into a huge toothy grin, saying, "I'm big pfella snake plenty good tucker, Shoon,' me cook im tonight, 'ave a big feed." Uncle Charlie never could say my name right, and I loved the way he said "Shoon".

I lost all interest in fishing. All I wanted to know was how Uncle Charlie knew what to do and how he did it. My mind was racing with questions, and my sister and I soon ran home to tell Mum how Uncle Charlie had saved my life. Poor Mum, she nearly cried and then berated us for spending so much time at the river bank, knowing the prevalence of snakes there.

Our Mum dearly loved Uncle Charlie. He would occasionally appear out of nowhere and show up at our house to hand over some fish or yabbies and rabbits to her and jabbering away in his mixture of Pidgin English and native dialect. Uncle Charlie never appeared when my father was there. He did not fear him; he just did not like him, and I overheard him once saying, "I'm no good pfella Mary; I'm bad pfella," at a time when Mum was sporting some fresh bruises on her face. I adored Uncle Charlie, and in my childish mind, I reckoned if Uncle Charlie had been a younger man, he would have flattened or speared the bastard.

Another sudden and uplifting bump of the plane brings me back to reality for a moment, and sitting in that modern aeroplane, bumping its way through the turbulences, and musing over my life, I realise the memory of that King Brown snake, or "Mulga snake" as it is known and Uncle Charlie, are permanently etched into my memory and often reappear like an old silent Charlie Chaplin movie I had once seen at the community hall for the local kids and families. Apart from the "old man" and his drunken, brutish ways, those childhood days were idyllic, fishing, swimming, and going on hunting expeditions with Uncle Charlie. The outside world was non-existent to us black kids and sun-browned, barefoot white kids, with only the dangers of nature and sometimes minor accidents from our wild games and playground mischief. Not having anything of great material value as children, we learnt to improvise and somehow got by. In later life, I realised the lessons learnt in my childhood gave me strength of purpose and the perseverance to get on with the job at hand, whatever that job might be and with whatever materials were available.

School was something to be endured; some kids hated it, but it seemed I had a mind that wanted to learn, so I really did not mind going to school and only "wagged it" on rare occasions, and that was usually when it was really hot and the river looked inviting. Looking back now, I realise that everything I learnt from Uncle Charlie on how to be bush smart and how to survive, coupled with the tough physical way we lived as kids, is what taught me to survive, and what I saw in my father taught me to dislike with a vengeance the many wrongs I was to eventually see and endure and try to do something about, and this came to me more so when I went into the outside world with the Australian military and experienced some of the brutality experienced by oppressed people.

CHAPTER 7

Brute of the Boxing Tent

At a young age, I realised that there would be times when I would be faced with difficult and sometimes dangerous decisions to be made, not realising then one of those times was coming my way. So the ensuing twelve months of my life passed in the usual way, by going to school, visiting Uncle Charlie, keeping out of the way of the old man's rages, helping and consoling Mum where possible, and by frequent escapes to the river whenever I could.

Looking after my younger sister at school sometimes was a problem. Older kids, particularly the bullies, would pick on her because she was quiet and shy. She did not speak much, nor did she mix a lot with other kids and tended to keep on her own or with me. I think our father's bullying had done this to her. As a result, I got a few bloody noses from bullies picking on her and me trying to defend her, and though I was not as big as the older kids, I could put up a fair showing and never backed down. The problem was that the worst bullies were also the biggest and strongest, so I copped more beatings than I dished out. Still and all, there was something in me that told me that one day, there would be a day of reckoning, and the way to do so happened most unexpectedly.

My best mate Jimmy also copped a share of the bullying, as he was always there to back me up and me for him. He was a game bugger, and even when beaten, he still would not give up. Jimmy had real strict Catholic Church-going parents who would not let him mix with us Koori kids. Although our father was raised by Irish Catholic parents, we kids were Church of England, the faith our mum had been raised as with the missionary family, but Mum was not strict about going to church. Although she was raised in a Christian family with regular church attendance, she had a questioning mind. I think it had something to do with the way the missionaries had raised her. However, they treated her well, loved, and educated her; she felt sometimes their manner was to force their religion upon the Aboriginal community in a manner of "either change your tribal beliefs and dreamtime stories, or you will go to a place they called hell." Mum had personally seen how many religious institutions had taken children from their mothers and tribal families and had, therefore, mistreated the Aboriginals in an endeavour to change and take away their tribal beliefs and ways. Jimmy could not come down to the river with us as much as he liked, but he and I and my sister still spent as much time as possible together, playing our games, building humpies in the bush, snaring rabbits and just mucking around.

While down at the river, late one evening fishing with Uncle Charlie, I was sporting my newest bruises and black eye from a stoush that morning in the schoolyard, when suddenly this big framed, tall black fella dressed as a stockman appeared out of the bush behind us. Uncle Charlie had heard a movement and suddenly turned to see who it was, and the next minute, this big black fella and Uncle Charlie were embracing each other and cackling away like a pair of sheilas at a wedding I once watched in town. It turned out he was a nephew of Uncle Charlie's who had gone walkabout when he was about seventeen. He had joined a droving mob out west and had grown to be a top ringer and stockman, working for some of the huge stations up in Queensland channel country and in the Northern Territory on the big cattle runs.

Uncle Charlie introduced me to him. His name was Angus, and he smiled and asked me how I got the "black eye". When I told him about my latest fight with bullies, he smiled again and winked at Uncle Charlie, saying, "Eh, Charlie, we better do sumthin' about that and make young Sean a better fighter". I immediately felt a strong liking for this big black man.

When Uncle Charlie asked Angus where he had been, I could hardly wait to hear some of his stories and asked Uncle Charlie if I could come back that night and sit around the campfire with them. He just smiled, saying, "Okay, Shoon, if your mum sez it okay." I raced for home and dinner. The old man had come home tired from a day's work in the heat, and because it was not payday, he was sober. As usual, when he was sober, he headed off to bed after dinner, leaving my sister, Mum, and me cleaning the dishes. In no time, there were loud snores coming from the bedroom. That was when I pleaded with Mum to let me go out for a few hours to sit around the campfire with Uncle Charlie and his nephew, Angus. At first, she resisted; being a typical mum, she was worried about me going out on my own in the dark, but knowing how much I loved Uncle Charlie and the fact that part of her earliest childhood before going to the missionaries, she recalled had been spent in the camp. She had seen Angus growing up, so she relented and gave me the big old torch she kept in a kitchen drawer. She made me promise to be back in a few hours and be careful not to wake the old man up when I came in. That night and the days that followed were to create a few more changes that were to lead to the eventful life that was to become mine. I sat enthralled, listening and fascinated, watching the flickering light of the campfire play on their dark faces as they talked about Angus and his adventures. I could barely wait to get to school the next day and tell Jimmy all about it and the stories I had heard, and then, a night or two later, I heard Angus tell the story that I remember most, and the big part it was to play in my future life.

In the time Angus had spent in the stock camps and on the big stations, he had seen and learnt a lot and had learnt to speak much better English than Uncle Charlie's pidgin talk, and he was really easy for me to understand. He had spent some time on the rodeo circuit and had won a few buckles and trophies in the saddle and bareback bronco riding, and had also had a go at bull riding. He had been subjected to a bit of racial aggression and insults in some of the stock camps and, because of it, had found that he was pretty handy with his fists. He didn't boast about his fights; he just said it as it was, talking openly about the few times he'd been knocked down when still a youngster and how he went on to win more than he lost. The story that captivated my young mind most was when Angus was at the end of a cattle drive that arrived at Mt Isa. It coincided with the time when the local Mt Isa Agricultural Show was on. Angus was wandering around sideshow alley with a couple of stockmen mates, when they heard a big bass drum booming, Boom! Boom! Boom! And strident above its sound was a shrill, loud voice inviting all to "come and see", "it's back in town, Willy Jardine's travelling boxing show", "the best boxing tent show in Australia". Willy Jardine was shouting through a loud hailer above the beat of the drum, "Who among you out there in the crowd is man enough to take on any of my fighters? I'll pay ten bob a round to any man who can stay three rounds with any of my boys and put on a good show. I'll pay ya five bob if you are knocked down and out inside the three rounds. And five quid to any man who can knock down and keep down any of my fighters in any round. C'mon now, two bob a seat, and the fights start when the tent is full."

Angus and his cobbers decided they would have a look at what was going on and stood there in the gathering crowd watching proceedings. Willy's sales pitch and voice seemed to be reaching a crescendo as he announced his prize fighters' names in the group, one by one, as they were standing on the platform in their boxing trunks, boots, and colourful dressing gowns. Willy's voice was fast reaching a climactic high. The crowd's attention was held, enthralled by his rising voice. "Here he comes!" Willy's voice was now screaming through the loud hailer. "Just ave a look at 'im, folks. It's 'im, the mightiest fighter in outback Queensland, and none other than Billy 'The Hammer' McLaren."

At the moment his name was mentioned, he appeared, strutting out from behind the curtain. He was a heavy-built, swarthy man, about heavy middleweight size, somewhere between twelve and a half stone, maybe thirteen stone. He was wearing a brilliant scarlet dressing gown and similar coloured trunks, and with a sneering look on his pugnacious face that seemed to say, "To hell with the lot of you!" The sneering man on the stage took off his dressing gown and stood flexing his muscles. He was solidly built, with broad shoulders, a big chest, and a head that looked like you could crush rocks on it, and his nose looked like someone had. Lower down, it looked like he was inclined to some fat, for there was thickening around the belly and waist, like that of a man who loved his grog.

The more Angus looked at that arrogant, brutal face, the more a light of recognition dawned on him. Puzzled and curious, he pushed his way through the crowd to get a closer look at the man on the stage, and then a flood of violent memories hit him with a surge of searing anger. Memories of a brutal attack, long ago, and pushed to the back of his mind, now filled him with a white heat of memory of something that happened about five years earlier when he was somewhere between seventeen and eighteen. The story went young Angus had joined a station in the territory at the end of a droving run as a junior "Jackeroo". One of the ringers working on this remote outback station was an arrogant, bullying, racist, slurring bastard who started giving Angus a hard time from the moment he joined up. When Angus could take no more of his insults and retaliated with a few words of his own, the brute, without warning, attacked him and beat him with his fists and boots into unconsciousness, leaving him bleeding in the dry dust of the stock camp. The overseer stockman was away at the time, so nothing came of it. Angus, although severely bruised, cut and hurting, packed his swag a day or two later, and he left the station to wander on, thinking about the unfair brutality of some white people. The other stockmen and "Jackeroos" mumbled and groaned about the unfairness of it amongst them, but none had the nerve to stand up to the brute, and now that same man stood before him on the tent platform! Angus stood watching this arrogant white man, strutting and dishing out challenges to the crowd, challenging anyone to come up and fight him, if they were game. Angus felt the initial flash of hot anger turn into a cold rage building up inside of him. He felt himself clenching and unclenching his fists as the memories of that vicious, sadistic attack overtook his soul. "I could kill that man," he was thinking. Unexpectedly, the man on the stage was now standing directly in front of him, and looking down at Angus, he said in an arrogant and insulting manner, "Waddabout you black boy, ya wanna have a go?" Angus said at that moment he felt a cold calm come over him, and looking "Billy, The Hammer" in the eye, he said in a loud and clear voice, "Yeah white shit, I'll take you on." The brute almost screamed with rage at the insult thrown back at him. "Well, git in here coon". The watching, listening crowd roared with fiendish delight at what they thought would be the spectacle to come.

In the five years that had passed since the brutal beating from the fists and boots of this Neanderthal, Angus had grown; with wide shoulders and broad chest, he was lean and hard, with no spare flesh, and the muscles in his arms bulged from hard work and clean outdoor life. Angus, like his Uncle Charlie, had left the camp swearing he would never let the grog kill his soul and body like so many of his family and friends. He enjoyed being fit and strong and worked to keep it that way, and there was more to it than that at the huge cattle station where he was now the head stockman and horse breaker, and his best mate was a white man by the name of Geoff Lewinski, a man who in his youth, had fought as an amateur middleweight, and had taken out a Golden Gloves championship. Later, as a professional, he boxed his way into the top five middleweights in Australia and was leading up to be the main contender for the Australian middleweight title. A near-fatal accident saw his big opportunity ruined when, on a training run in a normally quiet street near his gymnasium in Brisbane, a speeding car hit him and kept going, leaving him sorely injured with numerous broken bones and head injuries, and as time went by with the slow healing process, so did his chances of reaching the big time in professional boxing disappear. He wandered around gymnasiums for a while, and realising his chances of making it to the top of the boxing world again were limited, he then went bush and turned to become a stockman and shearer.

Geoff and Angus had become friends, and as Angus taught Geoff many stockman skills, Geoff, in turn, took on teaching Angus boxing skills, and they spent many hours together in their "made-up gym" in a shed, where Geoff had Angus working out on a heavy bag, sparring, shadow boxing, and teaching him the finer art of ring craft, and there in that rough corrugated iron and timber shed, Angus learnt some of the finer points of boxing and how to convert his natural rough fighting prowess into something far more skilled and deadly. Lewinski saw that Angus had a long reach and pointed out to Angus that a good straight left could cut through a defence, gain points, and help win a fight. Angus worked more and more on that, learning how to cut through a fighter's guard and follow through with a lightning-swift right cross with deadly impact and learning many other and varied punch combinations. He learnt that a boxer never took his eyes off his opponent. He also learnt from Geoff Lewinski that many a fighter signalled with his eyes where he was going to strike with a punch by a split-second look at the intended point of impact. His opponent, if watching his eyes, would automatically ready their guard to block the blow. The secret was to launch the punch looking at the opponent's face and then midway across, divert the blow to the midriff. That principle could be worked vice versa. If done swiftly and covertly enough, it often worked well and would leave the opponent temporarily open for further hits. It worked exceptionally well when using a straight left aimed for the head and suddenly dropped to the midriff, followed by a right cross knockout blow to the head. In time, Angus learnt much about the power of skilled ring craft, as did Geoff about a stockman's skills and in time, Geoff Lewinski moved on to accept a position as head stockman at one of the famous Kidman stations in Western Australia.

Because of Angus's colour, and young age, he had to put up his fists on a number of occasions in the past to defend him in the various cattle camps where he had worked. As his skill on the stations increased, he rose to head stockman and overseer. As he was black and often younger than other stockmen, there were occasions when his authority was challenged. When that happened, he had to "face down" situations in the most familiar way of men in the harsh Australian outback, with fists. He could now handle himself quite well, bare-knuckle, street-fighting style, and had no fear of his ability to defend himself when faced with a physical situation. Because of this, he had earned the respect of his fellow workmen and some reputation as a man fair and honest and not to be put down or messed around with, and now, with the increased knowledge and skills of a professional boxer, he could hold his own in the boxing ring if he so chose to. Right now, at this moment, he knew facing the man looming above him on the boxing tent stage that now was the time to square the account.

Angus had learnt to read as a child from the Pooncarie missionaries. He liked reading novels, and in a recent crime thriller novel, he had read about the American "mafia" and their ruthlessness, and he remembered reading a mafia chief saying, "Revenge is a dish better eaten cold." Angus was suddenly very hungry, and his hunger was fed with ice-cold anger! With his insulting reply to the man on the stage, the howl of rage in return, and the shrieks of joy from the listening crowd, one of Angus's friends grabbed his arm and said to Angus, "You gotta be jokin'. This bloke's a pro." Angus calmly looked at his friend and said,

"You'll soon see why, mate," and strode into the tent with the crowd and his mates following.

Inside the main tent, Willy took Angus aside and said, "You sure you gonna fight The Hammer, boy?" Angus replied he was sure about it. Willy then said, "You put on a good showboy and last three rounds, and I'll pay you ten bob a round. But if you don't make the distance, you get five bob. If, by chance, you knock The Hammer down, and out of the fight, you get five quid. Now that orta make you fight real well. Okay, so shake hands on that. There's gonna be a couple of fights on first, and then we'll call you up. What name will we call you by?" Angus thought for a moment. His given English surname was McKinley. He then said to Willy, "Call me Mack Kinley."

Willy nodded, turned around, and called over an old fella who had the look of a broken-down pugilist. His bent and broken nose looked like a horse had kicked it across his scarred face, and he had a sly-eyed look about him. Willy said to Angus, "This here is Jock. He's gonna be your second, and he'll give ya some advice on how to handle The Hammer. Now go out back with Jock, and he'll kit you up for the fight."

A short time later, when Angus came out, he was wearing a pair of blue trunks that were a size too small for him, a pair of worn-out boxing shoes, and had his hands bandaged and taped. Jock handed him an old patched blue dressing gown to place over his shoulders. Angus was thinking calmly about the forthcoming bout. The Hammer had not shown himself, but what Angus had seen of him led him to believe that even though The Hammer was of a strong build and could pack a powerful punch, he looked to be a bit soft in the belly. He remembered his professional boxing mate Geoff Lavinski saying to him, "It's the engine room of a ship that makes it move. The captain on the bridge only directs it. Knock the engine out, and the ship stops," Geoff had often said. "Sum up your opponent. If he looks a bit weak there in the gut, then that's the engine room. Go for it." In his fights around the stock camps, Angus had remembered those words and had found out that most quarrelsome blokes that picked fights around the camps were also boozers and usually had a weak gut, and a good belt to the guts often stopped them.

The lightweight and welterweight fights were over, and the fans were certainly getting their two bobs' worth. None of the contenders from the crowd had won their fight, the lightweight had been knocked out in the second round, and the welterweight could not come out of his corner for the third round, and at that moment, Angus came out of his reflective thoughts, as he felt his assigned fight second Jock, prod him in the ribs with a terse "yer on". As Angus made his way into the main area of the big tent, he could hear the loud voice of Willy Jardine booming over the loudspeakers, "Come on, now give a big hand and a cheer for young Mack Kinley. Mack is gunna take on our unbeaten middleweight Billy The Hammer McLaren. Come into the ring, young Mack, and let everyone see you."

A loud round of whistles, cheers, and shouts followed Angus alias Mack and his fight second Jock into the square canvas arena erroneously called a "ring". Angus was being weighed in and had given some background about himself, which was being passed on to the cheering, noisy crowd in Willy's high, shrill voice. "This young Aboriginal lad, Mack Kinlay, comes from down along the Darling River in NSW. He currently works as the head stockman at 'Jabiru Station' southeast of Mt Isa. He ain't a professional but claims to have had a few fights in his time as a stockman and drover

over the last few years. He's weighin in at eleven stone eight pounds, an' looks to be fightin fit. He knows the rules an' rekkins 'e'll put up a good fight." There came another loud burst of assorted cheers and whistles, among which Angus could hear one of his mates, Danny, repeatedly chanting his name. Go, Mack, go Mack! At that, Jock ushered him from the centre of the "ring" to a stool in the corner and proceeded to give Angus a rubdown on the shoulders.

Again, Willy's voice shrieked to a climactic high, "An' now comin' inta the ring weighing in at twelve stone two pounds the mighty, and the unbeaten in his last fifteen fights, Billy The Hammer McLaren!" A cacophony of boos, whistles, jeers, and cheers rent the air as "The Hammer" parted the ropes and stepped through into the ring. Holding his gloved hands high in the air, he paraded around the ring like a human show pony, encouraging the motley crowd to whistle, boo, and jeer even louder. The more he paraded and strutted, the loader the raucous sounds became.

It seemed to Angus that the crowds at this showman's fighting tent always seemed to be on the side of the "outsider" or the "contender". He wryly thought, I guess, that's something at least to have the crowd on his side, especially when he saw that the referee who stepped into the ring was one of the showman's fighters who had been standing outside on the platform beating the drum.

The two fighters were brought into the centre of the ring for the referee's talk and to touch gloves, then back to the corner for the bell to ring. The touch of the gloves was more than a touch, with The Hammer arrogantly pushing Angus's gloved hands back to his belly with some force. The gong went for the opening round, and Angus was barely out from his corner after listening to his second Jock giving some final advice when he was met with a huge flurry of crushing blows, one of which crashed through his hastily put up guard and sent him flying backwards into the ropes off balance. The Hammer came in fast and eager to capitalise on his advantage, and another heavy blow hit Angus on the left side of the head, sending him spinning around and down to one knee. The referee called The Hammer back and started a count; the crowd was going wild, booing and shouting.

Angus was stunned and surprised by the speedy onslaught, but not out. He knew he had to get back to his feet and stay out of The Hammer's reach until he had cleared his senses to mix it with him. "Rough house" fighting at this stage would be too dangerous; he had to use ring craft and box The Hammer off. Pretending to be more hurt than he really was, kneeling and half slumped over the middle rope, he watched The Hammer through partly closed eyes; the brute was poised, ready to dive in for the kill or to throw his arms into the air as the winning gladiator if the count went to ten. The Hammer knew that he stood to get a bonus if he knocked his opponent out in the first round, giving Willie Jardine more time that night for the boxing tent to be filled again for extra fights.

Angus let the count go to seven, and then, with the unexpected speed and the agility of a Black Panther, he leapt into the air, onto his feet, and out of the range of the murderous raging rush of The Hammer, and from that moment Angus kept boxing him and holding him off at a distance for the rest of round one.

Angus was tough, fit, and fast and lightly danced around the ring, holding off the furious Hammer using his longer reach and, with his long straight left, breaking through The Hammer's guard to catch him on the nose, which was now bleeding. The crowd was roaring when they saw this.

The bell rang for the end of the round, and Angus went back to his corner. A splash of water sprayed over his head and face and a little in his mouth, then something the fast-talking sly-eyed second was saying sank in and made him realise that these fights were rigged and always set up in the favour of the showman's fighters. Jock was saying, "You've got him done kid. "Look at 'im 'e's worn out from those lefts o' yours. Get into 'im from the gong. It 'im wiv all yer got, rough 'im up from the start!" And sure enough, from all outward aspects, The Hammer was sitting slumped, looking tired, a trickle of blood being wiped from his nose. Angus now knew this was all part of the ruse to draw him in and throw away caution; The Hammer was a powerful brawler, an in fighter, who relied on his rushing charges and flurries of powerful blows, to wipe out his opponents early in the piece. Angus knew what his battle strategy was to be. His longer arms and height were an advantage. He was going to stay out of range of those lethal and often wild blows; he would outbox the brute, continuously piercing his clumsy guard with his stabbing and infuriating straight left, and keep The Hammer running after him, keep him running until he tired and slowed, and then the moment would come when his onslaught weakened, then Angus knew he could come in close with a combination of punches he had learnt from Geoff Lewinski, to pound the beast of a man senseless to the canvas. So for almost the whole of the second round, Angus did just that, coolly and effortlessly boxing and keeping the distance, straight left, straight left, jab, jab, right cross, dancing continuously around his opponent. The Hammer was now breathing heavily. Angus by now, realised the brute's condition was even less than he first thought. After one particularly straight and painful left to the nose, followed by a right cross that opened a cut above The Hammer's right eye, The Hammer seemed to go berserk, charging with arms swinging like windmills; one of those wild blows grazed the side of Angus's head with enough impact to make him realise the merit of his decision to fight from a distance. Keep cool and stay clear of those deadly flailing arms.

For a few seconds, they went into a clinch, with The Hammer attempting to pound away at Angus's kidney area, growling in an animal-like voice, "Stand, stand still and fight, you black bastard!" The crowd was howling its disgust at these easily seen foul blows, and the referee wasn't doing much to break the clinch. The Hammer was trying to foul-punch and wrestle him into submission.

Angus thought, "Ah well, give as good as you get," and with the referee for a moment out of sight behind The Hammer's back and still in the tight clinch, he brought his hard forehead down across the bridge of the already damaged nose of The Hammer, he heard and felt the bone of the nose crunch under the deadly impact. The crowd saw it, though, and went mad as The Hammer screamed a yelp of pain, released his octopus-like hold on Angus and reeled backwards, dazed and with blurred vision from watering eyes. Angus was now onto him with a flurry of lefts and rights. The crowd was roaring with delight, shouting for the kill and then the loud ringing of the bell, and the referee was pushing Angus back to his corner. A second was ushering a semi-dazed Hammer back to his corner. The crowd now had the blood lust and were repeatedly shouting: "Go Mack, go Mack, go Mack!" Jock, his sly-eyed second, had very little to say this time.

Angus had a puffy bruise coming up to the left of and just below his left eye from the wild punch that had connected. He was feeling some soreness to the side of his head, but was feeling exhilarated and in full control of his senses. The Hammer's second was talking into the ear of the referee, and both had a worried look on their faces. Looking around the ring, Angus saw the scowling face of Willy

Jardine, and he inwardly smiled, thinking, *I'll show you, you lot of bastards*.

The bell rang for the third round, and this time, The Hammer did not come out of his corner quite so quickly; he had cotton wool stuffed up his nostrils, and his eyes were puffy, red, and watering. He came out in a shuffling, boxer's type of walk with his guard well up.

They feinted a while with lefts and jabs, each looking for an opening; the crowd was unusually quiet, with an occasional heckler yelling for a return to something more gladiatorial. Old habits are hard to lose, and suddenly, The Hammer came in with a rushing lunge, throwing a left and right.

Angus was almost caught by this surprise attack but managed to dance out of reach of those crushing, wild, swinging blows. And then his left eye started to burn and sting, and then he sneezed. He suddenly knew what it was; it was an old street fighter's trick. The bastard had pepper in his glove, and Angus knew it was only the speed of his reflex movement rolling away from the punches that had allowed him to avoid the full amount of pepper in his eyes. These bastards would go to any foul length to win the fight.

His left eye was burning and partially blurred, but he was okay, and now he knew he had to win. He deliberately allowed his gloves to go up to his eyes, rubbing them both. To the watching crowd, it just looked like a fighter wiping the sweat from them. The Hammer was watching and waiting for this moment and charged in to take advantage of his opponent's temporary blindness from the pepper, and with arms wide open and swinging his rock-crushing blows, he ran into a stone wall.

With the speed of a javelin, Angus, standing firm left leg forward, threw out a straight left, and backed by the force of his whole weight behind his shoulder, it was a straight bone-crunching left to the already mangled nose of "The Hammer", then lightning swift he brought across a slamming right cross. "The Hamme" brought his arms and gloves up together to protect his battered face, and there, wide open, was his soft protruding gut.

With all his power and weight, Angus dropped low and threw a powerful left hook into it. There was a sound like a bag of gas that had been punctured as the air gasped out of tortured lungs, and "The Hammer" started to fold in the middle. His guard now dropped down to his gut. Angus saw the opening, and almost in slow motion, he lined up The Hammer's head and let go a murderous left and right hook to both sides of the brute's jaw; he was wobbling at the knees, remarkably still on his feet and made a feeble attempt to put his guard up, and there it was again, that exposed fat gut. Angus drove another powerful one, two combinations into it, and "Billy The Hammer" now totally winded, folded over and forward toward Angus, both arms clasping his stomach, and then came the coup de grâce, as with almost slow, deliberate, and deadly aim, Angus again in a semi-crouch brought up a right uppercut which seemed to come up from near the floor and collected "The Hammer" where the left side of jaw met the skull. Angus heard an audible crack, and "The Hammer" was down and completely out cold, with his jaw now jutting at an unusual angle.

The crowd was going crazy and was roaring with delight, jumping up and down in their glee. Angus went back to his corner and stood quietly in that canvas and rope square as the count of ten went ever so slowly out over the fallen man. "The Hammer" tried groggily to get to his feet at eight, but his legs buckled under him.

At ten, the crowd went absolutely mad; the noise could be heard all over Mt Isa.

Angus walked over with an outstretched hand to his fallen opponent at the same time as two of the other tent fighters, and The Hammer's second came into the ring to help him to his feet; they were holding him up, one on each arm looking amazed at Angus, he then spoke in a voice, loud enough to get above the noise, "Ay Billy, you remember that young black boy you punched and kicked to the ground five years ago at the Fitzroy camp? That fella was me. Now we're even, you white bastard!"

Angus stepped out of the ring to the frenzied acclamation of the crowd and his mates. He was confronted by Willy Jardine shaking his head in amazement. "Ay Mack, no one ever knocked Billy McLaren down an' out like that. I rekkin 'is fightin' days might be nearin' an end, an lookin at his jaw e might have trouble eatin for a while 'eres yer five pounds an 'ow would ja like a job, I could do with a fighter like you in me team." Angus just looked at Willy, took the five pounds out of his hand, and walked away without saying a word, just shaking his head from side to side.

Angus felt it was time to return home, back to his grassroots and his family on the banks of the Darling River.

CHAPTER 8

Learn to Fight and to Ride

Throughout the whole series of stories that Angus told, I had sat totally absorbed, enthralled by his tales of life on the droving tracks, in the stock camps and on the big stations where he had worked. I learnt how he had been a horse breaker on most of the stations he had worked. He talked about something he learnt about "gentling" horses from a man who was roaming from cattle station to cattle station using a unique way of breaking in horses that did not use the old traditional and often crueller ways of breaking a horse in. The man had said it was more like "earning the trust and respect of the horse," encouraging the horse to want to learn rather than "bully" it and sometimes break the horse's spirit. He said it was a more humane and natural way. This unique horseman said that if Angus could bring him a couple of good horses to break in, he would teach him about it. Angus readily agreed to this and spent the next couple of weeks fascinated by the massive change he witnessed from wild and never-handled horses to excellent, well-mannered riding horses. Angus then said to me, that one day he would like to teach that skill.

I was over the moon with excitement at the increased horizons of my life and of all his stories; I was absolutely fascinated with the story of how he fought and beat "The Hammer". In my mind's eye, I saw myself in a similar situation, fighting the school bullies and one day teaching my despised father a lesson. When Angus told me he would teach me to ride and handle a horse and also how to fight to be able to defend myself, I was ecstatic and looked forward to my daily lessons every day after school. My training started with fitness lessons and then learning how to box.

Through the rest of the summer and into early autumn, I would go straight from school to Uncle Charlie's camp almost every day. There, for a couple of hours, Angus would instruct me in the finer points of boxing. He said I had an excellent straight left and a hard-hitting right hand. He said a good straight left could break through an opponent's defence and then follow it through with a right cross. He and Uncle Charlie had rigged up a heavy punching bag and Angus worked hard teaching me a number of punch combinations. He said I was a good student, because I was keen to learn, and I learnt fast. He also said that to be a good fighter, I had to be fit, so long runs, rope skipping, and push-ups were part of the daily training.

About midway into summer, Angus disappeared for a few days, and Uncle Charlie was acting strange about it, not saying much. I was worried and wondering if something was wrong. Boy, was I in for a surprise! And the surprise came one day after school when, as usual, I sprinted over to Uncle Charlie's. There, in a temporary holding yard made of saplings and ropes strung between trees, were two beautiful horses. Angus said one was a Palomino, a rich golden-coloured mare with an almost white mane and tail; the other was a buckskin or dun gelding with a black mane, tail and hooves. They were real solid-built horses, with big chests and rumps. Angus said they were a stock horse/quarter horse cross and said they were about 14.2 hands high and explained to me how a horse's height was measured in the old days by the width of a man's hand, hence the saying it was a number of hands high. Angus had purchased these horses from one of the stations he had worked on, saying that he intended to teach me how to ride and handle horses. He said living in the country, especially out in the bush, a man should have a horse and be able to ride it.

That started a new and exciting chapter in my life. My boxing training became interspersed with horse training and handling education, followed by rides out into the surrounding bush and along the river bank bareback. Angus said, to be a good horseman you had to be able to ride a horse at all gaits, bareback. At the start, I had a few falls, but eventually, I could gallop a horse at a fair speed without losing my balance and even jump some dead timber that had fallen across the top of the river bank. To my way of thinking, Angus could ride like one of those Indians I had seen in American cowboy western pictures I had watched on a Saturday afternoon at the local "bughouse", the name kids used to describe the town picture theatre.

Angus was an incredible horseman. At full gallop, gripping with his legs, he could lean over and snatch his old battered Akubra hat from the ground, then sit upright to pull the horse to a sliding halt. Almost every day, we would ride over the sandy flats on the dry parts of the river bed, along the tracks that wound through the big red river gums, and then on the long sandy track back into town, we would race with Angus leading the way. Every day, every race he would win, and every day, I was improving my style and balance, determined that one day I would take the lead.

After every ride, we would wash the horses down, and Angus would teach me about the anatomy of a horse, how to trim and shoe horse hooves, and the finer points of handling a horse. One day, Angus said, "We gotta go to the railway station depot to pick up a big parcel." He then called Uncle Charlie aside and spoke to him quietly, not loud enough for me to hear. I was puzzled. First, we walked into town to the big Hong Lee Chinese-owned department store, walking into the cool interior where Angus directed us through to the menswear department. The young girl behind the counter asked if she could be of assistance. Angus pointed to the hat section and said I want a new hat and boots for me and for my "cobber" here. Twenty minutes later, we walked out with the two of us proudly sporting a new black Akubra hat and carrying boxes with new riding boots in them, with Angus laughingly saying, "Sean, if ya gonna ride a horse, you better look the part." I was over the moon with excitement; no one had ever given me a gift of such grandeur.

As we walked to the railway station depot, I did not notice Uncle Charlie with the two horses, now named Moonlight and Stardust, standing almost hidden by bushes behind the depot stockyards. Walking into the office, Angus approached the counter and, speaking to the ginger-bearded man, said, "G'day Bill, I've come to pick up that box you said you've got here for me." The man named Bill pointed to the big heavy cardboard carton sitting in a corner with a few other boxes, saying, "That's it, Angus. You just gotta pay the freight on it. It's fifteen bob." I wondered what it was that was costing Angus fifteen shillings. To me, that was an enormous amount of money.

Angus said, "C'mon, Sean, give us a hand to carry this box out onto the verandah where we can open it." I was a mass of curiosity and questions, with Angus just smiling at me. Angus took out his razor-sharp stockman's knife and proceeded to cut away the strong strapping around the box, and inside, packed in some sort of loose packing stuff that looked like straw, I could see the tip of something made of leather. At that moment, Bill came out onto the verandah holding a garbage bin, saying, "Ere Angus, put all the rubbish in this bin, an if yer don' mind, I would like to keep the box to store some stuff in." And as Bill finished saying that, Angus said, "Here, Sean, reach in and see if you can lift this out," and the next minute, I was holding a magnificent "Barcoo" stockman's saddle. Angus was saying, "That one is for you, and the one underneath is mine. Now, young fella, we's gonna see how good you have learnt to ride."

By the time we had got to the bottom of the big carton, we had come up with two bridles and bits, halters, lead ropes, and saddle pads, and I was in what I thought to be the nearest thing to heaven. Angus then looked up and gave a loud whistle, and suddenly, Uncle Charlie appeared from around the corner, leading our two horses from where he had been waiting for the signal. I was trembling with excitement as Angus instructed me in the art of correctly fitting a saddle pad and saddle to a horse.

Leaving the surplus equipment with Uncle Charlie and Bill, we rode off with me sitting tall in the saddle, imagining I was a top stockman heading out to round up cattle. We spent a big part of that day on horseback, with Angus frequently giving me tips on horse handling skills. My whole world now seemed to be opening up for me more and more as each day went by, and I found myself with a growing thirst for knowledge and experience in so many more things that had to be assuaged.

The day that I was forced into a situation to use my newfound fighting skills came on rather suddenly and unexpectedly and was finished almost just as quickly. It was a crystal clear winter morning. There was a cold nip in the air, and there was still a light frost on the ground in the shady sections of the schoolyard. A bunch of us kids would often get to the schoolyard before the teacher arrived and have a game of cricket or kick a football around. When my sister, my mate Jimmy, and I arrived at the schoolyard, there were a couple of the bigger kids including the worst school bully "Bluey Ellicott" was there. His name was George, but he got the nickname "Bluey" when he was born because of his bright red hair.

"Bluey" and his gang started slinging off at us with their usual slurs. Most times, we just ignored it and walked away to another part of the schoolyard. This day was to be different. As we walked past and away from them, Bluey lost his cool at us ignoring him, and in a fit of temper, picked up a stone and threw it hard. It hit my sister at the base of the neck between the shoulder blades, knocking her screaming with shock to the ground. I kneeled down to her and held her. She was sobbing from the pain and shock, and I saw blood showing just below the neckline of the blouse and jacket she was wearing, where a sharp edge of the stone had cut the skin. At that moment, it hit me in a wave of anger. It was a cold, calculating rage at the injustice of it, the type of inner cold rage that was going to affect me deeply many more times in my life. I did not recognise it then. All I knew at that moment, looking down at my poor, inoffensive sister, was that something had to be done to stop this cruel, persistent torment.

Jimmy was kneeling beside me, looking down at her. He had a pained look in his eyes. Looking at him, I said, "Mate, you hold her. Look after her till I come back." He looked at me and said, "Wotta ya gunna do Sean?" I just got up and walked away, not taking my eyes off that mongrel "Bluey" for a second, and as I got closer, he just stood there with a smirk on his face. I had seen that look before. It was a look that seemed to say, "What are you going to do about it, you little shit? I can lick you any time." This time there seemed to be a little apprehension in him, perhaps not a worry about me but worrying about the consequences if he had gone too far, should she be seriously hurt.

One thing is for sure: he certainly did not expect my deliberate and violent attack on him, which caught him totally off guard. Angus had said to me a few times when I had told him about the worst kids, about the ones that picked on us most, being older and bigger. He had said, "Sean, me boy, don't worry about that. The bigger they are, the harder they fall. You just have to know how to make them fall. You have learnt the correct way to punch, and you have learnt to punch hard, but that is not all. You have to learn how to use your wits to out-think and outsmart the other bloke." And now, as I walked across to Bluey, those words from Angus came back to me, and I suddenly knew what I had to do to make him fall.

"Bluey" was a good head and shoulders above me in height. He was a bit on the fat side and probably weighed nearly two stones heavier. Even in those few seconds as I walked to him, I knew that I had to outwit him if I was to bring him to the ground.

I stopped less than a yard from "Bluey". He stood there, hands on his hips, looking down at me with that sneering look that I despised on his face. "Bluey," I calmly said, "my sister's bleeding. She's hurt real bad. Just look at her!" He and everyone else turned to look at her on the ground, being comforted by Jimmy, and that was all I needed. I leapt low through the air in a flying crash tackle that hit him around the knees and brought him crashing down, with his head bouncing heavily on the hard-packed dirt ground, and I was astride him in a flash!

This time, I was not using the fist flailing, eyes shut, blind rage punch attempts of the past schoolyard fights; instead, as Bluey was trying to sit up, I was systematically hitting him with left and right crosses and then grabbing him by the shirt with my left hand, I yanked his head up away from the ground and just punched, punch after punch with my right fist into his face.

Everyone else in the schoolyard just stood around, looking in mute shock, astounded at the sight of the biggest school bully being pounded in this way. His cronies never made a move. I had fought a couple of them before, and although outweighed and eventually beaten by them, I had never given up. Perhaps watching now, possibly astounded and shocked at what I was doing to their leader, made them back off. Perhaps they were remembering my persistent attempts in the past to keep coming back at them and not give up. The next moment, though, I was flying backwards, held tight in the grip of Mr Davidson, the schoolteacher who had just arrived on the scene. He was loudly demanding to know "what was going on", and at the same time, a lot of the younger kids were talking at once, giving their version of the events that led up to this moment.

Strangely, none of "Blue's" mates said anything, nor did "Bluey", who was now sitting up and looking very dazed. Tears were flowing, and he was sobbing out loud and bleeding profusely from his nose. He now was showing two badly swollen eyes, and blood was flowing down his chin from a cut lip where his tooth had punctured it. Looking down at him, I realised that is where the cut across my right knuckles came from, the edge of one of his front teeth. I hadn't felt a thing. Needless to say, "Bluey" and I were ordered to our respective homes for the day with a report from the teacher to hand to our parents.

It's funny, though. I could swear Mr Davidson had a faint smile on his lips when he sternly told me it was wrong to settle arguments with one's fists.

I was fearful of what the old man would do when he found out, and Mum was a bit frightened to give the letter to him, knowing that if he was drunk or in a bad mood, he could blame her. Mum and I need not have worried. He was sober at the time, and the old man just laughed and said, "Good on 'im, it'll make a man of him."

"Blue's" father, though, did not so understand; he blew a fuse, especially when he found out that "Bluey" had copped a hiding from a much smaller kid and a part koori kid at that. Bluey then copped another hiding from his father's leather belt. In hindsight, now I reason that type of thing could have been the reason for Bluey's chip-on-the-shoulder attitude, and I almost felt sorry for him. The best thing after it happened was that Bluey and his hanger-ons left me and my sister alone and bothered us no more.

The cut my sister received was not serious, and Mum washed it with Solyptol and put a pad on it.

Back at Uncle Charlie's camp, Uncle Charlie and Angus shook me by the hand and congratulated me on standing up for my sister and me and taking Bluey on. Angus said that pretty soon, he was moving on and that he had one more bit of advice for me. He said, "Sean, as you grow and go through life, you are going to meet a lot of bad bastards, people who like to heap shit on others and put them down. Keep your head up, son, and stand proud. Don't look for a fight, but if it comes, hit hard. Hit first and fight your best. I've found that many of the 'would be tough blokes' who talk fight are cowards underneath. They try to stand over and scare you with words of what they are gonna do to you. They figure their bluff talk will make you an easy mark. My advice is to listen to 'em and get a look on your face like what they are saying is really scaring you. That puts them off guard, particularly if they are carrying a weapon like a bottle or a knife. Stand in close to them, don't argue back, just look like you are beat and shit scared. Watch their eyes, and when you see them relax a little, thinking they've got you beat, and they drop their guard, then you hit 'em as hard as you can and with everything you've got. And when you get them down, make them stay down. Make them see you are tougher and harder than they could ever be. I bet you, Sean, they won't bother you again."

He then said, "Good luck, son. I know that we will cross trails again someday." Soon after, Angus left Uncle Charlie's camp and moved on. It was some years that went by before we were to meet up again.

CHAPTER 9

"Mulga" The Nickname

The sun on that February day was a blinding orb of fire. The temperature on the school verandah at midday was 102 degrees Fahrenheit. A light, dry, hot breeze had dust devils swirling around in the yard of the old schoolhouse, and being inside the old schoolhouse with its corrugated iron roof was like being in an oven. The old corrugated iron water tank at the side of the building issued tepid, warm water into our tin mugs, and black crows were sitting listless like they were stuffed birds in a museum on the limbs of an old dead gum tree at the bottom of the schoolyard.

"Christ, it was hot." The double entrance doors to the schoolhouse were wide open, as were every window of the old schoolhouse, hoping to catch the slightest breeze. It was just after the midday lunch break. We were back in the classroom and had just started a mathematics lesson, and we were writing in our schoolbooks, I think, with no real concentration, disinterested, and half dozing with the heat when I sensed something. I think it was a slight rustling noise that caught my attention, a faint murmur or sound of something moving against a schoolbag sitting on the floor near the aisle between the old-fashioned two-seater desks. My desk was one down from the back of the class, and I sat on the side closest to the aisle. I heard the faint rustle sound again. Was that a faint movement I saw? It was at the back, in the shadows underneath the seat of the desk on the other side of the aisle, where Jimmy Collett and "Kenny" Wilson were sitting. Were they laboriously or perhaps sleepily engaged in studying the numerals and figures on the classroom blackboard? Jimmy sat nearest to me, and I focused my gaze on where I thought I'd heard the sound; then I saw what had caused the movement, and for a second, I froze.

It was a huge, deadly King Brown snake known colloquially as a "Mulga snake". It was partly coiled, and with its head up, its steely cold gaze was transfixed on the back of Jimmy's bare legs crossed at the ankles, its tongue flickering in and out. It must have slid quietly and unobserved in through the open doors. "Geez! For chrissake, Jimmy, don't move!" is what I wanted to scream out, but I knew that could create the movement I dreaded! The end of its tail protruded slightly out from under the seat, and without another thought, I leapt onto it, grabbing the tail with both hands and running fast the few feet to the open door, dragging it outside. The bloody thing was longer than me, and I remembered Uncle Charlie telling me that if you pick up a snake, you have to keep it up off the ground at arm's length, swinging it like a pendulum so it can't strike back at you until you can crack it like a stock whip or beat it against something so as to break its back. Although I was pretty good at cracking a stock whip, I certainly could not crack that snake like a whip. I was not tall enough.

I ran like a madman out into the yard, keeping it stretched out. Once out there, I was swinging it around my head like a helicopter's blades, keeping its body stretched out in an arc away from me, and then I slammed it hard up against the old dead gum, sending the sleeping flock of crows, flying off screeching with their raucous calls. Time and again I swung and slammed that snake into the tree until its lifeless form just lay there on the dusty ground. Then I stood there, exhausted and shivering with the shock, with the realisation of what had happened now settling in on me. I became aware that all the kids and the teacher were all around me. Jimmy had picked the snake up by the tail and was holding it half up from the ground, and he was saying, "Jesus, Sean! Look how long the bugger is. He must be nearly six feet long."

The teacher, who had witnessed everything from the front of the class and had run outside with the kids, walked over to me and said, "Sean, that was a very brave thing you just did. You have possibly saved your school friends, particularly Jimmy Collett and Kenny Wilson, from a snakebite that could kill them, seeing as how far we are away from a major hospital. I am going to report this matter to the education authorities and to our local newspaper. You deserve recognition for what you have done killing that dangerous Mulga snake." That incident and a graphic newspaper heading created the start of the nickname "Mulga" I carry today.

Because of that disruptive incident and the intense heat of the day, Mr. Davidson, the teacher, allowed us all to go home early. I packed the snake into an old chaff bag Jimmy had found and took it home to give to Uncle Charlie for "tucker". Snake baked in the coals of a campfire was one of Uncle Charlie's favourite foods. That afternoon, an excited group comprising my sister, Jimmy Collett, Kenny Wilson and me surrounded Mum, and all were talking at once, telling her how I saved Jimmy and Kenny's lives. Poor Mum was overwhelmed and mortified with fear of what could have happened to me or the others at my action.

My father was still at the pub rehydrating from the day's heat when a car pulled up outside, and a pretty young woman got out carrying a camera and a small bag. She introduced herself as Naomi Wilkes and said she was a journalist working for "The Courier Star," our town's twice-weekly newspaper. She said she wished to interview the young hero who saved his friends from a deadly snake and asked for Mum's permission to do so. Mum was beaming with pride as she pointed to me, and I went red and got all tongue-tied.

Naomi said they had been visited at the newspaper office by our teacher, Mr Davidson, and were very impressed by what he had told them. She also said that their head office, with a much wider distribution of newspapers with national interest, was interested in the story, and they would also be contacting me for an interview.

Two days later, our local newspaper appeared at the newsagent and shops around the town bearing the headline **"Young Schoolboy from the Mulga Saves Friends."** It was along with a picture of me and a King Brown snake. It went on to say how a young lad from the "Mulga" country along the Darling River was sitting in the classroom of their small school and how he had saved two of his classmates from a deadly King Brown snake, also known as the "Mulga Snake". It went on to describe in detail how it was done, along with photographs of us all. The teacher read the story out loud in the classroom, and I immediately became some sort of a hero to the younger kids, who later walked around the school grounds chanting, "Mulga Man, Mulga Man, kills a snake whenever he can." On the very same afternoon the news was published, the same car pulled up and out stepped Naomi with another man, who was introduced as a reporter from a Sydney newspaper. He said he wanted to run a feature story in their Sunday edition. There was a lot of photo-taking and a long interview.

It was while this was going on that the old man staggered in, swaggering in his usual drunken fashion and started big-noting himself about how he had taught me everything, to which the reporter and Naomi politely listened. Later, when the old man had disappeared inside, Mum had the chance to apologise, asking them to ignore what he had said. You could see they were all awake up to the old man and were probably a bit embarrassed by it all. Anyway, the following weekend, there was a huge write-up in a big Sydney and Melbourne newspaper with pictures. The mayor of the town organised an official function and dinner, and along with Sergeant Kennedy, I was presented with a plaque from our local council acknowledging my bravery. Kennedy, the policeman, also presented me with a letter of commendation from the commissioner of police. For the next week or so, the "old man" walked around, crowing like a rooster about his son until he was drunk and abusive, and then he would come home and take his shit out on us as usual. God, how I wished he would go away and leave us alone.

Mum was as proud as one could be, and she made up a scrapbook with all the photos and newspaper clippings in it, which I still have to this day, and life soon settled back into the same old routine of school, house chores, dodging the old man and idyllic times down along the river with my mate Jimmy and the koori kids. I also would help Uncle Charlie tend to the horses and occasionally go on horseback rides with him.

Mum was complaining about how I was growing out of my clothes, getting taller and stuff like that. Uncle Charlie still had the punching bag set up at his camp, and I had gotten into the habit of going there every afternoon after school, where I would work out the punching bag, skipping rope, and doing push-ups. Angus had left behind for me a set of boxing gloves, bag mittens, padded sparring gloves, a skipping rope and a book on how to train for boxing. Uncle Charlie had become my trainer; he would put on the heavy padded gloves and move around with me as I worked through the series of combination punches Angus had taught me and more that I learnt from the book. I had also taken up running and would jog at various paces on the mile-long dirt track between Uncle Charlie's and the Koori camp.

Up to this time, I had not had much interest in school sports except for a game of rugby and cricket, but I now found myself interested in the inter-school competition, and in my first marathon run, I took out the blue ribbon and landed a second prize in the five-hundred-yard sprint. It turned out I had good wind and endurance and could easily run long distances at speed. I won quite a few marathon events over the next three years until I left school. That was a skill that also would help me in the years to come.

Scholastically, I was above average with schoolwork. The teacher said in just about every end-of-year school report, "I had a very high intelligence and learnt easily but felt that I had no interest in the everyday schoolwork." My mind seemed to be occupied with dreaming about the outside world and what it had to offer. I wanted travel and adventure and was more interested in working on my physical prowess.

Ever since I was a small child, Uncle Charlie had taken me on his frequent tracking, hunting, and fishing excursions into the surrounding bush, and I had learnt to see tracks and trails that other kids could not. Uncle Charlie had shown me how to survive on bush "tucker", how to set snares and traps, and how to use a spear and other primitive hunting weapons. He taught me how to identify different birds and animals by their tracks and sounds. He showed me where and how to find water and to make a shelter. Uncle Charlie said I was as good as any bush "blackfella" at survival. He no longer called me "Shoon" but referred to me by the nickname I had acquired: "Mulga".

By the time I was fifteen years of age, when I had left school, I stood a bit over six feet, and Mum said I had shoulders and a broad chest "like a wild scrub bull." I was not sure then how I was going to use these accumulated skills and physical prowess, but I knew somehow that one day I would. Right now, my immediate aim was to find a job. I wanted desperately to help support Mum, ease her workload, and stop her from having to rely on our unreliable father. I did not know for sure what I could do, and in a small country town, work choices were limited. I thought I would start by wandering around town and calling every shop and business to see what work I could find. On that day, my life was to see another change and take a major turn when I ran into Police Sergeant Kennedy.

CHAPTER 10

Jackeroo to Head Stockman

About fifty miles from where we lived, there was a huge cattle station of about seventy square miles. It was renowned for breeding top-quality, big, beefy Braford cattle. The old man reckoned he had worked there for a while as a young Jackeroo—that is, before the booze took hold of him. Well, on this particular day, I was standing in the main street of town talking with Police Sergeant Kennedy when this big-built man dressed in typical country squatter fashion stopped to say hello to him. He said he was in town to pick up some supplies, and he was going to the newspaper office to place an ad for an additional worker for his property. He said he was going to advertise for a young bloke to train, starting as a jackeroo and working up to stockman. And he asked Kennedy if he knew of any likely young fellow that would be suitable for such a job.

Kennedy looked at me, winked, and, turning to the man, said, "Bill, let me introduce you to this young fellow. His name is Sean Molloy. Sean, this is Mr. Finlayson, owner of Argyle Downs Station to the northwest of here." I shook hands with the man, and Kennedy went on to say, "Sean has finished school and is looking for work." He went on to say, "You may remember two or three years ago, the newspaper story about a young school kid that saved his classmates from a king brown snake that had wandered into his classroom. They called him the 'Mulga Man'. The police commissioner presented him with a bravery award. This is him! You could not find a finer young lad; he lives with his family on the edge of town."

While all this was going on, I was shuffling my feet with my head down, looking at the footpath, and feeling shy from embarrassment. I looked up, and this big fellow, Bill Findlayson, was staring at me intently. He looked me in the eye and said, "Is that so, young Mulga?" I nodded, saying, "Yes, Mr. Finlayson," and felt an immediate warmth to the man. He then said to Kennedy, "You would recommend him, John?" Kennedy replied, "I most certainly would." Finlayson then turned to me and said, "Sean, I am in town for a couple of days on business, and I would like to talk to you some more. I have to go to the police station to organise a travelling stock permit for cattle we are droving to Bourke and with Mr. Kennedy's permission. I would like to talk with you there," and turning to Kennedy, he said, "John, what time would suit you to sign a travelling stock permit and for me to have a chat with young Sean?"

At three o'clock that afternoon, I walked out of the police station in a daze, with my mind slowly comprehending that I had a live-in job as a trainee jackaroo on one of the most prestigious cattle properties in the district. One of my first jobs was to ride as a "jackeroo" on a one-hundred-and-sixty-mile cattle drive from Argyle Downs Station to the sale yards of the town of Bourke with a mob of eight hundred prime Braford cattle, destined for the meat-hungry miners in this fast-growing silver mining town.

Before Angus had left to head north again, he had entrusted the keep of the two horses, Moonlight and Stardust, to me and Uncle Charlie, saying that if I ever got a job on a station or a big property where horses were used, they were to be mine. And I now had a job where I could use them and my newly learnt horse riding skills.

Every day after school, I would race home first, put on my riding boots and hat and then head to where the horses were, where they now roamed freely, although inside Uncle Charlie's now fenced-off camp. There, I would take some hay, and with a few loud whistles and calls, we would soon hear the sounds of galloping hooves. Sometimes, they would come splashing across the shallows of the river, from where they sometimes fed on the other side, if Uncle Charlie had let them out of the compound to feed there. It was easy to catch either one of them and slip a bridle on, then saddle him while he ate his reward. Most times, I would ride out on my own with the spare horse following along, and on occasion, Uncle Charlie would come along, but he used to complain he was getting too old, particularly if we went into a gallop. The horses were in excellent condition, perhaps a little overweight, but I knew that would be soon rectified when I started my new job.

I was dizzy with elation, a jackeroo, and I was not quite sixteen, and what is more, I had my own horses that Mr Findlayson said I would be welcome to bring along. On that day, I made a mental vow that I would work hard at that job and not let Mr Finlayson down, and at that jackeroo position, I worked hard under the supervision of the head stockman, a wiry, tough old bloke named Joe Duncan, he was a tough teacher but fair. His knowledge of a stockman's work had come from a lifetime of working for a number of huge cattle stations, including the massive Sidney Kidman cattle empire. Kidman was reputed to be the owner of the biggest cattle herd and landholdings in the world. His first words to me were, "Son, you work hard, listen and learn, and I will teach you all there is to know to be a good cattleman and stockman, but I won't bother if you show no interest." He need not have had any concern there; my heart was set on being the best stockman ever, and over the next three years, I was to excel at the job, rising to become head stockman. Sadly, though, this promotion came about through a tragic accident.

Joe Duncan was severely injured and later died when a young rank and wild Braford bull caught him unexpectedly in a fenced race leading to the cattle yards. It was after a muster of cattle so we could brand and dehorn young cattle and get them ready for a future cattle drive to Bourke. Joe and I were pushing up the cattle from the large overnight holding paddock and down the race to the yards on horses. There were two stockmen working the gates in the pen yards and three others working the branding forge, dehorning and castrating young bulls, when a small group of feisty cows and a large angry bull broke away, and I went after them. This particular young bull, excited and frightened from its first muster, suddenly wheeled around back to the mob that Joe and I were working along the race, and upsetting the group of bawling cattle already packed in the race near the yards, causing three or four more cows in the race to spook and to run back around Joe and me. I sped off after the cows to turn them back.

I did not see what happened next, but I heard the yelling and shouting. Wheeling Moonlight around, I saw Joe lying face down on the ground with that big bull standing over him and repeatedly goring him. The other two blokes working the pen gates were trying desperately to distract its attention when I came galloping up and drove it off with my stock whip. Joe was lying still, and blood was pooling in the dust beside him. He was unconscious. His hat was off, and I saw a nasty gash on the side of his head. Kneeling beside him, it was then I saw where all the blood was coming from; it was on the side of his body, away from me, and what I saw there horrified me. Just under his rib cage and exposed to the sun were intestines.

In later years, during my time with Special Operations in Vietnam, I saw men with serious stomach wounds, but nothing to date in my young life had prepared me for this. There in the dust and blood were portions of Joe's intestines in a small loop on the ground, already attracting dozens of flies. Joe was still alive, but his breath was coming in rasping, guttural gasps.

Mr Finlayson had hurried to the homestead and was trying to wireless the flying doctor base about one hundred miles away. We decided it was unwise to move Joe, and while I kept the flies away from his wounds, the others hastily erected a tarpaulin shade over him. Just before the plane landed and the doctor arrived, Joe passed away, and kneeling beside him, I was distraught with grief. In those three years working with Joe, I had developed a strong respect, a fondness for this tough, no-nonsense, likeable man; he had become more like a father to me, much more than my own father had ever been, and now he was gone.

Later, going over the events that had led up to the accident for Police Sergeant Kennedy's report, it was realised that the young bull was what is known as a "mickey", a scrub bull who had been missed in the last muster when all the wiener males were castrated and dehorned. He had run wild for another year, and his fear of man and horse when being mustered and run in for yarding had manifested itself into a frightened rage as the yards, the noise, and humans came closer into view. At that moment, his fear overcame him. He spun around and charged into Joe's horse, which was directly behind him, knocking it off its feet and throwing Joe to the ground. At that moment of his horse being thrown, Joe's head collided with a yard rail, stunning him. A Cobb & Co wire hitch on the rail, when examined, showed some hair and blood, the reason for the nasty gash on his head. The bull then vented its spleen on the unconscious figure lying on the ground, driving a long horn into his stomach and doing serious harm before we could drive it off.

Joe was buried with his stock whip and saddle in the little cemetery in town; his only surviving relative, an elderly sister, was there who, with her husband, had come up from Melbourne for the funeral, and everyone from Argyle Downs Station was there. There were dozens of others, many of them men who had flown, driven or ridden in to pay their last respects to a man they knew and respected. Many of them were men who had worked with and under Joe over the years.

Even my father was there sober for once; Mum was on his arm, looking sad. I had taken Joe home to meet my family on occasion, and she liked Joe. Mr Finlayson, with his wife standing beside him, gave a moving eulogy about what a good man Joe was. When it came to my turn to speak on the man who had been like a father, I choked on every tear-filled word, remembering the man who had played a big part in my young life, helping to turn a boy into a man.

Later, at the magnificent wake Mr Findlayson had put on at the community hall, my father stayed, to a degree, reasonably sober, not making a fool of himself in his usual way. He actually seemed a little in awe of Mr Findlayson, who was a big man and certainly had an air of positive strength about him who would not tolerate fools. Nearing the end of the wake, Mr Findlayson came over to where I was standing, chatting quietly with a group of workmates and stockmen from other stations. He stood talking with us for a while, then, seizing a break in the conversation, he quietly said, "Sean, can

I speak privately with you for a moment?" Moving a short distance away from the group, Mr Findlayson went straight to the point.

"Sean, over the last couple of years, I have watched you closely. Although you are only eighteen, you work as hard as any man here. You have learnt well all the skills that 'old Joe' could pass on to you. You also have the respect of all the men and my wife and I." He went on to say, "Sean, since Joe's death, I have thought long about this and have discussed it at length with my wife and two other of the leading stockmen." At that moment, I looked over his shoulder and noticed two of the men in the group of stockmen grinning back at me. Slightly distracted, I turned back to Mr Findlayson to hear him say, "Sean, we want you to take over as head stockman. We feel that Joe would want the same. He has always spoken highly of you, so what do you say?" I was at a loss for words. There was a lump in my throat thinking of Joe and his patient way of teaching, and I felt my eyes blurring again with tears I could not hide.

Mr Finlayson was holding his hand out. "Well, Sean, can we shake on it?" I managed to stammer out the words: "Mr. Finlayson, I would be proud to take on Joe's job." And for the next two years, I put my heart and soul into that job and loved every exciting and sometimes dangerous moment of it. It was hard work, and I was saving money and also sending money to my sister to bank for Mum.

After Joe's tragic death, the next two years of my life were spent doing the work of the head stockman and senior horse breaker and generally supervising the daily life, work, and maintenance of a huge outback cattle property. I particularly enjoyed the long cattle drives along the stock routes, taking the cattle to market or just following the feed and water in times of drought. On those magic nights, we spent camped out and sleeping in a swag under the stars, the enjoyment of sitting around a campfire, yarning and listening to the tales of the old timers of the huge outback cattle drives and the great horsemen of their days.

For all of that great and rewarding life, deep down, there was something elusive, something niggling at my soul. I felt that there was so much more to see and do in the world I had not seen and knew only through National Geographic magazines and newspapers that I had read or heard about on the radio. So much so that when the letter came from the Australian government informing me of the federal conscription of Australian youth for National Service duties, something in me told me that I had to go. Mr Finlayson told me I did not have to go as I worked in a protected industry and said he could write a letter to the government explaining that fact. I thought long and hard about my decision and finally decided it was time to move on. I decided I was going to be a "Nasho", the term used to describe men who were called up into the army to do national service training for three months of full-time service, and then followed by two years in the Australian Citizen Military Force. I was now just twenty years of age. It was 1954, and there was a big world out there to see and explore. I had often listened to the radio and had heard Mr and Mrs. Finlayson talking about a country overseas called Korea where some conflict was going on involving Australia. I now found myself listening more to the radio and started to read more about that conflict and other areas of the world that were being disturbed by aggressive communist infiltration. There was an uneasy sense of tension in world governments. A feeling that something had to be done by the free world.

First Love

Bloody hell! What had happened to me? I was in a euphoria of emotions. At this time in my life, I had not yet had a proper girlfriend, other than a wonderful one-night stand with a girl that I met at a local rodeo about six months previous. She was off a property and had entered in the barrel racing rides. She was good enough to win against some pretty stiff competition. That night, she and I had a wild, mildly intoxicated night together. I never saw her again.

But this next romantic interlude hit me strong at a local rodeo and camp drafting competition. I was with three of my workmates, standing at the bar having a beer between events, when I saw a most beautiful girl come in with three other girls, all dressed in their western rodeo outfits, boots, and spurs. The group stood a few feet from us and ordered drinks, and the girl who had caught my attention was gorgeous. We were close enough for me to see she was blonde, blue-eyed, and had a beautiful figure with her tight riding pants and a fringed satin shirt accentuating the voluptuousness of her figure. I felt intoxicated just by looking at her. I was not really a drinker, just one or two beers occasionally with my mates, and yet I felt light-headed just seeing her. I was still staring when one of her friends nudged her, and pointing at me, she looked in my direction and smiled. I felt my deep tan face go the colour of scarlet, and I averted my eyes, feeling bashful and stupid, and the country boy that I was with no experience of these things.

At that moment, Larry, who is one of my stockman mates whom I worked with, spotted the girls and yelled out, "Hey Clare, come and join us!" The girl he had called to in the group was a tall, redheaded girl with large breasts straining out through a satin, sequined and fringed cowboy shirt. She yelled back something to him that was lost to me in the din of the bar noise and my state of embarrassment. The next second, we were all together as a group, with introductions going all around. It turned out that Larry and Clare were friends from way back, on occasion meeting at and competing in country rodeos. I gathered from the conversation that they had been in a relationship for some time before going separate, friendly ways. The blue-eyed angel that had me feeling like a little boy caught doing something wrong by his mother was named of all things Angelica, but her friends called her "Angie". She was standing next to me as the introduction went around, and at my name, she put a hand as light as a feather into my hand, which to me had the size and roughness of what I imagined a bear's paw would feel.

From that moment, there was no one else in the surroundings for me, and as we looked at each other, I saw a reassuring smile of warmth directed at me. We—or I should say she—started the conversation with the usual, "And where are you from? Where do you work? What do you do?" and as time went on, I felt myself relaxing in her company, more and more. Over the evening, I learnt that she was a company secretary working for a big multinational corporation firm on the north side of Sydney. She was twenty-two years of age and had grown up in a wealthy north shore area of Sydney she laughingly called "S'nives" in a stiff, formal way of speaking. When questioned, she said it was a very upmarket residential area and rather snobbish, its correct name being Saint Ives.

She had gone to an exclusive and, in her own words, "a boring private school", done a university course, had a degree in economics, and had broken off an engagement to a boyfriend some six months ago.

Her father was a merchant banker; her mother was a Sydney socialite who did not like horses and whom she did not get on well with. She had owned a horse since she was eight years of age, disliked the city and her only real passions and relaxation in her life were horses, barrel racing, country life, and travelling to rodeos.

"Wow! What could I say?" I mentally compared my life to a life like that, so as she probed me deeper, I just told her about most everything as it was, just a boy from the bush, my family, life as a head stockman, and one who has been called up to go into the army. She listened intently throughout my story, and when I got to the part of my military call-up, she reached out and touched my arm, saying, "How sad." I was puzzled and said so. She explained by saying, "How sad it must be to leave such a wonderful life, friends, family, and horses to go off to wherever the military sends me." She said it with genuine concern in her voice, and at that moment, I felt my heart go out to her.

I had not thought of my call-up in that manner and only saw it as another change, another adventure, and another experience in life. Mustering courage, I put my hand onto her hand and softly said so, adding, "It was time for my life to move on." Her eyes looked sad for a moment, and she moved her head closer to me, saying, "Then I hope we will meet again. You are different from men I have met, and I would like to talk with you more."

At that stage, the party around us was getting louder and raucous, with much laughter and joking. There had been several attempts to draw us into the frivolity, but we had been given up on. Larry and Clare were now hanging on to each other and, being a little intoxicated, pushed through to us. Clare was saying we are going to have a party at Larry and Sean's camp. Was that okay with us? It certainly did not bother me. There were four of us camped on the rodeo grounds, and we had our swags with a huge A-frame tarpaulin on a rope stretched between trees over them. There was a plentiful supply of firewood for a campfire, and it was a great place for a moonlight party.

We did a quick whip around of a hat for money for liquor supplies, and armed with a few cartons of beer and some wine, we headed noisily back to our camp. Not far from our camp and parked under a large shady tree, Angie pointed out her camp. It was a Ford 250 utility with a gooseneck, three-horse float and accommodation area. I said something like, "Wow! That's a real flash", and laughingly, she said, "It was Daddy's twenty-first birthday present to me. The horses I have accumulated since my childhood when Daddy gave me my first horse." Standing there in the bright moonlight were three good-looking horses held in by an electric fence enclosure. I said I would like to come over in the morning to have a look at them in the daylight. She smiled as she said, "I would like that."

We soon had a good campfire going; Angelica and I were comfortably settled down on my swag with a drink in our hands. Larry was the life of the party. Standing by the fire telling a range of raucous jokes, Eddy, our singing stockman, had produced a guitar and was strumming away, getting ready to entertain us with his vast range of country western songs. He had a voice very much like Johnny Cash, and he was a hit wherever we went as an entertainer.

It was a night of nights to remember, and as the cool of the outback night came over us, we moved closer to the fire, warmed by the heat from it and mellowed by a few drinks and Eddy's singing. It seemed so natural for me to put an arm around her and feel her warm body come closer to me. We just lay there, her head on my shoulder, her face close to mine, listening to Eddy. We lay in that position for a while, when she put her lips near my ear and softly said, "Sean, I saw you looking at me when we walked into the bar." Again, I felt that surge of embarrassment and told her of it. She said, "Sean, don't feel that way. I saw it, and it was beautiful", adding, "I felt an immediate attraction to you. I have become tired of the suave and shallow men I seem to have met since my fiancé and I parted. I find it truly wonderful to meet a genuine, warm, and real man who does not have to put on a pose to get attention. I am tired of people who use subterfuge and pose to impress. I really would like to get to know you more. Can you tell me how long it will be before you go into the army?"

I told her that my "call-up date was about seven weeks away". She lapsed into a pensive silence. Eddy was strumming guitar and started a sentimental country song, something about lost love and loneliness, when Angie whispered softly to me, "Sean, would you mind if I left the party?" rather startled by this remark, I turned to her and said "no." She then said, "I want you to come with me."

No one seemed to take much notice as we stood up and slipped away outside the ring of firelight. It was late, and some were showing signs of drowsiness. Larry and Clare gave us a lazy wave as we went past; Eddie was concentrating on his song with a cute brunette sitting real close to him. We walked slowly, hand in hand, through the moonlit night, to her camper cum horse float. On entering it, she turned on the battery-powered lights; I was impressed by the layout. It had all the necessary amenities for cooking and sleeping. The large bunk bed had a colourful abstract bed cover on it and was the size of a double bed.

Gesturing toward it, she said, "Sit down and be comfortable. Would you like a cup of tea?" We sat there sipping tea and talking about her love of horses and rodeo competition. We talked about our vastly different childhood days and the differences between our growing up in the city and the country. She told me her love of horses started as a small child, on getting her first pony as a gift from her parents and how she progressed through pony club training and into classical dressage and the huge thrill she got when a girlfriend invited her to see her first real rodeo being held at a country show not far out of Sydney.

That rodeo visit changed her whole outlook on horse sports, and from that moment, she became addicted to barrel racing and endurance riding, travelling far and wide to learn and compete and gradually chalking up an impressive number of wins in both sports. The three horses resting contentedly in their electric wire enclosure outside her horse float were horses she had acquired for each particular sport she competed in. Her barrel racer was a powerful, built stock horse and quarter horse cross with appaloosa colouring named Cherokee. He was a gelding of stocky build and fast, about fourteen hands high. Her endurance racing horse was an Arabian mare of impeccable stud background from one of Australia's famous horse studs near Scone in NSW. Because of the mare's impressive number of wins, Angie had plans to breed from her in the future. The third horse was a magnificent-looking ex-racing thoroughbred, which she used in dressage events. Throughout her trailer were the various types of saddles and riding apparel needed for each sport.

It was getting late, and our exchange of conversation was starting to trail off. When our eyes met, looking deep into each other, we both reached out at the same time together, and the next couple of hours went by in a swirling kaleidoscope of emotional feelings and passion. Never had I known anything like what I was feeling as we made love. Later, lying in each other's arms, she told me of her fiancé, the man she had once loved and his betrayal of her trust, and the pain of it all, which took her life onto a different path up until now. I told her of the one night I had with a girl, that I had never been in love with a woman, and how the emotions I was feeling now were totally new to me. She then raised her gorgeous nakedness over me, saying, "Let me love you as I want you to love me," and again, I was lost in the swirling currents of an unquenchable passion within me, which slowly dissolved into sleep entwined closely together.

It was almost midday when we awoke to more lovemaking. Angie's barrel race competition was on at 3 p.m., and she needed to get herself and her horse ready. I lay there watching her naked beauty, moving around the small trailer and then putting on a terry towelling coat to head for the showers. I said I would tend to her horse to feed and groom it while she showered and dressed in her rodeo outfit. I must admit that as I tended to her horses, I was walking around with a cloud of beautiful images and feelings going through my mind, and I stood with the rest of my friends and proudly watched her come in with the top points score to win yet another blue ribbon.

Angie had asked me if I could come to Sydney and visit her before I went into the army. I had promised I would. I would ask Mr Finlayson if I could leave a week or more earlier so I could spend time with her. Even though I was not too impressed with what I had heard of big cities, the thought of being with Angie over an extended period exhilarated me. She had told me she had her own apartment in a quiet, tree-lined street not too far from her parents' luxury house. She laughingly told me there was a huge park at the bottom of the dead-end street with lots of trees and a creek running through it. She said it would be the closest thing to the bush you will find in Sydney. That night, Angie won her event, and we shared one more night of love. I had heard the expression "being on cloud nine", and now I know what it meant. We were both on an incredible high, only saddened by the thought that we had to part and go separate ways the next day.

We said sad goodbyes, filled with the memories of our time together and heartened by the fact we would see each other again soon. Angie gave me her phone number and address and said she would pick me up at Sydney's Central Station when I came in by train. When I asked Mr Finlayson, he agreed to my earlier departure date, which would be two weeks from now, and gave me a wry smile when I told him of my meeting Angie. Mrs Finlayson just hugged me and said, "She is a very lucky girl to meet you, Sean."

The Conscript "Nasho"

The survival skills I had learnt from Uncle Charlie on our many ventures in the bush were to come to the fore in the years to come when, at the age of nineteen, just before my twentieth birthday, I received a letter from the Australian government stating that I was part of the selection process to be conscripted into the Australian Military Forces to do my National Service. The letter stated that there was a choice of Army, Navy, and Air Force. I wrote back to the government informing them of my choice to go into the Army. They replied with a date to report to Ingleburn Army training barracks on the western outskirts of Sydney. It is a big city I had only read about, and I must admit to being a bit nervous about going there. All of that was tempered, though, by the thought of Angelica. My Angie would be waiting for me.

It was 1954. The national service call-up was to be for three months, followed by a period of twelve months in the Citizen Military force, which became known as the "weekend warriors". I had learnt from listening to the radio and in newspapers about the war that was raging in Korea and America's heavy involvement in it. The Australian government was not sending national servicemen to that conflict. I had followed this war with strong interest. It had made a deep impression on me, but I had not given any consideration to any military service. When my call-up finally arrived, I found myself in the Australian Army, and with it came the realisation that I loved it!

I thrived on the military training, shooting rifles, learning fighting skills and the ordered discipline of Army life. On the rifle range, it was found I had exceptional skill as a marksman. We were using World War Two .303 Lee Enfield rifles and Thompson sub-machine guns, and on the thousand-yard range, I always managed to get a close grouping in the centre bull's eye. This was brought to the attention of our commanding officer, and I was introduced to specialist training on sniper rifles. My first rifle was the SMLE Mk 111, and then onto the further conversion known as No 1 Mk111* (HT), equipped with a 2.5 telescopic sight and cheek rest. The training involved logistics of wind direction, range, and velocity. It was very intensive, and I loved it; I progressed in training and soon gained the rank of sergeant.

My up-to-now unused bush-tracking skills were suddenly put to the test one day in a humid, steamy, thick, rainforested area of the Springbrook plateau. It was an area used by the military for jungle training manoeuvres. Led by our lieutenant, we were on a three-day jungle march and training bivouac in a dense jungle area, when one of the boys in my platoon wandered away into the jungle from our camp without telling me or our patrol leader he was going. To make matters worse, this lad had shown from the start of training that he found the military life was hard going. Often late for roll call, prone to lag behind, slovenly in manner, he did not meld in with the other boys too well; it was obvious he disliked Army life and its disciplines.

It was late afternoon, and we had stopped in a small clearing to silent camp for the night, which meant guard duties rotated, sleeping on the ground fully dressed with a cape cover over us and a groundsheet covering a hip hole we had scratched out. It was a hard camp on hard rations, with no fire or lights, and we were surrounded by dense forest and scrub with vision in any direction less than ten metres. Our trek into this area was by map and compass, a semicircular route of about fifteen miles, to finally arrive at a designated area on a track to be picked up by the truck taking us back to camp at Canungra and with the work in occupying the campsite; it was just on dark when one of our platoons was missed. No one had noticed him leave the camp. The seriousness of this was highlighted by the realisation he was an inner-city Brisbane lad with no knowledge of the bush or its inherent dangers. An immediate search and loud calls of the surrounding area were implemented with the instructions to keep cooee calling to no avail. As I did not want boot damage to the surrounding area with the possibility of destroying any sign of track, we posted perimeter guards. We fired blank shots intermittently through the night until the first light.

Wisely, a latrine pit had been dug in the centre of the camp. As morning light strengthened, the lieutenant gave me the okay to start searching. I took two reliable men with me. First, crouching low, I did a close perimeter circuit of our small camp. I then moved further into the bush on the same circuit, and I spotted it, a small patch of earth and mulch with a half boot print showing on the soft earth. From there, it was a series of signs, a broken twig, trampled grass, and an irregular sign of boot prints on an irregularly patterned march, and then I saw it where the lad had squatted to defecate. Was that his reason for leaving the camp and the privacy of the bush? We were by then about a hundred metres in the forest, and looking back, there was no way we could see our camp, and that is where the poor bugger's problem started. Finishing his toilet stop, he stood up, looked around, and not being able to see the camp and not hearing a sound, he set off, but in the wrong bloody direction! Heading away further into the forest as night closed in, it was not too hard to pick up signs of his erratic, obviously panicked trail, and we found him. Our loud calls must have roused him into reality; getting up from where he was sitting with his back against a huge tree, he came stumbling toward us through the scrub, tears flowing down a grimy face, crying and babbling excited words of thanks for finding him. He said he could hear faintly the rifle shots but could not find where they were coming from. By this time, he was over a mile away in the jungle from our camp, but an estimation of his wandering trail away from us was closer to two miles. Fortunately, he had the sense in a faint glimmer of moonlight to stop where he did and go no further. We got him back to camp, gave him food and water, and the lieutenant in command decided to finish the bivouac and head back to the truck pickup. I believe that saw the end of this lad's military training, and he was sent back to his home. I was commended to our colonel by our lieutenant for my search skills in finding our lost companion.

Every leave I got, I spent happily with Angie, including a visit home to see Mum and my sister, where Angie came with me.

At the end of the three months of "Nasho" training, and in a moment of impulse, I volunteered to join the regular army. I had been thinking on and off about it for some time and realised how much I enjoyed life, although I wondered what effect my decision would have on my relationship with Angie. I took leave and caught the train to Sydney to see Angie.

Angie was bitterly disappointed when I told her I had joined the army as she was hoping I would move to Sydney to further build on our relationship. It did put a mild damper on things at the time, and we still enjoyed our time together, but now, with Angie's realisation that I would not leave the Army. It was bittersweet when we parted, with both promising to keep our relationship on hold, and that I would see her again in Sydney.

My achievements during National Service, the search and rescue, and my promotion to sergeant had been recognised, and through a highly recommended letter from my commander to the military hierarchy, I was to be sent to the officer cadet training school in Portsea, Victoria. I was excited and over the moon. So to say, a dream come true to be an officer in the Australian Army, recognised worldwide as one of the best. And for a time, in my excitement, I gave little thought to the beautiful girl I was leaving behind.

Officer Training Portsea Victoria 1956

After months of extensive training, I graduated from there as a second lieutenant, specialising as a weapons instructor. Unfortunately, for a time, the army put me into a deskbound job, which did not suit me at all. A good thing was that I had plenty of time to travel to Sydney to spend with Angie and even spent time travelling with her as her "strapper" when she set off to some rodeo competition.

It was 1956, the Korean War was over, and I was becoming bored with my army desk assignment. I put in an application to be transferred to an infantry division where I was assigned to training National Service troops coming in every three months for similar training to what I had done. I fitted right into this position, and with a batch of new men arriving every three months, I learnt quickly and corrected any mistakes made in the training with every new intake of "Nashos".

It has been said that the only things that one can be sure of are death, taxes, and change. I knew that change was coming again into my life. There had been a slight cooling off in our relationship. Angie was not happy with me in the Army. She wanted us to be together more often; I loved her, but I also loved my army life.

I had kept in touch with Angus, who was working as the head overseer on a huge pastoral station in North Queensland. He told me many things about Queensland, so, with my interest aroused, I decided to take leave and travel there. Angie also had some holidays and agreed to come with me. We were having a wonderful time seeing the sights and visiting Angus. One night, I put it to Angie that I could transfer from the Army in NSW to Queensland, and I asked her if she would come with me. She refused, saying as much as she loved me, she could never be an army wife. When we arrived back in Sydney, we agreed that our lives were headed in different directions. She had her career in the company she was working for, her home in the city, and her horse sports, whereas I had become absorbed with my military career. When we parted, I knew the depth of our friendship was still there, and I guess, with a strong measure of love, but would it be enough to stand the test of time?

It was now 1958 when I put in an application to be transferred to the 1st Battalion Royal Australian Regiment based in Queensland. Eventually, it was to be a great move for me, and time and distance, a great healer. However, I still kept close contact by mail with Angie, and there in Queensland, I was trained intensively in jungle warfare and got heavily involved with martial arts and hand-to-hand fighting. Again, it was something I thrived on. I became skilled with many weapons and excelled at close infighting with the bayonet and knife.

When I got leave, I would often meet up with Angus, on occasion in Brisbane, or sometimes I would head out to Mt Isa to meet with him, and we spent many happy times together, reminiscing and remembering the day he defeated The Hammer at the Mt Isa show. On other occasions, with extended leave I had been granted, I would join him on the 500,000-acre cattle station that he managed and would spend wonderful days as a part-time stockman, riding horses, working cattle, and fitting in wherever. They were glorious times, and Angus never seemed to change very much. From the first time that I met him when I was a young boy, and he was teaching me how to fight and ride a horse. Perhaps he showed just a tinge of grey around the temples, but still the same muscular build.

World politics and times were changing; Chinese communist guerillas were fighting the old Imperial powers in Malaya, who in turn were endeavouring to reestablish themselves in the country since the Japanese invasion of Malaya and its defeat and the end of World War Two on September 2nd 1945. What was now known as The Malayan Emergency (1948–1960) was about to start.

Britain was battling to take back their control and ownership over the country's tin and rubber industries; Britain and Australia had thrown in their military support with Specialised Army Support (SAS). The Communist Party of Malaya (CPM) had taken the opportunity to eliminate those whom they considered Japanese collaborators, and atrocities were taking place across the country. British officials had tried to disband the Malayan people's Anti-Japanese Army and hand over their weapons, which was not successful, and that was when the Communist Party of Malaya took advantage of this situation. It was 1947, and the British government was unprepared and losing its ability and credibility to rule postwar Malaya. There was social unrest within the Chinese community and the communist-dominated labour unions. The British Military Administration (BMA) introduced martial law that was unsuccessful, and by 1948, the (MRLA) Malay Races Liberation Army, allied with the CPM, were sabotaging plantation properties, terrorising civilians, attacking police stations, and murdering three British planters. The Communist Party of Malaya now mobilised ex-members of the Malayan Races Liberation Army to rally in the jungle to fight against the British to create a Communist People Democratic Republic of Malaya, inspired by Mao Tse-Tung's armed revolution in China.

About then, I was ordered to report to a jungle training camp in a rugged hill country south of the Atherton Tableland. On arrival there, I was informed that because of my previous outback training in tracking and survival in the bush, I was to be sent overseas on active duty.

After more hard, intensive training, I was given leave and headed back to Argyle Station, there to spend the next two weeks tidying up personal things, doing some work around the property, and although saddened by the thoughts of leaving the Finlaysons, my family and friends, I felt a surge of youthful exuberance to what may lay ahead. Mr. and Mrs. Finlayson were very sad about my decision, but said that they admired my principles and would look after my horses and gear for as long as it took.

It was a mixed sad and happy day when I left. The Finlaysons put on a huge barbecue with music and rodeo entertainment. All my workmates were there, and Angus, who had come down from Queensland, and Uncle Charlie and friends from all around the country, were there to wish me well. Angie had flown from Sydney to be there, and my dear mother was driven to it by my mate Jimmy Collett, who was now dating my sister. I was glad my father did not show up, my mother excusing him by saying he was too hungover from the night before, and most of us, including Angus, had a go, riding some horses yet to be broken in and some smaller bullocks, laughing and cheering at the spills. Apart from a few bruises, no one was seriously hurt. There were farewell speeches and sad moments when it came to an end, the saddest being when I kissed Angie goodbye at the airport.

A couple of years earlier, I had purchased an old Holden utility, and the next morning, with the Ute packed, I made my final farewells and headed back home to see my mother and my sister, whom I still retained close contact with. I was looking forward to spending a week or so with them and visiting Uncle Charlie and Angus, who had come back home after a long stint on a Central Queensland cattle station, and I was looking forward to catching up with them both.

I was not looking forward to seeing the "old man". According to Uncle Charlie, "He is still a mean drunk old bastard," and I knew that if I saw him mistreating Mum, I would do something about it. Mum would never ever tell me anything about him; I could never figure out why she covered up for him. I suppose in some way she still loved him, but damned if I knew why. Mum, when questioned, would only say, "He is still the father of my children, end of story." As I drove back to the place of my birth and childhood, I could not foresee the happy, the sad, and the tragic events to come, all in the next week before I went to Sydney, there to see Angie, and start my military training. It was good to be home again, to the good things and friends that I remembered, even for a short period.

My sister Irene had grown into a beautiful young woman and was now madly in love with and engaged to my schoolmate, Jimmy Collett. Jimmy had landed a good job with the local stock and station agent on leaving school and was being trained to be an auctioneer. My sister said you could hear his voice from here to Bourke when he was practising, and he had already been allowed to handle some major auctioneering duties at the Pooncarie sale yards. At a family reunion that night, they told me they had their eye on a couple of thousand acres of well-watered, good cattle country that was on sale from a deceased estate. It had an old homestead on it that needed some work; the price was right, and they were excited about the possibility of buying it. It was about thirty miles down the river, and they were waiting on a bank loan approval. The stock and station agent owner who employed Jimmy was going as guarantor for them. I was happy for them.

Jimmy was a good, hardworking bloke, and my sister Irene was working as a bank teller at the Commonwealth Bank and had organised the bank loan. They radiated happiness. It was good to see. Mum was looking a bit older and a little tired-looking, but her eyes were sparkling with joyous tears when she looked at me, and my heart went out to her. She was much better dressed now and did not have to go out and work anymore. Both my sister and I, from the moment we started working, started sending small amounts of money to her into her own private account, enough to improve her quality of life and not enough for the old man to get suspicious and start knocking her around in search of it. My sister had opened up a bank account for her, which she could access anytime when she needed cash.

When I arrived at our old home, I was not surprised by my father's absence. At the end of the day, when he had, had work and money, the pub, or his cheap wine stash called him, and with one or two of his drunken "yobbo" friends, he would spend most of his time. I had been told he was not quite so loud or aggressive nowadays as he got older. It was suggested he had got tired of having the shit knocked out of him by those who could not stand his attitude.

Uncle Charlie reckoned though, he would still come home on occasion and give Mum a rough time, and when I was told that, I swore the mongrel had better not let me catch him doing it. The problem was I was never there, and the sly bastard was careful when I was around. My sister and Jimmy were renting a small house together, so they could only guess what went on. Mum kept saying she was not lonely; she had our old blue cattle dog, which I had brought home as a pup, and my sister and Jimmy called on her regularly and took her out on outings and shopping.

We had just finished dinner and were washing up when the old man came in. He seemed only half drunk, and he probably had run out of money or wine. He did not say much, just a cursory hello. Mum got his meal out of the oven, placed it in front of him, and left him to it. We then retreated to the lounge room, with me thinking what a miserable, lonely life he had created for himself. He had alienated himself from a warm and loving family, and all that he had was his grog and no-hoper friends. It was not long after we could hear loud snores coming from the bedroom. Mum gave a smile and said, "Don't worry; nowadays, I sleep on the long lounge, or in your sister's room."

I moved back into my old room and spent a pleasant week communicating with old friends and making regular visits to Uncle Charlie and Angus, who, from his work in the territory, looked as fit as ever. And I also called into the police station to visit my old friend, now Senior Sergeant Kennedy, who was talking about retiring soon. Many hours were spent around a campfire with Uncle Charlie and Angus, where we swapped our tales of life in the outback, on the land, hunting, fishing, riding in rodeos and life on the droving trails, and on one special night, Senior Sergeant Kennedy joined us for an evening of swapping yarns. He was in his last year on the police force. He said he had purchased a piece of land to retire on, not far out of town along the river, and he was going to raise a few head of cattle and fish the river for the big cod and yellowbelly that frequent it. He introduced me to his assistant, a young constable about twenty-five years old, who helped him keep the peace. Kennedy said he had been offered transfers elsewhere but liked our little town and had resisted the change. When I asked him about my old man, he only smiled and said he was pretty much the same, although a bit quieter. He still pays the occasional fine, which we both smiled at, knowing who the final recipient was.

I did not know then that less than a week later, I would see them again at our house under tragic circumstances. On the day I had gone to visit Uncle Charlie and Angus, we had planned to go on a fishing excursion along the river. If the fish were biting, we were going to camp out. In hindsight, it was just as well the fish were not biting on that day.

As it was, I was late returning to our house and driving up to it at about 10:30 p.m. I parked the Ute, and as I walked to the front steps that went up and onto a landing on our old Queenslander-style house, I could hear muffled screams of my mother and the hoarse, angry voice of my father interspersed by loud thumps and the crashing of furniture. Racing up the steep flight of stairs and through the open door, the sight that met my eyes was my drunken, crazed father holding my mother by her long, greying hair. Her body was on the floor, squirming around, and he was smashing into furniture aimlessly, trying to put the boot into her. That was enough for me. I crashed into him and, grabbing him by his free arm, pulled him around to a hard fist, smashing full-on into his soft beer gut. He went down in a gasping, vomiting heap to the floor.

I picked my poor dear mother up and sat her down on the only kitchen chair left standing. She was shaking, bruised, and crying with grief and pain. I hugged her to me and felt my tears come, yes grief for her, but an almost uncontrollable rage towards him; it had to end.

I heard him groaning and turning around and saw him rising unsteadily to his feet. I knew this had to end now, and stepping over to him, I grabbed him by his upper arms, pulling him upright. I could see the fear in his eyes as I slammed him repeatedly, again and again, against the wall of the kitchen. All fight was gone from him; he was like a rag doll in the power of my fury. I was screaming at him, over and over again, as I slammed him back and forth: "Get out of this house and don't ever come back. If you come near my mother again, I will kill you! I will kill you, you evil bastard!" Letting him go, he collapsed slowly to the floor. He lay there, sobbing. His trousers were wet; the weak mongrel had pissed himself.

I went back to my mother and helped her, now crying broken-heartedly, into their bedroom, lay her down, and sat with her, consoling her for a while until hearing a movement in the kitchen. I said, "Stay there, Mum. I am going to get him out of the house." Walking back into the kitchen, I saw he was standing, swaying unsteadily, clutching the edge of the kitchen table. When he saw me coming toward him, his eyes widened with fear, and he turned for the kitchen door. Catching up with him, I grabbed him by the shoulders and spun him around. This time, hot anger had departed, and with cold fury, I held him at arm's length and said, "Go get in your car and leave this town now, you drunken bastard! I swear by everything that is dear to me that if I ever see you in this town, or in this house, or near my mother again, I will break every bone in your body before I kill you!"

I pushed him hard out the door and heard him go, crashing down the stairs. I watched him, unemotional at his fall and the fact that I may never see the man who was my father again. After a short time, he picked himself up, and now limping, he slowly weaved his way to his car. It took some time for him to start it, and with the engine roaring, he drove off erratically, almost wiping out the opened entrance gate on the way out.

CHAPTER 14

Death in the Family

That was the last that any of us would see him alive. The sun was rising hot and strong, and birds were trilling their calls outside the window as I sat lethargically, trying to eat some breakfast Mum had prepared. My mother, looking totally listless, was moving desultorily around the kitchen. The night's incident was hanging heavily over us both, like the sultry humidity of the Northern Territories' wet season. Mum spoke up and said she was going back to her room to lie down for a while. I just sat there thinking about what had happened when I heard the vehicle coming up the path to the house.

They came up the stairs and knocked, and I knew without them saying anything that something had happened. Senior Sergeant Kennedy and the young constable were standing with sad faces at the door when I answered it. I invited them inside. Mum was still in bed; she had said she was suffering a severe headache, probably caused by the way in which she had been dragged around by her hair the night before. Senior Sergeant Kennedy stood before me and spoke first: "Sean, I am sorry to tell you this, but it is about your father. I am afraid we have some bad news. Late last night, your father was involved in an accident from which he did not survive. Based on what we could put together at the scene of the accident, he was driving out of town at considerable speed. When he reached the narrow wooden bridge over the creek, he turned onto the bend approaching the creek bridge, and judging by the skid marks, he was travelling much too fast. He lost control and slammed into the side railings at the entrance to the bridge at high speed. The car crashed through the timber railings and rolled, landing upside down on the lower river bank, and it then caught fire. I'm afraid your father did not survive. The impact was so great that we believe he died immediately; he was not wearing a seat belt. His body was badly burned, his wallet was in his hip pocket, and we managed to confirm his identification."

I turned to a sobbing sound behind me. My mother had come out of the bedroom with a dressing gown on; she was standing motionless, hands cupping the sides of her face, her face a mixture of emotions. I saw her starting to sway and raced to hold her before her legs crumpled beneath her. Helping her to a chair, I stood beside her, my arm around her shoulder, my hand stroking her hair, as Kennedy explained again softly to her what had happened.

Senior Sergeant Kennedy said that he had to ask some questions for his report and did we feel up to answering them at this time? I looked at Mum; she nodded okay. He then questioned Mum and me about why my father was driving in the wrong direction and out of town late at night. I did most of the talking and told Kennedy everything, including how I had found my father attacking my mother, how I had hit him, my threats to him, and how I had ordered him out of the house, never to come back again. Kennedy just nodded sympathetically while taking his notes; we heard nothing more about it after that day.

Irene and I had saved a considerable sum of money from our jobs and arranged for our father's funeral with the local undertaker, and again, I could not help thinking, "What a terrible wasted life." The funeral was a small one; the sermon was simple and brief. Our father did not have many friends, there was no eulogy, and the people who were there were mainly for the support of my mother, my sister, and me.

For my sister and I, it was hard to show any deep grief. Memories of his brutality toward us all were too strong, but we did cry and feel grief for all those wasted years when we could have been a happy family together. Poor Mum, though, she cried, but I could not help thinking that it was more for the lost years of unhappiness with the man she once loved than for his death. We never talked again about the night leading up to his fatal drive, and my sister and Jimmy moved back in with Mum to keep her company for a few weeks, and I signed over my utility to Jimmy.

I had phoned Angie and told her the news. She expressed her sympathies for me, my sister, and Mum. I told her I would be a few days later travelling to Sydney; she understood perfectly and said she was eager to see me.

For those last few days, I was in and out of the house, calling on friends and saying goodbyes. It was particularly sad saying goodbye to Uncle Charlie, Angus and Senior Sergeant Kennedy and then organising things and generally getting ready for my call up date to go in the Army, and just about everyone I knew was at the station to see me off.

Angus said he was going to travel on the train to Sydney with me, saying it had been a long time since he had seen the "big smoke". Angus had a married sister living in Erskineville close to the Sydney CBD and two cousins living in Redfern, who he planned to visit.

Mum and Sis were teary-eyed; Uncle Charlie stood quietly by. At the last moment before I boarded the train, he held me and said something in native dialect. His eyes had a wet look to them, and his hands trembled on my upper arms as he spoke some words of his native tongue in a deep, husky voice. Then everyone was clamouring around me, shaking hands, and kissing me and Angus and we boarded the train.

Later on, settling into the journey and thinking about what lay ahead, I mused on Uncle Charlie's words that l faintly heard in the noise all around me as they came back to me. Puzzled, I turned to Angus, who had been standing next to Uncle Charlie when he had spoken in the dialect of the Barkandji tribe to me. I asked Angus what he had said. Angus replied, "Sean, it was a blessing and a warning. He had a vision. He had seen you in a strange country with big forests, rivers, and much danger. He wished you well. He gave you a special blessing, he said. Remember everything he had taught you to survive so as to return strong to your people and the land of your birth." Those words were to stay with me over the years to come.

Throughout the long train journey to Sydney's Central Station, Angus and I alternately dozed, chatted, played cards, and gazed at the gradually changing landscape, eventually in awe at the mountainous and green terrain as we got closer to the outer suburbs of Sydney. Alighting off the train at Central Station, I was a bundle of nerves when a vision of pure beauty appeared before me with arms wide open. Her eyes were glistening, and her beautiful face was smiling as she rushed into my embrace. We hugged, kissed, and hugged again, and then I suddenly remembered Angus standing sheepishly in the background, and on his handsome black face was a huge grin. Introducing him to Angie, I said, "This is my friend Angus, the man I told you so much about." Turning to Angus, she hugged him and gave him a kiss on the cheek. I had never known a black man to blush, and I swear Angus did just that. Angie said, "Angus, I have heard so much about you. I have truly been looking forward to meeting you." The way Angus looked at her and mumbled a shy reply, I knew she had made a friend for life.

It was midafternoon as we lugged our baggage to the parking area at Central Station, where Angie had parked her Ford truck. She said that she had booked a restaurant table for a celebration dinner that night; it was at a classy restaurant high in a building overlooking Sydney and its famous harbour. Angus did not seem comfortable with this arrangement and said he really should go on to see his sister in Erskineville. We both looked at him and realised why. We both knew what he was thinking. His presence was not appropriate; our first night together after many weeks should be for us. No amount of urging could get him to change his mind, so we settled on Angie driving him to his sister's house. Which was not very far from central, and with the use of a street directory, we eventually found the house his sister Elsie, her husband Jack, and two delightful children, Timothy and Lisa, lived in.

It was on a very nice, tree-lined street named Pleasant Avenue. His sister answered the door at the first knock. Angus, Elsie, her husband, and the kids were all talking at once at a hundred miles an hour, his sister alternately crying and hugging him with joy. We were invited in after introductions and sat drinking tea and chatting.

Elsie was a very gracious and attractive woman. She was a few years younger than Angus, and her husband, Jack, was a white man. Elsie was much lighter in colour than Angus, having had a white father. The full-blood aboriginal father of Angus had died in a droving accident when Angus was a small boy. Angus's mother had remarried a white mining engineer. Elsie had moved to Sydney seeking work in her late teens and had met her husband, who was a manager of a large retail store in Sydney's CBD. It was enjoyable sitting there talking when Angie reminded us we had a restaurant booking to get to.

As we drove away to a chorus of goodbyes, the late summer sun was setting as we drove back into the city. I was very thankful that Angie was skillfully negotiating the traffic, the likes of which I had not experienced before. I was amazed and a little nervous at the size of the city and the hordes of people swarming everywhere, but more than that, there was an exciting feeling of looking forward to some special time with my beautiful Angie, and that first night together proved to be a never to be forgotten night. The restaurant was circular at the top of a huge building in the heart of the city, and it revolved around continuously. Our table was right by a large window, looking out at the ever-changing views of this incredible, huge harbour city. I was like a wide-eyed kid in a chocolate factory as I took in all the sights of the surrounding city that Angie pointed out to me. She said the area on the outside west of Sydney was called the Blue Mountains and could be faintly seen in the distance on a clear day. Angie promised to take me there to see them and the massive Jenolan Caves. As the summer night darkened, the millions of lights of distant Sydney gleamed brightly. It reminded me a little of the fireflies one sees on occasion in the outback. It was a dinner to remember.

I ate food that Angie had to explain to me what it was on the extensive continental menu. We toasted with French champagne, and we had a dessert that came out on fire. Angie explained it was a flambe; the flame was burning brandy. It was all so new to this boy from the bush, but it all faded into oblivion when later we slowly walked to a huge flash city hotel, where Angie had booked a room on the top floor, looking out over the lights of Sydney, and there we fell into each other's eager arms, recapturing every sensation and feeling we had experienced on our first night together plus much more, where long-suppressed passions surfaced. The next day, Angie took me on her promised tour of the Blue Mountains and to the spectacular Jenolan Caves, where we booked into the Jenolan Caves Hotel for the night, where we were told of an old silver mining town out in the bush, and provided us with a map. The next day, we drove on the gravel and dirt road to the isolated and long-abandoned old village of Yerranderie. There, we marvelled at the old and dilapidated wooden buildings still standing. The remnants of what had once been a prosperous silver mining community, and I felt very much at peace in this beautiful mountain and forest environment.

Leaving the Jenolan Caves Hotel, we drove to spend a night in Katoomba, in a grand old hotel, and the next morning, we did the long drive back to St Ives to meet and have dinner with her parents, and next day, explore the northern beaches, with an introduction for me to surfing. I was a good swimmer but those huge waves rolling in from the ocean had me a trifle scared, and I envied all the swimmers on their surfboards riding so easily on what looked to be flimsy boards. Those wonderful few days together were to be among the happiest memories of my young life; it was to be a long time before we could relive them again, if ever, because when we said goodbye, I wondered if we would see each other again.

Malaya Training Guerilla Hill Tribes People, "The Orang Asli"

Malaya was to be my first mission. Known as Malaysia from September 1963, it had united with Singapore, Sarawak, and Sabah, a unification that was not accepted by Indonesia, a country that decided to confront the Malaysian government from 1963 to 1966. This is where I, as a SAS commander and part of a Commonwealth force, was sent in support of the Malaysian and British forces operating especially in north Borneo and known as Operation Claret, highly secret SAS, plus other special operating forces and cross-border operations designed to penetrate deep into Kalimantan areas searching for Indonesian military personnel and its proxy. This confrontation was to terminate when Jakarta changed its policy to favour Malaysia.

Part of my training in the jungle camp in Canungra was to learn to speak Malay. It was a language that I found rather easy to learn, perhaps because I spoke pidgin (Aboriginal English) and had learnt to speak the native dialect of the Paakantji people from Uncle Charlie—whatever, I had an ear for the language, and soon picked up a basic knowledge of it. The rest of my training was in leadership and organisation of native soldiers to train in guerilla warfare, use of all weaponry and explosives, and more personal training for me in jungle survival; this was because, for me, it was a different country I would be living in, and time had to be spent learning about and recognising what plants are edible and what to avoid, and studying what information was available on the Asli Hill tribes people, customs, and language whom I would be working with. There was also extensive training in the latest methods of bomb-making and handling of explosives, weapons, and equipment of the Communist Chinese. To my way of thinking, it was easy learning, and I mentally thanked my Uncle Charlie for all that he had taught me. When the time came to be flown into the Malayan backcountry, I knew I was ready for whatever would happen.

I readily adapted to working with the native Malays and training them to be jungle fighters and to act as our guides, finding them extremely adaptable to our methods of training. Having specialised in sniper weaponry, I had been issued a No.1 Mk 111* (HT) rifle and Periscopic Prism sights and was always on call for long shots of up to 800 yards at a senior officer or communist official. The theory was to take out the top leaders, therefore leaving an unstable soldiery.

In an effort to stop the ethnic Chinese Malays from joining the communist guerillas, the Australian and British forces adopted a tactic the British had first learnt in the Boer War, some sixty-odd years previous. There, they had created the original "Concentration camps", and in Malaya, the British and their Australian allies rounded up hundreds of thousands of Chinese Malays, putting them into heavily guarded camps surrounded by police posts, barbed wire and floodlights. There, they were well looked after, although there was a measure of resentment about the loss of freedom, but they were protected against Communist Chinese infiltration as much as possible, though I felt sure there would be some sympathetic spies amongst them.

I had been made a platoon commander, and it was an arduous yet enjoyable task over the next two years, pursuing Communist Chinese troops up and down steep, jungle-forested mountains, often carrying heavy equipment. Part of my job was to find and work with the various indigenous tribal groups called the Orang Asli—the Malay language words for the original people. These wonderful, resourceful people were looked down on as primitive savages by the ethnic Chinese and Malays. Much as the Australian Aborigines were by the white settlers, in Australia, It was something I had experienced personally, and I refused to look down on these men as I trained them, finding them to be incredibly resourceful, hardy, tough and strong, with a fierce approach to the Chinese invaders of their lands. They were able to stalk silently, tracking animals and humans, and live happily on what the jungle provided in water, food and shelter. My relationship and position with them were enhanced greatly when they became aware of the tracking, hunting, and survival skills I had learnt as a boy and, after a period of time, absorbed their ways and knowledge of the jungle and its differences from what I had known. I could hold my own among them as a tracker and found myself accepted warmly and with respect by them.

Earlier in the covert advance into this country by the communists, they too had acknowledged the skills and strengths of these Asli people and started infiltrating their tribes, living among them, and getting their forces resupplied by them. My job now was to entice them away from the ruthless and murderous Chinese and win them back to our side, then train them in modern warfare and arm them to fight back the communists, who by now were coming in over the border and the jungles of southern Thailand.

Because of my successful acceptance by the Asli Orang, the commander-in-chief urged me to stick with this type of work, and over the ensuing two years of training and patrolling with the Asli Orang tribe's people, I developed a strong respect and admiration for them, and saw them stop numerous communist incursions into their country.

My time in Malaya ended rather abruptly with an Australian military high command recommending me for Special Operations training. A new man who spoke Malay, a specialist-trained SAS officer, was to take over my job. It was a time when Australia was gearing up to send a military training team to Vietnam. I had been promoted to lieutenant and was sent back to Australia on a short leave and a meeting with senior command. There, I was asked if I would be willing to join a small group of officers and volunteers to go to South Vietnam as military advisers.

CHAPTER 16

Operation "Clam" Spy Training

It was now well into the 1960s when I made the decision to accept this appointment to Vietnam, and this was before Sir Robert Menzies, leader of the conservative-liberal government, announced in 1962 that Australia was sending a small army training team to Vietnam. At the time I was approached, I knew little about Vietnam.

I did not know in detail what problems they were having, and I figured it had to be something similar to what was happening in Malaya. If it was a jungle conflict, I knew I had the necessary experience for that sort of thing, so I became very keen to be a part of the training team.

Later, I learnt that another training team had been sent very covertly and much earlier than commonly known. As it turned out, I was to be trained to be put into a top-secret military operation. It was a real cloak-and-dagger type of spying and guerilla warfare, and

I was to be assigned as warrant officer to an Australian Army Captain in a remote and isolated region who was successfully banding together a group of Central Highlands tribal people known as the "Montagnard". This was a name that had been given to them by the colonial French, who had occupied their country many years previously.

When the opportunity arose to apply for a place for training with the Special Operations Branch, I jumped at it. I realised that this was what I really wanted, where my built-up military training knowledge, endurance, fighting, and jungle survival skills could be utilised. Eventually, when I was posted to Vietnam, that very same knowledge helped save my life and a few others on a number of occasions.

The day I received my orders, I was instructed to tell no one and to report to an address in Melbourne. I registered there and was ushered to a room where I was given a thorough medical examination. I received no hint of what was to happen, and I knew better than to ask questions. I was taken to a room where five men sat at a table facing a lone chair in the middle of the room. No one introduced themselves, nor did anyone say what I was being interviewed for. I sat down, and the interview started, which to me seemed to be more of an interrogation. Various questions were asked. When I asked when I would know if I had been selected, the answer was noncommittal.

It was some hours later when I was called back into the same room and told to wait. The leader of the nameless men gave me papers to sign. They were an official pledge that I would keep everything I was about to learn secret. It was the highest level of secrecy and classified "Oyster", and if I ever were to breach this agreement, I could be put in prison. The man who handed me the papers then revealed that he was a member of the Australian Secret Intelligence Service (ASIS) and that, in the near future, I might be working for them.

That was the beginning of my future life in the dark shadows of extreme covert services. ASIS had been formed in 1952 in absolute secrecy to undertake spying operations overseas. It was so secret that few in the government even knew of its existence for the next twenty years. It was so top secret that, in fact, officially, it did not exist. It was not answerable to anyone. There were no records, and its name was not to be spoken. The government denied its existence, and if any media learnt of it and asked questions, they were threatened with jail to keep it out of the news.

The identity of the head of ASIS was classified as top secret, and all its members were legally protected from being named in public. The bland, nondescript building I was in was code-named M09. It simply stood for "main office nine." The man who told me all this never divulged his name. He said ASIS ran the secret training school that prepared military men and agents for overseas clandestine operations. I was told that my name would be placed on a classified list of those who had been told the name of the Director General of ASIS, Major-General Sir Anthony Cartbury. I knew a little of that officer. He had a good reputation as an army officer.

I was informed that Australia's spy training school was at Swan Island—a small 1.4 square kilometre island at the mouth of Port Phillip Bay. It was connected to the mainland by a narrow one-lane bridge. During the Crimean War in the 1870s, a sandstone fort had been built there in case a Russian attack was ever made on Melbourne. Swan Island had long been used to train both civilians and the military for covert operations. During the Cold War, its first trainees were inducted into it. It is still used today to train secret agents and Special Forces in counter-terrorism operations.

My training started; it was an intensive course in spy craft, both sending and decoding operating codes, running surveillance operations, how to make message drops and collections, to secretly tape record meetings and conversations, how to follow someone unseen, how to spot someone following you. It was wonderful; I loved it, realising it was filling a void in my life, unrecognised until now. The small group of men doing this course with me told me they heard it was the same training as was given to the British M16.

While on the island, I was informed that I may be required to operate behind enemy lines and work with guerilla forces. That was something I knew well and could understand, and I was enthralled with the fact that, although I did not know where I would be sent or what I would be doing, there was a sense of excitement to it all. But! Being a spy was not as easy as I thought.

With a few others, I had a practice field trip. We were to be a group of spies entrusted with the task of gaining information about a small Victorian town without being detected. We checked separately into a small hotel and went about our business.

We thought we had been very secretive and clever, only to return to the hotel bar to overhear locals talking about these fellows sneaking around the town and asking questions. I was to find that it's much easier to hide in a big city than in a small town where strange faces stand out.

From there, I was sent to the Army Water Transport Division at Chowder Bay on Sydney Harbour. There, with a handful of other officers, we trained in commando-type nighttime landings and pickups along the Eastern Coast and did courses in seamanship, boat handling and basic mechanics.

Sometime after the course ended, I received a letter from a mate and fellow officer who, some months earlier, had been sent to Vietnam. He wrote that he was working for the innocuously named Combined Studies Division, which, in fact, was a cover for the American CIA's Covert Action Branch. He said that I would be his replacement when I came over.

I guess my own spy network was starting to operate. I now knew where I would be going and realised it would be a tough job and dangerous, with a high risk of being captured. I thought because of the boat training, it would have to be doing something along the coastline or rivers of Vietnam. Imagine my eventual surprise when I was sent to the Central Highlands of Vietnam. On my own initiative I volunteered to do one more course. This one was run by the military and was innocently named The Code of Conduct course, but to the soldiers, it was known as the "torture school". The School of Military Intelligence was situated at Middle Head in Sydney. It had the most magnificent views of Sydney Harbour and was an old installation built for the same reason as Swan Island Fort from the fear of Russian Naval invasion during the Crimean War in the 1870s.

Throughout the installation were underground storage rooms and numerous tunnels carved out of the sandstone rock for gun emplacements. In my time in Sydney, I found there were a number of these old forts around the harbour, all placed in vantage situations where they overlooked the harbour at Neilsen Park, Chowder Bay, Watson's Bay, and the tiny island, Fort Denison. This little fort of early Australian settlement is situated in a prime spot near the entrance of the wharf terminals of Garden Island Naval Base,

Woolloomooloo, and Circular Quay. To the early convicts transported to Australia by Britain from 1788, Fort Denison was known as "Pinchgut" because of the early colonial military ruler's habit of leaving unruly convicts chained on the Island on just bread and water. Later, I drew a similar comparison to the torture school at Middle Head after my experience there.

The Australian Military was gearing up for the Vietnam War, and the damp, dingy tunnels of the Middle Head installation were being used for training Australian soldiers to withstand interrogation if captured by the enemy. I now know it is impossible to train someone to withstand brutal physical torture, such as electric shocks, needles under fingernails, etc., but there at the torture school were frequent beatings, humiliation, sleep, food deprivation, and psychological torture designed to break down resistance and confidence. Much of the programmed techniques were based on what had happened to Allied soldiers taken as prisoners in the Korean War. The military's aim was to expose the men to what could happen to them if they were captured in Vietnam. The authorities realised it might not stop them from breaking down but have them realise the torture techniques, to perhaps help them withstand the horrors a little better.

I was one of a group of very nervous young officers who entered the course. It was early in 1963. I had been warned not to trust anyone in the course: not the friendly guards, certainly not the interrogators playing the good cop, bad cop roles, and not even fellow officers doing the course with me. They could be plants looking for information. I was told to say nothing other than my name, rank, and serial number. I became terrified that if I broke down, I would fail and not be allowed to serve in the Special Forces in Vietnam. I worked on building up my strength of will and was determined to keep my mouth shut, stare straight ahead, cut off the world around me, and succeed at the course.

On the first day of the course, we were addressed by the commander, reminding us we were volunteers and that we could leave the course at any time and would be released without prejudice. I very much doubted that. I felt that anyone who failed could say goodbye to any Special Forces assignment and would spend the rest of their military career on regular duties. The commander left the room, and suddenly, a squad of mean-looking soldiers burst into the room. They were armed and dressed in khaki with red stars on their caps. They were shouting and ordering us to stand and line up against the wall. One by one, our group was seized, marched out of the room, and down into a maze of underground tunnels and cells. We were forcibly shoved into the deepest and coldest part of the old fortifications, and once there, shouting guards ordered us to strip off our uniforms and put on bedraggled, dirty prison garb, torn, stained, smelly, and ill-fitting. There was no belt or elastic in the pants, and we prisoners had to clutch them to stop them from falling down.

Humiliation! This was the first step in the process of breaking down our resistance. We were thrown into separate cells, but that was not to be our own cell. Nothing was allowed to get to the stage where we would feel comfortable or familiar. We were constantly kept on edge and apprehensive about what was next. I got to know each cell, each with its own offensive characteristic. One cell constantly blared from a loudspeaker near the ceiling communist anthems, interspersed with piercing rants of communist propaganda; another cell had a speaker constantly emitting loud shrieks, making it impossible to sleep or think clearly and interrogation of a harsh nature was held in a room I called the "happy hour suite".

The worst was a pit-like cellar room accessed only by a ladder. The floor was covered by ankle-deep water, and we were kept in total darkness and total silence, put in isolation to ponder on the next step in their torture and degradation. For eight days, I was constantly dragged in and out of these cells, keeping me totally disoriented. Each time I was removed from a cell, a guard would place a calico bag over my head, dragging and shoving me along corridors, constantly spinning me around, taking a different route each time, standing for a time, backtracking, and then moving on again.

I was ordered to my hands and knees and made to crawl under something that wasn't there. It was all part of the disorientation, so I could not work out the layout or passage of time. The treatment got worse as the days wore on. This was no play-acting; it was ugly and sadistic. I was bruised, cold, filthy, in pain, and degraded. I had not slept for days, having only wet, cold floors to lie on. My clothes were only just hanging on me, but I was thankful for my previous fitness, which to date was carrying me through.

My jacket was too small, and my pants kept falling to my ankles. Spotting a disused light fitting, I worked a piece of wire loose from it to act as a belt. I knew it was against the rules, but it gave me a shred of dignity. The days and time blurred, and I was dragged back into the dank, cold interrogation room. There were no windows and it stank of stale, rotten air. There was a bright light shining directly into my face. There was a broomstick on the floor, and I was forced down to kneel on it just below the kneecaps. The pain racked my whole body; it was terrible. I was ordered to hold my arms outstretched in front of me until my shoulders were screaming in agony and increased the pressure on my knees. The pain was now excruciating.

The interrogator was barking out questions: name, rank, and number. I concentrated on giving only the regulation answer: "Sean Francis Molloy, lieutenant, Australian Army, number 13796." I could sense but not see the interrogator; I could tell there were others in the room, but the blinding light made them only shadows. They wielded batons and punched and prodded as I kneeled. The pain was bloody hell. The interrogator spoke sharply with a voice rasping and devoid of emotion, "Today, Molloy, you will tell us more." A second voice said, "Others have told us." This was repeated by the interrogator.

I stayed silent. I knew this was a trick. My body was on fire with pain, and I felt like bayonets were stabbing up through my knees and into my thighs, but I kept my back straight and my arms forward as ordered. I was determined not to break and to tough it out. Retreating to the traditional formula of prisoners of war, I gave my name, rank, and serial number. One word more, and the torturers would have found a tiny opening to work on and work it they would until my dam of strength burst, and words would come tumbling out. I kept repeating the army formula, name, rank, and serial number. I was told that I was putrid and stank. No wonder after eight days of no washing and lying in stinking human waste. The interrogator kept shouting, "You filthy dirty man, have you no pride, no decency?" I gritted my teeth, determined not to succumb, knowing that the torment must end. I knew I could end it by saying I had enough that I wanted out. I said nothing, but the physical toll was starting to show, and my arms started to droop with the strain.

A guard screamed, get them up, and a baton whacked me in the back just above the kidneys. It was an expertly placed whack! It was just above the kidneys where it would do no lasting damage, but still hard enough to cause a painful jolt to course through my body.

My trousers had fallen to my knees; the wire holding them up was exposed. Guards were shouting, "He's got wire, he's got wire. Grab him and get it off him." Violent, rough hands seized me, forcing me to the ground; another guard grabbed my pants and the wire. I was forcibly pushed back to my knees. "Where did you get the wire?" another demanded, the voice close to my ear. I said nothing. Another voice screamed, "You were going to use it to attack us. You broke the rules. Why did you do this?" Endeavouring to look straight ahead, I said nothing. "You know this means more punishment," the interrogator said softly. "Why do this to yourself, Molloy? Other prisoners are more cooperative". I thought this might be true. I had heard screaming from another cell. It sounded like the man was going out of his head, but then again, it could have been another trick.

Damn them. Again, I was asked for my name, rank, and serial number.

The guards dragged me to the deep hole for further punishment. This pit was like a torture cell in a medieval castle. The only way in was through a trapdoor in the roof. I was ordered to climb down the ladder to the floor. The guards pulled the ladder up, and the trapdoor slammed shut above me. My nerves were raw; I was weak and feeling exhausted from the lack of sleep and nutritious food, and still, day after day, the punishing and humiliating torture went on, frequently interspersed by interrogations and endless propaganda screaming out from hidden loudspeakers. To add to this mind-snapping holocaust of sound were the screams and ranting from other cells. Was it recordings or some of the other "prisoners" who had volunteered to subject themselves to this hideous training, whose mental control had collapsed from the onslaught? Night and day were as one, and there was no measurement of time. I never knew when the meagre amount of so-called food, a grey-looking sludge of rice, was given to me; sometimes, it seemed to be at short intervals, sometimes days apart.

I was now almost in a hallucinatory state of mind, starting to think it would never end. My imagination was starting to think that I was a captive of an enemy force. Then I would snap myself out of it, and a sheer bloody-minded attitude would take over my thinking, and I would will myself for the next interrogation to only say "name, rank and number".

Suddenly, without warning, it was over. I was taken from the hellhole and taken to a different place; I felt comfortable warmth emanating through the door as I was roughly thrust into the room. There was a friendly-looking bloke sitting behind a large, scarred, and stained desk smiling at me. I was gently told to sit on the chair facing the desk. I was offered coffee and a cigarette. The cigarette was easy to refuse as I did not smoke, but the coffee I could have killed for. I did not want to risk being compromised and refused both. When water was offered to me, I saw no problem with accepting that and drank greedily.

I was asked to recite my "full name, rank and number" again, and then, surprisingly, I was asked how I preferred to be called by my Christian name or surname, taken aback for a moment. I replied once more with my full "name, rank and number". I would not allow the thin edge of the conversational wedge to penetrate and lead to conversation, and I stayed silent.

This friendly interrogator kept asking questions about my family, my military career, personal likes and dislikes and offering food and coffee. I continued to stay silent. After what seemed an interminable amount of time, the interrogator brusquely ordered the guards to take me back to my cell, and there was a feeling of relief as I was shoved back into it. I believed I had not answered any of the questions; they had not pierced my resolve.

It seemed like a couple of hours later, I was dragged from the cell, blindfolded, and led along with a guard on each arm. I could hear cell doors clanging open and the sounds of other prisoners being dragged out of the cells. We were ordered to go forward, and we shuffled along a cold corridor. I smelled rather than felt the fresh air, and I gulped it down, puzzled by what was happening. What is next? Is it more interrogations or worse? From the guard's orders, I felt we were being pushed into a line, and suddenly, our blindfolds were removed with the announcement it was over; it was through.

Christ almighty, there in front of us was a bloody huge table laden with food and drink. I was suspicious. Was this another trick? We were now looking around at each other; we all shared a dirty, haggard and ragged appearance. We were each still looking just as suspiciously and warily at each other and the guards and officers.

We were still not assured it was over, and it was just another trick. A high-ranking officer in an Australian Army uniform stood in front of us and smilingly gave assurances to us that it was over. We had survived this brutal and I see now necessary training. There was a mob howl of laughter as we shook hands, embraced and clapped each other on the back. It really was over! Looking around, I did a head count. There were three missing from the original group. Had they succumbed to the pressure, broken ranks, and given in? Perhaps the screaming I heard was real and not recorded. Later, I found out two had broken down completely and had ended up in the hospital.

I had made it. My stubborn integrity had got me through. Subconsciously and deep down, I knew it was a horrid, cruel yet necessary training exercise, and I shuddered to think of those poor souls captured and put into that same environment with genuine, sadistic and brutal physical and mental torture from brutal guards. I now felt I was ready to take on whatever assignment the military was going to put me on.

CHAPTER 17

Saigon, Vietnam 1962

My assignment had been outlined to me. I was briefed by ASIS, and the briefing sounded like something out of a spy thriller novel. I was ordered to fly to Singapore via Qantas, wearing civilian clothes. From there, I was to fly Air France to Saigon. I was told not to change into a uniform, to stay in civilian clothes, and to stay nondescript and undercover. My mission once there was to go into even deeper undercover, in a manner so that no one could record another Australian military officer entering the country. I knew I was destined to do something extremely clandestine. I was filled with incredible excitement. I had been trained to the highest degree, particularly in guerilla warfare. I still did not know the true nature of my mission, yet I felt I was ready for whatever was to happen. It was November 1962.

I knew that President Kennedy of the USA, like many other Western countries, was fearful of the so-called Domino Theory. It had started with Korea, then Malaya. It was the fear of South East

Asian countries falling in succession to the advance of Chinese Communism. America, Britain, Australia, and any other Western-friendly countries were banding to stop this inexorable creeping spread of Communism and do it just as the Japanese had tried to do in World War Two, with their successful takeover of South East Asia and their planned invasion of Australia, there was a strong belief that the communist scourge could head south and into Australia.

The Qantas plane came into a smooth landing. Although I had become used to the heat of the tropical regions of North Queensland and Malaya, coming off the air-conditioned plane into the wet heat of Saigon, it hit me with the force of stepping fully clothed into a crowded steam bath. Saigon then, in 1962, was still a lovely city, and I instantly loved it. The typical smell of Saigon is of "*nuoc mam*," the fish sauce that was everywhere and used by the roadside food vendors in their cooking. I had been met by my contact Geoff Truso. As we drove through the streets lined with old French-style colonial buildings, I saw palm, mango, poinciana, and rubber trees. They seemed to be everywhere, and yet there was an underlying feeling of tension, for by 1963, the USA had a contingent of 14,000 military advisers in Vietnam. Their military advisers were training the South Vietnamese Army and militias, and in the Highlands, US Special Forces were training the Montagnard militia. From what I learnt from Geoff Truso, it was not at all going well, with the wrong information reports going back to the USA political and military hierarchy. Reports of successes and enemies killed were grossly exaggerated, and the practice of mass artillery shelling followed by large military formation movements was not working, with only a few Viet Cong captured or killed. The Viet Cong had their spies in every American camp feeding back information gained by them, as the Vietnamese worked in a number of various menial jobs for the military, and so, being forewarned by their spies, the Viet Cong would simply disappear into the jungles, or mingle with the civilian villagers, before the large force or artillery barrage arrived. It was a known fact that the Viet Cong were in control of large areas of South Vietnam.

Saigon in 1963 was a rather modest town, unlike the Saigon that came about after the massive American Military invasion of its streets. There were strict laws enforced by governing bars. Nightclubs were illegal. Women were not allowed to have bare shoulders, stomachs, or legs and had to wear the traditional "Ao Dai", a long tunic worn over trousers. The laws governing divorce, adultery, brothels, opium dens, boxing, and cockfights were rigidly enforced by the sister-in-law of the Vietnamese President Ngo Dinh Diem, Madame Nhu. She was a devout catholic and a very cruel hypocrite of a woman. She was known by many as the Dragon Woman. The previous colonial Catholic French had certainly imposed their strict Roman Catholic religion on them.

They were ruthless in their treatment of the predominantly Buddhist population and, in particular, the Buddhist monks, many of whom were practising self-immolation as a way of protesting against their merciless rule.

Strong Catholic supporters of the president were in many key posts of military, political, and administrative hierarchy. They also controlled a Gestapo type of Secret Police. From 1955 through to 1958, President Diem carried out brutal oppression to force the assimilation of the predominantly Christian, freedom-loving "Montagnard" tribe's people into South Vietnam in an endeavour to control the Central Highlands. In 1958, four major tribes united under the leadership of Y Bham Enoul to form the "Bajaraka" movement. The aim of "Bajaraka" was to peacefully achieve self-government. President Diem ordered his arrest, and Y Bham Enoul was jailed.

In 1959, a Viet Cong insurgency started to gain momentum, and Communist North Vietnam started a war to conquer South Vietnam. Because of the strategic significance of the Central Highlands, North Vietnam endeavoured to gain the "Montagnard" allegiance. They were promised autonomy. The "Montagnard" hill tribes did not trust the Vietnamese and rejected it, with the Central Highlands becoming a battlefield of opposing Western and Communist ideologies and the "Montagnard" hopes for self-determination led them to ally with the USA. At that time, there were approximately 1.5 million "Montagnard" tribe people, and President Diem allowed American "Green Beret" forces under their own CIA control, to go into the Central Highlands to train and arm the "Montagnard" for village defence and patrolling.

Apart from the 14,000 plus military advisers, the USA had thousands of CIA agents in the country carrying out clandestine actions against North Vietnam. A year or so earlier, Geoff Truso and another Australian had been annexed from the Australian Army Training Team in Vietnam and instructed to report to the Combined Studies Division. This was an innocuous name for an organisation that covered the CIA's subversive activities. They were to engage in specific operations near Da Nang, investigating how the Viet Cong operated and how they obtained supplies and weapon information. It was necessary they found out how the Viet Cong interacted with the South Vietnamese villagers.

It was an extraordinary job, and with extraordinary freedom to move anywhere to question US and Vietnamese army units, and it was a big breakthrough for two Australian officers to gain confidence and to be accepted by the always suspicious CIA.

I was introduced to the colonel of the Australian Army Training Unit and told I was being sent to Ban Me Thuot. It was a medium-sized town nearly 300 km northeast of Saigon in the Central Highlands, and it was the capital of Darlac Province. I was to be assigned to an Australian captain who had built up a formidable reputation training, and leading a tribe of Montagnard warriors. The Montagnard were a primitive tribal people with a fearsome reputation who had never conquered in the past and who had fiercely fought for independence for generations. I was told that even though we had our own field program, we would actively be controlled and working for the American CIA, which, of course, made me a little apprehensive. It had been known by those in the know for some time that the Viet Cong were winning the war. Thousands of North Vietnamese troops and political trainers known as cadres were moving freely south along the Ho Chi Minh trail and controlled most of the rural areas. The poor farming peasants had little or no reason to fight them. The regular South Vietnamese Army was poorly equipped and had poor-quality leaders, and they constantly avoided contact with the better-armed Viet Cong.

My contact told me that the CIA had allowed an Australian military officer to run his own field program in the training and motivating the Montagnard Tribesmen to become allies to fight the Viet Cong and to disrupt the advance of troops and supplies along the Central Highlands trails. I was to be appointed his warrant officer, and to work with this mysterious captain, and assist in the training and leading of these hill tribe warriors. I was surprised that in due course, I was to find out that not even the Australian government, and many of the Australian Army, and senior military officers knew of this alignment with the American CIA or that we were under its control.

My first introduction to various CIA field officers, not surprisingly, was not in military uniform. I was wearing a loose shirt over pants covering a pistol in a holster. It seemed to be the unofficial uniform, and after a considerable briefing in a fortress-like room with map-covered walls, I was told I would be going to Da Nang to view the huge military base that was being used to train the South Vietnamese soldiers and to have a few days break before moving onto my assignment. I was to meet more Australian military officers involved with the training of the Vietnamese troops. It was there I was kitted out with suitable military attire and a weapon. I particularly liked the Browning 9mm in a holster, which I wore under my loose shirt, as I had previously seen others do.

At the end of the week, watching the training and getting partially involved with it was most enjoyable after my previous inactivity. From there, it was back to Saigon to the "Air America" hangar to board a plane for Ban Me Thuot, and there I was a little surprised to find out that "Air America" was the "unofficial" airline of the CIA. I say a little surprised because each day, things I learnt and saw opened my eyes more and more to the unconventional things happening in this crazy Asian war. Air America flew regularly on no questions asked missions, carrying mysterious passengers and cargoes. There were only three passengers on the plane: myself, my Australian military contact, Geoff Truso, a quiet, nontalkative CIA man, and the pilot on this inconspicuous flight to Ban Me Thuot. The pilots of this airline, I learnt, were a motley bunch of characters; it seemed they were gleaned from all parts of the world. It was a short flight of a couple of hours. As we flew from the flat coastal country, the scenery gradually changed from paddy fields and villages, dirt roads, and forests to jungle-clad hills and mountains.

Vietnam was originally a French colony from 1887, originally known as French Indo-China. The Japanese then controlled Vietnam during World War II, and a Vichy French government until their defeat in March 1945 and then, the Viet Minh, a Communist organisation led by Ho Chi Minh, took over and declared Vietnamese independence. An all-out independence war broke out in 1946 between French and Viet Minh forces. In an endeavour to create an alternative to the Viet Minh, the state of Vietnam, led by former Emperor Bao-Dai, was proclaimed in 1949, and the French sought to reunite Vietnam, though it was unsuccessful. Following the Geneva Accord of 1954, the French withdrew from Vietnam, which had been split in two, and French Indo-China came to an end. The French saw the end of their colonial reign there in 1954.

As we flew over and into Ban Me Thuot, I could see the old government buildings, French colonial mansions and thousands of ramshackle houses of the villagers, and I was impressed by the scenery. The Central Highlands were imposing, rugged jungle-clad ranges some 1,500 metres above sea level. These highlands were interspersed by swift-flowing waterways, with here and there isolated clearings with thatch-roofed longhouses, homes to the Montagnard Tribe's people, I was told. Montagnard being the name given to them by the French, their true native name being De Gar Champa, descendants of the ancient Champa Kingdom, with an origin going back to an ancient homeland in Siberia and Southeast Asia.

On landing, we were met at a small out-of-the-way landing strip and conveyed by an old model car to a hotel in the town. Geoff informed me the town had a floating population of 40 to 45,000 people, guessing that it fluctuated with the fortunes of the yet-to-be-officially proclaimed war.

CHAPTER 18

Training the Montagnard (Moi) Hill Tribes

Some history I learnt was in 1962. There were two thousand American "Green Berets" mainly in the Darlac Province, where they had formed the "Rhade" tribe's people into militia units called "Civilian Irregular Defence Group", and of the approximately 200,000 "Montagnard" in the Central Highlands, there were many who were sympathetic to the Viet Cong because of the way President Diem had forced the resettlement of lowlands South Vietnamese into their Central Highlands tribal lands. These highland tribe's people did not relate to nor accept the South Vietnam lowlanders. Local police chiefs, who were mainly South Vietnamese, had become wary of the open hostility of the Montagnard and confiscated their spears and crossbows at any opportunity that they protested at being forced off their traditional lands.

Similar to the Australian aborigine dreamtime, the Hmong are animists in belief, believing the ponds, streams, rivers, hills, valleys, and wind have individual spirits. The Hmong are thought to have migrated from their ancient homeland in Siberia and Southeast Asia. They have settled in the mountainous regions of Burma, Laos, Thailand, and Vietnam. "Hmong" means free people. This is the only name they call themselves. By some estimates, over half of the South Vietnam Hmong population perished during the war and the subsequent flight to Thailand to escape genocide.

Here now was a big anomaly to my way of thinking. The Americans were supplying and training the Montagnard with modern weapons, and this is where I was to move into the overall picture. My assignment was to work with and under the command of a legendary Australian military captain. This Captain Henderson was a unique fighting man who had won the trust and respect of his growing band of Montagnard militia. Our meeting took place in the hotel the following night with Captain Henderson. It was obvious from the start that Geoff Truso was on good terms with the captain by the manner in which they greeted each other and later discussed matters of military importance. I was personally impressed with Captain Henderson. He exuded the quiet strength and confidence of a man who knew what he was about and with no mannerisms designed to impress. I knew before the meeting was over I was going to enjoy working for the captain.

It was arranged for the next day for Geoff to deliver me to Captain Henderson's headquarters to start my induction training, and dressed in my jungle greens, a Browning 38 pistol at my side in a webbing belt, I was determined to make a good impression and learn from this legendary captain.

It was obvious to me from the start that as Captain Henderson introduced me to his assembled "Rhade" tribe's militia, there was a healthy mutual respect. These wonderful primitive people were affected by the same disrespect I saw had been given to the hill tribes of Malaya by local Malays. In this case, they were looked down upon and known as *Moi* or savages by the lowland Vietnamese, yet they looked at Captain Henderson in an almost reverential manner. I knew of this captain, who had also learnt to speak Malay in his time training guerilla teams in anti-communist warfare in Malaya and who now verbally communicated with the "Rhade" in an excellent manner in their own language. The dialect was different, but there were so many words of similar meaning. It excited me to be told that my knowledge of the Malay language would help me greatly in training these men because of this similarity of words, and he offered me a Rhade language dictionary to help me in the months to come. An early Christian missionary had compiled this dictionary, and it became almost as important to me as the 38 Browning pistol in its webbing holster I wore everywhere.

As the days went on, I was to learn that "Rhade" customs observed leadership as being held by the senior women of their tribes. They were based on a matriarchal society, and the women held the land and the property and were the real power, with the men always consulting them on community decision-making.

These consultations also took place when it came to farming, public ceremonial duties, and whether to send their young men to engage in military duties such as the militia. In those cases concerning fighting activities, the women then deferred to the men on the final decision. I was impressed by the civilised manner in which this was handled.

Captain Henderson had appointed to me a young translator. He was a fit-looking young "Rhade" man who had attended a missionary school. He spoke perfect English, a couple of "Rhade" dialects and Vietnamese. Y Bam Minh was to become a valuable ally as an interpreter, friend, and bodyguard. His knowledge of local customs was to guide me often through potentially uncomfortable situations. Captain Henderson had been well supplied with weapons, money and equipment by the American CIA and gifts for the so-called primitive Montagnard. We both thought the gifts of trinkets, toys, and sewing kits were a bit of a joke and useless in winning over the not so naïve, or as they were considered primitive tribes.

The more I got to know the "Rhade" the more I was impressed by these tough, resourceful people of Malay and Polynesian descent. They were culturally and ethnically different from the Vietnamese people. Their reputation and skill as fierce and ruthless warriors with their spears and crossbows preceded them. Once trained with military discipline and the modern weapons of war, their skill and ferociousness were unequalled. It was no wonder they were feared by the more predominant Vietnamese. Y Bam Minh told me stories of their history and how the term Montagnard was used by the early French missionaries to describe the hill tribes that lived and thrived in the mountainous ranges that stretched from the Yunnan plateau in China and extending through Southeast Asia.

Borders had meant little to the Montagnard hill tribes. Their rugged jungle tribal lands had existed long before any arbitrary borders were created and drawn through the Highlands. Vietnam, Cambodia, Laos, and Burma all carried varying percentages of populations of these hill tribes who held large quantities of land as their own. Often, they were feared and hated, particularly by the Vietnamese.

The US government, in its fight against communism and to aid the corrupt South Vietnamese government under President Diem, had realised the hill tribes needed to side with them and the South Vietnamese and were pouring in money, supplies, weapons, CIA, and "Green Beret" advisers to win them over from the Viet Cong.

Captain Henderson had instructed me to do a tour of the villages providing the men for our small hundred-man militia. With a broad wink, he advised me to be careful with the customary rice wine that would be offered. You must not refuse and, therefore, offend your host. My interpreter, Y Bham Minh, just smiled at this and refused to elaborate, leaving me somewhat puzzled. I had already learnt that the Americans had often earned the disrespect of the villagers in the manner in which they drove their jeeps on the muddy tracks and their often "overbearing, we are the best mannerisms". I was determined not to make mistakes and at all times act on the advice of multi-lingual Bham Minh.

My vehicle was an old, small US military truck. With Y Bham Minh driving, we pulled up outside the gate of the first village. We walked through the gate and along a narrow lane, which I gathered to be the "main street" of the village. There were pigs, chickens, and small children scurrying everywhere. Adults and children were stopping to stare at us as we slowly walked to what seemed to be the main "longhouse."

These hill tribes lived communally in these thatched-roofed buildings built on high stilts, with each extended family having its own allocated living space.

Stopping below the entrance of one of these longhouses, we stood looking upwards as Y Bham Minh spoke a dialect I imagined was a greeting to an elderly tribesman accompanied by two women of similar age looking down at us. They were backed by what seemed to be a family group mix of young and old male and female, some breastfeeding babies. After what seemed to be an amicable exchange of words, Y Bham pointed to a pole with crossbars fastened to it, which was angled from the ground to the entrance of the longhouse, indicating we were to climb it. To me, it looked precarious. I gestured to Y Bham to go first, as a monkey walked up it. *Ah well*, I thought, *if he can do it, so can I*. Although not quite so nimble, I safely made it to be surrounded by a swarm of smiling faces, many with betel nut-stained teeth and tattoos. Once in the longhouse, we were soon settled inside the cool interior on the grass matting floor in a semicircular fashion. Surrounded by these friendly hill tribes people, I was totally unaware I was about to be introduced to the "Rhade" custom of offering visitors their fermented rice wine. Later, I was to be told by a laughing Captain Henderson that the "Rhade" did not need much of an excuse to open a few jars of this intoxicating liquor.

On many occasions, it also involved the ritual sacrifice of a chicken or a pig, and if the visitor was of "big" importance, they would slaughter a buffalo. He also emphasised the fact of how important it was not to offend the "host" by refusing to drink. To do so could bring down the wrath of evil spirits and bad fortune on the tribe. Having seen the evils of alcohol and what it had done to my father and too many of my Uncle Charlie's Paakantji tribe people had succumbed to it, I had decided long ago not to be a "boozer", so I found this custom a particularly hard one to deal with. It took me much practice to sip sparingly whilst looking as though I was gulping quantities from the proffered jar through the long bamboo drinking tube as the Rhade did. And even so, negotiating the pole steps down from the longhouse after each meeting meant a few misses and an uncomfortable landing to great hilarity and laughter from the assembled villagers. I noticed the first person to be offered the rice wine to taste was the senior lady of the village. She would take a sip, then offer it and the bamboo straw and jar to the honoured guest. Not being a drinker of anything more than an occasional glass of beer, I found it an unpleasant experience. Still, I was determined not to offend the Rhade, so I would accept it and persevere through the whole ceremony.

I was amazed at how cheerfully intoxicated these tribes people would become. And my perseverance paid off, eventually winning the trust and respect of these admirable people. I found out it was okay to go outside and throw up. As long as you came back for another drink, it was a real test of my endurance.

As I became more accepted in the different villages, along with Captain Henderson, we were recruiting more young men as recruits. The villagers were eager for protection from the merciless Viet Cong who were coming into their villages and taking their food supplies and taking many young men to join their forces in the jungle. Further up in the north, the Viet Cong were using murder and terror to force the villagers to support them and to kill any white Europeans suspected of being Americans.

At first, the villagers knew nothing of Australia and thought all white men were Americans. We knew many Montagnards worked for the Viet Cong, although they had no real political alliance. We gained much information on Viet Cong movements from Montagnard, who had relatives often forcibly inducted into the Viet Cong. As we trained more men, this information enabled us to plan our ambushes on the VC and the North Vietnamese Army regulars.

Our weaponry, munitions, camouflage clothing and other supplies had increased from our CIA mentors, along with regular cash supplies to pay our militiamen. I managed to acquire two USA sniper rifles; they were the Army XM21 and the Marine Corps M40, both chambered to 7.62 (0.30 inches) and equipped with telescopes up to 40x magnification. Remembering the successful kills I had in Malaya, I intended to pursue a similar path and see if I could find a top marksman in the "Rhade" militia for similar training.

As a warrant officer, I had taken over much of the responsibility of training these skilled warriors, hunters, and trackers and turning them into a mercenary fighting force trained in all modern weapons, including martial arts and hand-to-hand fighting. As they came to know of my well-learnt tracking abilities in childhood, they showed respect. Their famed abilities with their traditional crossbow also played a big part in stealthy covert operations where the aim was to silently pick off a North Vietnamese officer or cadre at close range, then disappear back into the jungle with no sound and unseen. The incredible catlike stealth of these tribesmen and their hit-and-run tactics never ceased to amaze me, and as I showed further my own tracking, shooting, and jungle skills, I saw the growing respect and admiration in their eyes.

In Malaya, my adaption to martial arts included the use of a knife for stealth killing and learning the key points of blade penetration, major arteries and organs, which had these tough hunters wide-eyed oohing and aahing! The professional use of a blade impressed them greatly. So much were they impressed that I asked Captain Henderson to requisition from the CIA, the special commando knives that were issued to their "Green Beret" Special Forces, one for each man. When they arrived, I took them to an engraver in Ban Me Thuot, who was given the job of engraving the head of a tiger on each blade with the "Rhade" words for "A Tiger Kills". The reason for a tiger being selected, it was the most feared animal in the

Central Highlands and was hunted by these brave men with a crossbow and spears.

The day after I picked up the newly engraved knives, a special parade was held, and nearly one hundred men stood proudly to attention as Captain Henderson and I marched up and down the ranks, handing a knife to each man in turn. That day was to be a pivotal point in our relations with these jungle fighters. It seems they felt a great honour had been bestowed upon them.

The American Military command was putting pressure everywhere to increase the body count of the enemy. The South Vietnamese Army was poorly led and equipped and was elaborating on and falsifying accounts of action and VC killed. The Middle American command, where the action was, was saying we are not winning the war the way it is, and the USA High Command wanted results.

Personally, the captain and I did not believe the Americans were going about this jungle war the right way, and there were many who felt the same. The allied bases were infiltrated with Vietnamese workers acting as spies for the VC, so every time a large-scale operation with artillery and aerial bombardment was planned for an area, the forewarned VC would melt away into the jungle or disappear down their numerous dugouts or blend into the various villages' miles away from the action.

Also, the heavily manned USA soldier platoons were too cumbersome and noisy and prone to warn in advance of their coming. They were often subject to mortar attacks from the Viet Cong, Captain Henderson. I agreed, seeing the way our men were practising their martial arts and stealth attacks, that the body count would increase from our section, but there was a problem in that the American guns supplied to us were mainly World War II vintage

M1 Carbines; they were more of a close quarter weapon, although we were supplied with more than enough ammunition. Fortunately, every ambush attack brought us more AK-47s captured by the enemy. They were prized by our men as a much better weapon. Each nighttime foray into the jungle and remote VC camps brought in more of these superb guns and ammunition. We were also issued with grenades that would be dropped into enemy dugouts. Y Bhan Minh informed me the men were holding competitions amongst themselves for each raid, where the man who brought in the most weapons and enemies killed won the accolades. The highest honour was bestowed on the man who could capture a weapon with his "tiger knife" and bring the victim's head back as proof.

The Ho Chi Minh trail was becoming a heavily trafficked route from the North. There were not only Viet Cong and NVA but all sorts of specialists in mines and booby traps, political officers, and medical and communication teams. We knew it was time for us to concentrate our efforts on disrupting this flow of enemy traffic.

Our men were being constantly told only to kill the enemy, not to indiscriminately kill villagers and to fight with honour under the Australian Army Military Code of Conduct principles. It was impressed on them to win over the peasant village people to our side.

The Americans had a totally different way of training their Montagnard. They would train their men to operate in thirty-man platoons and companies of hundreds. This they would call a strike force, their aim being to strike with an overwhelming force. Their men were rarely trained to ambush.

Captain Henderson and I worked on a different formula, forming our men into small eight-man, hit-and-run ambush teams. The larger American teams were more subject to being hit and then run by Viet Cong guerilla teams, whereas we took the same tactics to the VC with much success. Captain Henderson had studied extensively the guerilla tactics of fighting in Australia, Malaya, and the Chindit guerillas who had operated behind Japanese lines in World War II, and based on my own training and background, I endorsed his views entirely and considered it an honour to serve with this great soldier. While the CIA kept the arms and supplies coming in, we would fight.

One day, Y Banh Minh came to tell me that two "Nung" tribesmen had come into the area and had been received well by the elders at the nearest village. They were brothers, and it seems they were related by distant marriage to a senior woman of the local tribe. They had been part of a training camp at A Shau in the highlands near Laos run by the Americans but did not like or get on with the South Vietnamese Army regulars based there and had heard of our training camp. They had lost their mother and sister in a Viet Cong attack on their village and hated all VC. I spoke with Captain Henderson, who agreed to meet and talk with them. My interpreter, Y Banh Minh, said he knew enough of their dialect to understand them, and he would bring them to our camp.

We were standing outside of our quarters when our newest, recently supplied USA Forces Military truck pulled up. Stepping down from the passenger side were two almost identical, big, six-foot-tall men. We had heard of the "Nung". They were reputed to be fierce and absolutely ruthless fighters. Many of them were being used as personal bodyguards by the American Special Forces in camps scattered throughout their area.

As the interview proceeded, it was plain to see their intense hatred for the untrustworthy Vietnamese, and especially the Viet Cong. Later discussions with the senior woman relative to them indicated they could be of great value to our team. She was right.

From the very start, they fitted into our training routine and were soon interacting with the rest of our men, many of whom were at least a head shorter, which did not seem to bother anyone.

Our first action with these men proved their worth. We had formed them into an eight-man ambush, hit-and-run team. We were heavily camouflaged, squatting in the thick jungle in a perfect ambush position on a blind bend in the track, opposite a sheer jungle-lined drop-off to a fast-running creek below. We had previous information from a reliable source that a supply team of about thirty men carrying equipment with a small armed patrol would be coming through from an earlier night's camp in the jungle. All our men were well armed with AK 47s and grenades and their treasured "tiger knives". An inspection of their placement showed me one could walk right by them and would be extremely lucky to spot them.

It was early morning in the jungle, and a mist was still lying heavy when we took up our position. A silent hour went by when we heard the first sound of movement not far from where we lay. One had to hand it to the VC. They were certainly much quieter and laden with their equipment and supplies than their American counterparts. They were no more than fifty yards away when we spotted their forward scout, an NVA regular, walking slowly along the track. His eyes were looking around and then down, looking for any telltale sign of mines or traps. Our man at the end of our spread-out ambush line would see to him. I was to fire the first shots, preferably at an officer, and then all hell would open up from our concealment.

It worked. For two, maybe three minutes, we poured uninterrupted fire into the chaotic, shouting, screaming line of carriers and soldiers. Men were going down like flies hit with a powerful spray as the withering firepower consumed them. A couple of soldiers had made it through the trees and bush to the edge of the gorge, and it looked like they had been hit as they went over the edge to plunge to the bottom.

There was a moment of calm when it seemed the only movement was from wounded and dying men on the track when the sound of an AK47 opened up from the jungle behind us. One, maybe two, of the bastards had managed to escape the mayhem and slip into the jungle to circle around behind us. As I and the others spun around to face this attack, one of the Nung brothers knocked me flat with a massive push to my back, at the same time firing single-handed his AK47 at the NVA soldier who had shown himself for a brief moment from behind the trunk of a huge mahogany tree. I caught a glimpse of his head exploding into a crimson flower. A massive punch hit my out-flung arm as I sprawled head-first onto the jungle floor. I did not see this second NVA take a burst from the AK 47 of my big Nung protector.

I was temporarily laid up in one of the excellent American medical facilities in Ban Me Thuot. I was thankful to my lucky stars that the bullet that got me was a clean shot. It had gone completely through the muscle of my upper left arm, just missing the bone of the upper humerus. It was to heal quickly, leaving a nice neat dent in the muscle with a slightly bigger scar where the bullet came out.

Captain Henderson had been to see me and said the ambush had been successful. There were only four survivors of the enemy side, two NVA and two Viet Cong, all wounded and who had been detained by the American CIA for interrogation. One of our men had a leg injury caused by a bullet ricochet, which tore out a piece of his calf muscle from the attack behind us, and a huge amount of medical supplies, food and weapons had been captured.

He said that our men were hailing the Nung tribesman who had saved my life and whether I wanted to speak with him. I certainly did! And with the assistance of Y Banh Minh, I thanked him, and from that moment on, I was to have a personal bodyguard who seemed to be at my back in every future encounter. The two Nung brothers seemed to have earned the respect of the rest of our hundred-man team. After about six more months of intensive training and many covert actions with our small eight-man squads, I approached our Captain Henderson to nominate both Nungs as NCOs, which was accepted. There was no doubting their ability or their bravery.

Captain Henderson and I agreed that some of the most outstanding Montagnard Militia should be further trained and promoted to officers of their own men. We knew if this was known, there would be resistance from the Vietnamese province chiefs who feared the tough, fearless, and independent way of the Montagnard. They were intensely loyal and disciplined. It had been approved to build our force up to 300 and to establish a base camp at Lac Thien, which was near the main track of the Ho Chi Mien Trail.

I had noticed that whereas the Americans seemed to treat the highlanders as low-grade people, our way was more respectful, and we always made a point of letting them know we were Australian, not Americans. This seemed to work well for us.

After much hard work clearing the land and building the new base in the jungle near Lac Thien, I tightened up our training routine, introducing more M'Nong tribesmen into our unit. These men came from an area that was mainly around the more isolated Lac Thien area. They were just as hardy and fierce as any other Montagnard and could be relied upon. We built communal huts, and I shared one with a small group of these soldiers whom I had learnt to trust.

We were always fully armed and ready for any outside attacks and slept with loaded weapons. My AK47 was by my side with a full magazine, and on patrol, my webbing pouches carried at least 500 rounds. We slept fully clothed and with our boots on, with guards continually patrolling the camp perimeter. I learnt to sleep on my back with my gun by my side and my finger on the trigger guard.

Our patrols went out every day and night into the surrounding jungle country until we knew every square inch of it and we knew any movement in it. The Viet Cong were everywhere, and there were frequent hit-and-run skirmishes. It became obvious that the Viet Cong were not too keen on an open confrontation with our well-armed and trained M'Nong and Rhade men.

No large force could move in this region without us knowing about it. Even small groups found it difficult to bypass our men, who were proudly increasing their body count with each foray into the jungle. They relished the martial arts training and excelled with their hand-to-hand and knife-fighting skills. They reminded me of the Ghurka men who fought with the British in Malaya. Ghurka legend has it that if they drew their knife in battle, it had to taste blood!

Our combined Montagnard tribesmen proudly drew their prized "tiger knives" at every opportunity, often preferring a stealth attack into a camp and quietly disposing of guards and sleeping enemies wherever possible. Their fearsome reputation grew and spread as they became known as the "Ma Rung." Interpreted, it meant (phantoms of the night).

A few months before we had established our camp, a Viet Cong unit had wiped out the South Vietnamese Army outpost. Although, by now, we had managed to reclaim much of the area they had dominated, I felt it was necessary to go all out to eliminate this unit.

So, armed with some intelligence from local villagers, we went and tracked down the base they were operating from. Our small raiding party was merciless, the only survivor being the commander, who was in a fearful state of terror and was passed over to the CIA for interrogation.

Immediately after this successful raid, reward posters were being found on trees, offering a large sum of money for my capture and smaller amounts for any of my men. Although the money offered was small compared to Australian dollars, it was a very large amount to the impoverished villagers and was equivalent to a couple of years' wages to a poorly paid soldier. This reward caused me some concern, as South Vietnamese officers were known to have been murdered by their men on occasions such as this, but as time went on and I saw the respect and loyalty shown to me, I felt more relaxed.

It became obvious Captain Henderson was also making inroads into the Viet Cong when posters appeared wanting him "Dead or Alive". Soon after, we received word a small band of Viet Cong and NVA had gone into a tiny isolated jungle village and ruthlessly slaughtered every man, raping and killing women and children, except for one, a young girl of about thirteen who had fled into the jungle when the shooting had started and over a two-day period managed to make it to our base camp exhausted and hungry.

Her story filled me with an incredible rage toward these animals who would murder, rape, and then burn villages just for their meagre food supplies. No, it was more than just taking their food and possessions. This was no war fought for a noble political cause. This was pure genocide, where the North Vietnamese were exacting brutal revenge against a proud race of independent people whom they feared and could not control. My anger knew no bounds, and I knew they had to be wiped out!

When the poor child had been medically tended to, fed, and rested with the help of Y Banh Minh, we questioned her closely. It was terrible to see the pain in her eyes as she described how she watched from her hiding place in the jungle and saw her family being shot one by one and the brutal raping of her older sister before she, too, was shot in the head. It was then she fled on her long trek to safety. She had headed to our base camp because two of her village men were here with our militia. That night, the atmosphere in our camp was palpable with the intensity of anger and revengeful mood of the tribal soldiers around me.

The next morning, a special parade was held. Even though my knowledge of the dialects and language was improving, I needed Y Banh Minh to get my message across. I needed a small band of the best jungle trackers and fighters. I wanted the men who had proven themselves in every form of combat we had been engaged in. I was not going to order them into this extremely dangerous mission of search and kill. I was after volunteers.

My only order to them was to dismiss them from the parade, and with the aid of their NCO, the two Nung tribe brothers came back to me in two hours with thirty handpicked men from over two hundred soldiers, all eager for revenge.

In that two-hour period the previous day, the discussions were loud and sometimes heated as the men decided amongst them who would go. Every man among them would have volunteered for this dangerous mission in the heart of Viet Cong-held territory.

When I looked over the assembled volunteers that afternoon, I knew I had the best men. Men who were skilled in every facet of jungle tracking, knife fighting, crossbow use, and most of all, proven in the use of modern weapons with skill and courage.

Y Bhan Minh informed me that the end result of who would go on this mission came about when all the soldiers agreed to put the names into a hat of each man who was noted for his ability and military achievement. There were over fifty names. It was then agreed to narrow it down to the required thirty by a final vote. That night the sounds of the jungle were added to by the sounds of men putting keen edges on their knives and the dismantling, cleaning and putting back together of weapons.

Never before, even in Malaya, had I assembled before me thirty volunteers so eager to go on such a hazardous mission. The Nung NCOs were out in front, and I was told that both of the two men from the devastated village were in the group. One had lost his wife and two children, the other his parents. Although they were eager for revenge, it was necessary to impress on them that all commands must be obeyed if we were to succeed. Their emotions must not overpower their trained discipline. They resolutely agreed. They were to be our lead scouts, more than capable of finding the way to their village even in the dark.

From there, it was up to the best jungle trackers to pick up any sign of the Viet Cong unit's tracks. It was still dark when we set off from our base just after midnight. Moving silently through the jungle using night vision glasses, we rested just before sunrise. It was estimated we were about a day's march from the village. My thoughts went out to the young girl, the only survivor of that terrible slaughter, finding her way through this jungle and all its dangers of snakes, tigers, leopards, and VCs. Thinking about it further steeled my determination to succeed in this mission.

It was the circling vultures who alerted us to the proximity of the village. As we drew closer, the stench of death hung nauseatingly heavy in the humid air. I knew that going into the burnt-out remains of the village would be extremely traumatic for the men and the two surviving members even more so. I decided to skirt around and circle well outside the village surroundings, with all the men watching for signs of the enemy, hoping this would keep them alert to the job at hand. It worked.

Suddenly, a silent hand signal from our lead scout alerted us to something, signalling the men to go to ground; I belly-crawled my way to his side. He was pointing to a number of marks in the soft soil of what seemed to be an animal track leading away through the jungle. Most of the Viet Cong wore sandals of the type commonly seen throughout Asia; these marks were of boots. Military-type boots with a tread pattern similar to that of the NVA soldiers. I had no doubt that there would be a number of North Vietnamese Military advisers and regular soldiers with the Viet Cong.

Even though there had been a couple of light rain showers in the previous days, and there were reasonably fresh leaves lying across them in a couple of places, the tread pattern was still clear in parts. The tracks were pointing northeast, and signalling to the men to rise and fan out either side. We started on our tracking pursuit with the scout who had found the sign leading us and the rest moving along silently.

It was coming to dusk when I signalled to halt. There had been enough track signs to move along at a reasonable pace. It was hard to be exact, but a rough estimate said there were about twenty to thirty VCs and NVAs ahead of us based on the mix of sandals and boots.

Ordering out perimeter guards, I instructed the men to rig up fine fishing line and stones in food tins in a circle outside the perimeter of our camp. We then settled down for a ration meal and rest for the night.

The next morning, just before first light, we were away on the trail picked up the night before. By early sunrise, we heard the sound of running water and cautiously observed we had arrived not far from a shallow river crossing, with the trail going across the mud and sand to the other side. Keeping down low, I decided to stay hidden for a while and observe the opposite bank and jungle. I was hoping to see if there were any lookouts or guards posted. The two big Nung NCOs and I were carrying high-powered American-issue binoculars and spreading out into wide positions. We were to observe the opposite bank and signal if we saw anything. Checking to see if all our men were well camouflaged and hidden, we settled down to watch. It was just as well we did; about ten minutes had gone by when we heard laughter, and three half-naked men walked onto the sand on the opposite side. They were wearing loincloths, and it was obvious by their actions they were about to have a morning swim and wash. There was no attempt by them to be quiet; they were no doubt confident they had the place to themselves.

Sending silent hand signals down the line to all the men, I instructed them to crawl slowly backward, deeper into the jungle. I knew we had found their camp.

Now, at a safe distance, I told the men that we were going to launch a nighttime attack using our night vision glasses, crossbows, and knives to eliminate the perimeter guards. Our two soldiers from the village said they knew this place and the jungle around it. As boys, they used to come and swim in this river and later hunt the region. They asked for permission to scout the area, and come back with advice on the layout and manpower of the enemy camp. Emphasising they were not to engage the enemy at all and to only do a reconnaissance of the area, I agreed. Looking deep into their eyes, I knew they were eager to do the job, and so they were the selected trackers. They said they knew a place further downstream where they could cross and circle around to where they suspected the camp was. For the rest of us, it was a matter of drawing back into the thick shelter and shade of the jungle, post guards, waiting, eating, and resting.

It was late afternoon when a prearranged bird call signal alerted the guards to their arrival back at camp. Their eyes were glowing with excitement as they relayed the information about the number of enemies and equipment seen. The enemy camp was made up of twenty-seven men and four women. The women and fourteen men were Viet Cong in the traditional black pyjama-type outfits they wore, and the rest were regular NVAs.

They had built two communal huts, and it seemed to be a camp from where they branched out on their terrorist activities. They were well armed with AK47s, and there was a store pile of mortars, shells, and supplies under a thatched shelter. The camp was very well hidden in the jungle, but only about 300 metres from the river. I assumed it was the main source of their water supply, as there was also a well-tended vegetable garden, which I was informed they daily carried water to.

The women seemed to attend to most of the cooking. I could not help but wonder if they were there on the day of the mass slaughter, and if they were, what sort of pressure, if any, was applied to them to participate? I knew their being female would not matter when my hill tribe's militia attacked their camp.

It was decided we would silently place ourselves in position and attack the camp at 14:00 hours, the time when people are usually in a deep sleep, and guards tend to nod off if they are in a complacent situation, as they showed by their noise and relaxed attitude through the day. Our two scouts had spotted the guards' posts and noted trip wires on obvious tracks, which the camp inhabitants carefully evaded and walked around. This we would also do. All of us would be aided by our night vision glasses.

Our key crossbow men, there were ten of them, were also carrying AK-47s and their "tiger knives" were honed to razor sharpness. These men were to be placed, two to each guard, in opposing diagonal fire positions less than fifteen metres from each guard point to double the chances of a quick kill with the crossbows or to use their knives for a silent kill if the opportunity was there.

With the disposal of the guards, the rest of us were to split into two groups and file two abreast into the communal huts, firing repeatedly down into the sleeping inhabitants. This done, we were to burn the camp and blow up all weapons that we could not carry, along with munitions, mortar, and supplies.

It was all going well, and it was a very dark, moonless night. There was not a sound from any of the guards, and our crossbow men, some showing blood stains on their bodies, soon joined us.

We were positioning ourselves in a semicircle around the entrance of each hut opening. I was about to give the signal to move in when I heard the rustling sound of a grass mat and a light cough. I had my knife drawn and my AK47 on the ground as an inhabitant stumbled through the entrance right next to me, sleepily lifting the front of his loincloth. He did not make a sound as my left hand clamped around his head and mouth, and the knife blade slid between his ribs and into the heart. Holding him upright, bent slightly back, I held him for a few seconds until he was totally limp, and then, slicing across his jugular vein, I lowered him slowly and quietly to the ground.

I gave the signal, and we filed quietly into the huts. The only sounds were those of sleeping people—but only for about five seconds, then a massive thunderstorm of noise erupted as thirty AK47s shattered the stillness of the jungle night, and for over a minute, we poured a massive volume of lead into those sleeping forms. There was no resistance and no wounded—just shattered, dead, and blood-soaked bodies.

We found drums of cooking oil and poured it onto the thatch walls and roofs of the huts. As we were setting fire to them, our NCOs were setting explosive charges under the piles of mortar shells and any supplies we could not carry. We retreated to a safe distance back into the jungle and were well away when the massive explosion and the fire of the burning huts lit up the sky.

It was a most successful night's action. By late morning, we were drawing much further away from enemy-held territory and settled into a well-hidden rest camp for the rest of the day. I was aiming to march our men through the night back to our base camp nonstop. My Nung NCOs told me the men were saying there would be a celebrity welcome because of the success of this operation, with much-fermented rice wine and the ritual sacrifice of a buffalo, that being one of the highest forms of tribute.

It was nearing the beginning of 1965. Captain Henderson had expanded the Montagnard guerilla force to over one thousand highly trained men with Montagnard officers and NCOs. Our overall success was being recognised by the South Vietnamese high command as having achieved one of the best combat records in Vietnam. Captain Henderson had been issued with a gallantry award stating this. Our men had sustained a minimum of losses while inflicting heavy casualties and equipment losses on the Viet Cong.

One night, after a particularly wearisome jungle patrol and feeling very weary, I went to my hut and was soon asleep. I woke up with a start from a very vivid dream. In it, I had seen Uncle Charlie. He was beckoning me to come to him from a distance. I awoke with a start and sat upright as I felt a cold chill go through my body from the nape of my neck and down my spine. What a strange dream. It stayed with me all the next day.

Throughout my time in Vietnam, I had kept constant mail contact with my family, Angelica, Angus, and the Finlaysons. I would send letters to Uncle Charlie and my sister via my mother, who would relay them to him. Uncle Charlie had never learnt to read English, so Mum would sit him down and read and explain to him what was happening in my life and how everything he had taught me as a child had helped me in my work in the Central Highlands. Of course, military censorship would not allow me to tell everything.

That strange dream haunted me for days. Was everything okay at home? It took an urgent phone call home for my mother to assure me that Uncle Charlie was okay and was avidly listening to every word as Mum read my letters to him.

I had always known from childhood of a special connection to Uncle Charlie and eventually shrugged the troublesome dream away and got on with my daily life of training my men and doing jungle patrols and ambushes.

One day in early March 1965, we received intelligence that the Viet Cong were becoming increasingly irritated with the success of our ambush patrols and were increasing the size of their patrol units.

Wonderful news: our small eight-men, hit-and-run teams, who were almost invisible, allowed them to disappear easier into the jungle and then melt into a Montagnard village for a night's rest. The bigger the VC patrols, the more damage we could inflict. This decision by the Viet Cong showed us that the early guerilla strategy we had copied from them was successfully working.

One of our Montagnard spies came in with a report that one of these larger units of Viet Cong was planning an ambush of a large South Vietnamese convoy due to travel along a road in the southeast Darlac Province. It was decided to send two eight-man teams to reconnoitre this move. They discovered the Viet Cong had set up a series of ambush hideouts on either side along a length of this road, which were extremely well hidden. Their plan was to wait until the South Vietnamese convoy was well and truly spaced out along this stretch and then hit them. They had anticipated one thing that would help them in their ambush was the swampy nature of the road due to heavy rain, and the South Vietnamese troops needing elephants to pull their trucks through the bogs would be slowing them down. Elephants were a necessity then, as there was no heavy machinery available capable of pulling trucks out of bogs.

Our two eight-man teams successfully manoeuvred themselves into position behind the last foxhole in the line on either side without being seen.

The Viet Cong were waiting for the first trucks to appear when our two teams attacked the first pit nearest to them. Firing automatic weapons and lobbing grenades, the five or six VC in the pit were wiped out. Then the two teams ran from pit to pit, destroying five or six of these pits in a similar manner. The remainder of the VC fled, having lost the element of surprise.

We had not lost a man and had no injuries. Elated and perhaps a little careless with our success, I was organising our men to check the bodies for survivors to be taken in for interrogation and to collect weapons and any documents. Standing by the edge of one of the pits issuing instructions, no one noticed a seemingly dead VC officer raise a handgun and fire a single round before he was riddled with bullets. Unfortunately, that one round slammed into my back, entering my left side and passing through my body, just missing my left kidney. The massive punch downed me.

I vaguely remember our team medic attending to me, and then the morphine kicked in. It seems my teams got me to a point on the map where I could be airlifted from Darlac by Air America to the USA base hospital in Saigon.

One thing that must be said about the Americans is the quality of the medical treatment they provide is superb. Again, luck was on my side. The bullet had passed through me and fortunately missed any vital organs. Soon after I had been operated on, Geoff Truso and Captain Henderson came to see me. They were all smiles at my recovery, but the smile on their faces dropped when I told them of my eagerness to get back to my men.

Long-faced and sad, Captain Henderson told me that his time with our Montagnard Militia unit had been extended. More Australian training officers were being sent over, and I was to be relieved. At first, I was dismayed to learn that I was being sent back to Australia. Furthermore, I was being given special orders to report back to ASIS on the situation here in the Central Highlands of Vietnam on Captain Henderson's behalf. He added with a smile that I was being awarded the military medal for combat gallantry and was also mentioned in dispatches. He emphasised that due to my nearly three years of exemplary service and the fact that I had been wounded twice, it was time to leave Vietnam for an overdue furlough. When he and Geoff Truro left, I lay back with my mind in two fields of thought.

One part of me was like a mother who did not want to leave her children behind; such was the bond I felt between my trusted Montagnard and myself. Their acceptance of me as a *warrior* had deeply moved me. The worry of how they would get on without me and who would take over their training disturbed me, even though I knew Captain Henderson and Geoff Truro would see to it well enough. In my imagination, I felt as would a mother handing over a newborn baby to a stranger. But I knew I just had to let go.

The other part of my thinking was the joy I felt at the knowledge of going home. Here was the opportunity to once again see my family and dearest friends. A recent letter from Angie had indicated she had met someone, and her life was moving on. I felt the need to meet with her once more, if only to hear and see the truth and wish her well. Another thing was that "troublesome" dream I had had recently. It was a very vivid dream where I saw and heard "Uncle Charlie" calling to me.

In the dream, he was beckoning for me to come to him. I was strongly aware of the spiritual bond that had always existed between Uncle Charlie and me; it was something deeply "Aboriginal" and difficult to explain, but the feeling inside of me told me it was time to go home. It was early April 1965. I healed well and was soon on an American plane bringing the United States and Australian soldiers first to Brisbane for me, then onto Sydney for R&R, rest and recreation for the war-weary Americans.

Back to Australia and Home

Our Special Operations training teams were still highly secret, especially our involvement with the CIA, so I was wearing civilian clothes when I landed at Brisbane Airport. My orders were to switch planes and fly directly to Melbourne on the first available flight for debriefing by ASIS.

Due to a union dispute, all flights out of Brisbane were delayed for twenty-four hours, which gave me the opportunity to catch up with Angus, dear, wonderful Angus, my best friend. Although somewhat greyer, he still looked a picture of fitness. He was now a station manager and was married with one small child, a son named Charles. He smiled when he told me he had named him after that fine old man "Uncle Charlie". In conversation, I told him of the dream where "Uncle Charlie" was beckoning me to come to him. Immediately, Angus's face took on a serious expression. As civilised in the white man's world as Angus was, the beliefs, customs, and dreams of an ancient race were still strong deep within him.

Leaning his head close to me, Angus looked deep into my eyes and said solemnly, "Sean, you go to him as soon as you can". Those words did it for me. I knew as soon as I had completed my military responsibilities, I would head for home as soon as possible.

My orders were to report to the senior ASIS officers at Melbourne's Victoria barracks. There, I was subjected to a gruelling debriefing. They wanted to know how effective their methods of training men for missions in Vietnam were.

They wanted comparisons between the Australian Army training teams and the US Special Forces. They quizzed me on the relations with the Montagnard tribesmen, how they accepted our training, and how we handled them in comparison to the CIA and their Special Forces. All of this took the best part of a day.

I was then taken to the Director General of ASIS. That meeting was more of a discussion about how the war in Vietnam was going. One bombshell question was: "What did I think about Australian combat troops being sent to Vietnam?" My answer was simply, "Excellent if they are well-trained in jungle warfare." There were more meetings the next day of a similar kind where the question of Australian combat troops was again mentioned. My answer was the same. Train them well before sending them over.

I left those meetings with the strong suspicion that the decision to send Australian troops to Vietnam had already been made.

With all the debriefings over, I was now given permission to take a long leave from the Army. I could hardly wait to get from Melbourne to my family home by the Darling River. I had already informed my mother I was coming home, who had passed the message on to my sister Irene and her husband Jimmy and Uncle Charlie. I had collected a considerable amount of money from the army, and with savings, I had more money now than I had ever had in my life.

The first thing was to buy a decent car and then spend a day shopping in Melbourne for gifts for all my family. I had brought back with me a special gift for Uncle Charlie and Angus. It was the "tiger head knife" that I had supplied my Montagnard tribesmen militia with. I also gave them an embossed red and black ornamental "Rhade" sheath. Each time I thought of Uncle Charlie, the vision in my dream came back to me.

Travelling around the car showrooms of Melbourne, I was impressed with the latest model Holden Station Wagon. I selected a white car; it had red upholstery and was fitted with a radio and air conditioner. I could not help smiling at the look on the face of the salesman when I paid for the car in cash from my army duffle bag.

According to a map, it was close to 700 kilometres from Melbourne to where I was going, near the village of Pooncarie. I reckoned I was about halfway along the journey somewhere past Echuca and listening to the radio when a news flash interrupted the radio program. My suspicions were justified by the news. The prime minister of Australia, Sir Robert Menzies, had made a surprise announcement that Australia would be sending a combat division of troops to fight with the Americans against the North Vietnamese communist aggression in Vietnam. It was the 29th of April, 1965. He had made the announcement at 8 p.m. that night before a near-empty parliament chamber. I thought that was very sneaky; it was too late to make the evening newspapers that night, and the announcement hit the country the next morning with many surprises and plenty of shocks to some.

I was getting road-weary and decided to drive on to Swan Hill and stay in a hotel for the night. When I walked into the bar of the first reasonable-looking pub that I came to, the bar was alive with the pros and cons of Bob Menzies's announcement. The main topic was the possible implementation of training for national servicemen to be sent. I steered away from the conversations, downed a small beer, and headed to my room. I had heard and talked enough about Vietnam at this stage and needed to switch off.

I aimed to get off to an early start the next morning for the last 320 kilometres to get home; I had used a public phone to call ahead to Mum and let her know I would be arriving about midday. I had to drive through Pooncarie to get to our old house at the northern end of the village. As I approached the village, I could see in the distance a long white stretch of cloth with wording on it strung between posts. As I got closer to it, my jaw dropped in surprise as I read my name.

In large red letters was the wording: WELCOME HOME, SEAN "MULGA" MOLLOY.

I stopped the car and sat there only a few moments, staring at it as a warm flush of melancholy feeling went through me, and then I heard a high-pitched shrill of delight emanate from the door of the nearby pub. He's here! He's here! And in the next minute, the car door was flung open, and my sister, with tears streaming down her pretty face, was half in the car, smothering me with kisses. In no time and before I could extricate myself from my sister and out of the car to greet people, it seemed like the entire population of the village was swarming around my now road grimed new Holden.

Managing to step outside the car with my sister's arm firmly holding my waist, I was surrounded by a sea of people all wanting to shake my hand or kiss me on the cheeks, that is, depending on their sex.

All the old familiar faces were there, including Police Sergeant Kennedy, Mr and Mrs Finlayson, and Angus, and then there was a momentary hush of noise. There was my very dear and now very frail mother, leaning heavily on the arm of Uncle Charlie as he gently found his way through the throng toward me. Jimmy Collett, my best mate and my sister's husband, was leading the way, making a passage through the crowd.

At the moment I held my mother's trembling body in one arm with the other encircling Uncle Charlie, my stiff-lipped military reserve broke, and the tears flowed down my deeply tanned face. It was good to be home, my white man's home and my tribal home, with the people I knew and loved.

I will never forget the welcome given to me that day and into the night. It seemed the whole town and surrounding population had turned out for the occasion, with many dressed in their best attire. Uncle Charlie was particularly resplendent, wearing a brilliant white shirt with a red tie and sharply pressed trousers and was even wearing shoes, although he did seem to limp a little in them. I did notice the tie, and the shoes came off as the evening wore on.

Because they had learnt of my military medal award, being mentioned in dispatches, and twice wounded, I was being hailed as the hometown war hero, which I certainly did not feel I was. I was asked repeatedly why I was not wearing my uniform and medals. There was an immense amount of food laid out in the pub, and Hennessy, the publican, had donated an eighteen-gallon keg of beer to the occasion.

My welcome was only marred by two things. The frail and dreamy appearance of my dear mother and the concern I could see in Uncle Charlie's eyes as he looked at her. It was more than an hour before I could free myself from everyone and sit for some quiet time with my mother and Uncle Charlie. Taking her on one arm, with Uncle Charlie holding the other, we found our way through the crowd to a small parlour room off to one side.

Earlier, I had managed to engage my sister Irene in a private conversation and was overjoyed when she told me she was expecting their first baby; she said that she and Jimmy were as happy as they could ever be, but her face clouded over when I asked her about our mother. Looking deeply into my eyes, she said, "Sean, Mum would not allow us to say anything in our letters to you. She would say you had enough worries about what you were doing in Vietnam. Even now, I am not allowed to tell you. You will have to talk to her yourself."

Sitting now with the two people I loved most dearly, Uncle Charlie and my mother, I found my courage to ask the question that I must ask, quail, as I looked into their loving, dark eyes. My voice was now faint with perhaps a slight tremble to it as I softly said, "Mum, what is it? What is wrong? Irene would not tell me. Please tell me the truth, mum."

Tears filled her eyes as she took my hands in hers and said, "Sean, about three months ago, I felt terrible pains in my stomach. My doctor took some tests and gave me some painkillers, and some days later, he said I would have to go to a major hospital for further tests. Irene and Jimmy took time off from their work and drove me to Mildura Hospital. They kept me there for two days and then let me come home. About five weeks ago, I got sick again, and with bad pain, the doctor came to see me, and he looked real sad. He said he had received the results of the tests, and they were not good." At this, the tears were streaming down her face as she told me she had terminal cancer and had about three to six months to live, adding that she had to have injections of morphine to help quell the pain.

Morphine! I certainly knew what morphine was for. I had been injected with my share when twice wounded and had pumped enough of it into wounded Montagnard soldiers. Oh god, my poor dear mother. It was then I knew what my dream of Uncle Charlie meant. He was calling me to come home before it was too late.

Soon after, we helped Mum into Jimmy and Irene's car to drive her home. One of Uncle Charlie's female relatives, and a distant relative to Mum named Ella, had taken on the job of carer. It seems she had some qualifications for the job, having worked in her teen years and early adulthood as a nurse's aide at the Mildura Hospital.

When I visited Mum the next day, I was impressed with the cleanliness of the house and the obvious warm manner in which Ella fussed over her. I spoke with Ella about the medications my mother had to have daily, and she showed me the locked cabinet holding the Morphine capsules. Ella told me that as the pain increased, Mum would most likely have to go into the hospice at Mildura Hospital.

As I wanted to visit and spend time with Uncle Charlie, the Finlaysons, and the now retired Police Sergeant Kennedy, I decided to stay around for a couple of weeks. It was just as well that I did; it was seven days later that Mum passed away in her sleep. Uncle Charlie said, "Shoon, she waited long enough for you to come home, boy. Dat kept her alive. Now she in dreamtime, no more pain." Mum had told my sister she wanted to be buried next to the man she once loved. That was something I felt hard to understand after all the years of grief and pain, but we honoured her wish.

After the church sermon, the mourners left to gather at the graveside for her final farewell. I had seen Uncle Charlie at the church and then he suddenly disappeared. I was puzzled, and as we, the close family and friends, got out of the cars, we saw there were about twenty Aboriginals waiting there, men in loincloths, women in blouses and skirts, and all were face, body, and arms painted with white and ochre markings, and led by Uncle Charlie. As our dear mother's coffin was lowered into the ground, the parish priest's words were drowned by the rhythmic drone of a didgeridoo, the clicking of the music sticks, the wailing of the women and the men performing a funeral dance. My sister and Jimmy were standing with me, and we were all deeply moved by this, with our tears openly flowing.

The funeral was followed by the usual wake held at the pub, where many respects were offered about our mother. The next day, Uncle Charlie said to me, "Shoon, it's time we go bush, boy, it's good for healin,'" and I knew he was right. The next day, we wandered off for our bush walkabout. I stripped down to shorts with a belt carrying my own sheathed "tiger knife" and spent the next three days with him and Angus, snaring, trapping, fishing, and cooking our catch in the coals of a gidgee wood fire. The stamina of that wonderful old man never ceased to amaze me. At night, we sat around our campfire of "gidgee" wood as I told him and Angus of my time with the native tribe's people of Malaya and Vietnam and their similar hunting skills.

Uncle Charlie and Angus were also wearing a belt, the "tiger head knife" I had brought back for them. I told them what the engraving on the blade meant and the honour it meant to those tribesmen who carried it. I endeavoured to describe what the war was about and its associated horrors. I told him of my being wounded and how it happened and the valour of the men who saved my life. Through it all, Uncle Charlie just sat there cross-legged, looking gravely into the coals of the fire. There was a long silence between us, and then he spoke in a deep and emotional tone, "Shoon, don' go back there boy, you done yer bit. It's time to stay in yer own land, too much death over there, ole Charlie see bad things, don' go back boy!" His profound words left me unsettled for days after, and I found myself reflecting on everything that had happened over the past few years. I knew deep down in letters from Angelica that my commitment to the army had no doubt caused me to lose her and now Uncle Charlie's words. Had my luck almost run out? Was it time to stay in Australia? One thing was sure: I had to visit the Finlaysons and then hit the road for Sydney again, with Angus travelling with me to visit his sister and her family once more. The next few days, I spent travelling around, seeing family and friends and saying farewells.

By the time we reached the outskirts of Sydney, my mind was halfway made up to resign from my army commission, but first, there was one more person to see. Angelica knew I was coming. I first wrote and then phoned her, and we arranged to meet at a hotel in the northern suburb of Palm Beach.

Dropping Angus off at a railway station where he could catch a train to Erskineville. I knew that before I made any further decision about my life, I had to talk to her first. I had to look into her eyes and see if what we had before was real, even though I felt I had lost her. We made an appointment time to meet for lunch at about 2 p.m. at a plush waterside hotel on the Northern Sydney coastline. Angie had given me good instructions on how to get there, but not realising the distance to drive, I was running about fifteen minutes later when I reached the hotel. Parking my car, I walked around to the outdoor beer garden.

There she was, sitting there idly toying with a straw in a green-coloured drink. She was a picture of radiant beauty; her long blonde hair flowed out over her tanned shoulders to her waist over a low-cut, backless white summer dress. I felt my heart miss a beat as I stood for a second or two gazing at her loveliness, and then she looked up, saw me, and flashed her beautiful white-toothed smile. Many times in Vietnam, I had visions of her beauty and the love we had shared, sometimes tinged with a pang of regret at my decision to go overseas with the army.

Now, at this moment, I felt hesitant, uncertain, and very, very nervous. Angelica stood to greet me, and then we embraced with an almost paternal kiss on each other's cheek. It was obvious we were both nervous, almost like two people on their first date. We sat down and went through the usual greetings and how well each other looked, and then came the silence. It was the silence of two people, uncertain of what to say next. Who would speak first and give voice to the real questions of what has happened in our lives in the three years we have been apart? The growing distance that showed in carefully worded letters, designed so as not wanting to hurt. Looking at her now, I knew I had lost her. I saw the pain in her eyes for a lost love, a love that once had been so profound and real. It was me who spoke first.

I simply said, "Angie, have you found happiness?" She just nodded, and then tears began to flow as she said, "Oh, Sean, I truly did love you, and I wanted a life with you. I hoped you would come back to me, but deep down, I knew the love you had for the life you chose could not include me. You have been away for three years, and in this last year, about six months ago, I have met someone who I feel I could be happy with." The words then broke down into trembling sobs as she said, "Sean darling, please forgive me. I am so sorry." Tears also flowed down my cheeks as I reached across for her hands and held them tight as I said, "Angie, you were my first real love, and it is not for you to be sorry to me, but for me to be sorry to you. I truly loved you; you had captured my heart, but the army had captured my soul. With my decision for that life, I realise what I have lost, and deeply regret losing what may have been, so please forgive me." We were now both crying openly.

A waiter had come over our way and then veered away, sensing our emotional reunion. He was now hovering near, and I felt it was definitely time for a drink. Pulling out a handkerchief, I wiped my eyes and handed it to Angie, who wiped tear-smeared mascara from her eyes and cheeks.

She managed a sad smile and excused herself to go to the ladies' room. I signalled to the waiter to bring me a scotch and soda and another green drink, which turned out to be Crème de Menthe and soda. As sad as I was at the outcome of this meeting, I now knew we could both get on with our lives and, in time, find what we both needed to live happily. When she came back to me, looking refreshed, from that moment, our conversation flowed freely over the whole afternoon as we talked about ourselves and the happenings over the last three years.

Her new man was an upward-moving architect with a city firm. According to her, he was a well-grounded, family-type man with a love for children. That indicated to me, I thought with a twinge of sadness, that Angie was having maternal urges. It was easy to picture her as a beautiful and loving mother.

As we said farewells to each other that afternoon, we had one last embrace and kiss goodbye. We both knew there would be pain and memories for some time, but time is a great healer. I knew in my heart, and I truly meant it, when I wished her love and happiness in her new relationship.

It was time for me to start thinking about my future as I drove back through the traffic to Sydney. Now I was thinking, did I really want to go back to military life? Was it time for a change of direction? Although feeling sad at parting from Angelica, I had no fear of what the future held for me here in Australia, but deep down, there was a nagging question about going back to Vietnam. Uncle Charlie's words still echoed in my memory and were buzzing around in my head, almost like a prophet of doom, as I drove back toward Sydney.

As I drove, I remembered that before leaving Brisbane Airport, Angus had phoned his sister in Erskineville to say that he and I would be arriving in Sydney. I remembered my enjoyable meeting with Elsie and her husband, Jack, and thought that I would now drop in to see them. Spotting a phone booth in a quiet side street, I veered out of the traffic and made a phone call. I was planning to stay in a motel and make it a visit tomorrow night if it was suitable, but Elsie and Jack would not hear of it and insisted I come over right away. It was now 4 p.m. on a balmy summer afternoon, and I figured I would make it to Sydney by about 6 p.m., with enough time, hopefully, to be able to find my way through the maze of inner-city streets in daylight to their house in Pleasant Avenue.

Coming off the Sydney Harbour Bridge into York Street, the traffic was intense, and my concentration was totally taken up with finding my way. Next to me, on the seat, sat a Gregory's Street directory. A previous study of the road maps showed me if I could get onto George Street and continue south, I would reach the wide main thoroughfare known as Broadway.

Somehow, with more good luck than good management, I made it, with only a couple of car horns beeping at me. I admit to feeling more stressed in this busy city traffic than I ever did planning a Viet Cong ambush in Vietnam, but then again, the streets of Saigon were much more chaotic, but usually someone else was driving.

I was now passing the clock tower on Sydney's Central Railway station on my left, and the memories of the route taken by Angie when she drove Angus to meet with his sister- and brother-in-law kicked in. Yes! There, on the left, was the entrance to Sydney's biggest brewery, Tooth's Brewery, which had been pointed out to us by Angie as we drove past.

Taking a chance, I pulled over to a bus stop just past the brewery to check Gregory's map, an illegal move at that time of the day in peak hour traffic. A glance at the map showed me just a couple of kilometres further on a major road with a big park on the right corner, turned off the Broadway, and headed south through the suburbs of Chippendale and Newtown to where it became King Street.

Memory told me in Newtown, there was a street turning off to the left with a big old-fashioned post office on the corner. I was pretty sure Angie had said it was called Erskineville Road. It seemed no time at all when I spotted Erskineville Road and turned left. I was now confident I could find my way to Pleasant Avenue.

Where the Erskineville Road widened out, and just past a hotel on the left, I pulled over to the footpath edging what seemed to be a vacant block of land. Almost opposite me was a hotel named the Rose of Australia. It seemed closed. I vaguely remembered the narrow street alongside it, went down a hill and came out at the bottom opposite Pleasant Avenue.

Damn! I had hoped to buy some wine and beer and some soft drinks to take with me for Elsie, Jack, Angus and the kids. My watch showed it was 6:58 p.m. Looking at the rows of shops along from the hotel; I saw a milk bar open. I thought, okay, I guess I will take chocolates and sweets. Jumping out of the car, I sprinted across the road into the shop. After purchasing a large box of chocolates and some sweets, I asked the proprietor, who looked to be Italian or Greek. "Did he know what time the hotels closed?" In a heavy accent, he said, "With the new laws, the hotels have to close at six o'clock to clean up and then reopen at 7 p.m."

Thanking him, I walked out of the shop and the short distance to the "Rose of Australia", and sure enough, the doors were just opening. Already, there was a sprinkle of patrons walking into the bar. Beauty! I could now buy some beer and wine. Back in the car, another look at the Gregory's showed me the street I wanted to turn down was George Street, and it was almost directly opposite my car.

Finding a break in the traffic, I did a U-turn and headed down George Street, passing the hotel I had just left. It was now familiar to me, at the bottom of the street, and a slight turn to the right, then a sharp left, and I was in Pleasant Avenue and pulling up to park in front of their house, between two lovely green-leafed trees.

Elsie, Jack, and Angus were sitting on the veranda, and the two kids, Timothy and Elsie, were playing on the wide footpath with some other kids. And their welcome made me feel like I was part of the family. It was two very hospitable days before Angus, and I drove away from there, about 11 a.m. on a Sunday morning with the farewells from them all still loud in our ears, amid the calls of come back and see us again someday. I dropped Angus off at Mascot Airport and headed back toward the city. It would be some time before we would meet again.

CHAPTER 20

Fated to Meet
Jonathon James Strong QC

As I drove away, I knew it was time to move on. I had the urge to explore more of Sydney. When last together with Angie, we really did not come back into the inner city of Sydney before I went to Vietnam, preferring to visit the Blue Mountains and northern beaches. The opportunity was here, so why not? Angie had told me of the national museum, the art gallery, and the Mitchell State Library. She had told me stories of the famous, or was it infamous, bohemian side and strip clubs of King's Cross. I felt it was time to see it all.

Stopping to study the Gregory's again, I could see by going back to Erskineville Road and turning right. I could drive on through the suburb of Alexandria and onto Botany Road. Turning left there would eventually bring me into the inner-city area. I decided I would just drive and find my way around the city of Sydney. Being a Sunday, there did not seem to be as much traffic as I weaved my way in and out of city streets, and soon found I was now back on George Street and headed north toward Sydney Harbour.

On a side street near Circular Quay, I found a parking spot. It was now about one thirty in the afternoon, and I was hungry. Walking around Circular Quay, I spotted a seafood café. Yes, good old-fashioned fish and chips sounded good to me.

An hour later, I decided to walk off some of the excellent meals I had just enjoyed and started walking around the western side of the harbour and under the huge Harbour Bridge that I had travelled over a few evenings before. Standing there under the bridge, I marvelled at the colossal size of this beautiful, huge, engineered structure. At that moment, a ship's foghorn sounded, and I looked up. But where was the ship? Looking to the west, I could see a row of grey-painted timber wharf buildings, and the sound seemed to be coming from the other side of those buildings. Still carrying my Gregory's to help me find my way through this harbour city, I found the Sydney CBD map and saw I was standing on Dobroyd Point, and the loud blast of sound was coming from a part of the Harbour called Walsh Bay. Intrigued, I was about to move off in that direction when the foghorn sounded again. This time, it seemed closer, and suddenly, there it was, a large ship painted with a black hull and white superstructure just starting to round the point. Based on the number of people standing on its deck lining the rails and the number of broken streamers fluttering along its side from the breeze as the ship made headway, it was a passenger ship.

As a boy, I had seen the paddle wheelers operating along the Darling River and the American ships in Vietnam, but this was the first passenger ship, and as it drew closer to where I was standing, I could just make out its name "Wanganella", and I wondered where it was headed to. Later, in a book I found in the Mitchell Library, I saw that it was owned by Huddart Parker Shipping Company, and it was a twin screw motor vessel of about 10,000 tons. I also read it was a medium-sized passenger and cargo ship that had been used in the 1930s to transport the famous racehorse "Phar Lap" from New Zealand to Australia and the start of its illustrious racing career. The "Wanganella" and its passengers were heading out on its twice-monthly Tasman Sea crossing to the ports of Wellington and Auckland in New Zealand. It had me thinking that one day, I would like to visit New Zealand and would like to travel on this ship.

There were quite a few people who had stopped what they were doing to watch this ship go by, and on the opposite shore, prior to this ship passing, I had spotted a big sun-like face smiling across the harbour. Angie had told me about this fun park known as Luna Park and all its fun rides and carnival-type attractions, and as I watched, the shape of the ship was slowly blanking the sight of this huge face out. I was musing over it all when a faint sound came to my ears.

Having lived the last three years with my mind and body continuously tuned in to surrounding dangers, I was instantly on the alert. There it was again! It was definitely an anguished sound of distress, but where was it coming from? Turning around, I saw that nobody else seemed to be taking notice; the cry seemed to be coming from behind the massive sandstone block pylon supporting the bridge, very faint but discernible to my hearing. Again, the noise, but this time a little louder! Now, I was curious, and I decided to investigate.

As I made my way back across the road that looped around Dobroyd Point, I noticed a family group. They were obviously picnicking on the grassy slope just below the pylon, and they had their backs turned, and also had their attention focused in that direction. As I walked briskly by them, I now heard a much louder and definite female scream, accompanied by a man's voice calling for help.

Breaking into a run, I rounded the pylon to see four youths engaged in an assault on two people. Two of these cowardly bastards were punching and kicking a man lying on the ground; he was bent in the middle, with both his arms folded across his head, trying to protect it from the vicious kicks. There was another youth holding a woman from behind, while another was alternately hitting her with one hand while trying to tear a large leather bag from her grasp with the other. Furious at the sight of this attack, I launched myself into the fray.

A hard two-handed rabbit chop to the side of the neck and shoulder muscle of the lout who was hitting the woman and trying to snatch the bag quickly put him out of the picture. He was out cold. The one holding her let go and came at me yelling and wildly swinging punches, which I easily ducked under, and then chopped him with the side of my left hand, up hard and under his nose. He screamed from the pain of his broken septum, but that was nothing to the scream that erupted from him when my right foot swung up and around, kicking his leg at the side of the kneecap and snapping it at the joint.

The other two thugs, surprised by all this, had turned from kicking and beating the man on the ground. He was lying there in a dazed condition, bleeding from the nose and now holding his ribs. Expecting their attack, I was ready for them, positioned in a classic martial arts stance. They were circling me warily. One of the two was holding an empty wine bottle he had picked up by the neck. Good, I grimly thought, you are going to be the first to go down. The other was standing apprehensively, in a vague boxing-style stance, and he was looking worried, particularly when he looked down at his unconscious mate and the other bloke, who was still screaming with pain from his broken leg and nose.

By this time, a small group of onlookers who had heard the commotion were gathering to see what was happening. I called to them that I was okay, and would someone please call the police and look after that poor lady? The distraught, sobbing woman was kneeling over her fallen partner, nursing his head and wiping the blood from his face with the hem of her dress.

The moron who was holding the bottle by the neck, on hearing me call out, and no doubt thinking I was momentarily distracted, rushed at me, swinging the bottle wildly at my head. I'm sure the look on his face would have been comical as the bottle flew from his fist, accompanied by the dull thud of his arm breaking. As he rolled over my bent body and slammed down hard, there, he joined his screaming mate on the ground. As he tried to sit up, nursing his broken arm, a hard right punch to his jaw saw him lie back down.

At this turn of events, the would-be boxer, now in a panicked state, dropped all forms of defence, turned and ran like crazy in an ill-conceived sprint, running for his life and weaving through the crowd, when he came to an abrupt and no doubt painful stop caused by a bone-crunching body slam tackle from a big brawny fellow who had arrived on the scene. I recognised him as one of the members of the picnicking family.

Later, after the police had taken statements from me and other witnesses, I talked with this big man. No wonder he could tackle hard; he was an off-duty policeman and a well-known front-row forward with the Balmain "Tigers", a leading rugby league team. The bloke that had tried to run away was lucky he had got off with a tackle that just winded him; he was taken away in a "Black Maria" the others were taken to hospital under police guard in an ambulance. It seems there was no heat on me after the police had interviewed witnesses, although I was required to put my name to a signed statement, and was told I would be contacted in the future.

The man lying injured on the ground was taken with his wife to Sydney Hospital; although showing pain, he did not seem badly injured apart from possibly cracked ribs from the kicking and a lacerated nose, which happened when he valiantly attempted to resist the "mugging robbery" attack on him and his wife. And his wife was uninjured; apart from some bruising on the face and arms, both he and his wife were somewhat shocked and traumatised by this attack. Before they left in the ambulance, they thanked me profusely.

He was a well-spoken, obviously well-educated sort of bloke; both he and his wife Genevieve were in their late fifties. He asked me who I was, and when told, "I was in Sydney on military leave from Vietnam," he offered me his business card and said if we can be of service to you in any way at all to please call him. He said he would like to keep in touch with me if possible. Not having a fixed address at this stage, I gave him my basic military details and how he could contact me. He had told me his name, but not what he did.

Later, in a quiet moment in a Travelodge motel room at the top of William Street, King's Cross, I sat on the bed and read his card.

Lawrence & Associates, Criminal Lawyers

Anthony Lawrence QC

That put a big smile on my face; those cowardly bastards who attacked him and his wife Genevieve would not have a ghost of a chance of getting a soft sentence when they fronted court.

That type of mindless brutality filled me with anger. It had always affected me in the past. I felt no bad feelings at all over the injuries I had inflicted on the two of them. Reflecting on this, I thought deeply. Had my time in Malaya and Vietnam and the fact that I had killed and wounded others hardened me, perhaps made me callous? Yes, to some extent, that was true, hardened but not callous. I equated my actions with the reasoning that those I had injured or killed were perpetrating their brutality on innocent people and, therefore, deserved punishment.

Thinking of Anthony Lawrence QC, I knew that his esteemed position as a Queen's Counsel would put him in a position of defending and fighting for justice, using all the means legally at his fingertips to achieve justice for the innocent. I pondered some on what his thoughts would be, if his gut feeling told him the person he was defending in court was guilty. An interesting thought, something I would like to have an answer to. I was thinking I would give Anthony Lawrence QC and his wife a phone call tomorrow and see how they are feeling after their ordeal.

I decided I would stay in Sydney for a while. Although more crowded and noisier than anything I had previously known, particularly on this Sunday night in King's Cross, there was a heady excitement about it that appealed to me. I mused on the thought that I was perhaps suffering from Vietnam withdrawal symptoms.

No! It was more than that. I was experiencing things I had not known before and liked some of it. Yes! That was it; I was ready to experience a new style of life. A new form of excitement. Tonight, I would have a meal in the motel restaurant and later take a stroll through the notorious King's Cross.

Being a Sunday night, I was surprised to see so many people wandering up and down the main street of King's Cross. As I walked, there were a number of young girls and women soliciting from the doorways of shops and seedy-looking apartment doorways.

To some extent, it reminded me a little of the Saigon bar girls who were starting to become more prominent towards the end of my stay there as more and more American servicemen were coming into Vietnam. I also felt a feeling of sorrow about their way of life, knowing that it was mainly dictated by poverty.

I had been told on my arrival in Saigon that under the rule of Catholic President Ngo Dinh Diem, prostitution was not allowed with heavy penalties for those who practised it, and yet in other areas of his rule, corruption and brutality was rife, the president was overthrown, and executed in a US military-backed coup in 1963. From that time on, bars, gambling, and prostitution flourished with the influx of the mighty "Yankee dollar."

Ignoring the numerous "wanna girl mister" from the working girls, I kept strolling along, occasionally stopping to watch the passing parade of people and to watch the "spruikers" with their sales pitches endeavouring to entice business into the various strip joints along the way.

There must have been an American warship in port because of the number of American sailors I noticed strolling along, some arm-in-arm with girls. I would imagine Sydney would become an excellent rest and recreation city as the Vietnam conflict progressed. I passed a "nightclub" looking place that seemed to be rocking along in its crowded bars. It carried the name "Beef Steak and Bourbon Bar." I was sure the well-heeled American servicemen would love that.

I was now level with a park with manicured lawns, trees and a public toilet block; in its centre, it boasted a magnificent water-spraying fountain. It carried the name "EL Alamein" Park. It was a memorial to a historic battle fought in World War II. Looking at some of the human derelicts lying on the grass and park benches and some obvious "ladies of the night" plying their trade, I felt a tinge of sadness for those old "diggers" who fought and died in that battle and wondered how they would feel if they could see this now tainted memorial to their valour.

I decided to cross the road and wander down the other side, a short distance and soon was standing outside a multistoried hotel named the "Chevron Hilton." There was a colourful uniformed fellow with a gold braided officer-type cap standing at the entrance, hailing taxis and opening and shutting doors for patrons. He carried a silver whistle around his neck, and with a piercing blast, he saw a taxi come sidling to the curb to pick up a customer. His gold braided uniform reminded me of a picture I once saw of a South American dictator, in all of his self-appointed supreme commander military finery, with row upon row of decorations, very ostentatious and a little ridiculous, particularly in the summer heat of Sydney. Near the entrance and to one side, I could see through the windows that it was a rather plush-looking bar. Being a warm summer night, I had worked up a thirst and thought I would go in for a drink.

There, I met Melissa. I had settled on a stool at the bar and ordered a glass of beer. The first shock came when I tendered a ten-dollar bill, and no change came back. Ten dollars for a 15 oz glass of beer. Bloody hell! Inflation was certainly rife in this city.

The second shock came when a very attractive and elegantly dressed young woman sitting a couple of bar stools along the bar from me looked my way and smiled. I looked around behind me, puzzled. Was she really smiling at me? I smiled back and raised my glass in the form of a salute, and in the next instant, she was on the stool beside me. She was carrying a low-rimmed glass with a creamy chocolate-coloured liquid in it.

Her perfume flowed over me as she breathed out sensually, "Hi, I'm Melissa." Leaning provocatively forward, she extended a slender, manicured hand. It took all of my willpower to lift my eyes from her perfect half-exposed breasts to meet her eyes looking intently at me, eyes that were a rich jade green. At that moment, the country boy in me took over as I blurted out, "Sean! Sean Molloy!" Her smile widened as she said, "What a lovely-sounding name. Is it Irish?" "Yes. From my grandparents," I replied.

The next hour passed in a perfumed haze and about sixty dollars in cocktails and beer. In that time, she had learnt about where I had grown up, my military career, name and rank, my time in Vietnam, my battle injuries, and my breaking up with Angie, why, how and the sadness. Wow! Talk about having verbal diarrhoea. I felt like a schoolboy on a first date. In that time, all that I learnt about her was that she was twenty-six years old, worked in the hospitality industry, owned a home unit overlooking Bondi Beach, and loved to surf, then came the shock of the night when she leaned in close to me, with our faces no more than a few inches apart, and looking me squarely in the eyes said softly, "Sean, would you like to sleep with me?"

Then it suddenly hit me: the puzzle of this chance meeting fell into place. This Darling River country boy was learning fast. The hospitality industry simply meant she was a high-class hooker, and this bar was where she plied her trade. The massive disappointment I first felt in foolishly thinking she had been seriously interested in me was slightly offset by no! It was mainly offset by the erotic thoughts I was feeling in her presence. But how much would a night with this beauty cost? At this stage, I still had a considerable amount of money locked away in a Travelodge safe, but I had no idea how much money this gorgeous girl would want.

She must have read the question in my eyes because, taking my hands in hers, she said, "Sean, I like you. You seem different to most men, and you can have all of me for only four hundred dollars for the night." At that moment, my thoughts flashed back to my first night with Angie and her similar words when she said, "Sean, you are not like other men." That did it. I was hooked. We walked outside where the doorman, with a knowing glance at us, whistled up a taxi. Because most of my money was in the safe, she agreed to stay at the Travelodge motel with me.

Back in my room at the motel, we kissed. I then hurriedly and clumsily undressed, leaving my clothes in an untidy heap on the floor. I lay on the bed with an impressive erection as I watched her undress in a manner that would make a striptease dancer green with envy.

Holy Christ, she was beautiful, and when she came to me, everything else in my life, past love and all, faded into oblivion, as I felt her warm lips and fingers caress my body. That night passed in the most intense, erotic and sensual night of gratifying sex that a man could wish for, but there was more to it than that. The first glimmer of dawn light was coming through the window as we lay entwined, our damp bodies temporarily sated and feeling the beautiful exhaustion that comes from prolonged lovemaking.

Melissa suddenly rolled her moist body over mine and, bracing herself on her elbows, and with a furrowed brow, looked deep and quizzically into my eyes for a long moment. Looking at her, I enquired, "What?" There was no reply as she rolled over to my side and snuggled her warmth close alongside me. She was still staring, though with a most thoughtful look on her pretty face.

Lying with one arm folded under her head, she reached over my chest with her free hand and started to stroke her long fingers gently down the side of my face, yet still looking at me in this intense manner. I was now intrigued by her stare and her non-reply to my question, and I asked again, "What is it, Melissa? Is there something wrong?" She said, "No, nothing wrong, but Sean, there is something I want to say. Something I want you to believe, so please hear me out. I only do this on an average once each month. Sometimes two months to supplement the income I earn as a hotel receptionist; it enables me to live a better quality of life and own a reasonable home unit of my own. Sydney is an expensive city to live in." She went on to say, "I was married young to my first love and divorced. It happened within six months in Brisbane about two years ago. I have no regular boyfriend and have not had the desire to have one. My parents still live on the Gold Coast in Queensland." She paused to take a deep breath, "I was shattered by my marriage breakup with the man I had loved and trusted dearly and then found he was having an affair with another woman. After the divorce, I decided to come to Sydney to get over it. I am not trying to make excuses for what I do. I see it as pure survival, and I am very careful about who I take as a customer. The Chevron is the only place I frequent, and Eddie, behind the bar, looks after me. Eddie is gay and has a finger on the pulse of everything, who and what happens in the hotel. He tells me what well-heeled businessmen and overseas visitors are staying in the hotel. He checks them out first over the bar for their attitude and manners and then refers them to me. If I find them suitable, I pay Eddie a small percentage," adding, "I usually charge seven hundred dollars for the night."

"You might wonder why I am telling you all this, but when I saw you come into the bar, you somehow looked different, and then when I spoke with you for a while, I knew you were a decent man." She paused. "You were natural, definitely not city worldly, and there is an underlying quality to you that I liked." She stopped talking, silent for about a minute. "Sean, I have never said this to anyone before, but if you like me and wish to keep in touch, I will give you my address and telephone number."

I had listened intently to her words and, for an answer, took her into my arms, held the warmth of her tanned nakedness tight to me and said, "Melissa, I would dearly love to know you more." Rising over her, I plunged once more deeply into the abyss of rapturous passion and so started a loving friendship with Melissa.

CHAPTER 21

Magic with Melissa

We showered together, soaping each other over and giggling like a pair of school kids, and then we dressed and went down to the reception, where I got some cash out of the motel safe. Later, in the car, I handed it over to her. Holding it in her hand, she looked at it, and then at me, and said, "Sean, that is the last time you will ever pay me money. You and I are going to have a wonderful night somewhere with it." Melissa was due to start work doing a night shift at an inner-city hotel at 3 p.m., so there was time to drive her to her beach unit to change and then bring her back to the city to work, and we managed to make love again. The magic of loving feelings was starting to weave through my life once more.

It was Monday, and we made arrangements to meet for breakfast at 10 a.m. on Tuesday and again for dinner on Thursday night as she started back on the day shift on that day. I went back to the Travelodge and fell into a deep sleep for most of the day.

When I awoke, I lay there for a while thinking over the blissful night's events and rolling over, I spotted the card that Anthony Lawrence QC had given me sitting by the phone on the bedside table. I decided to give him a call and enquire as to their health. Glancing at my watch, it was a bit before 5 p.m. The number quickly answered, and a very professional business voice answered, "Lawrence and associates. Eleanor speaking". I asked for Anthony Lawrence to be told that "Mr. Lawrence was at home ill. Would I care to leave a message?" I declined, thanked her, and hung up.

His home number was on the card, and his wife, Genevieve, answered the phone. When I told her who I was, her greeting was warm and friendly over the phone, "Oh Sean, thank you so much for calling. And thank you so much for what you did for us. Please hold the line. Anthony wants very much to talk to you. He is just a little slow hobbling to the phone, the poor dear. There was a few moments' silence, and then a male voice boomed over the phone. I could feel the smile in the voice that said, "Sean Molloy."

"My wife and I can never thank you enough for saving us from those louts on Sunday. I can assure you they will be getting what they deserve when they appear in court. The particular judge on the case is a friend of ours. It seems they belong to a gang of bag snatchers, thieves, and muggers who have been operating around the Sydney Rocks area for some time." I interrupted his flow to enquire about how he was feeling. He assured me that apart from sore and bruised ribs and a nasty cut to the side of his nose that required a stitch, it was not broken, just sore and bruised, and laughingly said, "I'm sure those thugs are feeling much more pain than I." He went on to say that after some interrogation of them by detectives, one of them gave up on the gang, and a police raid uncovered an Aladdin's cave of stolen goods. Thanks to you, many of the owners will receive some things back. They are still being held by the police, and two of them are painfully nursing their injuries under police guard in hospital.

After he had finished telling me all this, I managed to get a word in and asked about his wife's health. He said that "it took Genevieve some time to recover and stop shaking from the trauma of the ordeal," saying, "she had never experienced any form of violence in her life before, whereas I had been a rugby union player in high school and university and had always been involved in physical contact sports."

Anthony asked me where I was staying in Sydney, and when I told him, he said that it was only a short distance from their home in Rose Bay. He added they had a spare guest room, and I would be welcome to stay there for the duration of my visit. I thankfully declined that offer, saying I was not totally sure of my future movements. He went on to say that on the following weekend, on Saturday, they were having a group of friends over for a poolside BBQ, and they would like me to be a guest at this function, adding he had told a few friends and family about me and they would like to meet me.

Although a bit embarrassed by this, I thought I would like to attend, and so I replied in the affirmative and said, "I have a female friend in Sydney. Would it be okay if I brought her along too?" He warmly replied, "That would be wonderful. We would love to meet her." He added, "We have a large house with plenty of room. Please stay the night with us if you wish so as not to drive home after a few drinks and bring your swimwear."

Writing down their address, I decided to broach the subject with Melissa the next day at our 10 a.m. breakfast meeting back in the Travelodge motel restaurant. She said she would be very happy to go with me. With our morning appetite for food appeased, we were holding hands over the table with conversation flowing easily, when it came to an abrupt end, and we found ourselves looking deep into each other's eyes, and our hands tightened on each other as she softly voiced the words that I had been thinking, "I want you."

Without another word, we rose and walked hand in hand to the cashier, then onto the elevator, passionately kissing and touching on our way up the various levels to my floor and the short walk to my room. It was only 11 a.m., and she did not have to start work until 3 p.m. A magic few hours now lay in front of us.

Melissa had made a reservation at the exclusive Rock Pool Restaurant at the "Rocks" for our Thursday night date. That night, we wined and dined to a sumptuous candlelight dinner, which Melissa insisted on paying for. At first, I hesitated, and then I cheekily smiled and agreed to it, knowing where the money had come from. After dinner, we strolled through the "Rocks" area. When we approached the area of parkland around the southern bridge pylon, I could not help my senses coming onto high alert, but nothing happened, and no one bothered us.

How strange it is how one's life and attitudes can change so dramatically. Just a few days ago, I was surprised and a little shocked to learn of Melissa's occasional nocturnal life. Now, driving back to my room at the Travelodge, listening to her bubbling and infectious humour and wit, it was as if she had never told me. It did not matter; I did not care. All I saw was a very likeable and lovable person, a survivor of circumstances. I was driving past the Mitchell Library, planning to drive down through Woolloomooloo, along the waterfront past Garden Island Naval Base, and then up Macleay Street to the Travelodge, when she squeezed my arm and said, "Sean, let's not go to the motel, let's go through to Darlinghurst

Road, and I will show you the way to my home unit, I want you to be there with me tonight."

The next day, when Melissa left for work, I drove to King's Cross, checked out of the Travelodge motel, and drove back to my new abode overlooking Bondi Beach.

My life now seemed so right except for the nagging worry in the back of my mind that soon I had to report back to the Military at Holds Worthy camp. I was still an active service member of the "Special Forces" Australian Military, and yet Vietnam and its wars were like a distant memory from a million years away.

I decided to put a call through to Geoff Truso in Saigon and to Captain Henderson. It was a long time before I got through to Geoff to be told Captain Henderson was out on a mission somewhere in the Central Highlands. He said that my replacement officer was doing well with the Montagnard Militia and that another captain would replace Captain Henderson in about three months' time. It's funny, I now felt quite relieved when told that all was running along well over there without me and realised I did not feel the need to go back there again.

Melissa had the weekend off work, and early Saturday morning, as the sun was coming up on the horizon, we went for a jog along the beach, followed by a swim. I was a strong swimmer, but surfing was something new to me and I was soon having a ball of a time with Melissa, surfing the waves on the two rubber surf floats we had hired.

I marvelled at Melissa's tanned bikini-clad body surfing on the waves, and I must say with a small measure of male pride, noticing the many, not-so-sly approving glances from other male surfers.

Right at this moment, life was good, with my military life put completely away into the background of my mind.

The BBQ invitation was for a 2 p.m. start at Anthony and Genevieve's house at Rose Bay, and it was only 10 a.m. and a beautiful, warm day. Using the beachside showers, we put on clothes over our still-damp swimmers and walked to one of the many beachside cafes along the main street fronting the Bondi Esplanade for an enjoyable light brunch. This was followed by a visit to a hotel bottle shop to purchase some good vintage wines to present to Anthony and Genevieve.

Hand in hand, with a carry bag of liquor in the other, we walked back to Melissa's two-bedroom unit with its balcony view over the beach and ocean. We both had a happy gleam in our eyes, knowing we still had time for a couple of sensual hours together before we had to leave.

Public transport being what it was from Bondi Beach to the city. Melissa had not found the need to purchase a car, although she said she could drive. I caught my breath when Melissa appeared wearing a low-cut, shimmering yellow and blue floral dress that accentuated her tan and her perfectly formed breasts and curves of her body. The dress went down almost to her shapely ankles, which sporting fashionable Italian sandals, she said.

Her long, thick strawberry blonde hair was held back in a ponytail by a colourful band. It was a style that accentuated her petite nose and fine facial features. Above one ear, she was wearing a flower pinned to her hair. She was wearing the same exotic perfume from our first night together, and again, I experienced that heady feeling. Exhaling a loud, indrawn breath, I simply said, "You are beautiful!" and it must have been the tone in which I said it that had her suddenly in my arms, with her gorgeous lipsticked smile, hovering just an inch from my mouth. Then she had to go to a mirror to redo the lipstick, as I wiped it off my lips.

Armed with my trusty Gregory's Street directory, we set off in the new Holden to find the Lawrence house in Rose Bay. Melissa was the appointed navigator; we had left at close to 2 p.m. and soon found ourselves outside a very large two-story old federation-style home, with what seemed to be enormous-sized grounds on both sides of the house and going around the back. Melissa told me that was the style of the "nouveau riche" homes of the 1920s; the grounds and gardens were superbly manicured.

There were a number of sleek motor vehicles, including a Rolls Royce and a Ferrari, parked along the tree-lined footpath. I mused on the fact that Anthony Lawrence had some seriously wealthy friends. Finding a shady spot to park the Holden, we debated whether to go to the front entrance and ring the bell or wander down the side to the back of the house from where we could hear the sound of voices and laughter.

Deciding on the front entrance, we pressed the button on the large, round, ornate brass plate on the wall. We could hear a gong sound deep within the depths of the house. About a minute went by when Genevieve opened the large embossed timber door, and with a loud, happy cry of greeting, she welcomed us in. Clutching our now gift-wrapped bottles of wine and a hold-all bag with a change of underwear and our swimwear in it, we stepped into the foyer of this huge old house with its heavy solid timber furnishings from over a century ago. I introduced Melissa and noticed Genevieve looking closely at her; I hoped with a look of approval. A woman thing, I thought. I had already learnt that beautiful women always assess other beautiful women.

Genevieve looked elegant in what Melissa described later as a plum-coloured hostess gown with a string of pearls resting on her ample, shapely bosom. She warmly led us through the house to a beautiful outdoor setting, where already about twenty people of various ages were assembled, some seated, some standing, and all were chattering away with a drink in their hands.

A booming voice suddenly sounded above the chatter. It was Anthony Lawrence, calling everyone to attention. "Hello, everybody. Here is the man I have been telling you about. I want you to meet Sean Molloy." As he stepped away from the small crowd, he was leaning slightly on a walking stick to walk towards us, and a white-jacketed waiter standing by reached over to relieve us of the gift bottles we were carrying. Anthony stood by for a moment and then reached for my hand, shaking it vigorously, at the same time saying, "Thank you for coming, Sean. All our friends here are anxious to meet you." I could see by the quizzical look on Melissa's face she was wondering what he was talking about, as I had not told her about the confrontation under the Harbour Bridge.

Turning towards Melissa, with all the charm of a veteran barrister in front of a jury, he slightly bowed and said, "Sean, you must introduce me to this gorgeous girl with you." The next thing, Anthony was steering us around his friends, introducing us and making comments like "Here is the man who saved the day" Melissa was puzzled; her curiosity was aroused. Melissa jabbed me gently in the ribs and said, "What did you do?"

At this comment heard by Anthony, he said, a little startled, "You don't know," and looked at me with a look of "Have I stepped out of line?" I answered his look with "No, it's okay," and apologetically looking at Melissa, said, "It did not come up in our conversations." With that cheeky grin I had come to know, she looked at me and said, "Well, someone better tell me now. I want to know."

I felt myself squirming with embarrassment as Anthony, with an okay nod from me and an introduction of Melissa and me to the entire assembled crowd, now intently looking in our direction, started to launch into a blow-by-blow expose of that Sunday's events under the Sydney Harbour Bridge. By the time he got to the injury toll of the four thugs who had attacked him and Genevieve after their arrest and hospitalisation, the others were looking at me with wide-eyed amazement. I found myself almost sheepishly explaining that it was only my military training that helped save the day.

Throughout all of this, I had noticed one man, a very big man, standing with an elegant, attractive woman I guessed to be in her mid-forties. He had a piercing stare and never took his eyes away from me as Anthony Lawrence QC enthralled his audience with the story of how I single-handedly saved him and his wife from a terrible fate. It was obvious to me that his elocution and style of delivery would be brilliant in front of a jury, determining the fate of someone in court.

Talk about embarrassed: I felt my face flush through my deep tan from the neck up, and catching the eye of the waiter, who was also listening with interest, I reached for my second beer with my free hand. Melissa so tightly held the other one, she squeezed it hard enough to almost hurt, as Anthony placed some emphasis on an aspect of the attack.

At last, it was over to much applause and complimentary comments, particularly from the ladies. Melissa was looking at me with wide, shining eyes. It was then I noticed the big man who was staring at me move with his partner to be alongside Anthony. He said something to his lady and then moved a short distance away from the group with Anthony. They stood for a moment talking and then walked outside of the undercover entertainment room and out into the spacious grounds.

I did not notice them come back into the room as Melissa and I were now surrounded by a number of questioning people, all wanting to know more about us. We had previously decided that to answer any questions about our relationship, was that we were old friends from Brisbane who had renewed a friendship when I arrived in Sydney.

I was relieved when Anthony interrupted the flow of conversation, asking if he could speak with me for a moment, excusing us to Melissa, and we left her to be the centre of attention to an admiring band of women and men. I left feeling confident that she could hold her own amongst this well-groomed Sydney social set.

Anthony led me over to the bar, where the big man was now standing alone. I noticed his lady had joined the group surrounding Melissa. Nearby the bar, a man wearing a chef's outfit and cap was preparing to start cooking on a large, elaborate type of BBQ range.

Facing this big, friendly-looking man, I found myself looking upward to maintain eye contact as we were introduced. I estimated he was at least six feet six inches in height, with huge shoulders and chest, and yet not fat. I could feel an aura of strength to the man as Anthony introduced me to Jonathan James Strong, commonly known to his friends as "JJ."

Anthony had said that "JJ" had wanted to meet me; he then slipped behind the bar to pour us another drink. We all switched to a scotch and soda. Anthony suggested we go outside onto the grounds. He led us into a tree-shaded gazebo, where we sat down to talk.

The conversation started with Anthony explaining "JJ's" background as a criminal barrister. Then it turned to questions about my military career and my time in Vietnam, my thoughts on that war, and our involvement in it. Of course, there was much that was still secret. I could not disclose at that stage, but I could enlighten them on my work to a degree as a military training adviser to an indigenous militia in Malaya and Vietnam.

They were particularly interested in the type of training that I had undergone, particularly in the martial arts and unarmed combat part of it. About a half hour of conversation went past when a dinner bell rang. Anthony made a move to leave when "JJ" touched me on the arm, saying, "Sean, I would like to renew this conversation later." I nodded agreement and said, "That would be fine," as we reentered the dining area to take our places at the long table that was set for eating.

It was obvious by the look on Melissa's face that she was having a good time being the centre of attention of an admiring bunch of males and females. She opened her arms wide to hug me as I walked towards her. Anthony and Genevieve were seated at each end of the long table. On Anthony's right was seated an elegant lady, Eleanor, who was "JJ's" partner, and "JJ." On his left were Melissa and me. Over the long and delicious three-course meal served by the waiter and the chef now turned waiter, the scintillating conversation on all subjects fluctuated up and down the table with much banter and humour. It was easy to see that there was a group of people well-known and friendly to each other, and we had been recognised as guests of honour. It had been a hot and humid day, and the noise and laughter of the group were getting louder as the wine and other drinks flowed. The table was now being cleared of the plates and remnants of food.

Someone loudly suggested that a swim would go down well. The warmth of the afternoon sun made the large swimming pool look inviting. Anthony had already informed us to bring some swimwear, so with Genevieve leading the way, Melissa and I were shown to a bedroom to change, with Genevieve saying, "This is your room for your stay here," adding, "It was our daughter's room before she went overseas after finishing university studying forensic archaeology. It had elegant furnishings and an inviting king-size bed. Wonderful, I thought!"

Stripping off our clothes, we looked at each other's tanned nakedness and the whiter areas normally covered by swimwear, and our eyes told each other why not? As we reached for each other, our passions aroused once more. A cool swim would be excellent later. The faint noises of voices and laughter abated as we lost ourselves in the consuming fire of our orgasms. Twenty minutes later, we were in the large pool with at least a dozen others tossing a huge beach ball around to each other.

Later, sitting on deckchairs around the poolside sipping a drink, Melissa had got into an animated conversation about things that were dear to women such as fashions and the sort of things women like to talk about. Anthony was in some sort of political discussion about Australia sending troops to Vietnam when "JJ" detached himself from the group and sat down beside me. He started the conversation by saying, "Sean, I'm intrigued by your background. Please excuse me for saying this, but I and others could not help but notice the scars you have on your body. My experience as a criminal lawyer indicates to me they are bullet wounds. Is that so?" I replied in the affirmative, "that they were". Melissa had also asked me the same question when we first were together.

"Would you mind if I ask you what it is really like over there?" Again, I had to be careful how I answered, but that evening, our conversation opened the door to further discussions when JJ nominated a meeting to be held further down the track. Before "JJ" left that night, he gave me his business card and a request to have lunch with him, to whom I agreed; I gave him Melissa's phone number, which he said he would call in the next couple of days.

It was Wednesday, about midday. I was just about to walk out the door when the phone rang. Mellissa was working day shifts this week, and I was meeting her in the city to have lunch at her favourite café. It was "JJ". He asked "if it would be okay to meet to have lunch with him tomorrow at 1 p.m. I said that would be okay". "He said he would make a reservation at the Rose Bay Golf Club, and could I meet him there?" I knew where it was. Melissa had pointed it out to me when we went to Anthony Lawrence's house, which was nearby.

I felt a little intrigued by "JJ's" wanting to meet me. Ah, well, it did not really matter. He was a nice sort of bloke, and I found his manner of speech interesting. Perhaps he really did have a strong interest in the growing Vietnamese conflict and military matters.

On the lunch date with Melissa, I told her about his phone call and "JJ's" wanting to meet me. She was not so puzzled and said, "I got the impression at the BBQ when we were sitting at the table and later around the pool that he really liked you and was impressed with what you did for Anthony and Genevieve, as were all of us, it is obvious that he is very close to them," and went on to tell me Genevieve said that she and Anthony were friends with JJ's wife Jane, who had died in childbirth, they had all grown up together as friends. Anthony and "JJ" had gone to high school together and later attended the same university studying law. She said "they were more like brothers than friends" I guessed that explained it. This was "JJ's" way of saying thanks for saving two dear friends from serious injury or worse. Whatever, I was looking forward to my meeting with him tomorrow.

The next morning at dawn, Melissa and I got out of bed for what had become our daily ritual of a brisk jog along the hard sand of the beach, followed by a plunge into the surf and a light breakfast at an esplanade café, then back home for a hot shower together, with a little tickle giggle and lovemaking thrown in. In a short time, she would be dressed, looking the perfectly groomed, attractive receptionist. Although I always offered to drive her to work, she would insist on catching a bus each morning, saying it was easier than me driving through the thick traffic each day.

About 9:30 a.m., I headed to Bondi Junction, where I had found a small gymnasium to join. I started working out each morning for a couple of hours. It was a typical boxer's gymnasium, and I soon found myself in the ring with the "pillows" on, sparring with an aspiring young boxer. It was great. Along with the shadow sparring, rope skipping, the speed ball and punching the heavy bag, I found myself getting harder and fitter. Melissa thought my getting fit was great too, but in a more personal way.

Arriving back at the unit, it was about 11:45 and time for a quick change, then drive to the Rose Bay Golf Club. Checking the mailbox on my way out, there was an official AMF envelope in the box, along with some junk mail. I had previously given Melissa's address to the Military Headquarters as my place of abode in Sydney. Stuffing the envelope into my jacket pocket, I jumped into the car and drove off to my lunch appointment with "JJ."

"JJ" was already there at the table waiting as I checked in at the reception and then walked into the restaurant area. He was all smiles as he stood up to welcome me. Funny, it felt like I was meeting an old friend. We ordered a large cold Toohey's beer and were soon into conversation, first about the excellent BBQ and the people at Anthony and Genevieve's house that Melissa and I had met; he touched lightly on how impressed people were with Melissa and me on that day. Again, being a little embarrassed, I was happy to let that subject lapse.

The conversation then turned to my time in the Army and what led me to my choice of career and the promotion to Malaya and Vietnam. I thought, what the hell! I've got nothing to hide, and over an excellent rare steak lunch followed by a few more drinks, I filled him in on my family background, my life along the Darling River, my time as a jackeroo, and my promotion to head stockman. I described to him my call up into the Army and how much I liked the life. I felt there was nothing too secretive about my work training the Montagnard Hill tribes to fight the Viet Cong, but at that stage, I said nothing about Australian involvement with the American CIA.

He seemed particularly interested as I described how my job was to train these primitive tribe's people on how to use modern weapons and the arts and skills involved in hand-to-hand combat. He only interrupted once to remark on how his friend Anthony had never seen anything like how I had handled the four thugs. I told of the pride the Militia had shown when they were given their "tiger knives" and how eager they were to get out into the jungle to use them with their newfound skills. "JJ" interrupted here with a direct question. Had I used such a knife to kill a man? Looking squarely at him, I said yes and briefly described the night we covertly stole into a Viet Cong and NVA camp and wiped them out, adding how that

Viet Cong squad had ruthlessly slaughtered a village of innocent people.

For some time, "JJ" sat there quietly contemplating what I had told him, or so I thought when he looked up at me and said, "The horrors perpetrated by some people on others sicken me. How do you feel about that?" I readily agreed, having already mentioned my father's brutality and his demise. Perhaps it was the alcohol that had loosened my tongue a little. I was never much of a drinker, and so I added, "Although alien to my true nature, which is basically a caring type, I found a certain pleasure in killing those who I believed deserved to die for their excessive brutality."

At that, "JJ" looked at his watch and said, "Sean, this has been a real pleasure to meet and talk with you, and I am hoping we can do it again. I have one more question: are you planning to stay in the army?" That threw me for a loop. What was he getting at?

I replied, "It's coincidental that you mention that. In fact, I have been considering the possibility of resigning my commission and going back into civilian life. But first, I would have to figure out what I could do. As much as I love the Army life, my time in Vietnam and Malaya and being wounded twice has had me thinking twice about going back. I believe it is going to be one hell of a long and nasty war over there." I have to figure out what I can do. My only skills achieved are from my work as a stockman and what the army trained me to do.

Again, there was a contemplative silence, except this time, he just sat there, looking directly at me before speaking. "Sean, for some time now, I have had the need to employ the right type of person for specialised work. I am looking for a man who can be trusted and who can hold his cards close to his chest. He has to be resourceful, tough, and capable of using initiative and decisiveness when needed and be able to think things through before making a decision. I believe your training and your personal nature make you suitable for that position."

He stopped speaking for a moment, then went on to say, "I am going to leave it there. I must leave now for a meeting at my office. Think it over, and if you are interested, give me a call on this number. It is my personal and direct line." He was writing on the back of a business card as he spoke. "Thank you for having lunch with me. It has been a real pleasure meeting and talking with you."

I was pulling my wallet out of my hip pocket to get money and to put the card back in when "JJ" said, "Don't worry about that. I have already arranged for the club to put the lunch on my account. Keep in touch, Sean," with that, he got up and walked away. I sat there for a while, thinking over what he had said.

Specialised work, whatever did that mean? There was no doubt that I was interested. I was very curious, and with that thought, I remembered Angus telling me of Uncle Charlie's vision and words when we were on the train bound for Sydney, what seemed to be many years ago. Angus had said Uncle Charlie spoke in the dialect of the Barkandji people, and said he saw mountains and rivers, strange people and many dangers and to remember all he had taught me to survive and to come back home safe to our land.

Those words were burned into my brain. Yes! I think it was time to come home. There were also visions of Melissa floating around amongst all of my thoughts.

Remembering the official military envelope in my jacket pocket, I reached for it and opened it to read. It was what I had been expecting for a while. It was a directive to report in one week to Special Operational Command at Holsworthy base camp near

Liverpool in uniform for further instructions; I decided to drive there first thing in the morning. My mind was made up. I was going to resign my commission.

That night, Melissa and I talked for hours about my meeting with "JJ" and his job offer. She said she was happy about me thinking of resigning from the army, but only if I felt it was the right thing to do, adding, "I would be worried sick if you were to go back to Vietnam."

That night, lying in my arms, she suddenly brought up the subject of how we had met. It was something that had not come up again in conversation after that night. The memory of that business transaction and a splendidly sexual night was still in the recesses of my mind, but I had brushed it into the "not to be remembered section", preferring to relive the many wonderful days and nights since. I knew why. My feelings for Melissa were getting stronger, and I did not want to think of her having had sex with other men. I wanted to feel she was now my woman and mine alone and know she would never again pursue her previous activities. I felt her body heave a little, followed by a sobbing intake of breath. At the same time, a wet tear trickled down my arm that her pretty face was lying on. Startled, I turned my head to look at her. She was crying, "What is it? What is it that is making you cry?" And in sobbing gasps, she blurted out, "Sean, oh Sean, I am so sorry about how we met, but not that we have met. I am falling in love with you, and I cannot bear the thought of you going away. I never want another man in my life. I truly love you." I pulled her to me, held her tight, and gave her heartfelt assurances that I felt the same.

That did it. From that moment, my decision was set in concrete. There was no way that I was going back to Vietnam. Pulling her warm, sobbing body even tighter to me, it was my turn to speak.

"Melissa, my darling, I am also falling in love with you, and I want to be in your life. I am not sure how hard it will be to resign my commission in the Army, but I am certainly going to try, and if I am successful, I will speak with JJ and find out more about his job offer."

For whatever reason, our lovemaking that night took on a new dimension, with a depth of feeling even greater than before. The whole night was spent kissing, touching, and loving every part of each other's body. How wonderful it is what love can do to one's emotional peace of mind.

CHAPTER 22

Back to Civilian Life

After JJ had offered me the opportunity of my unique line of work, it had not been easy to resign from the Army in this time of military awareness, and the conflict in Vietnam; I had to go through many channels and interviews. I think the only thing that ended it and helped me to leave the army was my former exemplary record and the serious nature of my war injuries. I was even sent for a final interview with the Director General of ASIS, Major General Sir Anthony Cartbury. After extremely strong questioning as to my reasons, he just nodded his head and asked "if there was any way he could induce me to stay in the service." I just simply said "no".

With that, he said, "Then it is my duty to inform you that you will still be bound by the military secrets act, and should you at any time be found guilty in the supply of top secret military information, you will be punished to the fullest extent of the law," at the same time pushing forward toward me an official legal document to sign.

He then extended his best wishes for whatever career path I chose to follow and shookay my hand. It was over; I was out with an honourable military discharge, a military medal, two now-healed bullet wounds, and a healthy sum of deferred pay.

Throughout the whole six weeks that it tookay to finally get my discharge papers, I kept in touch with "JJ", Eleanor, Anthony, and Genevieve. They had become like family to Melissa and me.

"JJ" had said that he would talk in detail and introduce me to my new position when my final discharge came through. I must admit the mystery of this "specialised position" had me a little worried as to whether I could handle the job. "JJ" assured me I would have no trouble learning and fitting into the position. He was convinced that I had the right attitude for it.

In an endeavour to annul any doubts I may have, he outlined to me that he owned or was in partnership with a number of businesses, some of them were in partnership with Anthony Lawrence and what he required for these businesses was a troubleshooter, a Mr. Fix-It. Someone who could be trained to go to that business, oversee its operation and, based on observation, confer with "JJ" and make the decisions needed to fix the problem. I reasoned that it did not sound too hard.

Melissa was overjoyed at the news that her "war hero", as she was prone to call me in loving moments, would not have to go back to Vietnam.

I must admit, though, there were times when I felt I had "let the side down" and truly missed Captain Henderson, Geoff Truro, and all of my Montagnard Militia. I had still kept in touch with Truso and Henderson, who kept me updated, within reason that is, on the fluctuations of that terrible war, which seemed to be escalating more each month, and with a larger number of body bags being sent back regularly to the USA, carrying the remains of fine young men who had lost their lives fighting for their country and its anti-communist cause. Both Captain Henderson and Geoff Truro had both expressed their disappointment at my non-return, but still wished me well. Military censorship being what it was, they could not tell me what exactly was going on, but reading between the lines, it was reasonable to assume that the Americans were losing the war in most areas because of their incorrect and often outmoded approach to what should be a jungle guerilla warfare.

Wherever Australian Special Operations military advisers were, they were having better results with their smaller and more manoeuvrable fighting groups based on the hit-and-run theory.

I wondered what would happen to the Montagnard tribes if the communist insurgents eventually tookay over their country, and years later, I was horrified to learn that after the fall of Saigon and the withdrawal of all allied military forces, the NVA, Viet Cong, and Chinese communist forces ruthlessly burned hundreds of villages and murdered thousands of Montagnard villagers in their reprisal raids for taking part in the fight against communism. I seethed with anger at this brutality and felt helpless that I could not help my hill tribe friends. All the promises of the Americans, the CIA, and allied forces to help the Montagnard Tribes people gain autonomy in their own country or repatriate them from this ethnic extermination did not eventuate.

For all they did for us, the most fiercely independent, freedom-loving people that they were left to submit to their new masters or die. Many died.

It was 7 a.m. on the Monday that "JJ" met me outside Melissa's unit and tookay me to his office for an in-depth discussion on my new position. Melissa was as eager as I was to learn more about the new job. This was my first introduction to his way of life. On our arrival at his Double Bay address, I was amazed at the up-to-date security he employed. First, he explained the lift and stairs set up for entry to the offices above from the parking area in the basement. We then stepped into what he called the workers' lift to be taken to the ground floor to introduce me around as a new employee.

We then went back down to the basement to step into the code-operated lift through to what he called the "inner sanctum". He showed me the code-operated pad on the wall outside the lift and said only his most trusted people knew that code. Anyone else requiring entry had to use the wall phone for the lift to be operated from the "inner sanctum", or if on general business for legal matters, they would use the other lift to the ground floor.

He then tapped a series of numbers onto the code pad, and we stepped into the private lift. He said the code was changed each month, and I would have to memorise each change. Stepping out of the lift on the next floor, there working at a desk surrounded by an incredible array of up-to-date electronic equipment. As "JJ" was explaining all the apparatus, a low alarm sounded, and a few moments later, the lift door opened, and I had my first introduction to Edith. She was a remarkable and impressive middle-aged lady. I instinctively liked her and her direct way of talking: she said she was looking forward to working with me. "JJ" told me later that Edith was as reliable as a Swiss watch. He said she was always the first of his staff to start work at 8 a.m. when she would switch on all the necessary equipment and go through the mail she collected from the mailbox on her way in.

From there, we went back into the lift and up to the penthouse with its magnificent views out over Sydney Harbour. The penthouse was luxuriously furnished, and as "JJ" pointed out, it was completely soundproofed and secure. It was fitted with everything that one would need for a comfortable living. By a huge desk set up to lookay out over the view, there stood a small bar and a couple of bar stools, "JJ" offered me a drink; I declined the alcohol but accepted a soda water. We stood at the expansive window looking down on the harbour, admiring the view and the boats cruising and sailing to and fro across the glistening waterways.

Turning toward me, "JJ" said, "Sean, it's time to get to the 'nitty gritty' of the business and the job I have in mind for you. I have told you a few things about the numerous enterprises operated from here. My main business partner is my friend Anthony Lawrence, and when he told me about you and your unique skills in handling those thugs, I was intrigued and insisted on meeting you. That part was easy because he had already made the decision to invite you to his house for the BBQ.

"It has taken some time for me to decide to open up and tell you exactly what our businesses are and what happens from here, but we must be totally sure about who we employ. I will start by giving you a basic outline.

"First, operating in every major city are gambling casinos. It is only a matter of time before the laws governing gambling are relaxed and they become legal. Right now, it is a bit like the prohibition times of the 1920s and 1930s in America when every crook, thug, and mafia mobster moved in and tookay monopoly over every bar, gambling and drinking joint they could throughout the USA.

"Well, here in Australia, everyone over the age of eighteen can drink alcohol but cannot gamble. And the result is these illegal casinos are a melting pot for the criminal element.

"For example, in Kellett Street, King's Cross, there are a couple of casinos operating, and there are various other gambling joints, including the infamous 'Thommo's' two up school not far from Sydney's Central Station, and behind the façade of a number of respectable nightclubs, there are a number of other gambling places. Our past experiences dealing with criminals and the law have shown us that the majority of the criminal world gambles much of their ill-gotten gains in these casinos and on women and alcohol. Therefore, a lot of inside knowledge of criminal activity comes from these places.

"As you already know, both Anthony and I are very much involved with criminal law, and because of our everyday dealing with criminals and our justice system, we tire of seeing criminals who we know to be guilty escape the justice system through loopholes in the laws and sometimes poor policing or corruption or both.

"We know it is our responsibility to represent, defend, and fight for justice, and when we lose a case because some criminal is found guilty beyond a shadow of a doubt, we are quite pleased. Yet, when we defend someone and know the non-admissible evidence we often have, which we have gained through sound informants and cannot use, allows them to escape justice, quite frankly, it sickens us, and the result is there are quite a few of these bastards roaming free without retribution whatsoever!"

Those last few words were said with considerable loud emphasis and startled me for a moment because those same words, to some extent, summed up my feelings about much of what I had seen in my life as a child at home in Pooncarie and in Malaya and Vietnam. The bullying, brutality, killing of innocents, drug dealing, paedophilia, corrupt and ruthless politicians, and dictatorial leaders of poverty-stricken countries, rich beyond compare from raping their own countries, it all sickened me, but what was this leading to?

"JJ" carried on, but now in a lower controlled tone of voice. "Sean, what I am going to tell you is highly secret and may shock you. It is illegal and, in the eyes of the law in this country, is wrong, but from a moral point of view, Anthony and I, and a few others whose names I will not divulge at this stage, feel that something must be done about this inadequacy.

"And we are not alone. There are a number of people, many in the legal profession, and some businessmen who feel the same way about this sort of thing. With the result, we have taken it upon ourselves to try to find a way to overcome this inadequacy and to find some way of administering punishment designed to meet the crime committed. The more heinous the crime committed, the stronger the punishment needed. I guess to describe it, in a nutshell, would be vigilante justice, illegal, yes, but we feel it completely necessary.

"We have trusted investigators working investigating all manner of criminality and numerous informants throughout the underworld bringing in information on all types of criminal activity. Quite frankly, we are an investigating body and law court, but outside of the law. In addition to us, there are many people who attend court expecting to see justice done to criminals who have raped, molested, murdered, or whatever to their loved ones. They hope to see them receive that justice, but often leave the courts with their illusion of justice shattered by poor policing procedures, weak judgements, non-admissible evidence, smart, in some cases crooked lawyers, etc. The list goes on."

Through various channels, I am occasionally contacted on behalf of these people, who often are well enough financially to conduct their own investigations. We then investigate further, and if these criminals are found guilty without a shadow of a doubt, we would like to see they are punished to the full extent of the crime committed.

By the time "JJ" had finished, I was wide-eyed and open-mouthed. Had I heard him right? There was no doubt about it that his views fitted in very much with mine, but this was private law, more than that, vigilante justice, with shades of the American Wild West, "e stole a 'orse! Let's string 'im up from that tree! That thinking was a bit melodramatic, and I smiled. The funny thing was, I was interested and liking what I was hearing and was wondering where it was going and how I would fit into it all.

"JJ's" words interrupted my thinking. "The bottom line is, we own an illegal casino in Kellett Street. It has its uses as a sounding board on the criminal element. From the denizens of the dark who frequent it, we learn a lot. The money it provides helps to finance the investigative side of our operation, which is supplemented further by a 'fighting fund' contributed by members of the group and other interested parties. It is highly secretive. We hope it will stay that way," and that comment had me thinking of my recent signing of a "secret of information document."

"To sum it up, Sean, based on your ability to handle situations, sum up a problem, make judgements, and your trained leadership skills, we want you to oversee our Kellett Street Casino. Can we count on you to join us?" adding, "You will be well-paid, plus bonuses for performance."

Usually, I like to sum up a situation completely, as I did in the army when training men and planning an ambush. My gut feeling said yes, go for it, but I simply said, "I'm interested. Tell me more", and "JJ" carried on, filling me in on the workings of the business.

"Our manager of the Casino is Mick Kelly, and he is an ex-heavy-weight fighter who got out of the game while his brain was intact. He is a tough bloke, honest, and reliable to our business. He is a good fellow who does not take crap from anyone.

"There are two senior croupiers, Jack Wither and Sam Capelli. They are expert dealers, street-wise, who have seen the seamier side of life and done it tough. Both now have family responsibilities. They are well-paid, and I believe we have their complete loyalties. They oversee and continuously check out our eight casual croupiers, who work on a rotating basis. Our two permanent doormen, Phil Munro and Frank Calhoun, have worked doors at places all over Sydney. Both are tough, capable men who have seen all types come and go. Both are ex-first-grade rugby league footballers and are very fit. They still work out in Ernie McQuillans Gymnasium in Newtown and are good men in a situation. They are not married; both are divorced and have girlfriends. We are closed on Sunday and Monday, and they take turns to work the doors on weeknights. Both of them work on busy Fridays, Saturdays, and nights. They have Sundays and Mondays off.

"We also have a number of casual, fill-in staff for all positions, plus additional casual bar staff, male and female. We rarely suffer from turnover of staff, even though all are aware of it being illegal. I believe we encourage loyalty with big wages, excellent working conditions, paid holidays and bonuses based on turnover, with an added incentive all staff and family members receive gifts at Christmas, adding with a smile, we also enjoy some covert support from a few members of the police force. To top this off, there is an additional perk: I own a seventy-five-foot luxury cruiser, moored near the floating aircraft base at Rose Bay, and on special occasions, such as holiday periods, birthdays and Christmas, I arrange to take staff and families on cruises. Feedback on the information we receive from them tells us they are better looked after than at any other similar establishment. "JJ" then tookay in a deep breath, pausing for a moment before he spoke again:

"Sean, me boy," he said, sounding a bit like a paternal father, maybe godfather, I wryly thought, "you would enjoy all of those benefits plus some extras." Already I was pleased with what he had said, and he need not have added the bit about the extras. My decision had already been made, and I whole-heartedly said, "Count me in. I like the sound of it!"

As "JJ" was talking, I realised what I was missing on leaving Vietnam and the army. It was the excitement of the action and the continuous adventure, the endeavouring to right wrongs, which I now realise in that particular Asian war may never happen. There would always be those who would suffer at the hands of the ruthless. I felt that perhaps now I was on the edge of some sort of self-fulfilment in this new position.

"Yes, 'JJ,'" I said again with more emphasis, "you can count me in. I want to be part of it. When can I start?"

There was no answer. He just leaned over to me and grabbed my right hand, which vanished into the grasp of his massive hand. "Let's shake on it, Sean, and I'll pour us a scotch and soda to seal the deal" He then said, "There is just one more thing to mention: because of the nature of the business as outlined, I repeat myself again, that secrecy is of the essence. No one outside of this room must know the true nature of your work. You will have business cards and documents printed nominating you as an administration executive of our various business concerns. You will be briefed and continually updated on the workings of all our businesses by

Anthony and myself. This will ensure you are knowledgeable if ever questioned."

That little lecture really made me smile. If he only knew the secrecy I was bound to when I was associated with the ASIS, Special Operations, and the CIA. He would not have to be concerned about secrecy. I really enjoyed this cloak-and-dagger stuff going right back to my early days of training. One day, perhaps, when I get to know him and the job better, I might let him know a little. Until then, my lips are sealed tighter than a fish's anus.

It was 9:30 a.m. when I left there, and less than half an hour later, I was back in our unit whirling Melissa around and onto the bed, kissing her and saying between kisses, "I'm an administration executive. Let's do something to celebrate." We were just peeling our clothes off for some celebration sex when the phone rang.

It was "JJ". "Sean, I was just talking to Anthony and telling him the news. He is very happy with it, it was suggested, seeing as it is such a lovely sunny and calm day, that we go down to the cruiser at Rose Bay, which is always kept ready for short-notice trips. We were thinking of heading out through the Sydney Heads and heading north to the Pittwater Basin. There, we can all enjoy a celebration dinner at the Pittwater Yacht Club. It will be just Anthony and Genevieve, Eleanor, and me. You and Melissa, there are more than enough sleeping facilities on the boat to sleep overnight. Tomorrow, we will have a lazy day cruising the Hawkesbury River. What do you say? Can you call in sick for Melissa? I hear there is a dreadful flu going around." I could feel the smile in his voice. "Ring me back if it's OK." He hung up.

I smiled at that. Melissa is so reliable when it comes to her work, but it was no effort to convince her that she needed a break. If this was to be the lead into my new job, I liked it. Two phone calls later, a meeting time at Rose Bay was arranged, and we still had time for a little celebration. There was no doubt about it; I was really starting to enjoy this start to my civilian life.

It was just one o'clock when "JJ" kicked the massive twin Chrysler engines over as Anthony and I cast off the bow and stern lines. We started gliding slowly away from the marina. Out through the numerous moored craft in Rose Bay and out in the Harbour's navigable waterway, soon we were passing Watson's Bay and heading diagonally north through the rugged sandstone headlands of the South and North heads. "JJ" gunned the diesels as we rounded South Head, and soon we were cruising through a low swell at around a steady fifteen knots. In a short time, we were cruising past the beaches and beachside suburbs of Manly, Dee Why, Narrabeen and Newport, with me soaking in the beauty and thinking what a beautiful location on the Australian east coast is Sydney with its northern beach suburbs soon we were approaching Palm Beach now, where seemed to me, more beach and coastal vegetation along this area, particularly as we moved in closer to the stretch of beach leading to the Barrenjoey Lighthouse and headland.

Rounding the tall three hundred-and-fifty-foot sandstone headland, we were soon in the huge Pittwater Basin and cruising much slower through the crowded inner area to our mooring at the yacht club and a night to be remembered at the Pittwater Yacht Club.

It seemed that "JJ", Anthony, their respective wives and the motor Cruiser "Celestial" were well known at the yacht club going by the reception we received from the dock where the diesel tanks were refilled by staff and later in the club's restaurant.

That night, we celebrated and toasted everything we could think of, including my discharge from the army, the saving of Anthony and Genevieve from the nasty brigands, and my new position of administration executive. "What a title, I thoughtfully mused, I wonder what it really means". I was soon to find out.

It was about 10 a.m. the next morning by the time we sleepily roused ourselves, had a light breakfast, then headed away from the dock and out of the Pittwater for the cruise around to Broken Bay and the entrance into the Hawkesbury River. In the distance, we could see an island that "JJ" said was named Lion Island and was soon entering the river for the long run to a small estuary he said was named "Smith Creek."

The night before, "JJ" had arranged for the chef at the yacht club restaurant to pack an ample-sized picnic hamper, along with numerous wines and beers. We soon broached the liquor supplies, with some "nibbles" organised by the girls, who were enjoying the passing scenery.

What an ideal day for cruising, I thought as the engines were slowed a little to safely cruise and enjoy the sights of the Hawkesbury River. "JJ" and Anthony certainly knew these waterways very well. The beautiful river was as calm as a millpond as we cruised up Milson's Passage, and JJ pointed out we were passing the Milson Island Correctional Centre. Did I hear Anthony right? A correctional centre? There were green-clad men standing along its length with fishing rods. There goes one now reeling in a fish. Milson Island looked more to me like a holiday farm than a prison farm.

Opposite, and on our port side, Anthony pointed out the small settlement of Milson's Passage; there would not have been more than twenty old-style cottages centred above and on either side of a ferry wharf. He said that some of them were oyster farmer's homes, and some of them were fishermen's homes. They were people who made their living from the river, along with a sprinkling of holiday homeowners.

Just then, I could hear a succession of male wolf whistles and raucous calls coming from the inmates clad in green lining the island's bank, and they seemed no longer interested in fishing. A glance forward showed us all why. Melissa was standing, long legs slightly apart, at the focs'le, her hands braced on either side on the cruiser's chromed rails and leaning slightly forward. With her long strawberry blonde hair streaming behind her and her tanned, shapely figure, just barely covered by the tiniest white bikini, she resembled a strikingly beautiful carved bronze figurehead. Some of the gestures and words of the inmates were quite rude. "JJ" laughed and said, "Poor buggers, it is the only time they see a woman; it's an all-male prison." We all raised our glasses in a salute to the cheering, whistling, and gesturing inmates as we glided past. Melissa was waving and teasingly blowing kisses. I felt that would really make their day.

We were now coming out of this passage, and there in the near distance, I could see coming toward us on our starboard side a two-storey, white-painted ferry. Anthony said it was the mail and passenger boat, which does a regular mail run-up to the various isolated River settlements because there are no roads into them. It amazed me that these small settlements were so close to Sydney and yet so isolated.

It was right 1 p.m. and lunchtime when we nosed into the beautiful tributary of the river known as Smith's Creek. Coming up slowly to a white-painted mooring buoy, "JJ" had me poised with a boat hookay to catch the floating rope of the buoy. In just a few minutes, we were ready to enjoy our surroundings. Anthony pointed out a nearby white sand beach and announced that "he and

Genevieve were going for a swim". With that, they peeled off everything and, stark naked, clambered over the boat's transom onto the duckboard and dived in.

They were closely followed by "JJ" and Eleanor in the same non-attire. Melissa and I looked at each other in amazement. It was obvious that "skinny dipping" was something they were all quite used to. "What the hell, Melissa? Let's do the same." In an instant, we were all splashing around like a mob of naked kids, laughing at each other's antics.

"JJ" started swimming the short distance to the narrow strip of sand beach, and we all followed. It was obvious by the watermarks that it went underwater on a high tide. The tide was out, and we all stretched out on the warm, damp sand, looking like a small colony of light-coloured seals drying out in the sun.

When I had made the phone call to the Hotel for Mellissa about being temporally ill, no mention was made of when she would return to work, and "JJ" and the others said they were in the clear, so it was unanimously agreed to stay moored here in this little paradise for the night. With a laugh, "JJ" announced that he was hoping this might happen and had arranged for ample food and drink supplies to be put aboard the "Celestial", so we had the rest of the day and night to enjoy, and it was planned to cruise back the next day to the marina at Rose Bay, stopping only for fuel along the way.

After we had swum back to the "Celestial" and clambered aboard, "JJ" called me aside, saying he and Anthony wished to talk with me privately while the girls, now suitably attired in their swimmers, prepared lunch. Grabbing a cold beer each, we stepped outside the main cabin out onto the deck and climbed the steps to the flying bridge to sit on the comfortable deck chairs there. "JJ" pulled his deck chair closer, sitting opposite Anthony and me. He opened the conversation by saying that Anthony had arranged for me to start at the Kellett Street Casino on Thursday afternoon.

"JJ would drive me there for a meeting to start at 3 p.m. There, I would be introduced to the major staff members, and the meeting would be held to discuss various aspects of the business, including a situation that had arisen recently that needed to be looked into. He went on to say we have a private entrance and an undercover parking area also code-operated for security purposes, where you can leave your car safely.

"Anthony and I only enter through this entrance, and outside of trusted staff, we are not known to club patrons. Our private entrance takes us through two heavy steel code-operated security doors and up to the second-floor main office. Again, this area is only accessible by trusted staff, Anthony and me. This area is behind a one-way shatterproof glass window, which allows us to lookay down on the club patrons, all gaming tables, croupiers, and bar staff. The ground floor has a restricted and guarded entrance where only known patrons and associates are admitted. This entrance is controlled by our expert doormen, Munro and Catelli. It is a double door entrance, only opened by electronic means, and with a special cubicle room with an array of photographs of undesirable customers. There is a secret camera that photographs every person who enters the establishment. Unknown persons, young teens, and obvious drunks are definitely not admitted. The whole area is totally soundproofed. The games we offer are "Baccarat", "Roulette", "Mini Baccarat", the American dice game known as "Craps" and "Blackjack". We have six croupiers working these games each night. Your job will be to oversee the lot.

At 3 p.m. that Thursday afternoon my eyes were completely opened to the meaning of "executive administrator". At the meeting,

I was formally introduced to the "most trusted staff" and the innermost workings of the business operation. Summing it up I was to be the floor manager. It seems that all the staff present had been wised up to my arrival, and from the greetings, they seemed pleased to meet me. However, I did notice some wary glances from time to time, a sort of "sizing me up, one could say," particularly from the manager, who was introduced as Mick Kelly and the doormen Nick Munro and Rory Catelli.

It was the same lookay I remembered getting some years ago when introduced to Captain Henderson and later to the Montagnard tribal leaders when I arrived in Vietnam. If these men were as good as they were proclaimed, I knew I would have no problems and neither would they. The meeting was conducted in a semiformal way. "JJ" acted as chairman as the basic business routine was outlined and previous happenings discussed. I was still wondering about the "special situation" that was mentioned when we were sitting on the "Celestial." "JJ" and Anthony were studying some notes, and for a short time, things were quiet, then "JJ" spoke up.

"I have received some information that a Melbourne syndicate involved with illegal gambling, prostitution and numerous other rackets have infiltrated another casino in this area and in a forceful manner, with intent to disrupt it and eventually take over its operations. There is a good chance that their advance spies may have already checked us out by establishing a relationship with one of our regular patrons, more than likely one who is in considerable gambling debt to them. My information, which comes from a strong source, says they arrive in three's, though at separate times, and with a known gambling patron. Once inside, their 'modus operandi' is to bet on different games, and one of them will find a reason to start a 'blue, and when the doormen rush in to break it up, the others join into the ruckus attacking the doormen, and proceeding to cause damage to the place, and disturb the patrons forcing them to leave. My informant also said the men who do this are professional thugs, usually big men, handy with their fists and occasionally revert to weapons such as bottles and knuckle dusters.

"There has been no sign of knives or guns. It seems their main aim is to cause mayhem and damage to the business and to break the nerves of the casino workers. Soon after this disturbance, the casino manager receives a letter telling of this event with a strongly worded message that it would be wise to ring a certain phone number to arrange an appointment to discuss protection so that something similar does not happen again. It seems that once this is accepted, they gradually move in their own men and take over; if denied in any way, they use physical violence and threats to property and family.

"I want all of you on high alert for strangers coming in and keep a sharp lookout for anything suspicious. Sean here," "JJ" said, pointing to me, "was a military officer trained to observe and act; he has been highly trained in all aspects of unarmed combat and weapons and the training of men for battle in Malaya and Vietnam and has been decorated for such.

"His job will be to work with you in all aspects of control in any emergencies. He will report to our manager, Rick Kelly while here, and he will be on roving commission to other areas of our business under my control. Tomorrow morning at 9 a.m., Sean will report here to Mick Kelly and Jack Wither to start his training in all aspects of the business and the running of the games. This will be followed up each day with further training as necessary, and any questions.

CHAPTER 23

Executive Administrator

Three weeks had gone by in my new job, officially known as executive administrator, a fancy name for a glorified bouncer is what I thought. Each day, I had turned up on time for the necessary training by Mick Kelly and Jack Wither; they were a pair of good blokes who bounced off each other readily, with dry wit and humour. There was no doubt they were "hard boys", they were men who had grown up in a tough environment in the city, and I was enjoying their company.

Mick had been on the rise in the heavyweight boxing division, but when he saw one of his best mates, a middleweight boxer named Jack Hassen, die as a result of being knocked down in a 12-round bout with Archie Kemp, he decided to quit the game, he still worked out regular and would be a tough man to toss. He had an incredibly agile mind with a real knack for figures. As I got to know him I reckoned he could have been a brilliant accountant if trained. He said he had "left school when he was sixteen to take a job, any job to make money, and he ended up as a wharf labourer then tookay up boxing and then one day because of a legal problem, and through a solicitor, he met "JJ". In discussions with Mick, "JJ" recognised his unique talents and offered him a job, first running the bar and working him up gradually to manager. He had a wife whom he adored and two primary school-age sons, and he reckoned "JJ" was the best boss he had ever known. That statement showed the level of his loyalty to me.

Jack Wither was a totally different character who had been born to drug-addicted parents. He had been involved with street gangs from childhood, in and out of juvenile detention and eventually sent to Pentridge prison for a number of petty crimes. In there, he learnt every card sharp trick and game possible. Blessed with a retentive memory for cards dealt, he started around the illegal gambling games of Melbourne "remembering cards" is a unique skill few possess, and it helps those who can win large amounts of money. One night, he was caught out in an illegal casino, and he did a "runner". He headed for his room in St. Kilda, where his winnings were stashed. Hurriedly packing, he looked out of his window in time to see three "heavies" getting out of a car. He knew what they were after! If he stayed around, he would be crippled for life or dead. Running out of the back door with his bag of money he jumped a back fence and escaped and managed to get to a main highway where he thumbed a series of lifts to Sydney. He laid low for a while, living off the money, and one day, walking through Sydney, he was spotted by one of the thugs in Sydney on a "job". This bloke tookay off after Jack, who was crookay with the flu at the time, and soon ran out of wind.

Cornered in a dead-end lane behind Liverpool Street, the thug went for him. Jack knew it was over for him. In his condition, he was no match for the powerful bastard. What the thug did not know was Jack had taken to carrying a switchblade knife in his hip pocket, and as the thug came in fast, he was swinging punches, one of which landed hard, knocking Jack to his knees. Jack managed to pull the knife, and as the thug came in for the kill, he drove the knife upwards, into his stomach and through to the heart.

As luck would have it, a police patrol car had spotted the two men running, gave chase and came to the scene as the attack tookay place. The dead thug was carted off in an ambulance, and Jack was taken to police headquarters in Darlinghurst to be charged, and that is where "JJ" and Anthony Lawrence came into it. Although Jack was illegally carrying a prohibited weapon, in essence, he was defending himself. The police prosecution had laid a charge of murder against Jack. His case was argued extensively in the court hearing by his solicitor, who then referred it to Anthony Lawrence QC.

The charge was reduced to manslaughter and then successfully argued further by Anthony Lawrence QC, that based on the dead criminals' extensive violent record, which included extortion, armed robberies, and various assault charges, totalling about 12 years in various prisons, Jack Wither be declared innocent based on self-defence.

In his summing up, the judge said that based on Jack's previous juvenile convictions and the carrying of an illegal weapon, and the knowledge provided by the arresting police that Jack was acting in self-defence, he would waive the manslaughter charge and sentenced Jack to twelve months in prison on the weapon charge, to be reduced by the three months already spent in detention. With good behaviour, Jack Wither was out for six months.

The most remarkable thing was, whilst in prison, Jack saw the light, so to say, and became a "born again Christian". He came back to the attention of Anthony Lawrence when he wrote a most articulate letter to Anthony thanking him for his assistance at his trial and stating that his life had changed and that when released, he would seek employment and give away his previous life of crime. Anthony then referred the letter to "JJ", suggesting that knowing his incredible memory skills, they could give Jack Wither a job. "JJ" now had another intensely loyal member in his "tribe". The more I got to know "JJ", it was obvious he was a collector of people, people who needed help and, in return, reciprocated with their loyalty.

Definitely, "JJ" and Anthony were remarkable men, moral to the highest degree, crusading helpers to those who deserved it and yet capable of dishing out punishment and of the ultimate kind where and when required.

As time went on and I got to know in depth the real nature of my work, the only problem that I had was keeping its true nature secret from Melissa. I told her because of my training in business and financial management as an executive administrator, I would occasionally be sent away interstate on assignments to businesses that Anthony and "JJ" had a vested interest in. She was suitably impressed with my high-powered title, so that was okay.

In a discussion with "JJ," it was decided to tell her that my night time work was also associated with an illegal casino soon to become legalised, and she was happy with that.

As she had no inclination to go anywhere near King's Cross nowadays, I had no worries about an unexpected visit. When the basic training was over and my roster system was worked out, we analysed it, and then Melissa approached the hotel where she was employed to have her night shifts matched up with mine. It worked out satisfactorily for us. Apart from the times when I may be sent away, we could share the majority of our nights and days together.

Often, we would spend days on the beach or go for long drives. "JJ" had given us permission to camp on the cruiser when we liked, so occasionally, we would take wine and food and spend a romantic night looking out at the lights on the harbour. He said as soon as he could get around to some instruction. I could get a boat licence, he and Anthony would allow us to take it out, and when I told him of my seamanship training with the Army Water Transport division at Chowder Bay, he was suitably impressed and told me to apply to the Maritime Services, and get my licence. Little was I to know then that licence and the "Celestial" were to come in very handy in the future. At this time in my life, things could not be better. That was about to change, but only for a short time.

It was a Tuesday night at about 11 p.m. Catelli, who was roistered to be on the door, had called in that morning to say he had come down with a severe dose of the flu. Mick immediately rang around his casual doormen and eventually got one of the newer men named Jack Noble, a man who used to be in the fight game, as did Mick. After a briefing from Mick and showing him the rogue's gallery of undesirables, he had left Jack at his post and went off to relieve one of the girls behind the bar. Being Tuesday, the games area was less than half full. I was upstairs studying some game information and brushing up on my knowledge of Roulette and Baccarat.

There is always an audio phone hookay up with the doorman and a speaker relaying voices softly from the games room. Being the first time and totally absorbed in my studies at first, I tookay little notice of raised voices in the games room until a crash that sounded like something breaking and Mick's voice thundering on the speaker,

"Sean, get the hell down here quick". Racing down the short flight of stairs, three at a time, I saw Jack backed against a wall with two hefty blokes throwing punches at him. Jack was ducking and weaving and throwing punches back. Mick Kelly had another big bloke in a headlock in his left arm and was punching a bloodied face hard with his right fist.

Looking at Mick, the thought flashed through me, "No worries there", and I focused my attention on the heftiest one of the two blokes attacking Jack. Using a flying karate kick, the same as I had used on the attacking lout many weeks ago, It hit that big bastard with full force just below the kneecap. The crack of the leg breaking could be heard above the noise. Startled, the other bloke turned in time to walk wide open into a barrage of chops and punches, stomach, face, stomach, Adam's apple, punch, chop, punch, chop, and he collapsed into a gurgling heap. He sure was choking hard with his ruptured Adam's apple.

Mick Kelly was still holding in a headlock the other third fellow, and a couple of hard punches to the thug's kidney region from me soon saw him slump. And with that, Mick let him go and finished him off with the beauty of a right cross to the jaw.

Looking around, I could see there was very little collateral damage done to the games room, nothing that could not be fixed, although patrons were huddled back against walls and in corners with that wide-eyed lookay of frightened onlookers. Mick yelled out, "All you lot get outta here, and walked to the code-operated double doors and opened them. They tookay off like scared rabbits, and turning to the two bar girls semi-crouched behind the bar, he said, "You girls knock off, you'll still be paid in full." They, too, were very quick to retrieve their jackets and purses and heading out the door.

All the while this had been happening, our three on-duty croupiers had been standing by the tables as best they could to guard them: Jack Wither, Sam Capolli and a tall, broad-shouldered Jamaican known only as "Jimbo". Their job was not to get involved, but to guard the tables in case anyone helped themselves to the cash.

Mick called me to him and started advancing on two very scared-looking patrons whose eyes were darting around in every direction, looking for an escape route. Standing about five feet from them, he said, "These were the two bastards that brought them in", and pointing to the one on the left, a tall skinny-looking bloke with a large hookay nose and a beer gut, he said, they are both regulars, and this skinny piece of duck shit vouched for two of 'em", then pointing to the one on the right, who was a shorter fatter and dark-complexioned fellow, said, "This arse'ole came in about fifteen minutes later and vouched for the other one."

There was a strong, pungent aroma of urine wafting through the air, and Mick's deep voice cut in, "The weak bastard pissed himself" and laughed. The lookay on the boy's face now looked like he was also about to shit his pants. I turned to Nick. What do you normally do in a situation like this? Nick cupped his square jaw in his hand, thoughtful-like, looking hard at the two shaking and scared patrons.

He turned to me, and in a voice that sounded like a dog growling, he said in this vicious undertone, "I reckon we orta do 'em in", at the same time, giving a sly wink to me that they could not see. Turning to Jack, he said, "Jack, get the Ford transit van outta the garage." With those words, the dark fat guy who had pissed himself dropped to his knees, tears streaming down his face. He was pleading, "for god's sake, Mick, don't do this. I gotta wife and kids." The tall, skinny bloke had gone as white as a sheet and looked on the verge of collapse.

All of this was emphasised when the bloke that Mick had knocked out moaned and started to get to his feet until one of Nick's size twelve boots got him squarely in the ribs. He was gasping and vomiting as he went down. Turning to me again, Mick gave his sly wink as he said. "Sean, upstairs in the desk there is a locked drawer; you know where the keys are. In the middle drawer, there is a short-barreled .22 calibre pistol. Next to it is a silencer. Go up and get it while Jack gets the car, and I will get the rest of the patrons off the premises. With all the patrons now gone, the two soon-to-be ex-partners were grovelling at his feet. And while this was going on, the big bloke with the snapped leg was lying there moaning with the pain. He was a hard boy and had wised up to what was going on. Glaring at the two on the floor begging for mercy, he started to yell, "You two weak bastards, shut up, he ain't gonna!" and his words were cut off by a size twelve boot smack into his teeth. I winced, thinking of the dental bill.

I went upstairs and brought the gun down to Mick. It was a perfect short-range executioner's weapon with its snub barrel and silencer; I knew what Mick was up to, and I was sure, looking at the two almost comatose weasels lying on the floor, it was going to work. Jack walked in and said, "The van's ready, Mick. I threw one of those blue plastic tarps in the back." That was the final straw for the two poor bastards on the floor, and I was starting to feel a bit sorry for them. It would take them months to get over this trauma.

The three croupiers just stood with their arms folded with mean looks on their faces. I thought, well done, boys, that certainly adds to the effect. Mick was looking even meaner. I just stood by watching. This was Mick's show, and I would certainly give him top marks for his excellent performance. All the while, the scenario was enhanced by the three semi-conscious thugs lying and moaning with pain. I thought I would keep a close eye on them, and catching Mick's eye, I said, "Mick, do you know if there are any reels of strong sticking plaster or anything we can tie these blokes up with?"

Mick called back, "In the maintenance cupboard under the stairs, you will find a reel of grey tape. It's bloody strong." Jack went over to the cupboard, and came back to me with a reel of 3M duct sealing tape, excellent for the job to be done. We soon had the three hoodlums' wrists tied and gagged, except the bloke that Mick had kicked in the face; he was minus teeth, spitting blood, and his jaw was extremely swollen. There were only gasping sounds of pain coming from him. There was no need to gag the bloke who had copped the rabbit punch to his Adam's apple; he could only breathe through his nose. I wondered what they would eventually say to their boss when they eventually reported in.

Mick was now sitting in a classic pose with the chair turned around and his brawny arms leaning on the back of the chair with the gun dangling loosely on a finger. I had a vision of a Mafia hitman I once saw in a film. He started talking to the two on the floor, who were nonstop weeping. The only way you blokes are gonna save your miserable selves is to tell me everything you know: who are these pricks, where are they from, and where are they based? NOW TALK!! That came out so loud and fierce we all looked up startled, and out of their dribbling mouths, slurring words started to flow.

"JJ's" information was right on. These hoodlums had taken over a small casino operating near Central Square; their intention was to slowly build up taking over each casino in turn as they got stronger. The two poor bastards who were grovelling did not know the name of the boss, except he was from Melbourne. In turn, they said they had been approached by the bloke on the floor with the swollen jaw and promised five hundred dollars each to get them inside or face a beating if they did not. Mick simply said, "Get out of here, tell no one what happened here tonight, and don't ever come back." They almost fell over each other in their haste to dive out the door being held open by Jack.

Mick pulled me aside and said, "I gotta private emergency number to "JJ"; let's pull the sticky tape of that mug's mouth and see if he can tell us something." I was starting to like Mick and his style more and more. The mug on the floor nearly popped his eyes out of their sockets as Mick ripped the adhesive tape slowly off the bloke's face, and half of his moustache went with it. "Ouch," I could feel that myself. Mick just said, "Oh, sorry mate, did that hurt?" as tears rolled down the bloke's face. "Now lookay pal, we really don't want to hurt you, but you understand, we need to get a little information from you or your mate, and if you go along with us, you'll be okay, but if you don't, you might be going back to your loved ones in Melbourne as a paraplegic or worse if ya get my drift." Any firmness or resolve that bloke might have had vanished when Mick started to push the fat, silenced barrel of the little gun up the tight nostril of the thug. He screamed with pain as his stretched nose started to bleed. Nick went on, "Aw, lookay what ya done to me gun, yer snots on me barrel," and wiped it off on the remaining moustache." The bloke was sobbing like a baby now. He would be an easy mark to get information from.

Mick then turned his attention to the thug with the swollen jaw, who was having difficulty saying something through his injured mandible. In a voice that was putting out slurred words resembling someone mentally retarded with a speech impediment, we made out, "shuddup yer mouth and say nothing." He was obviously the toughest of them.

Mick turned to me and said, "Sean, get me that notepad and pen that's behind the bar under the counter and take some notes. Okay, old mate," he said, first thing, "what is the name of your boss of bosses?" With the thug's speech problem, I did not have to write fast, but I had some difficulty catching all of the words as they came out, and then I got him to repeat them to make sure. It was "get fucked you arseoles" This bloke was obviously the toughest of the group.

Mick said, "We want a phone number and an address of where he is living and about the gamblin' joint ya tookay over. I know old Freddy Mills, and I want to know waddya done to him. The bloke with the swollen jaw just glared at us." Mick then turned his attention to the thug, now missing bits of his moustache, and saying, "I hope you are going to be a bit more friendly, as he stuck the barrel of the twenty-two calibre pistol up the other nostril, this time he didn't just sob. No, this time he screamed, as Mick twisted the barrel around, drawing blood, and in between sobs, out poured the information we wanted. He admitted, "Yes, they did touch Freddy Mills up a little, but he is okay and is now on their payroll. Yer bloody lucky then," Mick said, "because if ya hadda done him in, you would have joined him, I liked old Freddy."

Having gained the information we wanted, Mick said, "We will call 'JJ' and get things moving with some information on this Melbourne mob." I remembered that "JJ" had informants and spies everywhere. Now Mick said, "We better do something with this lot," and headed for the doors. The next hour was hard work as all of us dragged, carried and loaded three heavy, groaning hoodlums into the back of the transit van. There was also a nasty smell coming from the bloke, minus some hairs off his moustache, and we had to drive to the back lane behind the gambling joint near Central Square with all the windows down.

It was about 4 a.m. when we unceremoniously dumped the three of them in the rubbish-strewn lane and rang the number that "half moustache" had given us. The message given by Mick was terse and to the point when the number called was answered. It was a gruff, sleepy voice on the other end. "If ya want ya three gutless wimps who work for ya you'll find em in the lane behind Freddy's joint, an if ya don go back to Melbourne, your next!"

Mick hung up the public phone and said, "That orta stir im up, lets head back to the casino and clean up." By 4 p.m. Wednesday afternoon, "JJ's" network of informants had the news we wanted. Frankie Gardiner was the name behind his thugs. He had a record as long as an arm and had spent a third of his life in prison. He was registered as a habitual criminal. His record included armed robbery, assault with a deadly weapon, drug trafficking, manslaughter, extortion, and prostitution pimp, but worst of all, he was arrested for a brutal rape and murder of a teenage girl and was released when two witnesses for the prosecution conveniently disappeared.

We now knew where he was living. Frankie was renting an old two-story terrace house in Foveaux Street, Surry Hills. He was sharing it with his thugs. It was not far from Freddie Mills gambling joint. "JJ's" contacts had indicated that a gang of six had left Melbourne intent on establishing themselves in Sydney. All had criminal records. We knew that three of them were not in good condition. All three were hospitalised early Wednesday morning at St Vincent's Hospital, Darlinghurst and were being questioned by police. Needless to say, they told the police nothing. The police were arresting one of them, Billy Hobson. He was the one with the ruptured Adam's apple. It seems he could not speak at all. There was a Melbourne police warrant out for him, and he was being extradited back to Melbourne.

I suggested to "JJ" that the best form of defence was offence. This was more in the line of my training in Vietnam, an ambush, hit-and-run tactics, but "JJ" felt that would be too public. At this stage of their Kellett Street Casino, they had operated under the radar of police scrutiny, and he wanted to keep it that way. An outright attack on their Foveaux Street headquarters could bring unwanted attention. The difficult and slower, but safer solution would be to single them out individually, administer suitable punishment for their transgression and send them back to Melbourne with their tails between their legs.

There was no doubt that the remaining three would keep a low profile in Freddie's joint, but for how long, we did not know. We were under no illusion that Frankie Gardiner would not run and would stick it out for a while in Sydney. In the Melbourne crime circles, he had a fearsome reputation, and many criminals lived in awe of Frankie and his brutality. The other two, Bruno Gavotte and Lenny Delaware, also had extensive police records.

Lenny Delaware was a vicious pimp notorious for beating, raping, and slashing with a razor any prostitutes reluctant to part with the money they earned. Both were gunmen; Gavotte also favoured a razor or a knife and had served ten years for manslaughter.

Yes, we had a dilemma to solve. We had no doubt they would be out for revenge if left alone, and "JJ" wisely did not want an open war. His thinking changed dramatically when old Frankie's brutally beaten and mutilated body was found. The bastards had cut out his tongue. His body had been found in the Sydney Botanical Gardens. The police investigation showed he had been taken to an isolated section near Lady Macquarie's chair, already bound and gagged, with his body wrapped in heavy black plastic.

He was then systematically beaten to death with a weapon that could have been an iron bar or jemmy. The plastic cover would have eliminated blood splatter. Every leg and arm had been broken. Freddie's head was left to last when the gag was removed from his mouth and his tongue severed by a sharp weapon. It was probably done with a razor. The police report said the tongue, which was nearby, showed signs of being pulled out to its fullest extent, possibly by a pair of pliers. We knew what that meant: it was a punishment reserved for those who talked. Freddie was one of "JJ's" informants.

We then learnt both casino patrons who had been coerced into bringing the three hoodlums into the casino were in Sydney Hospital. Both had been brutally bashed. Both had broken limbs and various injuries, and the one that had been called "fat boy" had been slashed with a razor from forehead to chin, and it l looked like he might lose sight of an eye. In light of all this information gained by "JJ" from his police contacts, we wondered what would be the fate of the thug who gave us the name, phone number and address of Frank Gardiner, and the remaining two criminals. No doubt Frank Gardiner and the others would sort that out in time. We didn't like "half moustaches" chances of pursuing a criminal career. Perhaps we may be able to save him from an inevitable fate and make him see the light. But first, it would be necessary to do something about Frank, Lennie and Bruno.

CHAPTER 24

Mulga Man, the "Justifier"

Mick Kelly was shattered when he got the news about Freddie Mills. It turned out that they had a history together going back to Nick's earliest boxing days. Mick had started his boxing training at Snowy Robbins and Theo Greens Boxing gymnasium in Erskineville when he was seventeen years old and getting into a lot of street fights around the streets of Erskineville where he lived.

Freddie Mills had been a renowned street fighter in those same streets in his youth, and had turned to boxing with moderate success and become a trainer for Theo and Snowy. One day, Frankie witnessed Mick punching the shit out of two Alexandria gang louts, who had attacked Nick outside the Rose of Australia hotel, a short distance across the road from the gymnasium. When the louts were laid out and just before a "Black Maria" police van arrived, Freddie managed to talk to Mick and convinced him to walk over to the gymnasium with him for a talk.

Leaving the dazed and bleeding Alexandria boys still there on the footpath surrounded by onlookers, they scarpered off down the street opposite where Frankie lived, kept walking out of sight, then circled the block and into the stairway leading up to the gymnasium. That was the start of Mick's boxing career.

Over the years, as Frankie aged, he gave away the training and started working at SP gambling and a sly grog joint owned and run by a mate. When his mate was killed by a hit-run driver, Freddie tookay over the running of the operation with a couple of his old boxing mates, and that is where Mick Kelly came into it. He was one of those mates. It was a small operation that grew in time to become an illegal gambling casino. Freddie was well known and liked by all who frequented it. Freddie Mills, now aged, would have been a pushover for the likes of Frank Gardiner and his brutal cohorts.

Mick was angry and wanted revenge, insisting that we go in on the attack, but "JJ's" common sense won out. Taking Mick quietly aside, I said to him, "Mick, I know what you are feeling. I have also witnessed the same brutality and feel the same as you. I have an idea I want to discuss with "JJ", and if he accepts it, I will need your help. Do me a favour now, mate. Sit tight, and don't make any rash moves. There is a good chance you will have your day.

"JJ" sat back in his office chair as I outlined what I had in my mind. His stare never left my face. Eventually, he spoke, "Are you sure you want to do this, Sean? Are you sure you are capable of doing it?" Damn it, I thought, now is the time to open up and tell all about my past, my training, how I have killed and the cold rage that fills me at senseless brutality. I had no compunctions at all about getting rid of bastards like Frank Gardiner and his kind. When I had finished my tell-all story going back to my childhood and my father's brutality and eventual death, "JJ" just sat right back in his padded chair and exhaled a deep breath, and then he spoke. "Sean, there are some things I want to tell you; for some time now, those same rages at the injustices we see and know of have been within Anthony and me. There are a couple of trusted ex-senior police also frustrated with the system who work with us and have endeavoured to punish to a certain degree, but not to the extent of execution. One would have to be trained to it and capable of it. What you have just proposed to me is exactly that. Could you be, would you be, our Mulga Man, the killer of the deadliest snakes?" That put a smile on my face, "JJ" bringing into the conversation the nickname I had earned many years ago and told him about.

After what Mick had told me about his old mate Freddie Mills, I did not see it as a problem, particularly knowing that Frank Gardiner had beat a sentence on vicious rape and murder charge. No doubt, the two major witnesses who had disappeared had gone the same way; I would not imagine Frank Gardiner paying them to keep quiet. It was time to start working on my plan. "JJ" had one of his ex-policemen doing surveillance on the Foveaux Street house and the other keeping an eye on old Freddie's gambling place.

I had estimated that a two-week surveillance would give me an idea of their comings and goings. First and foremost, security at our Kellet Street Casino would have to be tightened right up. Frank Calhoun was over his bout of flu, and with Phil Munro, they agreed to do extra shifts on the door together.

"JJ" had an extra camera installed, which gave good coverage of all movements on a wide area of Kellett Street. At this point, Gardiner and his cronies had shown no inclination to visit their two mates still in hospital, no doubt because of police visits, or was it lack of honour amongst thieves, or was it both? Maybe it was both.

In the meantime, I questioned "JJ" about the little snub nose .22 pistol. "He said it was clean and could not be traced, and it was okay to appropriate it." It was only kept there for self-defence in an emergency. He added that "anything I required in weaponry, he would get it for me no problems." He certainly was a remarkable man.

When the first week of surveillance reports came in I was starting to see a picture. The small gambling operation was closed with police tape across the entrance, as it was being investigated as a crime scene, so there was no activity at all.

The Foveaux Street terrace house was a different thing; the crims were certainly holed up there. No doubt wondering if there were going to be further reprisals from us and no doubt planning their next move. The report said that the two cronies with Gardiner were taking it in turn to go out and buy food at a supermarket in Crown Street, and pick up a case of beer at the nearby Clock Hotel. They kept a late-model Ford station wagon parked in a yard at the back of the terrace house. A light seemed to be switched on day and night in the downstairs entrance, and an upstairs light was on until late at night and sometimes into the early hours of the morning. There were indications they were late risers and late to bed.

By the time the second report had been read, an interesting feature was showing up. Each time Lenny Delaware went for supplies, before he picked up the case of beer he would stay in the bar lounge area having a few drinks. The Clock Hotel was a favourite haunt of the office workers from surrounding businesses, and because of their happy hour with cheaper drinks, there was always a large number of girls and women when they finished work to go there to enjoy a drink. The hotel was always packed, in particular, on a Friday night, which happened to be one of the nights that Len did his supply pick-up. It had been observed that Len Delaware spent a longer amount of time attempting to chat with different girls in a manner that indicated he considered himself to be a ladies' man. Len was younger than the other two and was no doubt starting to get a little restless, perhaps "horny" with the enforced stay in the house, and although viciously "pimping" prostitutes in Melbourne, there was no sign at this stage he was seeking relief from his tension in that area. This piece of news had me thinking if it could be of benefit. A chat with "JJ" convinced me it could. Crown Street had recently been made a one-way street, and just a short distance back down the street, on the opposite side was a wine and cider establishment. It was just a small bar, a very dimly lit bar with the benefit of upstairs rooms, which were available to girls and their consorts. When Len drove the Ford up from Foveaux Street, he had to turn left onto the one-way Crown Street facing away from the Clock Hotel and the Cider bar.

The owner of the Cider bar had been a client of "JJ" through a lengthy and expensive divorce battle. "JJ" in his way of appropriating favours had gained the upper hand for him in the divorce and also "whittled" down some of the bills. This latest report had me seriously thinking of how this could be used to benefit.

In my time working with horses as a jackeroo and head stockman, we often had to sedate and knock out horses to treat serious injuries and castrating. There was one particular drug called Rompen, which was very effective. I needed to find out if it would work on humans or if there was something better. The next thing I needed was a recent photograph of our lover boy Len.

Also, did "JJ" have on his list of acquaintances? An attractive "lady of the night" who, for the right incentive, could lure our would-be Casanova to this room above the cider bar where I would be waiting? And finally, find out if there was a back entrance to the cider bar where a semi-conscious or unconscious man could be bundled into a vehicle.

"JJ" is certainly a man of great resources; he had a positive answer for everything. He certainly did know the perfect lady for the job and she was an undercover policewoman. More than perfect, she was excellent. Just to ensure that the trio was still lying doggo on the terrace, it was decided to throw a scare tactic toward them. In the early hours of a Monday morning, not long after, the lights in the terrace upstairs rooms had been turned out. A lone figure alighted from a car in a nearby lane. He was carrying a high-powered rifle with a flash and noise suppressor hidden under a dark trench coat.

Creeping silently up the shadow-lined lane, there was just enough moonlight to make out the narrow rectangle window of the upstairs bedroom. Adjusting his military issue night vision glasses, the figure tookay aim, three muffled shots phoof, phoof, phoof! Through the window and into the ceiling, that should be enough to keep them thinking retribution was coming without waking the entire neighbourhood and keep them undercover a while longer.

There was no doubt about them not calling the police, and if they had any brains, they would see it as a warning to stay away from our casino. On Friday afternoon, our boy, Len, very furtively came out of the back door, trying to lookay in every direction at once. A movement of the drawn blind at the shattered window indicated to the watching ex-copper that the others were just as nervous. Satisfied no one was waiting for him, he went to the car, looking into its interior of the car, then trying all the doors, satisfied he got down on his knees to lookay for anything unusual underneath the body of the car.

Unlocking the driver's door, he released the catch for the bonnet. Stepping outside he lifted the bonnet and had a close scrutiny all around the engine. Satisfied once more, he dropped the bonnet and, standing upright, waved his hand in the direction of the window and got into the car.

Lenny was back into his usual routine, driving up Foveaux Street; he worked his way around and into Crown Street and found a place to park. It was not that far for him to walk to the Greek supermarket for supplies, which were the usual: meat, vegetables, various tinned food, bread, and milk. Loading the supplies into the station wagon, a short walk again, he was into the Clock Hotel for a drink.

She saw him walk into the lounge bar. Taking a sip out of her drink, she waited until he was seated and ordered his middy of beer. Draining her small glass of orange juice, she walked around to the ladies' room. A sidelong glance told her he was watching as she passed him. Putting an extra hip movement into her seductive way of walking, she disappeared through the door-marked ladies. The intuition of a street-wise woman told her he would be watching as she came out. Lowering her low-cut Spanish blouse a little lower, she walked outside into the lounge. Loverboy Len wasn't the only one watching.

As she came out, there were a few other men looking as she went by, including me. Jennifer was her real name, Carmen Del Rio was her working name, and she certainly looked the part. Her sultry gypsy appearance came from a Romanian mother and a Portuguese father. With long curling black hair, large round gold earrings and a gorgeous long-legged figure, she certainly looked the part. Her skirt was just short enough to have any red-blooded man wanting to peek under it a bit further.

It was still a little early for the Friday afternoon rush to start, so there were plenty of vacant bar stools. Perching her gorgeous backside on the edge of one, she was about three stools from Len, who by now was positively drooling.

Pretending not to notice him, she ordered a vodka and orange. When the drink arrived, she paid for it and casually looked all around as if expecting someone; turning her eyes toward Len, she smiled and said, "Hi". I swear Len almost swooned, I would have bet money his underpants were wet. "JJ" certainly knew how to pick them. Dolores was the perfect undercover policewoman. She had been working the vice squad for three years and had seen it all. She was sickened by the perverts, paedophiles, and deviants she encountered in her work and herself a victim of a sexual attack in a park near her home as a small child. She earned a university degree in law and joined the NSW Police Force. She had met "JJ" and Anthony in the courts and somehow formed an alliance. It did not matter how. All that mattered was Len was being sucked in like he had never been before. They were on their third drink; she had excused herself from drinking full shots of vodka and orange and insisted that Len only order half vodkas and orange. I was sitting close enough to hear her laughingly say, "If I have more than four full shots, I am anyone's." Len was totally hooked.

Her voice was getting a little merrier and louder, as if being affected by alcohol. I knew it was for my benefit. "Lennie, Lennie," she said again, "I like that name," leaning in closer to him, letting him lookay deep into her well-rounded, half-exposed breasts. "This place is too noisy. Just a little way down the street, there's the cutest little bar. I love it. There are comfy cubicles and soft lights, and they sell a bubbly wine that I love. Let's finish these drinks. I'll go to the ladies' room, and we'll go down there." Lennie's eager reply said he was more than ready. Lenny was 'hot to trot'

Good, that gave me enough time to get to the cider bar, get the spare key and position myself in the room. Mick would be positioned by now with the transit van with false number plates and ready to assist.

A few hours earlier at the cider bar, Earl, the owner, told me it is always very quiet until about 10 p.m. when he gets an influx of customers from the various hotels, he said he would put a reserve sign on a private cubicle to the back of the room. Telling his bar assistant "to hold the fort," he tookay down some keys and led me up some narrow stairs from the bar to the upstairs rooms. Stopping at a room, he said "Use this one," and opened the door. It was the furthest one from the stairs. It was very basically furnished with a double bed, a small shower toilet cubicle, and a large old-fashioned wardrobe. There was a window overlooking Crown Street, which was shut. He then showed me an alcove with a locked door almost opposite the room, saying, "This goes through to a stairway down to the back. There is a back door which will give you access to your car." He then handed me two keys, saying, "The one with the number four tag on it is for the room; the other one will open both the alcove door and the backyard door." Thanking him, I went in and examined the room again. I was thinking what would be the best way to handle this.

Should I hide in the wardrobe and spring out at the appropriate moment, or lay under the high old-fashioned bed and do the same, or wait behind the alcove door, then quietly let myself into the room? Policewoman Jennifer Ainsley, alias Dolores del Rio, was due to meet me here in about ten minutes; I felt it would be a good idea to get her opinion. I am glad I did. As soon as she saw the layout of the room, she said, "Wardrobe, no! Bed, no!" She went on to say the bed is sideways to the door. It has the street window on one side and the entrance door on the other. The hall light is directly above the doorway. So this is what we do. One, unlock the window and open it with the curtains closed. The aim is to let street noise in and light out. We will only leave the dim bed lamp on and the bedroom light off. Two, remove the bulb from the hall light above the door to make this area of hallway dark with just enough light from the other hallway light to see the way to this door, and three, I will tell him to get his clothes off as soon as we get inside, he has a flick knife in his jacket pocket, I want him naked with his clothes well away from him, while I freshen up in the bathroom. I will then come out in my "very skimpy underwear" and lay beside him on the window side of the bed. By now, he will be so hot he could burn a hole in the mattress. This will place his body facing away from the door. He will be on his side, and that way, he will have his exposed arse facing you, or wherever you want to jab the needle, turned towards you.

When we enter the room you be ready and waiting inside the alcove. Wait five or six minutes. The signal to come in and jab him will be when you hear me say loud. "Take me, Lennie, I'm ready, then come in quiet and quick. If that stuff is as good as you say, there won't be much fight in him and remember, I am also trained in martial arts so don't worry about me. If, by chance, he does get violent, and a ruckus starts, and you hear that, come in as quick as you can and between us, we'll sort him out."

One way or another, he'll get his shot, and with the noise that goes on in the bar, no one will hear anything. I have to hand it to "JJ". He certainly knows the right people. The professionalism of that beautiful girl had me thinking how I would have liked to have had her with me in Vietnam doing the covert work that we did. I reckoned she'd beat the CIA at their own game.

In my pocket was a syringe with a large dose of Fuxamephonium. "JJ" had told me Northern Territory Police used this potent sedative to quieten down and subdue aggressive and violent drunks in the various isolated aboriginal communities in the north. It was also used to sedate horses before castration and with as fast an effect as Rompen.

I was standing across the road from the cider bar watching the entrance when they came walking down the street. They were holding hands and walking with a slight stagger to their steps. Carmen del Rio nee Jennifer Ainsley was laughing loudly, while Lennie seemed intent on getting to the bar.

She had told me to wait about half an hour before positioning myself in the alcove. She wanted Lennie to stay drinking for about an hour before they came up to the room. Her aim was to get him drinking some of the potent cider they sold there and perhaps some of the 11% alcohol "bubbly" as she called it. She said "she would have no trouble stalling his ardour, and when the time was right, she would lead him up like a dog on a lead after he had purchased a key to the room." At the half-hour mark, Mick and I parted; he went around to where the transit van was parked, and I wandered into the bar. There was a fair crowd in there now and it was easy to sidle in and blend with the noisy throng. The bar had enough light for the staff to serve drinks by and a soft red glow barely lighted the outside. However, I did wonder what his mates would be thinking about him taking so long to get supplies.

Positioning myself with a glass of cider in a dark corner, I could just make out Lennie and Carmen sitting close together. By the time I finished my drink it would be time to position myself upstairs. I don't think anyone noticed me in the gloom as I moved over to the stairs and went up them. Our undercover policewoman was right; with the light bulb removed I could only just see the alcove and door number four. There was also considerable noise from the patrons coming up the stairwell. Opening the alcove door, I slipped inside. It was as "black as a duck's guts" as Uncle Charlie would say.

As I opened the door, I noticed a light switch. Turning it on, I saw a short hallway and a flight of stairs going down a flight to a heavy steel-clad door. I guessed it was a fire escape of sorts. Moving quietly down to the door, I turned the key in the lock it opened smoothly. Looking out into the yard, I saw four vehicles, three of them Earl and staff and the bigger outline would be the transit van. Leaving the door ajar, I strode the few steps to the side of the van.

Mick jumped when I tapped on the window and then relaxed when he heard my voice. "Creeping Jesus, Sean, ya frightened the shit out of me." I laughed and said, "Just checking, Mick, see you soon." About fifteen minutes went by when I heard voices and laughter coming up the stairs. Peeping out around the corner of the alcove, I saw another couple coming onto the landing; in the faint reflected glow of the hall light behind them, I could see he had his hand up under her dress, and she was giggling and saying, "don't be silly", after a clumsy fumble at the lock they disappeared into a room off to the side of the landing.

Less than five minutes had gone by when I heard voices and footsteps again. This time, the sound of Carmen's voice and laughter was unmistakable. Peeping out again, I could see that Lennie had a bit of a stagger to him. He had one arm tight around her waist and the other holding a bottle. She had an arm around his neck and the other hand was extended as if holding a key. So far, so good, I thought. Closing the alcove door to a slight crack, I stood quietly waiting. The fluorescent hands on my watch ticked over at seven minutes, and then I heard the loud exclamation, "I'm ready for you, Lennie. Take me now!"

Lennie for the Deep Six

Lennie never knew what hit him. Carmen was right; she had lain beside him, and he was clumsily groping at her crutch with his face buried into her breasts. He would have barely felt the prick of the needle as a large dose of Fuxamephoneum started its surge through his bloodstream. As his startled head turned toward me, the full weight of my body behind a short right-arm punch to the side of his jaw assisted the flow of the drug. Lennie slumped unconscious back onto the bed. In less than a minute, Dolores, now Jennifer Ainsley's undercover policewoman, was dressed.

Two minutes later, Mick was in the room with a body bag, and we were rolling Lennie's totally unconscious and gagged body into the bag, leaving the zipper open enough for him to breathe. Unless he had difficulty breathing through his nose, he should survive okay for the voyage ahead. Jennifer had been briefed to leave the keys in the room and disappear back to the bar and leave, after locking the back door, once we had loaded Lennie into the back of the transit van.

I was glad Mick was along to help. Lennie was a solid-built bloke and heavy. Even though I am physically strong, it would have been an effort to get him off the bed, down the stairs and into the van. We did not want Jennifer involved with this part of the operation. Mick did not seem too concerned about bumping Lennie a bit on the stairs on the way down. I really liked Mick's humour.

We had a long drive from the city over the Harbour Bridge and through the northern suburbs of Cremorne and Mosman to Clifton Gardens. There, "JJ" would be waiting at anchor just offshore with the "Celestial" and its dinghy towed behind. Mick was driving; I was in the back with Lennie and another shot of Fuxamephoneum in case he came around too soon. I had suggested Clifton Gardens as an appropriate place. When I was doing the seamanship course at the nearby Army Water Transport base, I had noticed how isolated Clifton Gardens was, being situated well down below houses, and there was an excellent wharf going out and around the old swimming baths. Our timing was right; it was a full high tide at 1 a.m., which meant the Celeste could be reversed close to the shore alongside the wharf. The dinghy would be rowed onto the beach where I knew the van could be backed near to the edge of the beach and very close to the dinghy, and when the coast was clear, Lennie would be dumped into the dinghy, the dinghy would be fastened to the transom of the Celeste and "JJ" would take over the van.

Mick and I, with our cargo, would head out through the heads to the open sea. Mick was no seaman, so I would take the wheel. We were well out to sea off the continental shelf, with the depth sounder showing very deep water when I stopped the engines and slowed down to the rolling motion of a gentle swell.

Going to the back of the boat, we pulled the dinghy alongside the duckboard. Lennie was almost awake and making strange sounds. This was the most difficult part. It was quite a struggle for Mick and I, as strong as we were, to lift the semi-limp body of Lennie out of the dinghy and onto the transom duckboard. By the time we had achieved this, Lennie was wide awake, staring at us, with his eyes wide open as big as 'dog balls' Mick had said, as they shone bright and lit up by the light shining from the deckhouse. They got bigger as he watched my hand over to Nick assorted heavy house bricks and scrap pieces of metal, which had been conveniently provided by "JJ' on recent frequent visits to the Celeste, and with each trip, carrying a heavy hold-all bag. Those same contents Mick was packing into the body bag with Lennie and not too gently going by the grunts. With that done and the zipper closed up to Lennie's neck, I climbed onto the transom with Mick. I was holding the .22 calibre pistol, and I was saying it's time for me to do my job, Mick; you might want to climb back into the boat. Mick looked at me with a hard look and shookay his head saying, "No, Sean." This one is on me. Taking the pistol from me, he placed the muzzle angled upward between the now terrified eyes and said. "This one is for old Freddie, you bastard. He was my mate." He squeezed the trigger, pulled up the zipper and pushed Lennie overboard. The Celestial's depth finder showed a depth of about six fathoms.

As policewoman Jennifer Ainsley walked up Crown Street towards Lennie's car, she was thinking about what had transpired. She had no idea what was going to happen to Lennie, but she really did not care. Deep down, she was hoping it would be his end. The world was better off without vermin like Lennie; it was a filthy mongrel like him who had got to her as a child. She was also thinking, I liked that Sean fellow, I liked his style, and I think I would like to work with him again. Taking the car keys out of her purse, she opened the door. Wiping away any fingerprints with a dainty handkerchief, she placed the keys on the seat as instructed. She then pulled the envelope Sean had handed her out of her purse and placed it on the seat alongside the keys.

The night was over for her, she thought as she headed back to her car and headed for home to her boyfriend and a long sleep; a smile lit her face as she thought of the beautiful man waiting for her in their bed. Thank god, her childhood experience and her time in the vice squad had not spoiled her for love.

There was at least a half-hour silence between Mick and me as we cruised back toward the lights on the distant shoreline. Mick was the first to speak, "I had to do it, I had to do it!" I really loved that old bastard Freddie." There were tears glistening on his cheeks in the glow of the navigation lights. "I've fought and beaten a few men, but I've never killed a man before."

I simply said, "It's not easy. I have killed many men, but there has to be a strong reason, and you had one, and you certainly did have one!" The sun was now coming up on the horizon and shining on a beautiful calm sea. "Mick", I said, "do you know anything about ocean fishing?" He said, "I do" I then said, "Are there fishing lines and bait on the boat?" "Nick said yes, and in the freezer, there usually are some frozen prawns. I said, let's go fishing. It's something I have never done before in the ocean." Nick's face lit up. "Yes, why not?"

We caught a few reasonable-sized fish in the next hour that Mick called Snapper, and it was a great release for the both of us after the past 24 hours. Mick looked like a great load had been lifted from his shoulders as we increased speed and headed for home. I was at the wheel, steering our way carefully as we rounded South Head, past

Watson's Bay and into Rose Bay, when I heard Mick say rather softly, "Thanks, Mulga." I spun around to see a big grin on his face, "Hope you don't mind me calling you Mulga. 'JJ' let me in on it."

It was my turn to smile, "Not at all, Mick." I was rather proud of that nickname as a boy. Turning back to the steering wheel, another smile came on my face as I thought, "Mulga, the snake killer." And that is how it was going to be. Two more deadly snakes to go.

I would have loved to have seen the lookay on the faces of Frank and Bruno when the voice on the phone told them where their car was, and they read the typed message which simply said. **Sorry, I am leaving this life for good! Lennie xxx**

It was time to start working on the next move. The surveillance men had reported to "JJ" that almost twenty-four hours went by before Bruno Gavotte furtively let him out of the back door of the rundown terrace house. Again, the movement of the upstairs blind covering the shattered window indicated Frank was there watching. It was obvious they were running scared and, no doubt, getting hungry. It was reasonable to assume that Bruno, knowing that he and Len had shared the shopping chores at the same Greek shop the first time, would head back there first to lookay for their car.

Looking nervously all around him, Bruno stood in the tiny backyard for almost five minutes when a taxi drove up the lane to the vicinity of the back gate. Bruno was almost running as he jumped in beside the driver, and the car reversed out of the lane and sped off up Foveaux Street in the direction of Crown Street. Bruno was back within the hour with their vehicle and carried two bags of presumably groceries into the back of the terrace house, followed by another visit to the car for a case of beer. One could only imagine what went through their minds when they read Lennie's note.

Where the hell did Lennie get a typewriter from? The bastard wouldn't know how to type. "JJ" had previously received a report to say that "half moustache", or Norman Clune, had been shifted to another section of the hospital after a lot of vicious threats from his much tougher mate with the broken leg and jaw and smashed teeth. The report said he was terrified for his life but still refused to talk to the police. He could no longer be kept in hospital and released.

Surveillance on him said he tookay a taxi to Central Station and boarded a train for Brisbane. He would keep until another time and another job, or the gang got him.

The tough bloke with the broken leg who had threatened the two patrons to shut up before Nick's boot smashed into his mouth was still in hospital under police surveillance. His name was Joseph "Joey" Barker. He was also wanted and was being extradited back to Victoria when his face and skull fractures healed well enough to travel.

A fingerprint check had shown matching prints, found at a murder scene in Footscray five years earlier when a prostitute had been razor slashed, and her pimp shot twice through the head, followed by the same fate to the prostitute. Joey Barker had been a stand-over man and extortionist, and soon after the double murder, he disappeared from the police radar until now.

That just left Frank Gardiner and Bruno Gavotte to think about. If I were Frank and Bruno, I would be having second thoughts about leaving Melbourne to muscle in on the Sydney scene. It was another week of surveillance, and the pair had not made a move. Joey Barker had been taken in police custody to Victoria. Apart from Bruno doing two shopping trips, things still remained the same. One could only assume that Bruno and Frank were starting to feel the heat was off them and becoming claustrophobic because, on the second trip,

Frank was with him, and this time, they checked the Ford before climbing in.

It was about 11 a.m. when they drove to the Crown Hotel and were there drinking for the best part of the day. One of "JJ's" men had followed them and was sitting as close as he could safely be to where they were sitting at a table and, to all appearances, looking like a normal patron, reading a newspaper and having a drink occasionally. He reported they were in heavy and quiet discussion with an occasional loud word. He said he thought they were talking about going home.

The solution was now obvious. In my time with the Special Operations Branch, explosives of all kinds were a big part of my training. I needed to discuss with "JJ" my new plan and seek what I needed for the job.

On the second night after the meeting with "JJ", in the early hours of the morning, the same dark-clad figure this time, armed with a car key made from a mould in putty, taken on the night of Lennie's kidnap, opened the driver's side door and quietly released the bonnet catch. He played for a while with wires attached to the starter and then planted a magnetic, electronic-operated bomb of Military grade C4 explosive under the dashboard. An explosive powerful enough to convert the late-model Ford station into scrap metal.

The Sydney evening newspapers the next morning reported on a massive explosion in Surry Hills where two persons, as yet unidentified, were blown up in their car. Police were investigating, but at this stage had no leads or suspects in their investigations. An anonymous phone call made to police HQ in Surry Hills identifying them matched with information given to police by the owner of the terrace house they had rented from. It was two days later that the news report stated they had been identified as well-known Melbourne gangsters Frank Gardiner and Bruno Gavotte.

Things were back to normal at Kellett Street, and Melissa and I managed to catch up on some quality time together. Lying in bed, she mentioned hearing on the radio and later reading in the newspaper about the terrible bombing in Surry Hills and saying, "How can some people live like that?" I answered with something like, "Yes, probably rival gangs quarrelling over each other's turf. The world is better off without them," and tookay her into my arms again, enjoying the warmth of her body and knowing that soon I would be on the move again into a warmth of a different kind. It would be the warmth of a tropical climate and a hotbed of criminal activity.

Information sent to me indicated that North Queensland would be my next call, starting at Cairns.

CHAPTER 26

L'Onorata Societa (Honoured Society) Calabrian Mafia

It was little known to the Australian public, and the police for that matter, that the branch of Calabria Mafia in Australia, known as the Honoured Society or "L'Onorata Societa" or "N'Drangheta" and on occasion referred to as the "Black Hand" was becoming entrenched into Australian society in certain states. It started in the early 1920s when, in 1922, an Italian ship named the Re D'Italia arrived in Adelaide. It was carrying three godfathers who would set up cells in Melbourne, Sydney, and Perth, one being Francesco Guglielmo Femio. They were soon followed out from the old country by family members. In South Australia, they were to become known as the Seven Families of Adelaide. Within a decade, those seven families were starting to exert control over the fruit and vegetable trade in Australia. Francesco Guglielmo Femio ventured to far North Queensland.

The 1920s had seen an increase in the domestic and world need for sugar. In Australia, the sugar cane fields started in the 1880s saw an increasing amount of land clearing, especially in the growth of the North Queensland cane fields and the physically hard hot work cutting sugar cane, which was once done mainly by the indentured South Pacific Island "Kanakas" was being slowly phased out with many of them being repatriated back to their islands with the implementation of the white Australia policy.

This new work opportunity seemed to attract these hardworking Southern Europeans of Italian extraction. By 1924, there were 4,286 Italians in Australia, and by 1934, this figure had increased to over 8,000. The majority of these immigrants were impoverished, hardworking people off the land, many of them from the rural villages of Sicily, and many of the villages were under the control of the Calabria Mafia. The Mafia had been able to grow in Calabria in the 1800s because it was then a very lawless part of Italy, and it was easy for committed criminals to take over towns through corruption and intimidation. Among those that went into North Queensland were some hardened criminals, gunmen and assassins' of the "N'Drangheta" who sometimes left the Black Hand logo of death on a victim.

They brought with them the traditions of violence, intimidation, and macabre initiation rituals into their way of life. An example of a ruthless revenge killing was a murder in Brisbane in the 1920s when one Italian immigrant was butchered for cheating on the daughter of a mafia chief. His heart was cut out and taken back to Italy to show the aggrieved woman.

Their method of extorting money from their hardworking fellow man was simple. Either pay a regular gratuity to the L'Onorata Societia or be punished, such as burning a crop, or a beating, perhaps torture or even death. As the strength of the so-called "Honoured Society" grew, so did it infiltrate into other areas of Australia as members branched out into other areas in Australia, and by 1940, there had been more than ten murders and thirty bombings attributed to the N'Drangheta, and by the end of the century, their power had infiltrated some corridors of power, business, and politics and into the aisles of huge national supermarkets with their vicious control of the Melbourne vegetable and fruit markets. Sydney's seafood markets, controlling them with an iron fist. Their method of controlling supermarkets was simple. It involved bribing the purchasers to take fruit and vegetables at inflated prices from Melbourne market stall holders, who, of course, had been forced to pay a levy of 50 cents per case directly to the "Honoured Society" or Mafia. This scam would net millions of dollars ultimately paid for by the consumers. A similar racket that operated out of Sydney's seafood markets was only different in that it was in control of the supply chain for prawns.

The Mafia control of the Melbourne fruit and vegetable market was to eventually prove to be a training ground for two young Sicilian boys who were about to leave their homes in Griffith. One came from a hardworking, honest family and destined to be the more ruthless of the two young men was Franco "Frankie" Colleoni, and the other, whose father was a "Capo" (boss) in the Griffith Mafia and more of a follower than a leader was Renaldo "Ronnie" Medici.

With all of the information supplied to me by "JJ," it was not too hard to track down Vincenzo Franco Colleoni, commonly known as "Frankie", a self-styled drug lord living under delusions of grandeur, by controlling a small gang of pimply faced teen runners and part-time pimps, carrying the drugs supplied to them from Frankie and his henchman Ronnie to all parts of Cairns and beyond. Looking at his criminal record, he had grown up mainly in a large Sicilian immigrant family in Griffith, NSW, basically honest hardworking parents growing stone fruits and apples. Still, unfortunately, young Franco was one apple who fell far from the family tree. He was the youngest of a brood of six who went to school and then doubled as field hands working with their basically peasant parents. Well, that is what his older brothers and sisters did, and there were two brothers and three sisters who willingly complied with the rigid family demands of Papa Giuseppe Vincenzo Colleoni and his wife Maria to help with the work and to succeed in this wonderful and new country they had moved to from their native Sicily in 1925. Two brothers, Giuseppe and Roberto, and one sister, Maria, had been born in the village they lived in, but Carla and Franco, who was the youngest and the last child, were born in Sydney before the whole family moved to Leeton, and then to Narranderah and then onto Griffith, where they lived in a ramshackle three bedroom old farmhouse they rented and worked as share farmers.

Because he was the last baby born to his loving parents and extremely cute, he was doted on through his childhood by the older sisters and brothers and his mother, and in no time, Franco was a thoroughly spoiled and nasty demanding brat who would scream the house down if he did not get his own way.

As he grew, Franco's parent kept telling him they were living far better than what they would have had in their Calabria village of Santa Cristina D'Aspromonte. A village tightly held by the Calabria Mafia in that lawless part of Sicily, even though he had to pay a monthly amount of protection money to the local mafia "Don" Domenici Medici, and Franco as a toddler believed him, but growing up his early teens, he saw and learnt things that made him think there was something much better out there and was learning how to get it.

By the time Franco had reached school age, nothing had changed in his demeanour. Selfish and demanding, and being of a solid and strong build, he became an intimidating school bully and fond of truanting with a few of similar ilk, and with one of similar nature a year younger named Renaldo "Ronnie" Medici, he learnt about the money his father Domenici Medici a mafia "capo" was making growing a plant that was sold into the major cities and towns, and sold for big money, and at ten years of age Franco, now called Frankie dreamed of being rich with plenty of money and not from growing apples.

Frankie was the bigger, nastiest and cruellest bully of the two, and Ronnie seemed to idolise him and follow along with whatever Frankie suggested. At Frankie's instigation, they had taken to extorting money, mainly lunch money, from other kids, administering a "Chinese wrist burn", and punching and threatening with a pen knife that Frankie carried if they did not hand it over.

Caught by a teacher one day, administering their torturous wrist burn to one of the smaller kids, the young thugs Franco and Ronaldo were disciplined by the schoolmaster and thrown out of school.

This ruling was suddenly changed after Ronnie's father and an uncle who worked for his father paid a visit to the Principal, and from that visit, the schoolmasters backed down from his ruling. Frankie and Ronnie had learnt about the benefits of the power of the "L'Onorata Societia", and Ronnie's father's prestigious position in it.

Soon after, they vowed to have a blood brother alliance, and on one of their truant days at their favourite hiding place in a grove of trees near an irrigation ditch where they fished for yabbies, there Frankie tookay out his penknife and though wincing at the thought of cutting himself he did, and as did Ronnie, pressing their bleeding thumbs together, their alliance was formed. They were blood brothers for life.

As young as they were, they were determined to learn everything that they could about this "get rich plant", and from that day on, at every opportunity, they would endeavour to listen in on conversations and meetings that Ronnie's father and uncle had on regular occasions with other men who met at Ronnie's house.

The Medici home was a larger and far more luxurious house built on high piers. Over the site of the previous old farmhouse that Signor Medici had bulldozed down, Frankie and Ronnie had built a cubby house of sorts directly under the main living room where the meetings were held. So they enhanced their knowledge of growing marijuana, how to hide its growing among other plants such as oranges, and the best ways to transport it to the Melbourne market hidden under vegetables and fruit, and to where, and also to where the best prices were paid. They listened and learnt about the best plants to grow, and on hearing where some seed was kept in the house, Ronnie crept in one day and tookay a small handful of seed. Their plan being was that seed was to be the start of a business adventure at some time in the future.

Ronnie had often told Frankie he was tired of planting tomatoes on his family farm. Frankie had expressed the same feelings about working after school on his families' apple trees, and marijuana seeds can be kept for a long time. Ronnie and Franco, now at the restless ages of fifteen and sixteen, were tired of school and working at home and decided it was time to run away from home.

It was early spring, and in the early hours of one morning, each of them carrying a flour bag packed with a few clothes and a small amount of money Ronnie had taken from his father's hiding place, and with the seed sown into the cuff of a pair of trousers Frank had stolen from an older brother, they set off to hitch a ride to the nearest railway station, to buy two one way tickets, and finally made their way by train to Sydney's Central Station.

They did not know or realise that leaving home would have been as simple as talking to Ronnie's father Domenici Medici. Then the way would have been paved for them to leave with substantial money, blessings and an introduction to a cousin and his business in the Melbourne market. The mafia world operates with a strong code of family first. Domenici had plans for his growing son and possibly fit into it his son's best mate Franco, who he liked, and although Franco's father, Giuseppe Vincenzo Colleoni, was a hardworking and honest Sicilian who paid tribute to Domenici Medici, any objections to his son's possible line of work would be brushed aside by Medici. Still, with the ignorance and precociousness of youth, they snuck off into the night. Signor Colleoni and his family were suitably distressed. Godfather Medici was furious at the thwarting of his plan to bring them into his family's business and blustered and threatened them with dire consequences when they were found. Still, time and parental love are great healers, and when they eventually made contact and needed help, Medici was thrilled to see them and was just the man to talk to.

The two boys were excited about their new adventure, although Ronnie, unaware of his father's intentions, was a little apprehensive of his father's wrath if he found them because of conversations he had overheard of his father's methods of dealing punishment to those who go against him.

CHAPTER 27

Becoming Street Smart in Sydney

On their arrival in Sydney, it was in the late afternoon, and coming on the night. It was hard to find accommodation in this city that they did not know. They resorted to sleeping the first night in Belmore Park opposite the Central Railway Station, and there they had their first encounter with Sydney's homeless, a brush with the law and an introduction to a low-level drug dealer. The brush with the law came about when they tried to take a couple of blankets one cold night from another park sleeper. A yelling fight started, which erupted into violence, and they were caught in the act of bashing senseless the poor fellow and taken to Central police station, where they were charged as minors with common assault and sent away to Yasmar reformatory for a month. So their parents would not know, they concocted a story about running away from their home a few years ago and refused to give any further information other than a false name and their age to the arresting police and in the courtroom. Already, they had learnt the strict code of "Omerta" never to talk to the police or people in authority. When questioned about the small amount of money they had, they said they had earned it picking fruit and veggies in their travels along the way in Victoria.

It was in this juvenile reformatory they met a hard-case kid aged seventeen named Casey McGuire, and he was in there on a similar charge of assaulting someone and also for peddling marijuana. It seemed the person he had assaulted was the person he was selling to and who had refused to hand over the money. Frankie and Ronnie attached themselves to Casey McGuire. Frankie still had the stolen marijuana seed sown into the cuffs of the pants being held by the reformatory authorities to be handed back to him when his sentence had expired. Frankie kept his fingers crossed and hoped that, by some chance, those seeds would not be found. At this stage they had still not contacted their parents.

By coincidence, their release date from the reformatory coincided with the release of Casey McGuire, and he told them that if they stuck together, he would be able to show them city life and where to go and how to survive in the streets. He told them of a contact he had in King's Cross who could help them make some money.

They boarded a train together for Central Station using the last of their money and some that Casey had to buy food and cheap boarding house accommodation and were soon broke, so they tookay to wandering around Sydney's shopping areas, shoplifting from the big stores like Mark Foys, Anthony Horderns and Grace Bro's, stealing anything that they could pick up and sell in hotels, on in the pawn shops that Casey knew of and who asked no questions. It had not taken them long to find somewhere to live on the cheap for a while, and with two others of the same ages, named Tony and Pedro, who they had met and befriended and who were living in a similar manner. Soon after this meeting, their little gang moved into an abandoned terrace house in Eveleigh Street. It was a street of dereliction doomed one day for demolition that they heard about that run alongside the Eveleigh railway shunting yards, and close to the largely aboriginal community in Redfern.

The side of Eveleigh Street, with its long stretch of railway shunting yards, was opposite a long row of condemned terrace houses destined for future development by the state government. It was one of these they commandeered for their own use, furnishing it to a basic extent with sleeping bags stolen from a Sydney-wide store, various stolen trappings and hurricane lamps for lights, and a gas BBQ they cooked on, on occasion.

One day, they came back from their escapades around Sydney CBD to find two men and a girl carrying bundles of belongings, some piled into an old child pram, walking into the house, no doubt looking at the possibility of moving into this old derelict two-story house. An argument started, and the two men were given a severe beating by its five occupants and ran off, leaving the girl about sixteen behind. She was given a choice to stay and have sex with its occupants or runoff. She chose the former, but disappeared a few days later, running away from the persistent abuse. She was probably destined to join the numerous street people roaming around Sydney, many of them begging for money in doorways and corners and sleeping wherever they could find a place out of the weather. Some girls found a pimp and sold themselves around the red light district of Kings Cross, along William, and the back lanes in nearby Woolloomooloo to the sailors off nearby ships and any other men wanting to pay for sex.

They had already taken to making some money with their shoplifting and nighttime stealing from cars and delivery vans around the Broadway, Haymarket, and Chinatown area, and bemoaned the fact that they had let Nicole, the girl who stayed a few nights getaway when they could have been her pimps and protectors and that is when Frankie said to himself "Live and learn, I will never let another opportunity like that slip past me again". They were prophetic words because, in the years to come, Franco Colleoni was to run a stable of 100 girls in Cairns along with his drug empire.

Over the next two years they were always looking for anything they could steal to sell in the numerous Billiard and Snooker rooms and pubs that were in that area. By now, they were pool room sharks at games of snooker and pool in the various snooker rooms, often scamming a game between them to win a few extra pounds. It was in these places they learnt more about being street smart and basic survival and had their first encounters with Sydney's gangland and its often criminal youth, which led to their first brush with the law.

One Saturday afternoon, they had gone to the School of Arts Snooker and Billiard rooms at Newtown and wandered in singly. Not as a group, so as not to arouse suspicion, they would enter acting as strangers to each other. They got into a game of Kelly pool with some local Newtown boys and worked their well-practised scam signalling by covert signs their ball numbers to each other. There were eight players in the game; it was Frankie's gang of four, still acting as strangers, and four Newtown boys in the game. Their scam was simple: Frankie's gang, by knowing the ball number tossed to each of them by the dealer, would then endeavour not to sink that number ball, which would then give them a secret team of four playing against the individual play of the others and multiply by four their chances of winning. Usually, if done with extreme covertness, it worked, and on this particular day, each game was a five shillings charge per person to play, and they were winning a sizeable amount of money when one of the Newtown boys got suspicious with the realisation that over nearly three hours of play, it was always one of the four who won the pot.

Now extremely wary, at the next toss of the numbered marbles from the dealer, he watched closely the actions of the four as each got his numbered marble, and who then looked at it and put it into his pocket. It was then he noticed how Ronnie was nonchalantly leaning slightly forward and with his pool cue clutched between both hands, was raising a finger away from the cue a number of times. He counted five times that finger was raised and then lowered back to the cue, and now, watching from the corner of his eye, he saw that being repeated by one of the others with a different number of rise and fall of a finger. With that, he knew that was their con, and it was verified when again one of them tookay the pot.

Pretending he was going to the lavatory, he left the game. Frankie was suspicious of this, and by now street smart, he was suspicious of the absent player and his intentions and told the others he was going to the lavatory also. So he followed him, keeping a distance behind; he saw him walk outside the School of Arts building and followed the fellow around to the hotel on the corner and go into the bar where there were a group of young blokes who were obviously his mates. Peeking around the side of the door, Frankie heard him say to them, "These blokes are working a con on the Kelly pool game. I am gonna go back and get back into the game. There are four of them, they're all 'wogs', and there are seven of us, wait five minutes and then come in, and we'll get them, beat the shit out of them with pool cues."

Frankie, having heard this, moved quickly away, and running back down the street about a hundred yards, he hid in a recessed doorway. As the young bloke walked past, he never saw the king hit coming that dropped him to the footpath, and not content with that, Frankie viciously stabbed him in each thigh with the switchblade knife he had taken to carrying and ran back into the snooker room he yelled to his gang "let's get out of here quick". Ducking around a few side streets, they came back around into King Street Newtown and hailed a passing taxi to take them to Kings Cross.

Their brush with the law came near Chinatown one night. Frankie, Ronnie and their two newfound friends, Tony and Pedro, were hanging around not far from Thommo's illegal two-up school. And decided to see if they could get into this place which they knew was protected by the notorious gunman and stand-over man "Chow Hayes", but were told tersely by the bouncer, "fuck off and come back when yer grown up", and feeling a bit put off by this and not yet strong enough to challenge him, they decided to wander up town to near the Town Hall where the Crystal Palace snooker rooms and try their usual scam at a pool game. In conversation, Tony and Pedro had told them how easy it was to mug drunks, which they had done occasionally around the "Rocks area" and the waterfront, and so when they saw a man walking out of the building where the two up game was held, and noticed he was stuffing a wad of something into an overcoat pocket their interest was aroused.

Their intended victim did not notice the boys standing in the shadows of a doorway nearby, but they had seen him. It was obvious to them that what he was putting into his pocket would most likely be money he had won at the game, and they waited until he had walked a distance away from "Thommo's, and then they jumped him.

Unfortunately for the would-be muggers, their chosen victim was a hard case, a real tough bloke who did not go down easily, and the fight erupted into bad violence when Pedro pulled a knife and stabbed the man in both legs, just so he would fall down. They were caught in the act of kicking and bashing senseless the poor fellow when a police patrol car came around the corner. With drawn guns, the police managed to corner Frankie, Tony, and Ronnie, and missed street-wise Pedro, who was the only one to get away by escaping down a side lane.

Taken back to Regent Street police station near Broadway, they were separated and questioned, and when their place of residence was revealed, a police search was done. And under some loose floorboards, they found some articles of clothing and some expensive fishing reels still with the tags on them which indicated they had been stolen from Mick Simmons sporting goods shop in the Haymarket.

At their appearance for sentencing at the Central Courthouse in Bathurst Street, they were charged as minors with common assault occasioning bodily harm and shoplifting and sent away to Yasmar reformatory for two months month. They were now fingerprinted and on police records. Their life of crime had now started, and while in the reformatory, they were to meet another hard-case kid named Casey McGuire, aged nineteen. He was in there on a similar charge of assaulting a person with grievous bodily harm and also for peddling heroin. He told them the person he had assaulted and severely injured with a knife was the person he was selling heroin to, a drug addict who had refused to hand over the money. Frankie, Ronnie, and Tony attached themselves to Casey McGuire.

By chance, Casey McGuire's sentence was due to expire about the same time as Frankie, Ronnie, and Tony were due to be let out, and they made arrangements to meet outside when they were released. Casey had promised them he would introduce them to "the Man", who he worked for and see if he could get them work.

Frankie still had the stolen seed sown into the cuffs of the pants being held by the reformatory authorities, which were to be handed back to him when his sentence had expired, and kept his fingers crossed in the hope that by some chance those seeds would not be found.

And now, at the age of eighteen, their new career was to start soon after they had been introduced to the so-called "man" in a strip joint partly owned by him in King Cross.

Abraham "Abe" Williams was "the man". Born into a wealthy upper-class family and who, at an early became a product of Sydney's underworld, he was a man of some inherited wealth and who had his fingers in the many "pies" of prostitution, drugs, strip joints, and an alliance with the "bikie" gang who frequented an area in Kings Cross, and who were known to do errands for him.

"Abe" knew Casey and what qualities he had for future work, but he could quickly see that the new boys, Frankie and Ronnie, were still a bit wet behind the years. He did like their story and how they had run away from their homes in the country and how they had quickly learnt to survive, and offered the boys a job, where he laughingly explained that "they were to be gardeners working for him on land he owned in an isolated valley in the hinterland of the Central Coast", which was a large already established orange growing orchard with a large house, packing and storage sheds on it.

They soon caught his drift when he explained that he was in the process of establishing an elaborate hydroponic set-up growing marijuana there for distribution up and down the East Coast, for starters, and eventually supplying into the Sydney and Brisbane markets. At that meeting, they were introduced to a huge, burly man named Nick Caminos and were told that he was in control of the operation. He would be their "minder," Frankie and Ronnie, based on their previous experience back on the family farms would be his growers. The now twenty-year-old and street-smart Casey McGuire would assist in planting and growing and be a runner and delivery boy when needed.

To Frankie and Ronnie, the initial thought of going back to growing as they once did was off-putting until the benefits and the excellent money they would be paid was explained, with no expenditure on their part, and that, along with the knowledge and education they would gain about the shadowy drug world, changed their thinking, and they wholeheartedly agreed. Ronnie was extremely impressed when, on giving his name to Nick Caminos, he found out that Nick had enjoyed some dealings with his father and uncle in Griffith some years back.

They all were in awe of Nick Caminos, who had an impressive reputation for his strength as a weightlifter and professional wrestler. As a hard man who did "special jobs" for Abe Williams when required, and when the impressionable two country boys Frankie and Ronnie saw the shoulder holster and pistol he wore under a coat or in a calf holster on a hot day, they understood what "special jobs" meant. When Nick warned them about being "smart arses" and not to talk to anyone about the business, they listened close; they had already heard of Nick's ability to make people disappear.

Nick already had warned them that whenever they had time out to head to Newcastle for some fun or to make the occasional visit to their families in Griffith to keep their nose clean and their mouth shut, and as far as their families were concerned, they had regular jobs with a construction company which did building work around the country.

Over the next two years, Frankie, Ronnie and Casey worked diligently at their job. In particular, Frankie listened and learnt and absorbed every detail of this lucrative business, remembering every aspect of the plant growing. Harvesting and distribution methods, and Frankie, being of the bigger and stronger build than Ronnie, would be occasionally called upon to do a delivery with Casey, particularly if it was to a new and as a yet unknown outlet, and for this purpose, Nick had installed a small arms practice target range on the land and had supplied the boys with a .22 calibre pistol each to practice regularly with and to be carried only when doing deliveries, and to be always kept out of sight when travelling and never to be produced unless in a matter of extreme urgency if a deal went wrong.

To his mates Ronnie and Casey and even to Nick, Frankie, over these two years, had become very quiet. He seemed to become very introverted; he was quiet and never spoke much, and if he did, it was to ask Nick about some aspect of the business. There was no longer any outgoing casualness about him, and he had become remarkably skilled in handling the gun on the target range, even getting a rabbit on the run with a double-handed shot. Nick was impressed so much so that he remarked to Abe on one of his visits to Sydney to discuss business that Frankie was showing everything necessary to be a success in this business: he is intelligent, he listens, and I believe he would be tough and decisive where it was needed.

In actual truth, if Nick could read Frankie's mind, he would be worried. Frankie had become so obsessed with the business; his thoughts were not about working for business, but for the business to be working for him. Franco "Frankie" Gitano had become possessed by ambition. Although he had long outgrown the pants he had stolen from his brother some five years ago and sown the marijuana seeds into the cuffs, he had cut the legs off just above the cuffs and still had them hidden away in his personal gear. Those seeds were, to Frankie, his symbol of future success. Those same seeds created the energy that fed his burning desire to plant them for himself in his own drug empire. Those seeds were going to be the stepping stones to get him there, and so his delusions of grandeur grew.

It was another year that went by in the usual way. Casey was doing his normal delivery runs throughout the Central Coast villages and towns of Tuggerah, Wyong, Wamberal, and Gosford, driving on the newly completed F1 freeway. As he drove, he was lost in thought, thinking about the girl he had met on his last visit to Gosford and the fantastic sex they had. He was hoping for more to come on this visit, and as it was running through his mind like a Technicolor movie, he had a lapse of concentration, something he normally never did on these runs, and came back to reality with a start when he heard the police car siren, saw the flashing red and blue lights and looking down saw he was speeding at 145km and too late to do anything about it.

With the stash of about forty kilos of prime weed packed in small parcels in the boot, a pistol in the glove box, and about a thousand quid in cash in his jacket, he knew he could not afford to be caught and searched so throwing caution to the winds he tried to outrun the police pursuit car. He managed to stay ahead of them for about forty km further on and then lost control around a bend. When the police came on the scene, they spotted the guard rail smashed through, and down the bottom of a heavily wooded gully, they saw the wreck of the Ford station wagon. It was upside down, with the wheels still turning, and when they scrambled down, and through the scrub, they could see the roof was crumpled down to the seats and inside was a lifeless, bloodied body scattered around the car and in the surrounding bush and trees were parcels of prime marijuana. When the car was turned over and retrieved back to the road, and the gun and money were found, the heat was on to find from whence it had come and who was the driver.

It had to be handed to Abe Williams he ran a tight organisation. The car was registered to an unknown person, and the driver was carrying a phoney licence number. There was no way of identifying the driver, and the gun had no serial number. When Nick heard the news and read the newspaper reports, he went berserk for a while, calling Casey for every sort of fucking idiot there was, and then used it as a lesson to Frankie and Ronnie as to what not to do, and passed on instructions from Abe that we were to halt things for a while until the heat had died down. For about a month they just got on with the hydroponic production and no deliveries. Totally unaware while this was happening, another gang were attempting to muscle in on the operation and fill the gap in supplies.

Franco "Frankie" Colleoni was about to get his opportunity and it came about in a deadly way.

CHAPTER 28

The Rise of Franco "Frankie" Colleoni

It was 1955, and Franco Colleoni, now almost twenty-one, found out that he, Rocky and Joey's new careers were to start soon after they had been introduced to Adonis Caproni, a Sydney godfather, and Adriano Barbarino, a member of Caproni/Pignatore family alliance and the manager of a Kings Cross strip joint and night club, and part owner of a number of bars, coffee lounges, importing businesses and mansions, throughout the country owned jointly by the Caproni / Pignatore families where Frankie and Rocky were to work in the bars and coffee lounges.

They were told they would be alternating as doormen bouncers at the strip joint and nightclub on busy nights. This was to be their introduction to the Sydney underworld and was to be their training ground for the next two years under the guidance and grooming of Adonis Caproni and Adriano Barbarino.

Adonis Caproni, a godfather, had been born into an old established Calabrian family going back to the 1920s when they emigrated from Palermo and found their way to Melbourne and then to Sydney and who now lived in a huge luxury mansion high on the cliffs overlooking the ocean at Bondi in the Eastern suburbs of Sydney. They had become related by marriages in the 1920s-30s to the Pignatore family. Adonis Caproni, at an early age, became involved in the family's businesses, both legal and illegal. He was known to be a man of high intellect and business acumen with a university degree in business economics and who had accrued considerable wealth for the family. He was also known to be of the "old school" of Calabrian mafia power who was of a ruthless and unforgiving nature to his enemies and who had his fingers on the pulse of his various operations and in the many "pies" of prostitution, drugs, and strip joints in the region of his control, and also enjoyed a strong alliance with "bikie gangs", one in particular, was the gang who frequented Kings Cross, in the vicinity of the Beefsteak and Bourbon bar who were known to do many errands for him.

Caproni basically controlled the Eastern Suburb back to the Elizabeth Street fringe of Sydney's CBD and out to the coastal edge from the South Head through south to Cronulla, and worked with the Pignatore family to control the drug, prostitution, gambling, and extortion rackets along the Central Coast and into Newcastle and the fruit and vegetable market. "Adonis Caproni" also knew and respected Domenici Medici and told him he would personally assess the boys to see what qualities they had for future work. At first, he quickly saw that the new boys, Frankie and Rocky, were still a bit wet behind the years, but he did like their story and how they had run away from their homes in the country, eager to create a life of wealth and how they had quickly learnt to survive and he admired the punishment dished out to their former gang member Tony for daring to talk to the police.

Caproni did feel some uncertainty about Joey McGuire and felt he would hold him in abeyance until he proved himself, suspecting that Joey could be a loose cannon, which proved in time to be correct. After two years of training the three boys in the various and nefarious business dealings of the families, he was pleased with their willingness to learn and carry out willingly whatever work assigned to them. He particularly liked the way they had handled themselves in the nightclub and strip joint as bouncers when overly boisterous drunks annoyed the girls. Caproni eventually offered the boys a job. However, the boys were a little shocked at first when he laughingly explained that "they were to be gardeners working for him on land he owned in an isolated valley in the hinterland of the Central Coast, which was a large already established orange growing orchard and with a large house, with packing and storage sheds on it".

They soon caught his drift when he explained that he was "in the process of establishing, an building up an elaborate undercover hydroponic set up growing marijuana there for distribution up and down the east coast, for starters, and eventually supplying into the Sydney and Brisbane market."

At their next "work introductory" meeting, they were introduced to a huge burly man named Nick Capuzzi and were told that he was in control of the operation and who would be their "Capo" and "minder," with Frankie and Rocky, and based on their previous experience back on the family farms would be his growers, and street smart, Joey Maguire would assist in planting and growing and be a runner and delivery boy when needed.

It was explained to them to lookay upon this job as an apprenticeship and a gradual step up the ladder. To Frankie and Rocky, the initial thought of going back to growing as they had once done was off-putting until the benefits and the excellent money they would be paid, and future job prospects were explained, with no expenditure on their part, and that, along with the knowledge and education they would gain about the shadowy drug world and other rackets under the families control, changed their thinking completely and they wholeheartedly agreed. Rocky was extremely impressed when on giving his name to Nick Capuzzi; he found out that Nick had enjoyed some dealings with his father and uncle in Griffith a number of years back.

They all were in awe of Nick Capuzzi, who, in his youth, had built up an impressive reputation for his strength as a weightlifter and professional wrestler. In later years, as a "hard man" who did "special jobs" for Adonis Caproni when required, and when the two impressionable country boys, Frankie and Ronnie, got to know more about Nick Capuzzi, they understood what "special jobs" meant. So in the first hours of their introduction, when Nick warned them about not being "smart arses" and to obey the code of "Omerta" and not talk to anyone about the business or their personal involvement, they listened close. They had already heard of Nick's ability to make people disappear. Nick had warned them that whenever they had time out to head to Newcastle or Sydney for some fun or to make the occasional visit to their families in Griffith to keep their nose clean and their mouth shut, and as far as anybody was concerned, they had regular jobs with a construction company which did building work around the country.

Over the next two years, Frankie, Rocky and Joey worked diligently at their job. In particular, Frankie, who listened and learnt and absorbed every detail of this lucrative business, remembering every aspect of the plant growing and harvesting and distribution methods, and being of the bigger and stronger build than Rocky, would be occasionally called upon to do a delivery with Joey, particularly if it was to a new. As a yet unknown outlet, and for this purpose, Nick had installed a small arms practice target range on the land and had supplied the boys with a .22 calibre pistol each to practice regularly with and to be carried only when doing deliveries, to be always kept out of sight when travelling, and never to be produced unless in a matter of extreme urgency if threatened, or if a deal went wrong.

To his mates Rocky and Joey and even to Nick, Frankie, over these two years of training, had become very quiet, almost introverted; he was quiet and never spoke much, and if he did, it was to ask Nick about some aspect of the business. There was no longer any outgoing casualness about him, and he had become remarkably skilled in handling the gun on the target range, even getting a rabbit on the run with a double-handed shot. Nick was impressed, so much so that he remarked to Adonis Caproni on one of his visits to Sydney to discuss the business that Frankie was showing everything necessary to be a success in this business: he is extremely intelligent, he asks questions and listens, is a quick learner, and I believe he would be tough and decisive, possibly even ruthless where it was needed.

In actual truth, if Nick could read Frankie's mind, perhaps he could have reason to be worried. Frankie had become so obsessed with the business; his thoughts were not about working for the business, but for the business to be working for him. Franco "Frankie" Colleoni had become possessed by ambition, and although he had long outgrown the pants he had stolen from his brother some five years ago and sewn the marijuana seeds into the cuffs, he now had cut the legs off just above the cuffs and had them hidden away in his personal gear. Each time he looked at them, those seeds were to Frankie, his symbol of future success. The seeds created the energy that fed his burning desire to plant them for himself in his own drug empire. Those seeds were a constant reminder of what he wanted to be and the stepping stones to take him to get him there, and so his dreams of grandeur grew. Franco Colleoni Franco wanted to be more than Nick Capuzzi. He wanted to be a "Godfather."

The next five years year went by in the usual way. Frankie and Joey were now doing alternate delivery runs, and they all were amassing a large amount of money, some of which Frankie sent back home to his parents, who were now better off than before since "Don" Domenici Medici out of respect for his son Rocco and Frankie's friendship no longer tookay "tribute" from Giuseppe Colleoni, however, Frankie was bored with the same old routine and inwardly yearned for bigger things, he saw himself eventually as "Nick Capuzzi" and even bigger, perhaps as a "Don" like Adonis Caproni.

There was no question, though, of Frankie's loyalty to Nick Capuzzi, who he admired, trusted and learnt from, and he kept his impatience and thoughts to himself. Then a fatal mini disaster in their drug delivery business gave Frankie his opportunity to rise to a higher level. It was through the death of Joey Maguire while on his turn to do the deliveries to the dealers throughout the Central Coast villages and towns of Tuggerah, Wyong, Wamberal, Gosford and Newcastle.

Joey Maguire was driving on the newly completed F1 freeway. As he drove, he was lost in thought thinking about the girl he had met on his last visit to Gosford, and the fantastic sex they had. He was hoping for more to come on his visit to her tonight. As the visions of the last time were running through his mind like a Technicolor movie, he had a lapse of concentration, something he normally never did on these runs, and he came back to reality with a start when he heard the police car siren, saw the flashing red and blue lights and looking down saw he was speeding at 145km and too late to do anything about it.

With the stash of about forty kg of prime weed packed in small parcels in the boot, two kg of cocaine in small bags, about a thousand ecstasy tablets, a thousand quid in cash and a pistol in the glove box, he knew he could not afford to be caught, and throwing caution to the winds he tried to outrun the police pursuit car. It was about forty km further on and around a 75 km bend when the police came on the scene and spotted the guard rail smashed through, and down the bottom of a heavily wooded gully, they saw the wreck of the Ford station wagon; it was upside down, and the wheels were still turning, and when they eventually scrambled down, and through the scrub, they could see the roof was crumpled down to the seats and inside was a lifeless bloodied body and around the car and in the surrounding bush and trees were scattered parcels of marijuana, cocaine and tablets. When the car was turned over and retrieved back to the road, and the gun and money were found, the heat was on to find from whence it had come and who was the driver.

It had to be handed to Adonis Caproni that he ran a tight organisation. The car was registered to an unknown Sydney address and person, and the driver was carrying a phoney licence, and there was no way of identifying the driver. The gun had no serial number. When Nick heard the news and read the newspaper reports, he was furious and went berserk for a while, calling Joey for every sort of fucking idiot there was, and then used it as a lesson to Frankie and Rocky as to what not to do. Nick passed on instructions from Caproni that they were to halt things for a while until the heat had died down. For two months, they cut their losses and just got on with the hydroponic production with no deliveries. In this early stage of the delivery shutdown were unaware that another gang were attempting to muscle in on the operation and fill the gap in supplies.

Franco "Frankie" Colleoni, now appointed to be the senior delivery man, was about to unknowingly further his job prospects, which came about when he was faced with a situation that required him to take command in a deadly situation, and the ruthless manner in which he handled it, cemented his relationship with the "Dons".

For two months, they worked at planting and growing and generally lying low until the all-clear came when Nick got a phone call from Caproni to say that he and Pignatore were coming up for an urgent meeting with him, and Frankie and Rocky were to sit in on the meeting. A month previously, a new man, Adrianna Barbetta, had been sent from Sydney to report to Nick Capuzzi to be given a similar training apprenticeship and was to be included in the meeting, and what with the four trusted contract growers, they now had a full team again of growers and delivery men. Barbetta was a quiet, tough-looking man with eyes that darted everywhere, and at their pistol range practice, he proved himself to be a crack shot. Frankie figured him for a real hard case.

It was now early March 1960, and at the meeting held in a back room of an Italian Restaurant in Gosford with Adonis Caproni and Giovanni Barillaro, an enforcer for the Pignatore family. At that meeting, Franco Frankie Colleoni learnt that now, at almost 26 years of age, he was showing the qualities needed by the organisation. He was to be, not only the senior delivery man, he was to be the right-hand man to Nick Capuzzi and the "capo" when Capuzzi was away at any time, and Rocky was to be his right-hand man. It was a boost to his and Ronnie's egos, with them feeling they were on a climb up the ladder of success, and at the same meeting, this was emphasised to them when their boss Nick Capuzzi was given the name "the Ghost of Hades" Motorbike club, and the names of two men from the gang, who had attempted to muscle in on their drug business, and that these two men and the bike club had to be dealt with by any means necessary.

CHAPTER 29

The Croatian Connection

They were told the names of the two men who were attempting to take over their main Newcastle dealers and who had already converted this Croatian family of four to an alliance with them. Unfortunately for the Pignatore-Caproni syndicate, that family of four, which consisted of parents Josip and Anna Andric, in their mid-fifties, and their sons Juric and Geza, twin boys, who were in their mid-twenties, were the major dealers and suppliers servicing Greater Newcastle, and inland as far as Quirindi. This family had gone against the code of the Onorata Societia, and Nick Capuzzi was told bluntly to "go to Newcastle and eliminate the Ghost of Hades bike club problem and deliver a very strong lesson to the family who had switched over."

It was unusual for the Calabrian mafia to be allied with Croatians, and Josip and Anna's arrival into this country went back to the late 1940s when, along with many others of Croatian, Serb, Yugoslav and Italian origin, they migrated to Australia from their war-torn countries to seek a better life. Josip started work labouring in the massive Snowy Mountains hydroelectric scheme, and in his fourth week, he found himself working alongside a huge, arrogant Serbian named Marjan, a fact that was bound to lead to violence.

Throughout living history, the Croatians and the Serbians have fought and hated each other, and even in this new wonderful country, things were not to change. The Croatian Josip Andric and a Sicilian named Roberto Bartolino were working together in a gang of rock drillers. Even though there was a language difficulty, Josip and Bartolino had formed a friendship over some weeks, before the big Serb was introduced into the gang.

The three of them were now working temporarily as a three-man drilling team, separate from the rest of the work gang, and were deep down inside one of the many huge tunnels being constructed with heavy sledge hammers and hardened steel drills taking turns with drill and hammer to hit and twist the drill to make a hole deep enough for explosives to be packed into the hole to blow out rock to create the tunnels which were being blasted through the hard granite country, and designed to divert the enormous flow of snow melt waters into huge holding dams when an age-old argument flared up between Josip and Marjan about something that happened in Yugoslavia during the Nazi invasion of their country.

The Croatians were a highly nationalistic race and, unfortunately, had become deeply influenced by fascist ideology when in 1941, the Nazis set up a puppet government headed by Dr Ante Pavelic. His bloody rule saw the deaths of countless Serbs, Gypsies and Jews, and the fight in the tunnel started with the huge Serbian Marjan calling the much smaller Josip a dirty Nazi and continuously abusing and insulting him throughout the morning until Josip snapped and threw a piece of granite rock in Marjan's direction striking him painfully on the shin, and that is all it tookay to turn the big Serb into a raging lunatic and in seconds he was mercilessly pounding Josip into the ground. Roberto, shocked by this attack, could no longer tolerate this brutal attack on his new friend and, picking up the heavy sledgehammer they tookay turns using, raised it high and, with one wild swing, smashed it down on the hard hat the Serb was wearing breaking it and crushing in the back of his skull.

For some time, he and Josip stood in a state of shock, looking down at the body of the dead Serb, slowly realising the implications of what had been done. Josip spoke first, saying in his broken English, "Tank you Roberto, you save my life, now we fix," and they set to hastily reconstructing the scene. First, they picked up a large granite boulder, smeared it with blood, placed it in the pooling blood near the head of the dead Serb, and scrambled back through the tunnels to the main work gang calling for help for their workmate who had been killed by a rock fall. To the management, It was just one more death in a number of workplace accidents that were to take place over the ensuing years of that massive hydroelectric scheme.

From that incident, an implacable friendship grew between the two and led to an introduction of Josip and Roberto into a mafia connection when a second cousin of Roberto's arrived by ship in Sydney from a village in Calabria controlled by the Calabrian mafia and made contact with him. This cousin, Adolfus Bezio, proved to be a senior member of a Calabrian mafia family who was intent on making a name for themselves in this country of opportunities, and this did not include digging holes through the Granite Mountains. The reunion of the cousins was held in the village of Cooma where Roberto's cousin Adolfus told of contacts he had to make in Griffith with possible work opportunities.

Josip Andric and Roberto Bartolino left the Snowy Mountains and, with Josip's wife Anna, Adolfus Bezio travelled to Griffith to a meeting with the Medici family. This meeting was productive and proved lucrative when they were introduced into the world of cannabis growing and selling, and eventually, over the next eight years of growth as a team spent learning the drug trafficking trade, they were sent to the Central Coast as major dealers for the Pignatore/ Caprone syndicate.

Josip Andric and his wife Anna now had twin sons growing into their teen years and had settled onto a nice piece of land near Clarence town and built a beautiful house that acted as the base for the rapidly growing drug distribution network handled by the two cousins Roberto and Adolfus. Their allocated area of distribution was throughout the surrounding region from coast to inland, and a strong relationship had been established with Nick Capuzzi, who delivered regular supplies from the Hydroponic farm. Josip's two sons, Jure and Geza, now finished with their schooling, were being trained by Josip to eventually take over his part of the family business from him. He was ably assisted in this by Roberto and Adolfus who had become like uncles to the two boys, who also were sent to Griffith for further education in methods of distribution.

It all was shaping up to be a rosy, wealthy future for the Andric family and the two cousins Bartolino and Bezio, who had purchased land nearby and built two separate houses. It was making plans to bring from Calabria suitable wives and to raise a family. Then a major tragedy struck in the form of a light plane crash when the two cousins, Roberto and Antonio, were returning from a business meeting in Sydney with the Pignatore/Caprone families.

They were being piloted in a chartered plane, a four-seat Cessna, on a return flight from Bankstown Airport to a small private airport near Maitland. The weather was fine and clear on the day the flight left; it was early in the morning when they flew out, and soon after, the pilot received a weather forecast saying there was a large offshore and coastal build-up of storm extreme activity with possible gale-force wind gusts and hail stretching from the Sydney region to past Newcastle.

In an endeavour to avoid this, their pilot, a man well-schooled and experienced in all flying conditions, then made a decision to radio back he was making a change to his flight schedule to veer off his designated course to a northwestern inland pattern, which would take him on a circuitous route flying over a portion of the remote Wollemi National Park. It is an area of the largely unexplored wilderness of thick, high-canopied rainforest and deep impenetrable gorges. Unfortunately, the cyclonic low moved swiftly inland before the plane. Bankstown Airport control received one distress mayday call and then nothing. The plane and its passengers were not seen again and, to this day, have not been discovered.

The syndicate of the Pignatore-Caproni families allowed Josip Andric and his family to stay in business under their control and by the code of the Onorata Societia.

Although he missed his Italian friends and partners, he saw the increased profits to be made for his family, with him in control and with his sons running the business. Josip Andric was aware he was not Calabrian, but he was a proud Croatian, although somewhat greedy. He felt he was capable of running his own business, and did not understand or acknowledge their ridiculous codes and rituals. When an opportunity came along with the temporary downturn of supply from Nick Palluzzi's team and what seemed a better deal from the "Ghost of Hades" motorbike gang, he rolled over to them.

It was an unfortunate decision and a big mistake for him and his family.

The syndicate instructed Nick that the first thing for him to do after the "Ghost of Hades" bike club has been dealt with is to go and ascertain the strength of the syndicate's alliance with the other key dealer who, to their knowledge, had not been approached by the "Ghost of Hades" gang. This dealer was an old and respected Mafioso. One could say semi-retired from a wealthy Sicilian family. He was known as a venerated godfather and named Liborio Gitano who lived on a palatial estate near Port Stephens. A number of years ago, out of long respect for his Calabrian background, Gitano had been given an area of NSW to control by the linked syndicate families and, with it, the responsibility of servicing the drug trade from there to Port Macquarie and hinterland. Nick Capuzzi's job was to ensure that he was still on the side and prepared to take over the entire territory under the patronage of the Pignatore-Caproni family and with the physical assistance of Nick Capuzzi and his team.

Frankie and Rocky's eyes lit up when Caproni said to Capuzzi, "Take Frankie and Rocky with you, and carry these", and with that, Caproni handed over a large canvas bag he had been carrying. When Nick picked up the bag, he knew by the weight what was in it.

Caproni went on to say that Liborio Gitano had been contacted and told that some major change in distribution was about to take place, which would give him greater turnover, and that their emissary Nick Capuzzi, who is well known to him, would soon be visiting his family to explain the overall benefits.

That night back at the farm, Frankie and Rocky's eyes bugged when Nick handed to each of them a 9mm Walther P38 handgun, each with the original 4.9-inch barrel machined to take a silencer which screwed to the barrel, and then Nick pulled out of the bag a sawn-off Browning semi-auto A5 shotgun. It was at that moment Frankie and Ronnie realised the importance and possible danger of the impending mission.

As they sat examining these weapons, Nick said, "The bosses must have some excellent contacts to get these guns into the country, perhaps even in the Italian Military." He then went on to say, "This particular gun was originally designed in 1938 for the Nazi government, and Walther went into mass production in 1940 in their factory in Germany. It was to eventually replace the more expensive German Luger, and they were produced up until the factory was destroyed in 1945 near the end of World War II. By that time, a large quantity of these guns had been supplied to the then-Fascist Italian Government under the military dictatorship of Benito Mussolini. There were many thousands of them captured after World War II, and they were to become a favoured weapon, along with the similar Italian Beretta 92 by the N'Andragheta assassins.

The boys just sat there in silent awe as Nick went on to explain in detail the workings of this beautiful weapon, which had an effective firing range using the front and back sights of up to 55 yards, although the bulk of the silencer limits accuracy, and the gun then is really meant for close range shooting. When Nick was questioned on how he had so much knowledge on this gun, sometimes known as the "pistole 38", it was then the bug-eyed boys learnt that Nick had been a lieutenant artillery officer in the Italian Military and had been captured by the Australian Sixth Division force in the Middle East in World War Two. He was sent back to Australia as a POW and elected to stay on after the war ended, and he was released in 1946.

The 12 gauge Browning semi-automatic shotgun A5 model had been sawn off, and it obviously had been done by a skilled craftsman. With the surplus butt timber removed, it had been cut back to a comfortable pistol grip that fitted perfectly to Frankie's hand and measured about 20 inches in length; it would be a perfect close-quarter weapon. However, it produced a much louder muzzle blast than the pistols. There were also four hand grenades, and Nick, with his knowledge of explosives, explained them. Two were M67 military fragmentation type, and four were AN-M14 incendiary (thermite) hand grenades packed with 26.5 ozs of TH3 thermite mixture, which, as Nick explained, explodes when the igniting fuse sets fire to the thermite filler after the normal delay. It then burns for about 40 seconds at a temperature of 4300F, produces intense heat and will ignite combustible materials over a small area, with a portion of the thermite filler turning into molten iron that flows out of the grenade. This molten iron will then ignite or fuse whatever it touches and destroy all types of equipment.

As Nick was explaining all of this, Frankie felt an almost sexual experience go through his body. It was a vicarious thrill he got when he hurt someone or when exposed to extreme brutality, and he was thinking how much he liked this tough man and the weapons of destruction he was unveiling to them and how badly he wanted to use them.

They spent the next two days practising marksmanship, loading, unloading and cleaning the weapons, pulling them apart and putting them back together, they now all felt confident that they would be ready for the job ahead. It was now time to research the information given to them on the background and habits of the "Ghost of Hades" Motor Bike Club, its club members, their clubhouse, and where their drug supplies were kept, then do surveillance and plan our method of attack. Carrington is now part of Greater Newcastle, but back in the early 1800s, it was known as Bullock Island and was an area of swamps, small river islands and mangrove flats located over shallow and deep underlying beds of coal, and for over 150 years or more, far-seeing politicians and townspeople saw its true worth. The land and mudflats were slowly reclaimed with massive landfill projects starting with the dumping of sailing ship ballast and the filling in of waterways and tidal flats.

It was only natural for it to become a major coal shipping port because the coal seams could be continuously mined, and the coal then directly loaded onto ships once huge wharves had been built to take the many ships of the world. The rich seams of coal extended in many directions and even out under the Pacific Ocean. Bullock Island grew to become a coal miner's town and arguably the biggest coal shipping port in Australia and then renamed as Carrington.

It reached its zenith when a railway was put through to it from Newcastle with rail turnarounds, shunting yards, conveyor loading facilities, and access to the massive BHP Steelworks. In the earliest days of its growth, it was a colourful port, a motley brawling community of coalminers and seamen, and local citizens of every race and colour frequenting the hotels that grew with the population. By the 1950s, it had mellowed and grown up. But still of a dismal, shabby and dusty appearance with its huge coal port facilities and the crisscrossing network of railway lines, with long rows of railway coal wagons queued to get their fill of coal and which could be a hazard to drunken seamen haphazardly wending their way back to their ship after a night on the booze, in one of the hotels.

In fact, it was recorded that in the 1950s, a sailor, possibly drunk, was crossing the innumerable railway lines that spread like a spider web over the area, either tripped and fell or, perhaps drunk, collapsed and fell asleep between two wagons in the long line with his body lying across the rails. It was after the pubs closed, possibly about midnight, when he fell, and in the very early hours when the trains started their movements, the result was inevitable. It tookay some time for the authorities to remove the body parts and clean up the mess.

As Frankie, Nick, and Rocky absorbed all the relevant information on where they were going pertaining to the job in hand and the locality of Carrington and its waterside area dense with mangrove scrub, Frankie found all of these little bits of information entertaining. The sadistic and cruel side of his nature was starting to surface more. When he had been told about Joey Maguire's high-speed crash and death, although he showed on his face suitable commiseration, inside his mind Frankie was smirking, actually pleased, because he saw Joey Maguire's death, as an obstacle removed from his own climb to power, and as he read on about the sailors body being crushed under the wagon wheels he imagined what it would be like to watch his body being chopped to pieces and again felt a shivering thrill go through his body.

Frankie may not have known it then, but a psychiatrist would have recognised the signs of a psychopath, and an impending event was soon to prove that so.

CHAPTER 30

Not a "Ghost of a Chance"

It was about 5:30 p.m. on the 24 of December when Nick, Frankie and Rocky, set off for Carrington with Nick driving a stolen van with false number plates. With it being Christmas Eve, there was no doubt there would be a police presence on the roads, so they were in no hurry and eventually turned onto a side road at about 8:30 p.m. and drove for a short distance into a thick mangrove forested area on the outskirts of Carrington. It was Nick's plan to have a short rest, and to once more go over the plan of attack. Three weeks earlier, Nick and Frankie, driving an old model Ford utility loaded with camping gear and fishing rods and pretending to be fishermen, had explored the entire area around and in Carrington.

They had found the "Ghost of Hades" motorbike club. It was an old-style large weatherboard house set on high timber posts, similar to the Queenslander style, with a verandah on three sides and a high under section ideal to keep their Harley Davidson motorbikes out of the weather and under shelter. The house was painted in a garish red and white, no doubt the "Ghost of Hades" club colours. Close by the house was a padlocked steel shed. It was surrounded by a high woven mesh galvanised wire fence, similar to what is seen around airports, and boasted a sign on its padlocked gate that said in big letters in red on a white background: THE GHOST OF HADES MOTOR BIKE CLUB with a logo showing a ghost-like red and black Satan astride a motorbike, with the wording "PRIVATE CLUB ENTER AT YOUR OWN RISK". It was on a remote corner of Fitzroy and Darvall Street, with vast areas of mangrove flats around it and facing a huge mangrove swamp. It was ideally situated for any nefarious bike gang activities and, on closer examination, ideal for Nick's plans.

Two weeks earlier, Nick and Frankie had stolen the white Ford transit van late at night in Gosford. They drove it back to their secluded Central Coast property and concealed it in one of the lock-up sheds where the number plates were removed, and before fitting a false set of plates, it was spray-painted a nondescript mid-brown colour. The van had no side windows and, therefore, ideal for their coming nocturnal excursion of murder. Inside the van, it was carrying their arsenal of weapons, including an incendiary hand grenade, bolt and wire cutters, a twenty-litre drum of 50/50 diesel petrol mix and two firelighters of the type used by bush firefighters.

It was a dark, hot, humid night with mosquitoes buzzing around them in this mangrove swamp area, when the three men put black ski masks on and pulled down over black high neck long-sleeved cotton T-shirts and black pants and black sandshoes. With daubs of black stage makeup on what one could see of their faces, they were unrecognisable. If anything, they would appear rather frightening to an observer. They did a final check of their Walther pistols, loaded the semi-automatic shotgun and a silenced .22 rifle, put on tight-fitting, soft black leather gloves and drove to their destination. About six or seven hundred metres from the clubhouse, there was a noisy Christmas celebration going on in another house with similar noise coming from the biker's clubhouse interior, which would be in their favour as they cut through the wire mesh fence.

As they approached the immediate proximity of the fence and the house, Nick was reminding them of information given to him recently that there were about twelve active members of the club. Still, intelligence reports he had received said that a few of them had families and would possibly be home with them, being Christmas Eve, and there should only be a small number of the single men in the house, which they often slept in and used as their base of operations. If there were too many club members present, we were to abort the mission. Nick then said with a smile, "It should be a small group inside, but whoever is there tonight, don't give them a ghost of a chance to get away. We all laughed at his 'ghostly' reference. The Ghost of Hades bike club was about to be sent a very special Christmas present."

Now, less than fifty metres from the fence, we could see that all lights were on in the house and shining out through the open windows and doors, which were covered by fine gauze fly screens. There were also burglar lights on three sides, giving a wide spray of light to three areas of the yard, with one side shining a bright light across the nearby padlocked steel shed. Nick guessed the shed was holding drug supplies and possibly weapons. A couple of neon tubes were showing a strong light under the house, illuminating and reflecting light spots on four polished and shining 'hogs'. The bikers certainly adored their Harley Davidson motorbikes. There was a low fire burning under a hotplate on an outdoor BBQ. Obviously, they had cooked some meat and were now inside eating and drinking and by the sound of their loud voices, doing a lot of drinking! Listening keenly to the variety of voices, we could make out one loud, harsh, and rasping female voice. Nick said with a laugh, "She must be a biker moll who smokes too much", and said, "there's only four men inside. This should be a piece of cake, and tonight's Christmas gift will pass on a lesson to the others." Nick went on to say, "Let's go around to the back of the house, which backs onto the thick mangrove swamp. There are no back steps there, and it will be better cover. We will cut the fence wire there, get in under the house where the bikes are, and pour the fuel all over the floor and the bikes and trail it back a metre or two outside, and then we hit it with the firelighter.

"Rocky, you get around to the front yard outside the circle of light and watch the front steps. If anyone comes out of the screen door and down the steps, fire away with the shotgun first, that should keep them inside, and then keep your pistol ready, that will give us enough time to double around and join you with the guns". "Frankie, you shoot out the yard lights, with the silenced rifle. If no one comes out, sit tight. I will join you and wait to see what happens when the fire hits the bikes and starts to burn upwards." "They might have weapons; stay outside the range of light coming from the house, and as they run down the stairs, shoot at them, but not at the woman. I want the girl alive to send a message."

There was now a big red flash of light coming from under the house as Nick ignited the fuel mix, and it only seemed like a matter of seconds before it was creeping up the walls and then the first of the Harley Davidson's fuel tank exploded with a whooshing roar, followed in sequence by the other three bikes, and upstairs the occupants started streaming out of the only doorway to the stairs, in dazed and drunken wonderment, pushing, yelling, and falling over each other in their haste to get down the flight of stairs, only to be met by a fusillade of bullets from the three silenced barrels of the Walther P38's Three were killed instantly, a fourth lay wounded.

Telling Frankie and Rocky to keep covering the steps, Nick quickly strode the short distance to the padlocked steel shed and, with the heavy-duty bolt cutters, cut the chain and threw open the door to survey an Aladdin's cave of stacked marijuana and numerous cartons packed on top of each other, no doubt holding a huge variety of illegal drugs, and what looked to be a large gun cabinet in a corner. Nick laughed as he said, "I hate to do this; such a waste of product, but it will teach them an expensive lesson," and without further hesitation, he pulled the pin on an AN-M14 incendiary grenade. We ducked down for cover, and a few seconds later, there was a massive whoomph of white-hot heat followed by a raging inferno inside the steel shed.

It had taken less than ten minutes, and it was over. Their cache of drugs was gone, and there were four bodies; three were draped dead around the bottom steps where they fell from the fusillade of bullets, and two were on the ground, one dead and with some painful groaning coming from one of them, which stopped when a.38 from Frankie's gun shattered his head.

The woman was a hysterical mess. She had fallen heavily down the last few steps and was crawling on her hands and knees just past the bottom steps, screaming and pleading "not to be shot" until Nick shut her up with a hard punch to the jaw and picked her up under her arms like a rag doll said, Frankie, grab her legs, and we'll carry her through the front gate, and we'll tie her to the gate with this, pulling a short length of cord from his hip pocket. Dropping her not too gently on her ample rump, Nick made her sit with her body upright and stretching her arms out wide in a crucifix fashion along the fence, got Frankie to hold them, and using Frankie's flick knife, he cut three lengths of cord, two pieces he used to tie her outstretched arms by the wrists to the wire mesh. Intrigued by this, Frankie watched as Nick forced her mouth to open and then put the third piece through her mouth, pulling it firmly into the cheeks of her mouth, and tied both ends of the cord together through the wire mesh, effectively holding her head upright, saying "I have got an idea of what to do with her. That will get a message across to the other bastards in the gang," and going back to one of the bleeding bodies on the ground he placed his gloved hand, with fingers spread and palm down into the pooling, congealing blood. Walking back to the barely conscious woman, he tore her blouse open and slit the front of her brassiere apart with the knife, exposing an expanse of chest above her breasts. Nick then placed his bloodied hand against the white skin of her chest, leaving a bloody handprint just above her breasts and saying, "This is the sign of N'Drangheta, the mark of the Black Hand. Now they should get the message." Frankie was watching this procedure with extreme interest and again felt his body shudder with the same erotic like thrill feelings he had experienced before

All of this, by now, had taken maybe twenty minutes, and it was now time to move quickly to get far away. No doubt the fires had been spotted, and it was time to move. Rocky already had the van ready with the motor running, and piling into it, they headed away in the opposite direction. They soon reached the outskirts of Carrington and were headed for Newcastle and home on the Central Coast when two fire brigade trucks went hurtling past with sirens blaring, closely followed by two police cars.

Nick congratulated us as we sped along and said, "We will wait a few days before settling the score with the family at Clarence

Town, who had switched over to the bikers." He went on to say, "Now we will visit the old Godfather Liborio Gitano, who would no doubt realise as soon as the news is released that there would be a huge business increase for his family fortunes."

The next morning, and for a few days after, the news of the shooting dominated national and regional newspapers, the radio, and the new black and white television news, now the most recent form of news media, which was growing in popularity in the 1950s. The media reports on Christmas Day were all about the Christmas Eve massacre, and it was the major news for the next couple of days.

It created ripples throughout the nation about the possibility of an outbreak of gangland violence, particularly in the Greater Newcastle region. The news about the shooting murders of four members of an outlaw bikie gang, and with a woman gang member, who is suffering shock and severely traumatised in hospital, and the destruction by burning of their clubhouse certainly shocked the nowadays normally quiet suburb of Carrington. This horrific incident has been followed by the disappearance of the remainder of the "Ghost of Hades" motorbike club from the area. They are believed to be disbanded and are being looked for by the police in the hope of gaining information as to this massacre. The hospitalised woman refuses to talk to the police.

The police suspect the crimes of being committed by a rival gang probably over drug deals gone wrong, as the "Ghost of Hades" motorbike gang was known to have links to organised crime. The police say they have no leads to follow at the moment.

Nick Capuzzi and the boys arrived back home early in the morning on Christmas Day to the secluded valley, Nick had cautioned the boys not to discuss the mission with anyone. All were elated with its success as Nick locked the van and guns inside a heavily padlocked shed, and they all turned into their beds for some sleep, that is all except Frankie; there was no way he could get to sleep as he relived over and over again the night's events right down to the last detail.

Late that afternoon, Nick tookay them all to his favourite Italian restaurant in Gosford to enjoy a massive Christmas dinner which he had prearranged. When Nick came out of a back room dressed in the outfit of a rotund Father Christmas, Ho, Ho, Ho'ing, he had the restaurant clientele, its staff and everyone else in stitches of laughter. Nick was dressed to the part and complete with a red velvet bag filled with expensive gifts for everyone, including a pearl-handled switchblade knife for Frankie, who now never went anywhere without one, seeming to prefer a knife to a gun. When presented with it, Frankie was laughing and thinking, "Here is a skilled assassin in a Santa Claus suit," Nick had already noticed the use of a knife as a personal preference by Frankie Colleoni, which was to show itself in a bloody manner in the near future.

A few days later, Nick spoke to Frankie and Rocky, saying, "It is near the time to talk to the family who will be taking over. We will be going to Nelson Bay to see the old 'Don' Liborio Gitano with a gift from the Pignatore-Caproni families and to reopen our supply lines as soon as you get back from seeing your family and in the New Year, we will be back in business."

Nick Capuzzi, accompanied by Frankie and Rocky, was driving an expensive new Statesman car, a lavish gift from the Pignatore-Caproni families, to show their trust in his loyalty from this old Godfather Liborio Gitano, who welcomed them like long lost family to a sumptuous dinner. Methods of distribution and accounting of monies were discussed and toasted with good wines and "Grappa," and with Nick assuring Gitano and his sons Mario and Pietro of the loyalty of the families he represented and of his own strong protection and support where needed.

Caproni informed Nick that the Pignatore and Caproni families were pleased with the outcome and the fact that no evidence of what had happened on the "hits" could be traced back to them and had arranged for a very generous bonus to be paid to each of them with best wishes for the Christmas and New Year.

Along with that message was the instruction to lay low for a couple of weeks and take some holidays, as they felt there would be no more moves on their territories in Greater Newcastle and beyond, and the Josip Andric family, who had switched over to the bikers could be taken care of at a later date, who of course, would no doubt be wondering what was going to happen to them, knowing the old saying in the mafia "that revenge is a dish that is better eaten cold." Nick was instructed to let them sweat for a while, we will work out what to do with them soon. With no supplies going into them, nor going out from them, they won't be having a money-making Christmas or New Year, and with no contact or signs of repercussions from us, they may think all is forgiven, and that is what we want them to think, and then we will hit them hard.

That old Croatian piece of shit and his family will soon learn about the code of "Onorata Societia" and what it means.

A New Year Blood Bath

In the restful days after the Carrington incident and over the Christmas and early New Year holiday period spent with their families in Griffith, Frankie was like a cat on a hot tin roof, restless and overactive. He could not settle down nor derive much enjoyment from being with his family, whom he had not seen for so long. As much as he loved them and wanted to see them, his mind was a whirlpool of violent and yet salacious thoughts, continually dwelling on the Carrington murders and shootings and then jumping to protracted colourful images of the coming visit to the traitorous Andric family. Simply put, Frankie could not wait to get back to work.

An insatiable blood lust was building up in him; it was a thirst that needed to be quenched, and it was not until the second week of January 1961, after Nick Capuzzi told him and Ronnie of his planned attack on the Andric's family, did Frankie settle down into any degree of normalcy.

Nick had been studying the weather patterns and reports. He knew that violent wind and rain storms, along with thunder and lightning noise, were common along the Eastern coastline at this time of the year, usually in conjunction with the start of the Northern Territory monsoon season, and he was looking for such a night to visit the Andric family home.

Adonis Caprone had passed on some information that the Andrics had put their house up for sale, no doubt in an endeavour to leave the area for places unknown and hopefully escape any retribution for their betrayal. To the mafia code of conduct, that is never permissible. The instructions to Capuzzi were to hit soon and hit hard.

It often takes time to sell a house, and before getting this news, Caprone had already organised for regular surveillance to be done by a private investigation business owned by his family, and daily reports had been coming in.

The Andric family lived in a luxurious two-storey home on about a hundred acres of land which backed onto the Williams River and only a few kilometres distance from Clarence Town and alternated their shopping forays between Maitland, Dungog, and Raymond Terrace. Their house was well back from a secondary road and semi-isolated from neighbours. They employed a part-time gardener and handyman, also a Croatian who worked on the property and gardens an average three days per week. They owned two handsome appaloosa horses who were kept in stables and were seen to be ridden by the two sons on occasions and on some weekends. They were seen on occasion to go riding with friends from the surrounding areas, but in recent times, since Andric's partners Roberto and Adolfo disappeared in the plane crash six months ago, there had been no activity in that area.

The two houses owned by his now considered deceased Italian partners were on sizeable land nearby and side by side to each other and were still empty, probably being held intestate until a coroner verdict on their deaths was reached.

All drug supplies in the past had been delivered to them from the Hydroponic farm by Joey McGrath, which ended after his fatal crash, followed by the temporary shutdown of business and supplies by Nick Capuzzi.

An important fact that showed now was the entire family rarely left the house, unless as a group in one car, and that was to do a food shopping excursion to the nearest town, and one teenager and one adult always stayed in the car parked in a most public place. They did not have any visitors and no longer rode their horses, and obviously, that meant that their street dealers had got the message there were no longer any drug supplies and to stay away. Each time before entering and leaving the garage it was noticed a person peering covertly from behind shade windows.

Aerial photographs showed the necessary details of the house layout and from where a covert approach would be made to gain entrance. Close examination of photographs provided by Caprone showing front and back entrances had Nick thinking of a possible back door diversion noise by Ronnie and a sudden entrance through the front door blown open by a shotgun blast at the height of a thunderstorm.

On analysis of the reports, Nick reasoned that a bomb in, or under the car, or in the family home was out of the question, and as extreme punishment to the whole family was required, the individual execution of a single or two family members at a time had risk and associated dangers. No! It had to be one hit, with the destruction of the entire family in one go.

It was nearing the end of January when the Bureau of Meteorology sent out a warning of severe thunderstorms with gale-force winds, lightning, and possible hailstones, and they were ready, having been practising with their weapons and going over in repeated detail, the plan of attack.

Thunderclouds, heavy with the promise of rain, had been looming on the Eastern horizon all of that Sunday afternoon, along with the growling rumbles of thunder and distant lightning flashes. It was now a humid, sultry evening and at their farm, there was a tense expectant energy In Nick and the boys. It was the perfect night for the murderous work that lies ahead.

Nick Capuzzi had put a lot of thought and time into his plan of attack. He had outlined his plans to Caprone and requested some items not easily available, and in due course a box arrived, a trusted courier delivered it, and in it were three sets of night vision glasses as supplied to the Australian Military special services operatives.

There was still some faint light in the late afternoon sky when the three men left for the hour-long journey to the near vicinity of the Andric family home.

There was an air of silent expectancy in the van as they drove along, a quietness only interrupted by the radio stations. Nick was monitoring for updates on the weather forecast. Frankie and Rocky were lost in their own thoughts on the coming night's events.

There was a humid, heavy feel to the air inside the van, and outside, violent wind gusts were starting to cause the van to sway somewhat as Nick drove along the highway and as the van rounded a bend and out of an area forested on both sides, the enormity of the coming storm could be seen.

Looming in the sky and to the northeast, and now almost above the van, was a huge mass of dark cloud. It was a cloud of the type with a greenish tinge with its threat of hailstones, which was now filling the horizon and lit with intermittent flashes of lightning, accompanied by loud cracks of thunder. "Christ help sailors on a night like this", Nick said; it was a saying Nick remembered, a flashback to something his seagoing fisherman father used to say to him as a child. Nick smiled to himself and then said out loud, "It's a perfect night for a murder," and Franco "Frankie" Colleoni felt the shiver of feeling again. An extreme, almost erotic feeling which sent a surge of blood through his body, he could feel himself getting an erection.

The van radio was now crackling with static as the latest storm warning was transmitted, telling of increasing wind gusts of up to 100 kms, accompanied by torrential rain and heavy hail, and warning people to stay indoors or seek shelter, and advising motorists to watch for flooded causeways and roads, and possible hail damage. It was anticipated the full brunt of the storm would reach the coast between Taree and Newcastle at about 9 p.m. and would move swiftly inland. Nick spoke again: "Perfect timing," he said, "we will be in position when the worst of it hits about 9.30" as he turned the van off onto a side road.

The van was now hidden on a side track and screened off from the main thoroughfare. After handing out their pistols and ammunition and waterproof coats, Nick tookay a large black plastic bag out of the van, saying we will need these too, and they made their way cautiously through some open forest and toward the back fence boundary of one of the houses, previously owned by one of the now deceased cousins.

Standing temporarily sheltered from the mounting fury of the storm behind a southern wall of the house, they could clearly see by looking around the corner of the wall the Andric house with its outside front lights on and with upstairs and downstairs house windows showing light through. They had donned the long black coats Nick had handed them. The night was now pitch black and only lit by incessant lightning flashes accompanied by the deafening sonic booming rumbles of thunder, and heavy rain was coming down in spasmodic torrents.

In the early preparation for this job, Nick, in visualising what would be required if his wish for bad weather eventuated, had purchased long black water-repellant coats similar to what men of the land and seamen wear and now with their black ski masks covering their head and faces they resembled three black crows cowering in the dubious shelter behind the house from the full blast of the windswept rain, while Nick gave last minute instructions followed by saying, "Rocky, you wear this" and opening the plastic bag, handed over a leather belt carrying an army ammunition pouch and a hand sewn canvas sheath, saying with a laugh, "It tookay half a day to cut out and sew this together, I don't think I would qualify for a seamstress job in a clothing factory!" We all laughed, his flash of humour cutting through the growing tension at what may lay ahead.

The waterproof sheath contained the loaded, sawn-off twin-barreled semi-automatic shotgun. The ammunition pouch was full of 12 gauge heavy-load shotgun shells. He reached deeper into the plastic bag and pulled out three AN-M14 incendiary grenades and then, in a most serious tone emphasising his words, said. "No matter what happens, whether this 'hit' goes well or not, these babies must be used, the house, everything and everyone in it, must be destroyed," and pausing for a moment's silence, added, "and that includes anyone of us, if mortally hit, there must be no recognisable evidence left behind, do I make myself clear! He repeated emphatically, "anyone of us! With that last profound statement, Frankie and Rocky stood in quiet shock, now fully realising the seriousness of this mission and, as one simply said, "yes!" These were the same incendiary grenades used to wipe out the "Ghost of Hades" motorbike clubhouse and drug stash. No doubt this was to be a very serious message to send to any dealers who don't toe the line.

In the large side pockets of their coats, Frankie and Nick were carrying their silenced Walther P38 pistols and ample ammunition, and their pockets were now weighing heavy with the AN-M14 incendiary grenades; Ronnie was struggling to strap the leather belt heavy with the ammunition pouch and shotgun around his coat and still leave the flaps of his coat pockets free to be able to reach in for his Walther P38 and ammunition, and was still fiddling with it as they were about to move out into the deluge of rain, when Nick stopped and turning to Frankie, quietly said, as if to reaffirm his previous words "Frankie, with these grenades, we have to make sure the house burns to the ground with everything, including the bodies in it, nothing must be left." As they walked on, Frankie puzzled for a moment, wondering why the emphasis; Nick had certainly already made himself clear. The house and all in it must burn! They were now outside the white-painted post and rail fence surrounding the house when the hailstones came, some almost as big as golf balls, started to rain down on them. There was a foul curse from Nick and then another curse from Ronnie, as they were hit on the head by these deadly missiles, and as quick as possible, they scrambled over the low post and rail fence with no fear of making some noise and went for the cover of the inset back veranda and BBQ area, thankful for the blackness of the night and the thunderous sound of the hail coming down on the roof of the house and its masking all other noise. In the shelter of the indoor/outdoor barbecue entertaining area, they could see some light filtering through shaded windows and had their pistols ready in case someone should appear.

Nick's plan was for him and Frankie to make their way around to the front of the house, and after a five-minute interval, Ronnie was to turn off the switch in the power box, which was in an alcove and now visible to Nick's pencil torch. Ronnie was to hide out of sight after throwing the switch, and when someone appeared to check the power box, he was to blast them with the shotgun the moment they stepped out and through the door. At the sound of the shotgun blast, Nick and Frankie were to use their Walther P38s to shoot through the lock on the front door and go in with guns blazing at anyone they saw in the house.

Adjusting their night vision glasses to be ready for the blackout, and just as Nick and Frankie were about to make their way around to the front door for their grand entry, there was a mighty explosion of thunder and lightning and turning in a split second to the sound they were to see the incredible sight of a tree about two hundred metres away, hit by the lightning, and split in two with one part slowly falling and a line of burning bark running from top to bottom of what had been a tall hardwood tree. At the same time, all the lights went out in the house. The power surge from the lightning had fused the power box.

There was temporary blindness for a second or two through the night vision glasses to eyes struck by the unexpected brilliant flash of light, and Nick said hoarsely, "Fucking hell! Change of plan, quickly now, go for cover and get ready for when they come out and shoot first!"

Nick had taken shelter in the power box alcove, Ronnie was crouching behind a built-up garden area of flowering leafy plants, shotgun at the ready and Frankie was well hidden behind a gas barbecue area built onto a raised concrete block stand when the door opened, and the two brothers Juric and Geza stepped through the wide open door with their torches flashing toward the alcove. That was when Nick stepped out, squeezing the trigger on his Walther P38, and at the same time, a fusillade of bullets and shotgun pellets from Frankie and Ronnie hit them both. They were dead before they hit the ground, and Nick was running through the open door, shooting at someone within the house as he ran, with Frankie hot on his heels.

Frankie was just in time to see Josip Andric, still alive with a rifle sagging in his hands and slowly slumping to the floor, blood pouring from his chest. His gaze was fixed on Nick, spluttering blood from his mouth as he said, "fuck you", as Nick finished him off with a well-placed bullet through his forehead.

In the moments of silence that followed this incredibly quick extermination of the male Andric, there must have been little thought given, or perhaps it was a lapse of judgement, from all three on the whereabouts of the wife and mother of the men, Anna Andric. Later, Frankie, in hindsight, was to vaguely remember words he once read or heard, such as "hell hath no fury as a woman scorned" or something like that. Still, they were all shocked into a moment of inactivity when they heard a high-pitched wailing scream at the same time as a succession of high-powered automatic rifle bullets ploughed into Nick's body from high in a dark section of the stairway to the upper floor, with one of them grazing the fleshy part of Frankie's upper right arm who was standing just behind him.

Although Anna Andric could not see in the dark who had murdered her men, it was guessed she aimed at the small muzzle explosion of light as Nick fired the final bullet into Josip Andric's. She knew how to shoot and did not miss, and Nick was dead, his body riddled with four of five bullet holes, one of which had penetrated his heart. Through the night vision glasses, Frankie could make out an outline up high on the stairs on a small landing and fired a quick shot at it. He heard something hit the landing floor, and then the vision disappeared; at that same moment, the lights came back on, and for a second or two through the night vision glasses, the flash of light temporarily blinded him.

The power box had not fused at all; it was the lightning strike, and its surge of power had simply caused a temporary power blackout and power was now restored. Taking his night vision glasses off, Frankie turned to Ronnie, saying, "Cover me with that shotgun. I am gonna find that fucking witch and make her suffer for this," pointing his gun toward Nick as he said it. The murderous glint in his eyes said it all; the psychopathic urges previously lying beneath the surface were about to emerge, and Ronnie knew without knowing what was about to happen.

Frankie went slowly up the stairs to the landing where Anna Andric had fired the automatic rifle from and stopped at the sight of an automatic rifle lying there; he picked it up and saw the magazine was empty and, crouching down, saw what he was looking for, a few drops of blood and a succession of blood drops going further up the stairway. Frankie was sure his one shot had hit her, and he was right; she had dropped the now empty rifle and gone further up the stairway, and now he had to follow the trail.

At the top of the stairs, the top floor landing branched off to the left and right. Ronnie, who was following Frankie about five steps behind, saw him hesitate as he looked first to the left and then right and then bent down to the carpeted landing. To the left of the landing was one door and a large wall area covered with pictures, to Frankie's thinking, it was probably the master bedroom with an en suite. In contrast, the blood drops were headed to the right, where there were three doors, which Frankie surmised were the entrances to the bedrooms occupied by Juric and Geza and a communal bathroom between. "Just as well she was bleeding," Frankie thought, "without that blood trail, it would be a more dangerous search," as he slowly turned right and headed for the door on the left.

Treading lightly and carefully, with pistol ready, he was about to take the last step to the door to turn the door knob when a loose board under the carpet gave out a creaking noise, he hesitated for a second and instantly stepped back, and it was just as well he did, as two shotgun blasts within a fraction of a second from each other blew the top door panel apart at the height where Frankie's chest and shoulders would have been.

Frankie leaped forward, crashing into the light panelled door with his shoulder and the weight of his body behind it, which flew open just in time to see Anna fumbling to load two more shotgun shells into the open breech of an old-style twin barrel shotgun. Frankie saw in an instant blood pouring down her arm from a bullet wound high in the arm. She was having trouble fitting the cartridges into the opened breech as Frankie hit her hard to the side of her head with the silenced barrel of his Walther P38. Her scream was stopped mid-breath and she hit the floor and lay there moaning with a slow trickle of blood now coming from the head wound just above the right temple.

To Rocco, standing inside the open doorway, shotgun at the ready, the next few minutes seem to be a movie slowed back to half speed as he watched Frankie methodically lay his P38 pistol on a nearby bedroom dresser and then bend down to the floor and put one arm under Anna's knees and the other under her narrow shoulders, and using brute strength lifted her off the floor, and onto the bed. Frankie stood there watching her for a few moments and then turned to a door that opened into the communal bathroom previously shared by the two brothers; he went into the bathroom and came out carrying a large glass of water and a hand towel.

Placing them on the dresser, he looked around the room and saw the elaborate, rich burgundy curtains draped on either side of the French window doors, which opened out to a terrace veranda; the curtains were held back on each side by scarlet velvet cords with tasselled ends. He pulled them off the curtains. Rocco just stood there mesmerised, watching this; he felt he knew what was coming and was intrigued momentarily watching as Frankie stretched Anna's arms out, and slightly above her, and methodically tied each wrist to the ornately carved posts of the bed head and then did the same with her ankles to similar corner posts at the end of the bed, she lay there spread-eagled, her blood from her right arm staining the bed cover. With Nick gone, Rocky was now urging Frankie for them to fire the place and leave, but Frankie's insane eyes were blood red and thirsting for revenge.

Anna was just coming around as Frankie forced her jaws apart and stuffed the small hand towel into her mouth, and she became fully awake as the glass full of water poured over her face. Muffled sounds passed as screams were now coming through her gagged mouth, and she was staring at Frankie through wide open and terrified eyes as he slowly withdrew from his pocket Nick's Christmas gift to him. It was the pearl-handled switchblade knife.

Rocco remembered Frankie telling him once about an ancient torture he had read about somewhere. It was known as "the death by a thousand cuts," but never in his wildest imagination did he ever think that he was about to witness it happen.

First, Frankie used his razor-sharp knife to cut through Anna's blouse and brassiere, as he had witnessed Nick do to the girl at the Carrington shootings before leaving the Black Hand imprint on her chest. He then slowly and not too carefully ran the blade of the knife up the inside seam of the stretch tights she was wearing, cutting them away at the crutch and cutting away her underwear, tearing the clothing away from her and throwing it to the floor until her body was naked and fully exposed from head to toe.

The slow motion movie had now turned into a horror film, as Anna's first muffled screams sent a shiver of horror through Ronnie as he watched Frankie slowly sink the point of the knife a half inch deep into the inside of her thigh just below her crutch and proceeded to slice along the length of her inner thigh and down her leg to her ankle stopping only long enough to button shut the front of his wet weather coat as her blood started to spurt out.

Initially intrigued by Frankie's preparations, Rocco was now sickened and starting to feel nauseous, and by the time Frankie was onto her other leg and was halfway along with his cut, he was physically sick and went outside the open doorway and vomited on the landing. He could no longer tolerate the agonised muffled screams coming from the room and went downstairs and outside and into the storm-swept yard and threw up again.

It was at least fifteen minutes before Frankie came outside to where Rocco stood. The storm fury was abating, and in the flashes of intermittent lightning still happening, Rocco thought he looked like some monstrous creature from a horror movie, as the lightning showed his dark waterproof raincoat to be glistening from neck to mid-calf from the red blood that covered it. He was still holding the glistening knife in a bloodied hand and seemed in an almost catatonic state, before he slowly spoke saying, "We'll get the incendiary grenade out of Nick's pocket and his gun. We gotta do what he said and torch everything, including Nick, and beat it out of here." Frankie folded his bloodstained knife and put it in his coat pocket as he was walking back inside the house.

Frankie stopped at Nick Capuzzi's body lying close to that of Josip Andric. Taking off his now scarlet, glistening black coat, he first removed his pistol, knife and incendiary grenade from the pockets, placing them on the steps of the stairway, and did the same from the pockets of Nick's coat. Rocco watched as Frankie stood silent for a few moments, looking down at Nick, head bowed as if in silent prayer. He then draped his coat, now a bloodstained shroud, over Nick's body and disappeared into the downstairs guest bathroom. Rocco heard the shower running.

It was about fifteen minutes before Frankie reappeared, clean, refreshed, with no trace of blood showing, and with a smile on his face, looking like he had just had a night of wonderful sex. Rocco was now looking at this transformation and could not believe it was the same person who had just performed the most monstrous murder imaginable and felt sick again. Rocco thought that it would be a long time before he stopped having bad dreams about what he had just witnessed. He also threw his coat over Nick's body and crossed himself with a silent prayer for Nick.

With the storm now passed, they knew it was time to move. Frankie threw the first incendiary grenade into the upstairs bedroom where Anna's mutilated body lay and then did a quick run down the stairs, reaching the bottom as it exploded and slowed long enough to throw the second grenade into the centre room of the house. The storm had now passed over, and the rain had stopped, as they were getting into the van, they turned and saw the house explode into a blaze of light as they drove away.

Frankie was driving and had not spoken a word since throwing the grenades. And Ronnie turned to him to say something and stopped when he saw Frankie's face, faintly illuminated by the dashboard lights. Frankie was still smiling and now had an almost angelic lookay on his face. Rocco shuddered and felt nausea again as glimpses of the blood bath came back to him. For the rest of the journey back to the Central Coast, they hardly spoke except to stop for fuel, and that suited Rocco; he was left with his own now disturbing thoughts about the sanity of his friend Frankie.

Their next meeting with Caproni proved to be most fortuitous for both of them. First, Caproni was extremely sad about the loss of Nick Capuzzi, saying, "Their organisation had lost a great man, and he personally had lost a great friend, and then he was ecstatic at the success of the mission," saying, "the police have no idea about exactly what had happened, and no suspects other than a gangland massacre possibly aligned with the Carrington shootings." He then went on to say, "After a break of two or three weeks, we will be back into full production and supply to the 'old Don'", as he called Liborio Gitano, and then came the biggest surprise of all, which came as a nice shock to Franco Colleoni and Rocco Medici.

Caproni asked the boys to stand in front of him and to listen closely to what he had to say. He spoke to Rocco first, saying,

"Rocco Medici, Nick Capuzzi spoke highly on how you worked and learnt the business of the hydroponic growing and the supply and distribution to the overall market, and we, the Pignatore-Caproni families want you to take over from Nick Capuzzi, as the leader, the new 'Capo' with the new man Adrianna Barbetta, as your delivery man whom you will train in all aspects of the supply business. You will be in total control reporting to me."

He then turned to Frankie, saying, "The reports Nick gave us on how you handle difficult and dangerous situations and your ability to think out and make calculated decisions when needed, no matter how hard the situation is, lead us to believe you are the man to take over this new opportunity that has arisen in Cairns. The combined families want you to take over as the new 'Don'. Your job will be to eliminate the uninspiring riff-raff gutter rats who are trying to move in and take over. You are to rebuild and bring under your control every aspect of the business, which will be an extensive portfolio of drugs, gambling, brothels, prostitution, night clubs, etc., you name it, it's all there, and you will control all of it and of course report to our families."

Reaching out to each man, Caproni, in true Sicilian style, embraced them in turn with a kiss on each cheek and stood back, looking at their dazed expressions. Franco "Frankie" Colleoni's dream was coming true, and Rocco had a flash of thought that he was glad he was going to stay on the Central Coast and would not go with Frankie. He had a strong feeling now that he wanted to distance himself from Franco Colleoni forever and was happy that Cairns was a long way from the Central Coast.

Mulga Man's Justice to Cairns Dealers

It had taken me a long night's reading to absorb all the information sent to me by "JJ", and admittedly, I knew wading through the known facts about Colleoni, there was a lot of supposition on other happenings, such as the Carrington shootings and the elimination of the Croatian family near Clarence town, but on close analysis of all of the facts, the suspicions of the police, and the whispers of numerous informants on the known activities of the Pignatore-Caproni families and associates it would be naïve not to see Franco "Frankie" Colleoni's part in the known murderous activities, and the knowledge of his growing fame and power in Cairns and the number of murders that had taken place in Cairns since his arrival, all of which convinced me he had to go. The latest suspected murder was of a young prostitute, a drug addict who had turned informer. She told police enough to suspect Colleoni and was then found naked on a beach, slashed and mutilated beyond recognition, and Colleoni was known to carry and delight in using a knife.

In the 1950s and 1960s, along the Queensland coastline, the various sugar ports from Mackay through Innisfail, Townsville and Cairns were known as the "Barbary Coast" and, in particular, Cairns, and it was easy to see why. My first impression of Cairns was when I was doing my SAS training with the military and taking leave breaks in Cairns, and the 1960s, it had an almost frontier town type of atmosphere. In the cane-cutting season, the town was filled with throngs of people associated with the sugar industry. The waterfront pubs at night, particularly on payday, were a seething mix of cane cutters, a seaman of the ships of the world waiting for their cargo of sugar, the seasonal wharf labourers' who loaded the sugar, the Australian passenger ships, crew and tourists doing their runs along the eastern seaboard, and the drovers and stockmen of the hinterland pastoral stations and cattle droves, in for a holiday to spend their hard-earned money.

To add to this mix of humanity, there were the numerous women who seasonally arrived looking for their share of the "sugar" from the free-spending, "women-hungry" males. These women thronged into the sugar towns each year, and there were plenty of "work" opportunities to be had. The good times, alcohol, drugs and money were a big incentive to these ladies of the night. They were a polyglot mix of prostitutes from the major cities. There were also aboriginal and white Caucasian women, Palm Island girls, and, of course, girls who wander into Cairns and just get caught up in the atmosphere, looking for good times and fun, with drinks and drugs, in the wild waterfront pubs with their wooden shuttered and barred windows. Colleoni and his thugs would soon take in this supply of women, an enforced offer of protection to supplement his "stable."

When a tough-looking female bar attendant in the Barrier Hotel was asked casually by me "why the lack of glass windows," she looked at me in a quizzical way and said, "ave you ever been in Cairns in the cyclone season, or in this pub on a Friday night, and pay night when the men have been paid, and their all competing for the girls, and vice versa, a glance or word in the wrong direction, could buy you a fight, and then this place can explode like a volcano." She tookay a deep breath and in an exasperated tone said, "why only last week, a coastal passenger ship named the Manoora was here tied up opposite the pub, a crew member came in to have a drink and was chatting to one of the Palm Island girls who comes in regular, and next minute, he was surrounded by three pommy seamen off a ship that was in port for a cargo of sugar, 'Skauses' they were, who had come in to the pub looking for this girl, one of the 'Skauses' said something nasty to the 'sailor' who tookay offence and decked him, and then it was on, the sailor was fighting off the other two and seemed to be doing okay, when the one he dropped got up and pulled a razor on him, and just at that moment, a mate of the sailor who was fighting them off came in, and he had a gun, a pistol it was, and he threatened to blow the razor blokes head off, this was serious shit! People ran everywhere for cover, and I ducked under the bar. It had got too serious for me."

There was no doubt about it; Cairns was the perfect atmosphere for a drug dealer and his "mules" to operate in, but they had gone too far by supplying kids and murdering women. It really got to me how this scumbag, Colleoni, now king of vice, could live a life of great wealth and luxury in Cairns while others suffered. It was time to get rid of this arrogant, bloodthirsty psychopath, Franco "Frankie" Colleoni.

My mission now was to cut the heads of these this merciless snake. The "Mulga Man" had arrived, and by disposing of the "kingpin" drug lord in Cairns, Franco Colleoni, his thugs and established chain, supplying marijuana, ice and ecstasy to young people, and worse, inducing young girls to inject heroin first by supplying free to them. Once they were hooked on the drug, forcing them into his prostitution ring, forcing them to make money and to buy more heroin from him. For Colleoni, it was a win/win situation. Making money from the girls prostituting, plus money made from the heroin supplied to them, keeping them forever indebted to him

To me, that alone was a bad enough crime to warrant the death penalty, and I knew what had to be done. But first, I intended to do an intensive interrogation of Colleoni before disposing of him.

I believed his network was extensive enough to warrant at least a week, or maybe more, tracking down his chain of dealers in this tropical North and information sent to me had indicated that Port Douglas could be my next call.

I would have loved to have Melissa with me to enjoy some of this tropical paradise, but unfortunately, that could never be; her involvement and knowing what I did would be too great. That information in the wrong hands would endanger her life.

The low-level, low-life "mules", first I had to punish. For want of better words, they were mainly teenage hooligans, some hooked on the drugs they purveyed and all looking for easy money. It was necessary to clean up this rat's nest.

I figured I would check first with "JJ", who had given me the main client in Cairns, wanting me here to solve a problem. He was a wealthy businessman who had two sons in rehabilitation because of their weakness for the drugs sold to them by Colleoni. He readily agreed to further financial assistance. Although my payment was only for the coming hit on the so-called drug lord, there would be a hefty bonus for me if I could break the supply chain to its lowest level, and all expenses would be paid, so I decided I would start at the bottom level and work my way up to Franco Frankie Colleoni, my aim being to first give them some major money problems, with a breakdown in drug supplies, before I got to terminating his existence.

The car I had picked up in Brisbane had the newly introduced 3M tinted side windows, and difficult for those outside to see in. I decided to first start tracking the various young dealers. There were known to be five of them, including one who delivered drug supplies to them, who was known to be armed with a pistol and also acted as bodyguard for Colleoni and the "working" girls when needed.

Not far out from Cairns near Mareeba, there was an old house they used for holding deliveries of drugs, meetings, and parties. Two of them, a young bloke and his girlfriend, lived there in that house, and two lived in a waterfront shack on the northern edge of Cairns. The one known to be the delivery boy and bodyguard, a man in his thirties, lived on his own, sometimes with one of the girls, in an expensive-looking unit on the waterfront not far from Colleoni's very flash villa.

It was mentioned in JJ's report, gained from his contacts and private investigator, that there was one other, a recent new arrival, and surmising from the clothes he was wearing when his picture was taken, he was from a city. They had surmised right; JJ had searched through his computer files and found it was Rocco Salvatore, a notorious thug, hit man, and stand-over man from Melbourne, a man entrusted with the task of collecting monies from the fruit and vegetable vendors of the Melbourne market and numerous other businesses and who was a second cousin to Domenici Medici in Griffith. He had been appointed to assist Colleoni in any difficulties associated with his takeover of the cairn and regional market.

He had been the man that Domenici Medici considered entrusting his son Rocco and his friend Franco to for education in the Melbourne market and drug distribution; that is when those two lambs eventually came back to the fold, so to say, by quitting their reckless gallivanting around Sydney and returned home to Griffith, which of course did not eventuate with the new path they had taken under the Pignatore-Caproni sponsorship. Rocco Salvatore was a hardened criminal, an N'Drangheta assassin, and well-schooled in the mafia ways, the code of the "Honoured Society" and the law of "omerta". This was a man I would have to watch very carefully.

It would be easy enough to match the descriptions given to me and follow each around for a few days and nights. It was obvious to me that when the "dealers" and "mules" went to the address of Colleoni a few times to pick up more supplies and found they weren't there, they would be suspicious of trouble and possibly disappear, whereas when their boss Colleoni was to find their dealers including the "heavy" I suspected of being their bodyguard, had been beaten up, and in the custody of police, they would stay close to home, knowing the mafia code of "Omerta' and the fear of reprisals even death if any of their minions spoke to the police, would save them from investigation.

So, thinking deeply about what mode of attack I would take, I decided against being an opposition drug dealer from Brisbane, here to take over their business. No, that could trigger Colleoni to prepare for war and possibly go into hiding. No, the dealers were not high enough in the chain to warrant execution, but they were definitely in need of a painful lesson, but how painful and what? As I thought long and hard on this, a glimmer of an idea came to me, a totally ridiculous idea it seemed at first, but the more I thought about it, it put a smile on my face about how they could be punished without alerting Colleoni and Salvatore, into taking cover and hiding. I figured that if my idea was successful when the newspaper reports hit the streets, it would deeply puzzle them, and they would stay in the open yet go into conference over it, and that would be the time to "hit" them.

My idea was taking shape. It was going to be a "lone wolf" attack on the dealer network. Some irate person from everyday life, who was totally pissed off with the amount of drugs and associated crime on the streets and was out for vengeance. Someone with enough intelligence to gain information from street level, and then it hit me!

There were a number of charitable and religious institutions that helped those in need, such as homeless street people, drug addicts, alcoholics, the list goes on, and who better to gather information on drugs and dealers than a religious, self-righteous zealot attending to the poor and weak, who listens to the poor abused, and who decides to tackle the problem as a self-styled vigilante imposing the "wrath of the Lord" on the evil one's, "hallelujah" I thought, that's the way to go.

The more I thought it out, the more I liked it, and I decided to throw a dash of humour into the job at hand. I was going to take up the "sword of holy righteousness", so to say and administer a few good hidings along with stern warnings of a repeat performance to the dealers should they stray from the path of the "Lord". I thought a few days of hospital treatment, with some stitches here and there, along with bruises and a few fractured or broken bones, would help them see the light of redemption and hopefully break down the will to participate further in the drug supply business.

I smiled again, thinking of myself as a "self-righteous religious holy roller". It would be easy; I would play the part of some fanatical, religious, anti-drugs, crazy guy, taking on the responsibility of saving the community from the evil of drugs. I was still laughing to myself as I started my car and drove off to start off on this godly mission of punishment, to disrupt, even hopefully terminate the drug supplies.

Wearing a black ski mask, long-sleeved black T-shirt, and black pants, I cornered the first two in their beachfront shack. There, I systematically administered a severe beating, leaving them both unconscious, with a couple of bone fractures and lacerations, and then used their phone to ring for an ambulance and police before ripping out the phone line and tying them together with it and planting their cache of marijuana, ecstasy tablets, heroin, and methamphetamines in a tidy heap by them with a note placed on the top which said **repent sinners from the evils of drugs, or I will be back the Grim Reaper.**

The third victim was the bloke I had some concerns about. Knowing he was armed, he certainly was of a solid build, colourfully tattooed and strong-looking. This was the one I knew to be a bodyguard and main delivery man, who I had spotted leaving "Colleoni's" house, and followed him until he turned into a darker part of the dimly lit street and parked his late-model Ford station wagon in the driveway below the top floor unit where he lived. Checking to see that no one was around, I quietly got out of my car and caught him unawares as he was unlocking a garage door, and within seconds, he was lying unconscious in the back of his station wagon car. I drove the car into his garage and shut the door after I had removed the Berretta 9m gun he had in a calf holster on his right leg. There were more boxes in the garage.

I saw a number of cartons in the back of the station wagon and guessed they would contain various drugs that he would have to share space within the back. So, pulling him out of the wagon, to make sure he stayed unconscious, I administered another rabbit chop to the side of his neck and gagged and bound him with the trusty 3m duct tape, the perfect multipurpose product, after seating him on a heavy wooden chair that was there.

By the time he was conscious, though a little groggy, he was sitting bound to this chair in his garage. I was still wearing a ski mask and was slapping him around a little to bring him properly awake, and now he was looking at me, through dazed though inquiring eyes, as I proceeded to lecture him on the errors of his ways. He now came more awake, eyes widened as he looked at me, as if he was off my head; obviously, he was older than the "dealers" and of a tougher mould, and as I told him he must repent, he said sneeringly "fuck off." I was shaking my head sadly at him, as I put some duct tape over his mouth to muffle his screams, which I knew would come, I then told him to nod his head toward me if he could accept redemption and change his wicked ways, he shookay his head obstinately and negatively, and I heard repeated three times a very muffled, f—ck you, f—ck you, f—ck you!

I can only guess that he changed his attitude some when I bent his fingers back, breaking one on each hand, and then taking off his shoes, bent his legs back under him at the knees, and when in position, I held them still, to enable me to crush a big toe with the butt of the Beretta pistol, I had to knock him out again to kill the muffled screams. Even with his broken fingers and crushed big toe, I needed to make certain he would not move far, so to make sure, I further duct taped his arms together and taped his legs to the chair. I was sure over the next few weeks, he would regret his hasty answer. Dragging the chair and its weight back against the garage wall, I left him propped unconscious with a note pinned to his shirt stating, **"Jesus loves you, even if you are a drug dealer." Please search the car, garage, and premises upstairs.** I then finished by taping a package of the drugs he had picked up from Colleoni to his legs; I placed the gun, minus the bullets, next to his unconscious form, turning the light off and leaving the garage door partly up enough for a policeman to see under, I then drove to a phone booth a short distance away, to anonymously call the police and tell them there is a man unconscious, who looks severely beaten, and who is tied up, and gave them his address. I watched from a safe distance, and within minutes, the police arrived, soon followed by an ambulance. I was sure the messages I'd left would get the police thinking. Who was this religious crazy person doing their work for them?

Now, I felt it necessary to "strike while the irons hot" before any alarm bells rang and headed for the next dealer, the boy with the girlfriend. I knew she was in on his dealing, but as always, I was reluctant to hurt women. No, I thought, the beating would have to be severe enough to make her repent her ways, then perhaps go back home to mother. It had to be more than just a slap or two. There was no one in their flat when I arrived, and just to make sure, I knocked on the door. It was now past midnight. I waited in a dark side lane for about an hour, and then I saw a car pull into the driveway, and a porch light switched on; going by their noisy laughter and the way they walked from the car to the porch, they were a little drunk.

"Good," I thought, that will make things a little easier. I waited some time, and until after the lights went out. Putting a small roll of duct tape into my jacket pocket and donning the ski mask, I made my way cautiously to the entrance, thankful the porch light was not an automatic switch-on type.

Using my skeleton keys, I crept into their darkened flat. There was only a very dim bed lamp with a red globe showing a soft light through the half-closed bedroom door. They were on the bed noisily copulating, well, it was not exactly coitus. He was lying on his back spread-eagled with his eyes closed and moaning as she kneeled between his legs performing oral sex; they were both totally engrossed in their enjoyment and out of this world.

Looking down, I could see the untidy pile of clothes on the floor at the end of the bed, and a bong nearby, and I reasoned the slurping noises, moans and groans coming from them would cover any noise I might make, spotting his jeans in amongst the pile of clothes, I bent down and silently retrieved a wide studded leather belt from them. It was the perfect thing for the crazy punishment I had suddenly thought of, and so, rising above her wide, white, ample-sized backside that was pornographically displayed in front of me, I brought the belt down with one almighty thwack! The muffled scream from her was nothing compared to the high-pitched scream that came from her lover, as her "pearly whites" clamped shut, sunk deep into his well-endowed and inflamed organ. I chuckled, funny! I had not considered any side effects like this of that whack.

She collapsed forward onto his body, screaming and writhing in pain and effectively pinning him down, but her shrieks were nothing compared to his. I leapt to the side of the bed and cut off the screaming from both with a couple of well-aimed hits to nerve centres. First, I gagged their mouths and covered their eyes with duct tape, binding their wrists and ankles with the tape. I then laid them on their backs naked, side by side, thinking she certainly was a buxom lass.

I winced, feeling the pain myself as I looked at the bleeding teeth marks and deep lacerations on his now withered member, saying out loud, "It might be a while before you get around to using that again, cobber!"

Going out to the kitchen, I found a plastic bucket and filled it up with cold water. I was thinking this ought to wake them up to the realities of their situation. They both rose off the bed a few inches when the cold water splashed over their partly awake, moaning, warm bodies. It's not really a humorous sound listening to cries of anguish coming through gagged mouths.

I just sat on the edge of the bed for a while listening until the sounds started to die away into sobbing intakes of air through their nose, and then I spoke in deep, sombre "evangelical tones."

"Now, my children, you have sinned against the laws of this land, and you have been selling your poisonous filth to the children and adults of this fair city, and for these crimes against decency and humanity, you must be punished. Your punishment, this time, is of a minor nature compared to what will happen to you should you transgress from the path of righteousness ever again. All of your drug dealing friends have been dealt with most firmly, and your suppliers will vanish from Cairns, forever gone from this world." Amen to them.

Now shake your head from side to side to show me you have heard my words. With that, I swear I thought their heads would snap at the neck. They were shaking so violently. Now, in an even deeper tone, I said, prepare for your punishment. Their bodies stiffened, and the forced-out grunts of pain from behind the duct tape were pitiful as I first laid into him with the wide leather belt, with the metal studs which were leaving an interesting pattern, first on their thighs and stomach, then forcibly rolling each one over onto their stomachs, I left the same patterns from shoulders to ankles with particular emphasis on their bare arses.

There were no more sounds coming from them. Putting my head to their nostrils, they were still breathing heavily, but unconscious, they both had fainted. I felt that was enough punishment for them to remember my words. I did wonder what they would say to the police when taken to the hospital about their naked state and his mangled love rod. And though she might have to find another lover to satisfy her needs for a while, for I doubted his equipment would respond to much action for a considerable length of time, going by the blood on the sheets, he possibly would be weak from blood loss.

I did a quick search of the house with no luck, and then as I walked around the bed on the side that he was lying on, I felt a creak of a board under my feet, noticing it for the first time and pulling the edge of the rug back, I found a trapdoor cut in the floor about two feet square, and on lifting it, discovered a box built into the floor between the floor bearers and it contained a large stash of various drugs, prescription drugs of various sorts, including morphine, oxycontin, small packets of heroin, syringes and needles and a sealed tin of white powder I presumed was cocaine. A further search showed another trapdoor with a similar box filled with packaged marijuana. It was a good haul for the police to find, and I left another note on the exposed drugs that said.

The wrath of the lord has found these sinners. May they seek forgiveness, or they will be found again.

Holding back laughter, I modulated my voice and rang the police, giving the address, giving details of the drug cache and suggesting they send an ambulance along, and left the flat with grim satisfaction at a job well done and the sincere hope their lives would change for the better. The idea to use the belt was an impulse decision hard to resist at the time; I could remember similar punishments being dished out to male and female drug law offenders in Malaya and Vietnam and also Indonesia, where drug peddlers were beaten with the Rattan cane. I do admit to some sadness, perhaps pity for the girl, I hoped the end result would warrant the painful means.

CHAPTER 33

Cairns Terminate Colleoni and Salvatore

Now, it was time to deal with a dual problem in Colleoni and Salvatore. Knowing Medici was back on the Central Coast, I would deal with him and his cronies another time. Rocco Salvatore was a key member of the Calabria mafia, and I had no doubt he would be in Cairns to oversee Colleoni's performance.

I knew the shit would hit the fan when the morning radio news came on and newspapers were delivered. My unusual method of punishment would certainly raise questions from law enforcement and possibly a few smiles from some of the general Cairns population, and no doubt Colleoni and Salvatore would be in a furore as to "who is this masked evangelical avenger?"

It was about 9 a.m. the following morning. I was parked at a safe distance from the lavish waterfront villa that Colleoni lived in when I spotted a car, a dark blue coloured car coming fast along the waterfront road, which almost skidded sideways into the driveway of the villa and one man got out. Through the high-powered binoculars, I could see his features; I knew that face and double-checked the picture sent to me by "JJ". The big man with the hard, swarthy features was none other than Rocco Salvatore.

Franco "Frankie" Colleoni and "Rocco" Medici had been good apprentices and learnt fast, earning much recognition from the Calabria mafia families, with Colleoni's efforts being rewarded when the mafia capo in Cairns got careless and was executed by an unknown assailant who blasted him with a shotgun in the back using "Lupara" pellets, the same type of shotgun pellet used to kill wolves in Calabria. The families in Calabria actually approved Colleoni's posting to Cairns and Medici to take over the Central Coast.

After a period of two days' surveillance, I managed to follow Colleoni and Salvatore to a quiet, secluded mangrove-lined cove on the second night of watching. I anticipated this could eventually lead me to the "Mr. Big", whoever and wherever he was, and hidden amongst the thick bush, I kept watch through night vision glasses. After a short wait, I could see the navigation lights of a boat starting to show in the distance out to sea. It came to a stop about 300 yards offshore. I guessed this was because of the shallow coastal waters of the Cairns shoreline, and soon, a large dinghy was heading to shore, obviously propelled by oars; it was very quiet. I could make out two shapes in the dinghy. Obviously, they were the delivery men, and nosing the dinghy onto the mud flat, which served as a beach, the three I had followed walked to it and started unloading cartons handed to them from the dinghy and then carrying them over the mudflat to where an old ex-military Jeep 4WD was parked on a rough track, probably a fisherman's path. I also had a hired vehicle parked hidden a short distance away, and I was soon following them with no headlights on, using the night vision glasses to find my way.

Reaching the outskirts of Cairns, I saw their vehicle turn into the driveway of a rundown old-style "Queenslander" house built on high posts, with the driver reversing the vehicle into a shed that was obviously serving as a garage.

I could not see what they were doing and could only assume this was where they unloaded what they had picked up from the boat. I had seen enough and now had this address for future reference. I headed back to my car and waited. I still had a clear view of the house and garage, and after about an hour, one of the men went back to the house, and the jeep backed out of the garage. The driver got out and padlocked the entrance door shut. The driver was Rocco Salvatore. The remaining man was standing with him when the driver shookay his hand and then embraced him, kissing him on each cheek as if he was someone important. That someone would be his right-hand man, I guessed it would have to be Colleoni, and that opinion was confirmed soon after. I sat and waited, knowing that the Jeep would have to go past me. I could now make out the two men in the car; the passenger was Colleoni, the figurehead "boss" of the Cairns operation, and I figured they would now lead me back to his address. These scum were selling their wares to a large clientele of school children, teens, and others, but I knew there would have to be someone higher up the ladder who owned the boat I had seen anchored offshore? The drugs coming in from the sea by the boat I had just witnessed, but from where? Following the Jeep along the bush track at a distance was easy enough by using the night vision glasses, and on reaching the city lights, I switched the headlights on and followed it to the luxurious-looking bungalow along the waterfront, owned by Colleoni, not far from the old iconic "Barrier Hotel".

Sitting in the plane on the way to Cairns, I had been examining the evidence given to me with photographs; I saw the man, Salvatore, thought to be the Sydney boss of this operation, was a well-known criminal, originally connected to the Calabrian mafia, operating in the Griffith, and Mildura region of NSW and was well known to the police in that area, and also the suspect in the murder of a prominent businessman who was extremely vocal about the criminal operations and drug plantations owned by the predominant Calabrian Italian community in the region, and also in later years Sydney and Brisbane.

Then, Salvatore had vanished suddenly about two years ago from the Sydney and Brisbane drug scene, with suspicions he had been killed in a gang feud. Such was not the case, from the information received; he was alive and well and was now operating in Cairns, now with an alias, and sporting a beard and moustache. It was clear now that Salvatore was a senior Mafiosi of the Calabrian Mafia sent to Cairns to oversee Frankie Colleoni's takeover of the Cairns and regional crime network. Fortunately, one of "JJ's" Brisbane underworld contacts from Sydney, who was enjoying a holiday in Cairns, spotted him in the Barrier Hotel, saw through the disguise and passed on the information to the "JJ" that Rocco Salvatore was very much alive and going by the name Roberto Luciana.

They had to go! It was to be a few more days before the right opportunity came. It had to be a dull, overcast day, which looked like it would turn into a dark night with no moon. Originally I had decided not to use a knife or gun but would be flexible. So I made up a "garrote" of strong 100lb fishing line, fastening a piece of wooden dowel for a handle at each end, a very efficient and quick method of killing, cutting off oxygen and blood to the brain in a very short time. A fond method of disposal, I believe, that was used on occasion by the Mafia, and of course, the suspicion would be, if by chance he was found, it was a professional hit, for whatever reason, from his former compatriots. Hopefully it would be Colleoni to go first.

For the body disposal, I had booked a cabin cruiser with a motorised dinghy for a three-day fishing trip to be picked up on the afternoon of the night I planned to give Frankie his sendoff. First, I would fill a few large hold-all bags with rocks, and do a couple of journeys to the boat looking like I was loading it with grog and supplies for a fishing party. Then I would cruise at a reasonable pace in daylight to the drug pick-up cove. Measuring the distance covered as I went and the time taken to be able to do the same distance and time in the dark to lessen the chance of not finding the cove. The cabin boat I had selected had a large spotlight mounted on the cabin roof, which would help me in the dark to find the cove. I had selected this same beach because the rest of the coastline was all mangrove swamp, and it was the only suitable place to take a boat out to sea, and hopefully unseen.

I had watched and followed for three more days, Luciana and Colleoni and noticed each afternoon at about 6 p.m., his various street dealers would go to the back of his bungalow in Cairns, singly over an hour, obviously to pick up their supply for their evil night patrol distributing their poison around the streets of Cairns.

On the fourth day, after the dealers had left and after dark, I had followed them to the house out on the bush track near the sandy cove, and from where Colleoni Salvatore was waiting to help unload another shipment that had come in on the dinghy from the sea. Again, they reversed the jeep land into the garage, and the two men went inside. About a half hour after that, they drove out, padlocked the door shut and drove to Colleoni's bungalow, obviously to unload fresh supplies.

On the days that the "Mules" were supplied and had left to deliver their night's supplies, Colleoni would disappear inside the house where I could see the flickering light of a TV screen through the drawn shade of a window and venturing close could hear what sounded like the world news, and then between eight and eight thirty Colleoni would go to his car in the garage, and drive out to travel the short distance to the Barrier Hotel. There he would eat and drink while chatting and playing cards with a few old cronies, Italian-looking men, probably locals from the cane-cutting days around Cairns when all of the sugar cane was cut by hand. He would sit with them until closing time, then drive back home. Although Colleoni had a stable of girls prostituting he would gratify himself with as the whim tookay him, he obviously preferred a bachelor life, and that was a good thing, no one else to worry about in the house, but I did wonder what he did, or would do with all of the money he made from the drugs and vice, perhaps saving it for an early retirement and a life of luxury, maybe back in Italy, at forty years of age, he still had a lot to lookay forward to living off his ill earned money, and I knew I had to do something about that.

I figured that on the chosen night, I could lock-pick my way into his garage and hide by the land cruiser; there would be more than enough time to do the job, put his body into a body bag and into the boot of my car, and take it to the spot where he was getting the drugs delivered to. There, in the bushes, I would hide the body. I would then head back to where the hire boat was moored and motor back to the same spot. Stop offshore; take the dinghy in, load the body onto the dinghy, and head out to the sea and deep water.

A good plan, unfortunately, "Murphy's law was to come into the equation, if it can go wrong it will." It all went well up to a point, and by 8:45 p.m. on the fifth night. Frankie Colleoni, the drug boss of Cairns, breathed his last. I knew he was in the habit of feeding his German shepherd dog each night around 5 p.m. He was puzzled to find the dog unconscious in its pen; a couple of crushed rohypnol tablets in a pound of raw minced beef saw to that. Stepping inside and leaning over to the dog, he did not hear me coming as the garrote slipped over his head; a short struggle, and it was over very quickly, and I soon had his body stuffed in the boot of my car.

Stopping at a pay phone, I left a message at the pub from Frankie saying he would not be there to play cards that night as he was not feeling well and possibly got the "flu." By 11 p.m. I was hiding his body, now zipped into a body bag, in the thick jungle-like vegetation behind the mangroves near the little beach, and by 12 p.m., I was cruising at a slow speed up the coastline in the hired cabin launch using a stopwatch to measure time and distance. At the correct time of forty-four minutes, I turned my nose toward the shore and approached very cautiously with the powerful spotlight turned on, closer, closer, but where was the little cove?

All I could see was a thick growth of mangrove trees and no entrance into the small beach. Had I made a mistake with the timing and the spot that opened up to the tiny beach? As I was questioning this problem in my mind, it happened. There was a bump, followed by a grinding scraping noise coming from underneath the boat's keel. Stopping the slow revving engine, the vessel ground to a stop. What the hell has happened, I thought? Where did I go wrong? And then it hit me: I had not allowed for the run-out tide, the speed of flow and the depth the tide drops, and no amount of revving the engine and propeller speed would move me off this mud bank.

I was stuck here until the tide turned; that was now obvious to me. Also, the current flow had added to my estimated speed and distance and I had gone past the point where I had to turn in toward the cove entrance. It was now 1 a.m.; I pondered on what time the tide would turn. On the cabin wall was a navigation chart but no tidal chart. Surely there would be one somewhere for fishermen hiring the boat to work out the tide movements? I started rummaging through drawers and cupboards and there in a small cupboard by the steering wheel and hidden under some magazines was a current tidal chart for this month.

Some quick calculations showed the tide was almost at its maximum low. Sunrise is about 7 a.m. at this time of the year and in this part of the world. Allowing for the ebb tide of one hour, there should be enough water under the boat by 6 a.m. to be able to head back along the shoreline and find the cove. Fingers crossed, there would be no one in the cove when I found it.

This time, lady luck was with me, and at 5:45 a.m., I was cruising back three-quarters of a mile or so to where I spotted the entrance to the cove. Dropping the anchor in reasonably deep water, I was soon sliding the dinghy with its small 4hp outboard motor a short distance onto the part sand, part mud flat. The tide was still rising, nearing its peak, when I dug the dinghie small anchor into the mud and sand. There was no one to be seen, about fifteen minutes of physical labour, and I had Frankie laid out in the bottom of the dinghy, a bit more effort to put the anchor back aboard and to pull the nose of the now low floating dinghy, and I was aboard motoring back to the hired cabin boat.

I was about two hundred and fifty yards away from the beach and just about to nose alongside the cabin launch, with the first glimmer of daylight just starting to show, when I heard an engine sound and looked back to see the headlights of a car coming down to the firm patch of ground behind the beach I think it was an adrenaline surge of superhuman strength that enabled me to throw "Colleoni's" now stiffening body aboard the cabin launch, and then tying the dinghy onto the after the end of the cabin boat, I jumped aboard started the engine and headed out to sea. Looking back through my binoculars, I could see it was an old model 4WD with a number of fishing rods fastened to racks on the roof. Whew, that was too bloody close, I thought! Because Cairns is inside the Great Barrier Reef, the inside waters along the coastline can be fairly shallow. I had plenty of fuel and had decided to cruise out into the deepwater shipping lanes, and there I would say farewell to the well-weighted-down Oscar. Because of body gases inflating the bag, I felt it necessary to drive a long-bladed knife into his abdomen a few times and open the heavy zipper a little. Once on the bottom, in time, the creatures of the sea would see to the rest. I had read of the old days on sailing ships and how sailors who died were buried at sea, so I gave Colleoni a sarcastic salute as he slid down into the depths, and now something had to be done about Salvatore and the remaining dealers.

On returning to the hire boat mooring, I decided to see if I could get the boat for another few days and gave Angus a call to see if he could come down to do some fishing or just relax on the boat for a couple of days. Angus said it would take the best part of three days to free himself from the property to get there, so I booked the boat up again in three days' time and decided to spend the next three days resting and doing a little sightseeing around Cairns, but this plan was not sitting right with me. First, something must be done about the stash of high-grade marijuana and various other drugs in the luxury bungalow and the garage of the old shack. My first thought was to phone the police and give directions to both places; certainly, that would get rid of the drugs and any money that was stashed inside, but I was uncertain if the "mules and street sellers would all be caught and they certainly would not find Salvatore."

No! They all would have to be in one place, and what better place would be Colleoni's bungalow? Could a meeting be called by his number one henchman, a man who was obviously the main pick-up man and guardian of the supply hidden in the garage of the shack not far from the little beach? He and one other resided in an old-style "Queenslander" and occasionally lived in a luxurious though smaller bungalow about ten minutes drive from Colleoni when they were off duty and entertaining. I reasoned it could be a meeting of extreme importance to discuss the mysterious disappearance of Colleoni. Why was he not there when his dealers called in? Why was he not answering his phone? By now, Salvatore could have phoned or called in on him and could be starting to wonder where he was. But I felt that it was too soon for him to be worried over, knowing of the regular dalliances Colleoni had with any one of his girls that tookay his fancy, but another day or two would be a different matter. I knew I had to act now.

A call to "JJ" some time back had led me to a pharmacist, previously a doctor who had worked on the edge of Sydney's underworld and who sometimes was involved in repair work on shot and injured criminals. "JJ" had helped him out of a serious situation once, and the esteemed doctor retired to Cairns and opened a large pharmacy, and was now another one of "JJ's" unique collection of people. A couple of hours later, I walked out with a small package containing two syringes, each loaded with a strong dose of "flunitrazepan", commonly known as "rohypnol" or the "date rape drug, plus a spare bottle of small white pills of the same drug, I thought might come in handy? I walked away with the drug, and he was five hundred dollars richer. When I saw the excellent results later, I would have given him a thousand dollars. I had told the "doc" the two men the syringes were for were fairly solid, strong-looking blokes, and he replied if it didn't stop their heart and kill them, the dose he gave would certainly knock them out and make them extremely tractable and non-resistant. It was a chance I would have to take, I wanted the names and phone numbers of everyone involved in this consortium of crime.

My surveillance had shown where the bulk of the drugs were being stored under the guardianship of these two men. It was about three am when I silently picked the lock on the back door of the shack, although it was more of an old-style Queenslander style set up on low stilts at the front and built back into a rise with the back verandah at ground level. It was obvious to me that the occupants were now sleeping soundly, going by the snoring coming from each bedroom and the empty Bourbon and Coca-Cola bottles sitting on the kitchen table, along with a pack of cards and some small change. For hardened criminals their lack of security amazed me, no doubt, that they had become complacent, probably from having successfully run their business for a long time and without interruption from the law or others. This complacency would be their undoing. It was a warm tropical night, typical of summer in that region and both bedroom doors were ajar, and above each bed was a slowly rotating fan, its soft whirring sending a gentle flow of cooler air down onto the drunk and sleeping forms. Each bedroom had a window opening to the outside and screened from insects. A careful lookay around with a pencil torch in each room showed a snub-nosed pistol, probably a .38 calibre, sitting on a bedside table in the first room. I looked into the other, and a similar pistol in a shoulder holster was slung over a chair in the other. I quietly removed both and, slipping back outside, left them under some bushes to be retrieved later.

It was now time for the real work to begin. The "Doc", as "JJ" called him, had said that the best result would come if the entire dose of "Rohypnol" in the syringe was administered direct into the ceratoid artery in the neck. I went to the bedroom, which I had seen to be a little more luxurious with an en suite toilet, and figured that would be the room the "boss man" would take. He was most accommodating. I knew where the ceratoid artery could be found from my medical training getting ready for Malaya and Vietnam, and he was lying on his side in a fetal position with the artery area clearly exposed and lit by the tiny light spot from my pencil torch. A quick jab with the syringe and my hand clamped hard over his mouth, and a slight heaving of his body, and within a few seconds, his body went limp; he was out cold. I could not help thinking that, what with the bourbon he consumed and the massive shot of Rohypnol, he was going to wake up with one hell of a headache.

The next bloke was not quite so accommodating; he was lying on his back, and his snores were echoing throughout the bedroom. I had to get down on my knees to pencil light the right place to jab. Still and all, the results were the same, and in no time I had both sleeping bodies bound hand and foot and thought I would have a bit of relaxation myself after I had retrieved the guns. I had to shut the bedroom doors to cut down the now extremely guttural snoring. The couch in the kitchen looked comfortable, and I thought I would catch a couple of hours of sleep. It was about 8 a.m. when the strident ringing of the phone woke me up. It was an excited, almost hysterical voice on the other end and it was saying "Fredo, it's Jack" is "Frankie there" and without stopping the voice went on to say I've been to his house twice, and so has "Johnno" and "Mikey and he doesn't answer his door or answer the phone, and we need more stuff", and in a flash, I saw a simple answer to my quest for knowledge. Pretending I was hungover and just woke from a deep sleep, I slurred my voice into a low monotone and said, "fuck you, waking me up this early, I gotta bad hangover, wassamatta wit you." It worked; the voice was suddenly voicing abject apologies. I pretended a coughing fit and, between coughs, said, "es not here, get out and round up everyone of the boys for a meeting" and tell them to meet me at three o'clock at the back of the bungalow and make sure no one sees you there "we'll kick the door in if we have to". A couple of anonymous phone calls then told police of a huge drug cache and of its dealers who would be meeting at a house in Cairns, and by 5 p.m. that same day, every street dealer in Cairns, was in the Cairns lock-up, being questioned. One hour later, another police raid found two, tied up and still coming out of a dope haze, incoherent drug dealers, who were picked up along with the garage full of various illegal substances and plant material.

The evening news media was, again, all about some anonymous mystery vigilante-type person who led police to premises, which allowed them to capture and break up a major drug ring. The mystery still remained of the whereabouts of the owner of the bungalow Frankie Colleoni, where the drugs, street dealers and Roberto Luciana were arrested, and the following investigation and questioning of the gang showed the police now knew about Rocco Salvatore, alias Roberto Luciana, still being alive. Suspected of being the Mafia boss of the entire gang and wanted by the law for questioning in a few states. I was pleased with the results and Colleoni was now many fathoms underwater.

Perhaps now, the citizens of Cairns and the authorities would not have to put up with the growing number of robberies, muggings and criminal activities that had been happening around Cairns, crimes which often are associated with drug addiction. I did think that Cairns would be wise to spend money on a drug rehabilitation centre.

The expected arrival in Cairns of Angus saw us spend a couple of days in the sun on the hire boat, relaxing, fishing, and catching up on the news on what he had been doing. This helped put me into the frame of mind I needed to get on with my next job, deep down, I had a gut feeling where that would be. "JJ" would pay me well for the Cairns operation, but I had a feeling the next one could be bigger.

The mysterious cruiser I saw offshore that loaded its illicit cargo into the small boat had to come from somewhere. Who was the main supplier? Who owned the big cruiser? Where were the "MJ" grown, and the pills manufactured? There were a lot of questions to be answered and perhaps "JJ" might be able to give me a few more clues. First, I'll take a short break and then head back to the "big smoke."

Angus and I had a few days fishing and relaxing on the hire boat, and after dropping Angus off at the hire boat dock to head back to his work on the outback station, I was still feeling the need to unwind some, so I spent the next two days, relaxing in Cairns, and taking a boat cruise out to Green Island, and decided to stay there a couple of days. For a short time, I found my mind thinking about Angie and what might have been, wondering how she was doing, but those thoughts soon diminished as visions of Melissa filled my mind. There lying on the beach soaking up the sun, my mind started reliving again many of the people I had known, the places and dangers of my life in Malaya and Vietnam, and some of its horrid brutality, the terrible persecution of minority ethnic groups, and I knew without doubt it was that life, and what I had seen and experienced, that had set the wheels in motion, and put me on my path in life today. Malaya and Vietnam, it seemed so many years ago, and yet, the memories are still strong.

CHAPTER 34

The Breakthrough: Head to Port Douglas

Having satisfactorily disposed of Colleoni and seen the incarceration of Rocco Salvatore and the punishing of various drug dealers, thereby interrupting drug supplies in Cairns, I knew there was much more to the chain of supply to be dealt with at a higher level. It was two words uttered during my interrogation of Colleoni before tightening the "garrote" to close off his wind; although he had remained staunchly silent for a time, he broke at the last moment and then in one gasping breath before the final tightening of the "garrote" I heard the words "up north."

That led to some enquiries from one of "JJ's" informants who knew a Cairns police superintendent. The information gained from questioning dealers arrested had led to one, a senior dealer breaking the code of Omerta (silence), saying Colleoni had told him the major supplier was based in Port Douglas.

I now had learnt enough to warrant at least a week in that tropical paradise and start tracking down the supplier suspected to be operating from here. This knowledge, plus some, was then confirmed by "JJ" that he had received from a businessman in Port Douglas, who was having trouble with his two teenage son's drug addiction.

To make sure of details, I figured I would check again with "JJ", who in turn contacted his informant, and in two days, I learnt that the man I needed to speak to was a wealthy, self-made businessman, land owner and land developer who had two sons in rehabilitation because of their weakness for the drugs that had been sold to them. "JJ" contacted this man and asked if he could provide any information on the person suspected, which, in due course, he did by hiring a private investigator in the hope of getting a picture and details, along with descriptions, names and habits, of anyone concerned. In the morning mail I just received was a package with photographs, names and all other relevant details from "JJ" and with it was a terse warning to be very careful. The private investigator that had been hired was now in hiding. He had been spotted, and late one night, a fusillade of bullets had been fired into his home, scaring the life out of him, his wife and young children. They have since departed for parts unknown. A wise move, I thought, getting divorce evidence on cheating husbands or wives and scam insurance claims would be much safer for him to pursue in the future.

Packing my carry-all, including the gun JJ had provided, I departed Cairns at daylight for the scenic sixty-mile drive to Port Douglas; I always preferred to keep a low profile wherever I went and would usually bookay a room in a small motel and sometimes in a pub in smaller towns. To any other people, I was just another tourist seeing the sights of Port Douglas, which was much more subdued and quiet than Cairns, and I thought it an ideal place with its access to the sea and offshore islands to be a perfect place from where to mastermind and run a drug smuggling operation, capable of supplying from there south to the more populated cities of Cairns, Mackay, and Townsville, with their larger populations, and possibly supplying the smaller towns to the north.

I had done considerable reading on these North Queensland towns and recalled that in the 1950s and 1960s, along the coastline of Townsville and Cairns, it was known as the "Barbary Coast" it was easy to see why. In my time in Cairns when doing military training, it had an almost frontier town type of atmosphere. In the cane-cutting season, the town was filled with the throngs of men associated with the sugar industry. The waterfront pubs at night, particularly on pay da, were a seething mix of cane cutters, seamen off the ships of the world waiting for their cargo of sugar, the seasonal wharf labourers' who loaded the sugar, the Australian passenger ships doing their runs along the eastern seaboard with crew and tourists passengers and the drovers and stockmen off the massive size hinterland pastoral stations and their cattle droves, in Cairns for a holiday to spend their hard-earned money.

To add to this mix of humanity, there were the numerous women who arrived looking for their share of the "sugar" from the free-spending males thronging these sugar towns when the season was on, and there was plenty of work to be had, the good times alcohol, drugs, and money were a big incentive to these ladies of the night. They were a polyglot mix of prostitutes, aboriginal, white Caucasian women, Palm Island girls, and just those caught up in the atmosphere and looking for good times and fun. In those wild waterfront pubs with their wooden shuttered and barred windows.

When a tough-looking female bar attendant was asked casually, "Why the lack of glass windows" she quizzically looked at me and said. "ave you ever been in Cairns in the cyclone season or in this pub on a Friday pay night when the men have been paid, their all competing for the girls and vice versa, and a glance or word in the wrong direction could buy you a fight, and then this place can explode like a volcano." She went on to say "why only last week, a coastal passenger ship called the Manoora was here, tied up opposite the pub, a crew member came in to have a drink and was chatting to one of the Palm Island girls who comes in regular, and next minute he was surrounded by three pommy sailors 'Skauses' they were, who had come into the pub looking for this girl. One of the 'Skauses' said something nasty to the 'sailor' who tookay offence and decked him. Then it was on; the sailor was fighting off the other two when the one he dropped got up and pulled a razor on him, and just at that moment, a mate of the sailor fighting them off came in. He had a gun, a small pistol it was, and he threatened to blow the razor-block's head off. People run everywhere for cover, and I ducked under the bar; it had got too serious for me."

There was no doubt about it: Cairns was the perfect atmosphere to set up a major mafia-controlled drug supply and prostitution business, considering its early 1920s association with mafia control of its cane fields, but they had gone too far by supplying to kids and getting them hooked, and then prostituting young girls. It really got to me that this scumbag, whoever he was, the kingpin of this criminal network, could live a life of luxury, peace and tranquillity in a quiet and beautiful place like Port Douglas. My mission was to cut the head of this ruthless and merciless snake. The "Mulga Man" had arrived.

I would have loved to have Mellissa with me in this tropical paradise, but unfortunately, that could never be. It was necessary to clean up this rat's nest, and as much as I loved her, I did not need the distraction.

That night in my motel room, I found not only did I have a list of names of dealers and "mules", but they were in one photograph; getting out of a Mercedes with his head turned toward the hidden camera was a face I recognised. The last time I saw that head, it and its body were lying on the floor of the casino in Kings Cross, and Mick Kelly was removing 3M duct tape from its face, pulling part of its moustache out with it, and then jamming the barrel of a twenty-two pistol up one nostril and then the other. This was the face of the "pussy" that sobbed and squealed out the information on his fellow crims and then did a runner. It was Norman Clune, or "mustachio" as I now referred to him; I had a big smile on my face thinking of Mick ripping the duct tape off his face and part of his moustache with it; this visit to Port Douglas going to be a lot more fun than previously thought; first, I will clean up the town mules and low-level dealers and then take out the boss, and "mustachio", and the other two thugs mentioned in this report, Jeff Richards and William Dalton.

I had returned the hired Holden to its pick-up area and, in turn, had hired another vehicle of a type I had seen getting around along this northern coastline and which I felt would be more suitable for off-road travelling. It was a fully reconditioned American Jeep. They had been left behind in quantity after the war ended in 1945 by the American Military, who had established an Air Force base in Townsville and who had many servicemen established throughout this entire region from 1943 in an endeavour to stop the possibility of a Japanese invasion of Australia, and to service the allied troops who were fighting the Japanese in New Guinea and other Pacific Islands, and many of the local communities were making use of them and I felt it would be ideal if I had to do any backcountry driving.

After thoroughly reading this report, I decided to start tracking the various young dealers named and work my way up the ladder. There were four of them, each with a section of Port Douglas to service. They were not hard to find. Not far out along the main road north from Port Douglas CBD, there was an old house they used for receiving deliveries of drugs, meetings, and parties. One of them and his girlfriend lived there, and the other two lived at separate addresses; one lived on his own in a cheap flat, and the other seemed to be a couch dweller, staying sometime in the same flat and sometime in the house or wherever else he was offered a bed. It was easy enough to match the descriptions given to me and photographs and follow each around for a few days and nights.

I now knew who the top man was. His name was Joseph Marconi. He was a millionaire from down south with suspected connections, as did the deceased Frankie Colleoni with the Calabrian mafia community. The report indicated Marconi, although a Sydney-born thug from Sicilian parents, grew up in the Sydney criminal world, growing up with extortion, prostitution, stand and drug dealing, through which he made frequent visits to Griffith, no doubt to gain further knowledge and valuable contacts for his future career.

The dossier Edith had sent me on Joseph Marconi must have been an expensive one to procure. It covered every aspect of his life from childhood. Finding a shady tree-lined street opposite a park, I stopped the car to study again this extensive report.

Marconi was born in St Vincent's Hospital Darlinghurst in 1912. His father's name was Luigi, and he was known as Louie, an honest and hardworking Sicilian; he scraped a living working as a barrowman's offsider buying fruit and vegetables at Sydney's Paddy's markets. His mother, Katarina, worked as a washerwoman in a laundry in Brougham Street, Woolloomooloo. They rented an upstairs section of a rundown rat infested terrace building, a short distance up from Woolloomooloo in Palmer Street, in the brothel area of Sydney. Joseph was two years old when his father, feeling that he owed a debt of gratitude to his newly adopted country, Australia, joined the army and was signed up to go fight with the 13 AIF battalion in World War One. He was killed at Gallipoli in the failed Allied invasion of the Turkish peninsula.

His mother, Katarina, after four years of struggling without her man, and trying to lookay after an uncontrollable son, gave up. With the need for money to survive, she became a prostitute working for Kate Leigh, a well-known "Madame" of the area. Young Joseph ran wild in the streets of Woolloomooloo, Kings Cross and Darlinghurst. It was the era of the razor gangs and their hold on crime in Sydney. In 1918, when the Tradesman Arms hotel was built almost opposite the terraced slum they lived in, six-year-old Joseph was already acting as a lookout for his mother and the molls and prostitutes of the area by accosting pedestrians and sailors, asking if they wanted a girl. He already was a nimble thief and was continually truant from school. By twelve years of age, he had his own small gang of pickpockets, who were fond of rolling drunken sailors, who frequented the pubs nearby, where their ships were moored at the wharves of Woolloomooloo. Their method was to swarm around a man seen to be drunk and continually harass the victim until he fell down, and then they pounded him senselessly.

Joseph was not averse to knocking any who resisted over the head with a wooden club he always carried. The razor gang toughs who frequented the area around the "rocks" area and Darlinghurst were his heroes, and by fourteen years of age, Joseph was in and out of trouble with the law.

Caught smashing a window of Mark Foy's department store to steal clothing, young Joseph was arrested. When the magistrate was sentencing Joseph to six months in a juvenile detention establishment for his misdemeanours, he screamed out across the court, "When I get out, I'm gonna get a razor and cut your fuckin' ears off." Joseph Marconi already had a reputation as a vicious and dirty fighter; he would use any weapon he could put his hands on to win. At eighteen years of age, Joseph was carrying a razor and did not worry about using it if offended by anyone. This seemed to be often and was now pimping two girls, fifteen-year-old twin sisters, mainly to sailors around Woolloomooloo shipping wharves and the nearby Naval Base at Garden Island. By the time Joseph was twenty, he had a number of prostitutes working for him, and he had an extensive police record covering a vast number of crimes.

One night, he slashed with his razor the face and neck of an American sailor, who was a tough man and who fought back as the gang were trying to roll him. They were caught in the act by a police patrol. That offence sent Joseph to Long Bay Jail for ten years on a murder charge. Joseph had cut too deep and severed the man's jugular vein; he served six years of hard labour, and when released, he was by then a hardened criminal with much knowledge of underworld dealings.

After another stretch in prison on an assault and robbery charge, at twenty-six years of age, Joseph was declared to be a habitual criminal. On his release from prison, he landed a job as a doorman bouncer at Phil Jeff's Fifty Fifty Club on William Street, near Kings Cross. It was a sly grog and drug den.

It was there that Joseph, now nicknamed "gorgeous" by the many molls and prostitutes who frequented the club because of his rugged good looks, was made aware of the profits to be made from narcotics, in particular cocaine and the new arrival on the market, Heroin. Joseph Marconi decided to branch out on his own, starting with a small stable of girls he had charmed, and then stood over to work for him, and he opened up his own brothel and sly grog den in Bayswater Road, not far from the Rushcutters Bay, Sydney Stadium.

It was December 1939, and World War II had just started. "Gorgeous" Joseph Marconi, resisting the call to arms for men to join up in the fight, had an entrepreneurial spirit and saw much profit from servicemen coming to his establishment, but it all came crashing down when three men from a rival chain of brothels stormed into his establishment and started knocking the girls and customers around. Joseph came running in, brandishing a handgun, and shot two of them, wounding both of them. One was seriously hurt with a bullet near his heart he managed to survive. Joseph got off both shooting charges, pleading self-defence, but got eighteen months in jail for carrying an illegal weapon, including heavy fines for owning and managing a brothel and sly grog shop.

When Joseph got out of jail, he found that his brothel and girls had been taken over. Endeavouring to reassert himself, he was badly beaten, then cross-slashed from shoulders to lower stomach by the gang now operating it. The wound required over two hundred stitches, and after recovering in hospital, Joseph disappeared from the Sydney scene. About eighteen months later, Joseph appeared in a Brisbane Court charged with carrying a deadly weapon and in possession of small bags of cocaine and was sentenced to another twelve months in prison. Thereafter, "Gorgeous Joseph Marconi" built up a long string of various charges that were mainly drug-related.

An armoured car robbery which netted the thieves two hundred thousand pounds, saw Joseph Marconi as a prime suspect, but it was never proved and has never been solved.

Soon after this unsolved robbery, Joseph disappeared from the Brisbane crime scene, re-emerging for a time in Cairns, and soon after, Joseph vanished again and was not known to have been seen anywhere else until he popped up in Cairns again, about ten years later, and this time looking and acting the part of a wealthy businessman with plenty of money. Co-incidentally, soon after his arrival back in Cairns, a drug scene was seen to develop, and cocaine, heroin, and marijuana started to emerge in large quantities. It was now obvious Gorgeous George had been promoted to be the "Don" of Port Douglas.

The "Don" of Port Douglas

At fifty-odd years of age, "Gorgeous" Joseph Marconi was now living in a luxurious Mediterranean-style waterfront Villa in Port Douglas with an attractive Chinese girl who was about half his age. He now has big investments in property developments in the Port Douglas region and other parts of Queensland and owns an importing company in Hong Kong, which brings into Australia by ship Chinese made ceramics. He changes cars every twelve months and is currently driving the latest model German made Mercedes Benz. Among his many other toys is a super-fast speedboat with twin outboard 150hp Evinrude motors and a sixty-foot luxury cruiser that was custom-made in Hong Kong and sailed from there to Cairns.

Reading all of this, I thought it was quite an impressive rise for a razor-carrying slum kid from the poorest parts of Sydney. The two muscle-bound men in the photographs were said to be employed ostensibly as gardeners, handymen, and pool cleaners; this, according to the information, also showed that both Jeff Richards and William Dalton had criminal records, including drug and weapon possession; both had served short terms in different prisons. The report went on to say that when George tookay his cruiser out to sea, often on overnight journeys, both men went with him. I thought, "Birds of a feather stick together." I suspected these overnight boat cruises had a sinister motive.

The study of a maritime map of the Queensland coastline showed me the proximity of the offshore shipping lanes. To my way of thinking, that could be the perfect way for his bulk drug supplies to be dropped off from a ship and then be picked up by a fast speedboat and loaded onto his cruiser for deliveries further south down the coastline, such as the cruiser I had witnessed in Cairns. What made sense and interested me further was that Jeff Richards had served in the Royal Australian Navy in an underwater demolition team, not unlike the US Navy seals. He had been dishonourably discharged from the Navy on drug smuggling and drug possession charges. Interesting? I was starting to see a picture here, but where did the new arrival, "mustachio", as I called him, fit in?

Later, I was to establish he was the "land man," responsible for distribution around the surrounding community and outlying townships and up to the "top end" as far as Weipa and Cooktown. It amazed me the octopus tentacle-like spread of this drug organisation.

Staying at home and minding house was Joseph's girlfriend, an ageing male Chinese cook and a young Chinese maid; obviously, Asian delicacies of every kind appealed to Joseph.

I was sitting in my motel room as I was reading this dossier, and I had read enough; my job now was to work out how to dispose of

Joseph and his team. It needed an in-depth plan, on how it would be done. One thing was for sure "gorgeous" Joseph Marconi had an appointment with his "maker" and perhaps too his scumbag friends, and so, I spent many hours analysing previous hits, endeavouring to work out the best approach. Port Douglas was too small and too remote from major population areas for me to simply blend in and do surveillance. It was a place where everyone knew everyone, and Joseph Marconi had built up a reputation as a philanthropic businessman who was very community-minded; a lot of awareness of strangers highlighted this in the town since the character known as the Grim Reaper had made an appearance doing his vigilante thing in Cairns.

Perhaps I had made a mistake there and overdid what I had thought would be something unique and somewhat humorous. Also, wherever he went, his minders, acting like fellow business companions, went with him. At the social Port Douglas functions they attended, his girlfriend was always with him, and two attractive young ladies accompanied these minders. It was obvious Joseph Marconi was always trying to improve his social and community image.

Thinking deeply on what mode of attack to introduce in Port Douglas, I knew JJ had been humorously impressed with the previous successes, and I was still an unknown person here, so I decided to stay with the "tried and true". Once more, to take up the "sword of holy righteousness" and administer a few good hidings along the way with stern warnings of a repeat performance to the low-level punks, should they stray from the flock. A few stitches and a fractured bone here and there would help to show them to see the light.

I smiled, thinking of myself as a "Holy Roller"; perhaps I should don a clerical collar? It would be easy to give these young ones a few light taps here and there, administering some soft justice, but for the head man and his henchman, I would favour something more severe.

Wearing a ski mask, I cornered the first two young blokes who were still in their late teens in the communal house, gave them a good hiding, tied them up with duct tape, gagged them, and laid out on the kitchen table their entire stash with a note for the police, saying the **"Grim Reaper has Arrived"**, and then used their phone to ring for an ambulance and police before ripping out the phone line, and my luck was in, because in the same afternoon, it was about 6 p.m., I spotted a third fellow who was an older man, probably a senior in the gang, who was leaving Marconi's mansion in a late-model Ford that was very heavy in the boot. I followed him until he turned into a part of Port Douglas, along the coastline, and to a darkened beach house with lovely views to be seen in the now dim light from the sun out over the water.

A few steps from the car, he was unconscious on the sandy path, lying by his car. I found he was carrying a .38 pistol. This was a bit more serious. By the time I had him inside the beach house, he was just coming around to a conscious state, conscious though groggy. I was now wearing the ski mask, and was slapping him around a little to wake him properly, and I proceeded to lecture him on the errors of his ways. He looked at me as if I was off my head and said sneeringly, "Fuck off." "Wrong answer," I said.

He changed his attitude when I turned his hands back and broke a couple of fingers. I was sure over the next few weeks, he would regret his hasty answer. I left him unconscious, tied up with duct tape, and strapped lying down on the kitchen table with a handwritten note pinned to his shirt saying, **"Jesus loves you".** I then laid the entire haul of marijuana out on the floor of his kitchen with the gun on top and another note saying, **"Compliments of the Grim Reaper"** I was sure that would get the boss man thinking, especially with his knowing by now his entire Cairns gang was out of action from similar attacks. I would phone the police later when I was well away from here.

No doubt by now, Joseph Marconi, the major supplier of these drugs in Port Douglas, would be wondering what was happening. Who was this grim reaper? And is he the same one who enabled his outlets in Cairns to get caught, and where was Colleoni? What had happened to him? There had been no contact for many days. His brain would be reeling from so many questions. I had no doubt his heavies would be getting around trying to find out what was happening and wondered if "mustachio" was in that level of hierarchy. I thought it was time to be a tourist and enjoy a tour out to the reef, and travel around and see the sights; I was now a retired Viet veteran, wandering around having a welcome holiday.

The next day I just rested and walked around Port Douglas, and when I walked into a coffee lounge cum restaurant, sitting there was a group of elderly ladies who were chatting loudly about some "hellfire and brimstone evangelist" who had gone through Cairns punishing known drug dealers, and he is now in Port Douglas. The radio and the newspapers were full of the news about his punishment to them and the huge haul of various drugs and a gun that the police had found, and one old dear piped up and said, "Wouldn't it be nice if we could get him to come and preach at our church on Sunday? A visual thought of that had me smiling for days."

The police were mystified as to the identity of this vigilante-type person, calling himself the Grim Reaper. Many townspeople were phoning the newspapers and going on talkback radio, and saying things like "find him and put him on the police payroll. Port Douglas, Cairns and Townsville need someone like that to end the drug problem." Authorities were saying that the actions of this "evangelistic avenger" were creating a massive wave of anti-drugs sentiment, which has the police stepping up their campaign to stop drug trafficking. He also said the police were mystified by the disappearance of the key dealer in Cairns and had extended their investigation into his known Brisbane acquaintances.

I decided to put a call through first to Melissa at the hotel where she worked and managed to talk to her; it was just long enough to tell her how much I loved her and missed her, and then get onto "JJ" on the public pay phone, and update him on happenings to find out that he already knew. I should have known with all of his monitoring equipment and contacts. He was laughing when he said to me, "Bloody genius that, it was a brilliant move, particularly the belting you gave the couple with his leather belt." He went on to say. "Our client in Port Douglas has extended his finances further and wants you to deal with the major supplier there. I now have a complete dossier on him for you to study, and from what I have read, he is another sick bastard. It will be in the mail to you in the next hour, and adding, we know by now Melissa would be missing you. So Eleanor and I are going to invite her to have a weekend with us on the "Celeste." "I will tell her you are caught up on a major business transaction with one of my clients up north. Gotta go. I have to race to the Supreme Court now. I'm representing a case for a shady solicitor whose client has an unsavoury reputation. It could mean more work for "Mulga"; I could imagine the smile on his face as he said that.

I knew I would have to hang around Port Douglas for a few more days to finish this job, and in between surveillance, I tookay a couple of tours. I liked Port Douglas and thought that perhaps I would like to settle here with Melissa one day.

The next few days passed in the contented bliss of a man who felt he had everything: the love of a beautiful woman, a job with a good income, where he felt that what he was doing was for the better, even though he knew the laws as they were, did not agree, and yet, there was something else, there was more to it. In Malaya and Vietnam, I had come to like the action, the constant danger and the "hit-and-run" style of ambushes we did on the Vietcong. That feeling, combined with the intense satisfaction of eradicating some of the brutal bastards that existed in that horror of war, was what had made it better. I wondered what a psychiatrist would have to say about that.

Frankly, I wasn't too worried. Some things were not worthy of a deep conscience; it was time to move on and track down the head of this drug network. Another evil bastard who was living a rich life while young and not so young died slowly, poisoning their minds and bodies and breaking the hearts of their families.

No! The only way I could get to Joseph was for Joseph Marconi to come to me. "JJ" liked my plan, and almost immediately, I started acting on it.

The first thing was to arrange for someone who could lookay the part, with a past criminal background that could be checked out, to go to Cairns and start to blend in with the locals and spread the word he was looking for supplies. Jack Withers would be the perfect fit for the job. His story would be that Sydney was getting too hot for him activity-wise, and he was looking for a quieter place to live. The information we already had would supply him with inside knowledge of Joseph Marconi's operation.

When contact with a supplier had been made, Mick Kelly would go up to join him as the "heavy", a minder, to be on hand for the hoped-for meeting with Joseph Marconi. We believed that the first negotiations would be with either Richards or Dalton or both. I did think back to the night of the disturbance at the casino and wondered if "mustachio" was in on the meetings, would he recognise Jack Withers or Mick Kelly? A short phone conversation with Jack and Mick confirmed this could be possible, and it worried me about how to handle this possibility.

I need not have worried; the matter was solved. It was through a lapse of carelessness on my part and Port Douglas being a small town. It was late in the afternoon, it was early afternoon, when I made a quick trip to a nearby supermarket to pick up some shaving cream along with some necessary supplies and walked back to my car, and as I was unlocking the door, I spotted "Mustachio". He had got out of his car and headed for the supermarket I had just left and was headed toward its doors. His Mercedes Benz was about fifty feet from my car. It had happened so quickly and unexpectedly that, for a moment, I hesitated, and he saw me. I was about forty feet from him and running, as he was rushing back to his car to get a door open. He was not quick enough, and a hard rabbit chop to the side of his neck, and a full-on blow to his jaw and he was down. Looking swiftly around, I could see that no one else was around, and we had not been noticed. Scooping his keys up off the ground, I opened the large boot and attempted to tumble him into it, but was faced with difficulty because of a very large canvas carry-all that was full of something, taking up some room and partially blocking me from getting his frame into the boot.

I think I might have come close to breaking bones, going by some grunts I heard as I squashed the now semi-conscious "Mustachio" in with the bag and was just lowering the lid as some shoppers were coming toward us. I had to get out of there quickly to a quiet place and then be faced with the problem of what to do with him. There was no doubt that he had to be disposed of; the latest information had shown that "Mustachio" or Jacob Green, had an extensive criminal record and was wanted in Victoria for questioning by their police, but to hand him over to local police was not an option, that would warn Joseph Marconi something was happening and blow the chance of him coming to me. Two, the knowledge of who Jack Wither really was could get to Joseph Marconi if "Mustachio", by any chance, was released on bail. No, he definitely had to go, and very soon, but how? I checked my watch; it was a few minutes past two, plenty of time for a drive somewhere.

Quickly retrieving my dropped bag of groceries, I put them into my car, I got back into the Mercedes, and it was then I noticed the black traveller's suitcase with wheels sitting on the back seat. Reaching around behind me, I pulled the zipper around its edge enough to see its content. The bag seemed full of various articles of expensive clothing. Was our bad boy planning a journey? Reaching over to the passenger side, I opened the glove box to find a pistol. It was a new model eleven-shot Glock. Wow, I thought, an excellent hand gun, but more important was a notepad with a list of names, addresses and phone numbers. This was definitely something I had to study, but first, I had to find a remote place away from prying eyes, study the notebookay in detail, and work out my next move.

Putting the note bookay back into the glove box, I turned the key on this beautifully made piece of German machinery, slowly drove out of the car park and headed for the main northern highway. Going by the faint bumps coming from the boot, "Mustachio" must be aroused from his slumber. I cruelly thought perhaps I could find a rough bush track to drive on, and I did.

I had driven for about twenty-five minutes before I saw the track. It was heading off through a stand of timber on my right, and it was a bit rough being packed with crushed stone and firm. I assumed it might be a fisherman's track as it was heading in the direction of the sea. I drove it for about ten minutes. Then I saw a glimpse of water and then another track heading off to the left and parallel to the coast. Stopping the car, I got out, and again, I checked the ground for its firmness to ensure the Mercedes could still travel on it. Obviously, the Cairns council or maybe the local people had packed it with a road base for better access to the sandy and softer coastal area. I most certainly did not want to get bogged down this far out. The ground was firm, and there were still muffled, although louder, sounds coming from the boot.

It was a reasonably hot day, and I thought Mustachio would be getting somewhat uncomfortable and perhaps a bit thirsty. Getting back into the car, and then a short drive of about two hundred metres and I was in a clearing with only foot tracks going to the mangrove-strewn coastline and patches of beach. I thought this must be a fisherman's campground and the perfect spot for Mustachio's final rest. First, I must check his notebook. After about ten minutes of reading, I knew that "Mustachio" was definitely heading off on a long journey. Going by the dates and addresses in his notebook, he had appointments all along the way north to Cooktown, and I now knew what was in the large bag he was sharing space within the boot. Later, looking at its size and testing its weight, I estimated it was about a hundred kilos. No doubt the far northern addicts will be having some withdrawal symptoms for a while.

Opening the boot, I could see that "mustachio" by now, did not have much fight left in him. He was in a lather of sweat and seemed a trifle faint. Levelling the Glock at him, I ordered him out of the boot. I reckon it tookay him a couple of minutes to unwind and extricate himself from the cramped position he was in, and when he stood on his legs, he seemed rather wobbly, poor fellow; it must have been terribly uncomfortable, hot and airless in there. Giving him a nudge with the point of the gun, I ordered him to start walking down a narrow foot track that branched off and went along in the direction of the mangroves. "Mustachio" was now blubbering and crying like a baby and pleading with me to let him go; it was almost heartbreaking to listen to him. "I did say almost". The track ended here, and just behind the mangroves, there was a ridge of small grass-covered sand dunes running parallel to the coastline. We had reached a small shady glade overhung with a thick band of she-oaks, casuarinas trees common to the eastern seaboard. I estimated we were about fifty yards from the Mercedes, which was out of sight.

Jacob alias "Mustachio" now seemed very tired; he was gasping for breath and in need of sitting down. Looking around, perfect, I thought, pointing to a raised section of a grass-covered small dune with a shade tree hanging over it. Dusk was now on us. "Sit down, Jacob and rest I said." He was now a pathetic mess and just sat there with no fight at all left in him, watching me as I walked around analysing where we were and if it would be a suitable place to say goodbye to him. Hearing the sound of wave action, I knew it was near, but I could not see the water because of a rise in the height of land, the bushes, trees and thick mangroves; I knew we were close to it, maybe fifty yards or less. I knew crocodiles inhabited these northern waters and did wonder if they came ashore here. Interesting thought!

Turning back to Jacob, I pointed the gun at his chest, pulled the trigger, and fired a finishing shot to the back of his head as he slumped forward to the ground. I then dragged him by his heels the short distance back along the track, and, opening the boot, I tookay the heavy carry-all bag out and placed it on the back seat, and then struggled for a couple of minutes to get Mustachio back into the boot. Walking back along the track with a broken tree branch, I scuffed away all signs of the bloodstained sand.

Satisfied, I walked back to this beautiful Mercedes and then thought, now I must dispose of it, and that was a sad thought. It was such a lovely car. A thought did flash through me; I wondered who paid for such an expensive car, the boss man or "Mustachio?" What a sad waste of money, I thought as I considered total disposal and burning the vehicle and its contents or driving it the sixty miles or so back to Cairns and dumping it there. Because I always wore gloves, I had no fear of fingerprints being found. I thought it better that police recover the drugs, so I made the decision to drive the sixty miles back to Cairns, park a reasonable distance from the police station, and the next morning put a phone call through to them, happy in the thought that it would be a day or so before "Mustachio would be missed", and when the car was found, Marconi would be in a state wondering why, and how? Did his top courier, his car, and the northern area drug supply end up in the south in Cairns, with him dead inside the boot? I was now looking forward to a big breakfast of eggs and bacon in the morning. I was famished. Finding a quiet, dark spot closer to Cairns, I stopped to sleep for a few hours. Just before daylight, I parked about 300 yards from the police station, putting the Glock pistol into his bag of clothing and checking to see if no one was around, I stepped out of the Mercedes, locked its doors and put my arms through the carrier straps on his bag. Hence, it sat like a backpack I did a slow jog to and along the esplanade on the waterfront to the Trinity Wharf, the deep sea terminal where passenger ships docked. Finding a shady tree in the stretch of parkland there, I sat watching a beautiful sunny day shining over the ocean and napped for another couple of hours before picking up the bag of clothing and walking over to the Barrier Hotel, now looking like a typical tourist, there to bookay a room, eat and sleep. In a few hours, I would make a phone call, and next morning, find a way to get back to my car in Cairns.

Joseph Marconi was hurting real bad and was in an almost apoplectic rage over this mysterious masked "bastard" beating and scaring the shit out his street dealers, the demise of his Cairns market, and now that fuck wit Jacob has disappeared, with over a quarter of a million quid of product in street value, and the bloody new car he had brought him. He was fuming, his blood pressure was through the roof, and he wanted badly to kill. The empire that he had worked so hard to build was crumbling around him. He wanted to shoot someone or at least carve them up with the razor he had kept from the old days.

It was about 4 p.m. when the final nail in his coffin of despair came. It was with a visit from the police, telling him that his car and its contents had been found, and could he please explain the drugs and the murdered body of an employee. His rage knew no bounds; he and his lawyer were now faced with convincing the police that Jacob was an employee, employed only on general maintenance duties around his estate, and about whom he knew nothing of his nocturnal activities. Strongly asserting that he could offer no reason why he had been found shot dead in a company vehicle with a large amount of various illegal drugs. Marconi's mind was now in turmoil; he knew the questioning and police attention would be on him for a while, and it was time to cease activities. The thought of the money he would lose just added to his pain, plus he was faced with the embarrassing news media publicity and the public humiliation his philanthropic and business reputation would face with this media exposure.

That prolonged break in Marconi's illegal activities was going to be ideal for the plan that we, JJ, Jack Wither, Mick Kelly and I had formulated and needed to be completed in detail and launched into operation. First, it was time for me to take a break, write to my darling Melissa, ask her if she could take some holiday time from work, and maybe catch up with Angus. Her reply came in a phone call to the motel where I was staying. A breathless Melissa was excitedly saying I've got three weeks holiday starting at the end of this week. It was Tuesday, by Friday a plane ticket had been arranged. Monday morning, she was on the first flight to Cairns where I was waiting at the airport as she came through the airport gates. I felt an internal flutter and a catch in my throat as I looked at her radiant beauty coming toward me, and in seconds, she was in my arms and we were rapturously and excitedly kissing and kissing. In that short time, I had made reservations for a stay at a couple of luxury resorts along the Barrier Reef coastline with boat trips to the reef, a yacht charter and a number of great places to visit, and I felt the tension and stresses of these past weeks fast disappearing as I held her in my arms. We were soon on a boat cruise to a resort hotel on Green Island, where we decided to stay and revel in some quiet, restful luxury for the entire length of her stay. They were to be idyllic, languorous days, dining, swimming, sunbathing, and a boat cruise to the outer reef followed by enchanted nights of love.

CHAPTER 36

The Final Sting

It did not take long for dispirited Joseph Marconi to prick up his ears when word got to him about a man with much money wanting to join forces by buying in with him to the currently expired Cairns market. First, he sent his two men, Jeff Richards and William Dalton, to meet and investigate Jack Wither and Mick Kelly. Too many bad things had happened lately, and he must be sure it was the police trying to set him up. "Fuck," he thought, "I want to kill someone real bad!" Even the police contacts that he had on his payroll could not help him with information on anything helpful. They were just as puzzled as he. Police enquiries had reached a dead end about what had happened to Jacob. There were a number of suspicions. Was Jacob doing a runner with his load? Had he switched loyalties to another mob? Did a deal go wrong? Did they shoot him, and, of course, was this evangelical avenger bastard involved in all of this; although he usually left a message, this time nothing? Marconi was seething as he thought, if it's the last thing I do, he would track him down, carve him up piece by piece and feed him to the sharks in the harbour. This and a thousand other nagging questions were going through his tortured mind. Now, his doctor tells him he has a stomach ulcer and should stop worrying about business matters, and to top all of this, his Asian mistress wants to fly back to Hong Kong to see her family.

Richards and Dalton were suitably impressed when they examined Jack's criminal rap sheet that their boss Marconi had obtained from his police contact. Their eyes bugged when Jack showed them a bank account in his name with 500,000 pounds in it that he claimed to be his earnings from past criminal dealings and enhanced by a bit of exaggerated bragging outlining some of his past criminal pals and misdeeds. Much of this they already knew when they received his police record and seemed impressed that it all added up. Also, Mick Kelly fitted right in as the tough guy, "minder", and collector of unpaid debts for Jack Withers.

Richards and Dalton first pushed for the money, or a large part of it, to be handed over for the first drug delivery. Jack pushed right back and said he would only put the money directly into the hands of the "man", meaning Joseph Marconi. Richards and Dalton seemed satisfied that Jack Withers was not a cop and went back to Marconi with a copy of Jack Withers's bank account and certifying the information on his criminal record was all okay; it worked. Marconi rang Jack at his motel in Cairns and arranged a date for a meeting. A week later, Marconi flew down to Cairns for a personal meeting with Jack Withers and Nick Kelly. They sat in the bar of a nearby hotel and talked for nearly three hours, where they agreed a payment of three hundred thousand pounds would be paid directly to Marconi at the transfer over of the first shipment of drugs before going to a seafood restaurant for a meal. Joseph had booked his team into the same motel as Jack for the night, and by the time Marconi, Richards, and Dalton flew out the next day for Port Douglas and were chauffeured to the airport in Jack's hire car, you would swear they were long lost brothers. Before they flew out, they went for a drive along the Cairns waterfront and Joseph showed Jack where the track into the delivery cove was. The seed was sown; it was wise now to let it grow for a while

The item that I was eagerly waiting on had arrived from "JJ's" northern contact and was personally delivered to me by a trusted courier. When it arrived, I could hardly wait to run my hands over the ugly beauty of a Remington 700 V bolt action in .308 calibre. The barrel action and even the screws were bedded in Devcon aluminium into black fibreglass and Kevlar stock, and were made to take a silencer, also included in the package. The rifle was purely ugly and beautifully balanced, and I loved it. I remembered one of the American "Green Berets" snipers in Ban Me Thuot had one, and he gave me a few shots with it on an 800-yard range. I was impressed with my five-shot, group 1 MOA (0.3 mrad) extreme vertical spread for all shots with this rifle, and when fitted with a silencer, I knew it was a magic killing tool. It was fitted with a Leupold 10 scope.

I almost caressed it as I gazed at this weapon. I tookay it to an isolated stretch about thirty miles into the hinterland and set up six hand-drawn targets. Lying down with my legs splayed in a perfect sniper position, thirty .308 calibre bullets later, I was totally satisfied with the six groupings; each of the five shots I had fired at about 600 yards was almost a perfect grouping, and the bolt action reload, was swift and smooth for repeat shooting, I was open-mouthed and amazed. It was better than expected, and I would be shooting at a much lesser distance, if things went entirely to plan

Five days from now on, starting on a Tuesday night, there would be a king tide at 6:35 p.m. with a moonless night, and on that night, the cruiser would head into the cove; because of the king tide, the cruiser would be able to anchor about 250 yards from the shore, where Joseph would come in with his men in the twin outboard speedboat which would be more than big enough for the three of them and the drug cargo. Jack and Mick were to meet them on the beach and hand over a briefcase with 300,000 cash in it for Joseph to count, and in turn, Richards and Dalton would offload the drugs to Jack and Mick.

This was an ideal situation for what I had in mind. I had managed to acquire from an Army mate I trained with in Sydney and sent to me in Malaya a pair of the military's latest version of night vision glasses that pick up distinctly any heat source, animal or human over a long distance and gave a sharp outline to the figure.

But, as luck would have it, Murphy's Law struck; heavy clouds started to roll in on Tuesday, and by Tuesday night, it started to rain. There was no wind, no storm, just rain, and when it rains in Cairns, it really rains; it was like being under a waterfall. The only good thing about the volume of rain was it certainly helped to eliminate the possibility of fishermen turning up. When Joseph had spoken to Jack Withers, he was told that his men always carried fishing gear at the cove to make out they were fishermen if anyone was around; he advised Jack to do the same. He said they also had a flashlight signal system to signal the cruiser if other people were in the area.

When in position, I had to keep wiping the night vision glasses free of the mist build-up as I checked them for visibility. Earlier that afternoon, with Mick's help and a couple of camouflaged army "hoochies", we had managed to rig up a shelter of sorts on sticks thrust into the ground and strung with strong fishing line. The roof had a shape to let the rain runoff, and duct tape held it all in place. I then positioned a tripod stand and a pillow for my elbows to rest on. We then laid a couple of ground sheets down. The idea was to lay stomach down with legs splayed in the perfect sniper position.

My "hide" was positioned on the rise in the bank covered with ti-tree bush, paper bark gums and other assorted bushes. By clearing a line of vision through the leaves and branches, I could lookay slightly downwards to the landing spot on the beach and had an excellent wide-angle view out to sea and the entire area where the cruiser would be anchored. There was no way a spotlight from the cruiser or the speed boat would be able to see me where I lay. Some camouflage netting would be draped over the muzzle. My army mate had managed to get for me a flash and noise suppressor which were now fitted to the muzzle of the Remington 700V. Although a flash noise suppressor reduces impact velocity over a long-range, at this short range, there would be a maximum impact. Half a dozen shots out to sea when it was dark confirmed that from twenty metres away, it could barely be heard or seen.

The Cruiser was coming from the north, and to the south, about a mile away, we had a thirty-foot hire cruiser at anchor. Mick and Jack had anchored it there about mid-morning and rowed ashore, hiding the dinghy in the mangroves lining the edge of the bank. I picked them up in the hired vehicle and brought them to the cove. It was still pouring rain. Mick then drove the short distance back to Cairns to pick up some food and drink. I lay in the hide and thought over the entire plan to eliminate gorgeous Joseph Marconi and his cohorts.

Actually, it was reasonably dry in the hide; the foliage around me was growing out of the sand, and the water, as heavy as it was coming down, did not run in over the ground sheet ends, with the ends being slightly buried in mounds of sand, resulting in the rain just soaking into the sand. It was really quite cosy. Pulling the pillow under my head I lay back and closed my eyes and thought about what was about to happen, and then fell asleep thinking about Melissa.

Just before I dozed off, I had one more thought; when this job is over, I will see "JJ" and check to see if it is okay to take the MV Celeste and then see if Melissa would take a couple of weeks' holiday from her job and go cruising the waterways of the Hawkesbury River with me, I had really liked those couple of days we had on the boat, seeing the small settlements along the way and the occasional waterside restaurant pointed out to us.

The sound of the car engine and its headlights shining through the bushes woke me up. It was Mick and Jack returning. Making sure the Remington was dry, I scrambled out through the rain and into the car. The smell of hamburgers and chips hit my nostrils as I dived into the car. A paper bag was put in one hand and a can of four x beer in the other; I had not realised I was so hungry. As I was about to take a sip of beer, Mick's deep voice boomed out. Cheers mates! Here's to a successful night. It was close to 10:30 p.m.

For the next four hours, we alternately dozed and kept watch, only getting out of the car to urinate. We went over the plan again in detail. At first sight of the cruiser navigation lights shining in the northeast; I would position myself in the hide with the gun ready. Mick and Jack would turn the car headlights on high beams as the cruiser got closer and give the signal number of flashes. 123 pause 123 pause 123, which would let them know it is okay to drop the anchor and come ashore. With the lights on the cruiser we would all be able to see if the three men got into the speedboat. Once into the speedboat, which I thought would only cruise in at quarter throttle, they would be out in the extremely dark night with rain falling. I would be the only one who could see them.

When the nose of the speed boat touched the shallows the car lights were to come on to low beam to show them the way. It was anticipated that Joseph would be driving, and Richards and Dalton would jump out and pull the boat closer for Joseph to get out.

At first, and having the night vision glasses, my plan had been to pick them off one by one as they neared the shore, but on second thought, it was realised that if by chance I did not hit the driver with deadly impact, the speedboat could spin around and race off to the safety of the cruiser. Discussing this with the blokes, I decided to reset the range down to fifty metres. At that distance, a man hit anywhere in the body with 7.62 x 51mm .308 Winchester blunt nose bullets would be flattened. I would be aiming for a maximum area chest shot. We would wait until the boat nosed onto the shallows and turn the lights on the high beam, causing temporary blindness to those in the direct beam.

Joseph's cruiser was due to appear at 4 a.m. At 3:30 a.m., we were all keyed up, waiting for the lights of the boat to appear. At 4 a.m., nothing. At 4:15 a.m., nothing. We started to wonder if something had gone wrong. It was coming on 4:30 a.m., when we spotted the lights of a boat in the distance. At 4:45, the cruiser's anchor rattled through its hawse pipe, as we flashed headlights, 123 pause, 123 pause, 123. Our signal was returned. It was still very dark and raining steadily. We would just have enough dark to carry out the rest of the operation, feeling relieved they were not much later. In early morning daylight, even with the rain, we faced the risk of being seen. Through the night vision glasses, I could see figures passing packages over the side of the cruiser to a figure in the smaller boat by its starboard side.

As soon as I heard the "Vroom Vroom" of the outboard motors starting up, I reasserted my body into the sniper position, laying flat on my stomach with legs splayed. I drew the rifle up into my shoulder in a smooth, practised motion, notched my elbows into position on the pillow, and locked my arms firm under the rifle's ten pounds of weight so it was well supported, and no movement of muscle or twitch of pulse could deflect my shots. They had to be quick, concise and on target.

The speed boat's twin outboard motors had now been cut off, and the boat was on a silent glide into shore; it was now about ten metres from touching the bottom when I released one arm, pushed the night vision goggles back over my head, and back in position, as the car headlights as prearranged came on full beam. There were three men, each with an arm up, shielding their eyes from the strong high beam; one was still sitting at the steering wheel, and two were leaning over the side and ready to jump over to steady the boat, as it touched bottom "shut yer fuckin' ligh" were the last words "Gorgeous Joseph" ever spoke as a 308 slammed into his chest through the low Perspex windscreen, smashing his heart and internal organs. In quick succession phoof, phoof, two silenced 308s went through the side of Dalton's chest, as he went to jump over the side, and as Richards spun around to dive down low, he was a fraction too late from another blunt round that smashed through his spinal cord, shredding his lungs, and forcing his body to topple over the side.

Action stations! It was time to move fast, and bringing the Remington with me, I jumped out of the "hide". At the same time, Mick and Jack got out of the car. We had about twenty to thirty minutes maximum before daylight would come creeping in. We had to pick up the spent cartridges, dismantle the "hide", and load the bodies onto the speedboat, thankful that two of the bodies were in the water, with no bloodstained sand to clean up, and for the rain that was still teeming down. I ran to the car, packed the Remington and night vision glasses away, and turned back to the speedboat.

Mick was first on the boat and was pulling Marconi's shattered body to one side and away from the steering wheel, as Jack and I were also struggling to lift Richard's heavier body by the arms and legs into the speed boat. Then Mick's massive strength was there with us, jumping over the side and lifting him from under his waist. Just a few seconds more, Dalton's lighter-weight body was lifted in.

As we did this, we could see the large packages wrapped in waterproof plastic and tightly bound with tape, that were packed in under the forward decking of the speedboat. Picking one up, I estimated its weight, at a rough guess to be about ten kilos, and a quick count of packages told me that about two hundred kilos of drugs would be going along with the three bodies to a watery grave at the bottom of the sea.

The heavy rain had put a considerable amount of water into the speedboat, and in the glare of the headlamps, we could see the water had a red tint to it. Mick and I jumped in, and as I was starting the motor, Jack was getting into the car. His job was to get to the dinghy, park the car near as convenient to the dinghy then row out to the hired cruiser.

Mick and I would board Joseph's cruiser and tow the speed boat behind us, after covering the bodies with blankets obtained from the cruiser and motor along the coast to meet up with the hire boat. Jack would then follow us out to sea into deep water, where it was planned to sink the cruiser and the speed boat once we were outside the reef and in a deep enough part of the ocean. In about thirty minutes, we had met up with Jack, and turning the boat around, we headed out to sea as the first of the dull morning light came up over the horizon and through the grey, moisture-laden sky.

It was a quiet and solemn cruise at about ten knots until we were about seven nautical miles outside the outer reef, and it was now daylight. Mick and I had not spoken much, no doubt the reason being we were feeling the tension of the past few hours. I was thankful the sky was so overcast and heavy with rain that we could barely see two hundred metres in any direction, and there was little chance that any other boats would be this far out on such a miserable day. I turned to Mick, saying, "I'm bloody glad we have got a compass on that hire cruiser, or we could be heading to New Zealand without knowing it." I had cut the engines of the cruiser back and they were just idling now, and the depth finder was showing we were in 300 fathoms of water. I said, "I think we will stop here. There is a bit of a smooth swell, but with all three of us, we should be able to lift the bodies out of the speed boat and onto the cruiser. We are going to lock them into the downstairs cabins and then open all the valve cocks and sink the lot, Cruiser, bodies, drugs and boat. Let's signal Jack to come alongside, and we'll get to work. Jack was soon there with Mick helping to tie the hire cruiser along one side.

Pulling the speed boat up alongside the transom duckboard of the cruiser and looking down at the covered bodies, I said, "This is a bit like déjà vu, like we've been here before" Mick just nodded and smiled at me as he tookay the soggy bloodstained blankets from me to bundle into the cruiser.

It tookay us about half an hour, puffing and straining, to eventually get all three bodies, the bundles of drugs, and miscellaneous articles stowed away down below. I stepped into the speedboat searching for and throwing all floatable material into the cruiser to be put below with the bodies, and then removed the bung at the stern of the speedboat. What with the water already in it, and the weight of the twin outboard motors, and still tied to the cruiser, the boat would soon slip below the surface as the cruiser slowly sank. We then went searching for the valve cocks on the cruiser. While Jack and I were searching the bilge area for them, Mick found Joseph Marconi's liquor cabinet and, when we returned, walked over to us with three bottles of Black Label Johnny Walker Whisky. He had emptied two carry-all bags of clothing and had filled them with various spirits and liqueurs, saying, "It's a bloody shame to let this good stuff go down to the bottom. We can celebrate later." We all laughed heartily at this comment, the built-up tensions of these past few hours dissipating as we laughed and tookay a drink.

With the cock's open, Marconi's luxurious cruiser had now dropped a few inches lower in the water, so we transferred ourselves and the booty over to the hire cruiser and then stood watching this magnificent boat, a beautiful example of craftsmanship, slowly sink deeper into the water. As I stood there watching, I felt a pang of sadness. This same feeling happened to me in Western Australia when I saw a luxury boat blow up in Mandurah Harbour.

It was the simple fact that I really appreciated these beautifully crafted vessels, and yet it seemed to be my destiny to destroy them; this was relieved by the thought that perhaps one day I might own one.

My moment of reflection was interrupted when an opened bottle of Johnny Walker Black Label was thrust into my hand. Turning around I could see that Mick and Jack were also holding a bottle of scotch. Mick, now speaking in his most solemn voice said. "A toast, gentlemen, here's to the men who go down to the sea in ships," that toast was followed by another when he said. "And here's to the 'Mulga Man,' may he strike hard and deadly wherever the snakes of the world hide, cheers." I smiled at his words as I knew there was truth in what he had said. There would be more such work ahead, and I knew I would soon be doing the necessary research on "JJ's" information to find and destroy an even bigger snake: The whereabouts of the suppliers and their network sending their poison into Australia.

The End

Author Steve Langley on his horse, Anglo Arab "Strongbow," pictured on his property Three Waters High Country Holidays around the time he wrote the original manuscript "The Mulga Man" 2019. He's now retired from that business, and his Horse Strongbow is deceased.

www.ingramcontent.com/pod-product-compliance
Lightning Source LLC
Chambersburg PA
CBHW050959180726
48291CB00006B/1902